Parachutes
& Kisses

By Erica Jong

Parachutes
& Kisses

by Erica Jong

NAL BOOKS

NEW AMERICAN LIBRARY

NEW YORK AND SCARBOROUGH, ONTARIO

NAL BOOKS TRADEMARK REG. U.S. PAT. OFF. AND FOREIGN COUNTRIES
REGISTERED TRADEMARK—MARCA REGISTRADA
HECHO EN HARRISONBURG, VA., U.S.A.

SIGNET, SIGNET CLASSIC, MENTOR, PLUME,
MERIDIAN and NAL BOOKS
are published in the United States by New American Library,
1633 Broadway, New York, New York 10019,
in Canada by The New American Library of Canada Limited,
81 Mack Avenue, Scarborough, Ontario M1L 1M8

LIBRARY OF CONGRESS CATALOGING IN PUBLICATION DATA

Jong, Erica.
    Parachutes & kisses.

    I. Title.   II. Title: Parachutes and kisses.
PS3560.O56P3   1984   813'.54   84-11530
ISBN 0-453-00466-0

Designed by Julian Hamer

First Printing, September, 1984

1   2   3   4   5   6   7   8   9

PRINTED IN THE UNITED STATES OF AMERICA

For Clayton C. C. Wheat

&

Grace Darling Griffin

I know that there are immense expanses
hidden from us,
. . . quartz in slugs,
ooze,
blue waters for a battle,
much silence, many ore-veins
of withdrawals and camphor,
fallen things, medallions, kindnesses,
parachutes, kisses.

—PABLO NERUDA
"Melancholy Inside Families"

I

We Are the
Older Generation or
Baby Boom Grows Up

I am delirious
because I am dying so fast.
—HENRY MILLER

(It is, of course, impossible to judge
what course evolution would take
after human extinction, but the past
record strongly suggests that the
reappearance of man is not one
of the possibilities. Evolution has
brought forth an amazing variety of
creatures, but there is no evidence
that any species, once extinguished,
has ever evolved again.)
—JONATHAN SCHELL

ISADORA, separated from Josh, is like a kid in her twenties. Only like the kid she never was in her twenties—almost carefree. At thirty-nine, she finds herself possessed of a demoniacal sexuality—which has no need to justify itself with love.

Once the wrenching pain of the first separated month is past, she runs around madly, as if that way she could outrun her despair. Nobody, she thinks at first, is as good in bed as Josh. And now that she's flush (though she never believes it) and famous (though she never believes that either), impotent men seem to be everywhere! Why didn't anyone tell us that if women got strong, men would get doubly weak—as if in spite? But still, she diverts herself—with a drugged-out disc jockey from Hartford (her Connecticut Yankee Mellors-the-Gamekeeper), a cuddly Jewish banker from New York, a blue-eyed Southern writer from New Orleans, a cute Swedish real-estate developer who owns (and is ruining) numerous islands in the Caribbean, a lapsed rabbi who wants her to be his congregation, an antiques dealer who drives a Rolls and never graduated from Erasmus Hall High, a brilliant, astoundingly well-hung, twenty-six-year-old medical student who can get Valium, Librium, quaaludes, and Sonoma County sinsemilla in abundance (and in his spare time is discovering a cure for cancer), a plastic surgeon from New York who's into oral sex, and so many others she's practically lost track.

Everyone is into oral sex, it seems. Everyone has discovered the clitoris. In the ten years since she took off from Bennett Wing and ran (briefly) away with Adrian Goodlove (then wrote a book about it that gave women everywhere permission to do the same), the world has certainly changed. For one thing, there is more oral sex. For another, more impotence. For a third, sex is ubiquitous and yet also somehow devoid of its full charge of mystery. For a fourth, the world is definitely lurching to its end.

Isadora's generation is middle-aged. Those irrepressible babyboomers, who thought they would never sag, bald, or die, are now sagging, balding, and dying at an appalling rate. A lot of them

3

have ex-spouses in abundance, children on alternate weekends, houses in the Hamptons, houses in the fabled counties of Fairfield or Dutchess, co-ops or brownstones in town. Some even have stocks, bonds, money-market funds, lawyers, accountants, business managers, and hemorrhoids. (These things apparently go together.)

They *are* the older generation now. They know it because they sign the checks. They know it because their parents are starting to die. They know it because their grandparents stare down at them from uneasy chairs in the clouds. (And the living are beginning to seem almost as glassy-eyed as the dead.) They have reached the age where they meet their new lovers at A.A.; the age where some of their friends are addicts, some of their friends are bankrupt, and some of their friends are dead; where their children want real horses, not toy ones, and where they no longer worry about their *own* pregnancies but about their daughters'. They have reached the age, in short, where they know they are going to die.

Isadora now lives in Rocky Ridge, Connecticut. Having left her native Manhattan for "the Coast," having done her time in Malibu, she has now completed the triangular path her kind is duty-bound to traverse: Manhattan, Malibu, New England (sometimes in that order, sometimes in reverse). But still, it's as inevitable a hegira for "successful" writers, actors, and media types, as the triangular trade route—England, the coast of Africa, the Sugar Isles—was for eighteenth-century "pyrates."

Isadora thinks of herself as an eighteenth-century type: a sort of pyrate of the heart. She's every bit as much a survivor as Moll Flanders or Fanny Hill. She left her self-pity somewhere back in the seventies. At the age of thirty-nine, she is *almost* convinced that all the pain one gets in life is somehow for the best, that one never gets more than one can cope with, that life is a process of tempering the spirit—so that when at last it flees the mortal body, it knows a little better which way to go than it did the first time around. She knows that her life is a journey toward self-reliance. She knows that she has always lived with her heart on her sleeve. She knows she has paid the price for that, but also reaped the rewards. When one follows the path with heart, one often bleeds. (But what is the alternative—a cauterized core?)

At times she is seized with a sadness so profound no tears can release it. Being separated in Connecticut requires so much driving! Sometimes she'll drive an hour on the Merritt Parkway just to get laid. Marriage is so much more convenient. She knows the

4

parkway exits by heart—up to New Haven and down to New York —and sometimes she wonders what a girl from Manhattan is doing at three in the morning, driving stoned down the desolate Merritt, past Shelton, Orange, Milford, Fairfield, listening to "easy listening" on the radio—a late-night habit she'd never publicly confess to, and feeling her soul empty as a thrown-away beer can that suddenly explodes your tire.

It is three A.M. on what used to be called a "crisp" October night. Since the heavens have poured with rain for two whole days, the sky is suddenly clear and winking with stars which look like pinpricks in black oaktag shining through some remembered gradeschool window. Isadora has reached the age of nostalgia—her dreaded fortieth year. She races toward that birthday from a lengthy tryst with her drugged-out disc jockey, a man more into pleasuring women than any she has ever met—despite the fact that he is only intermittently hard. He's the Count of Cunnilingus, the Lord of Licks, the Viceroy of Vaginas. He's the only man she's ever met—including Josh—who knows the rhythm of a woman's coming and doesn't stop just as the throbs begin. What's more, he adores her, has worshiped her and her writing from afar (one never can worship very long up close), and Isadora means to see it stays that way. She rations herself to him one night a week to make the pleasure last. And she often wonders if, unstoned, she'd find him interesting at all.

She still loves Josh, who moved out three months past after a year of unspeakable pain, upheaval, and guilt. Their seventh year. All the body cells change every seven years, she read somewhere —perhaps in *Science News*. Inseparable for seven years, they finally came to blows—over money, sex, competing for the love of the three-year-old daughter they both adore—all the usual shit couples come to blows over. Their intelligence did not spare them, nor their passion, nor the fact that they are linked forever in some Dantean sphere or other. They still love each other, but they can't live together—at least not for now.

"I will never come back—find someone else," Josh keeps saying. But Isadora doesn't quite believe it. She has purposely chosen lovers she can't take seriously. She is waiting for Josh to grow up. He's thirty-three—Christ's age on the cross. Dante's age when he descended into hell. *Nel mezzo del cammin di nostra vita.* The Middle of life—a dangerous age for a man. Or a woman, for that matter. At thirty-two she bolted from her second marriage, left Bennett for Josh. Now it's her turn to be left. Though she was the one who threw him out—after a year of listening to him say he wanted to leave. He provoked her into the decision so he could blame her. But the decision was more his than hers.

As for Josh, he thinks she's his noose, his albatross, the box he can't unlock. He's lonely in his rented house the next town over from Rocky Ridge. He lives in Southton, the low-rent district— which, in these parts, means the houses cost a mere $100,000 instead of $300,000. He's lonely, but he won't come back. Won't and can't. Nor will he take a penny from her. Out to prove it on his own. Writing novels, too, he is—and with some success, though her absurd renown dwarfs it. What can they do? They love their daughter and each other, but they can't write under the same roof. So they shuttle Mandy back and forth. Amanda Ace, their gorgeous three-year-old treasure—and they make do as best they can.

Now she is hurtling down the Merritt at three A.M. while the radio plays a sleazy rendition of "Stardust"—all tinny strings and soupy nasal horns. She only listens to "easy listening" when her mind is already gone, when it's so late that hard rock or jazz or baroque would tax the gray cells beyond endurance. She loves to drive. In her twenties both driving and flying terrified her; now she adores them both. Big planes, small planes, Pilgrim Airlines to Boston on what she calls "a de Havilland double rubber band." Private planes to Catalina Island whenever she gets the chance. (She has a friend in Los Angeles who flies a Cessna.) The Concorde if a foreign publisher's paying. Jumbo jets, Lear jets, Hawker–de Havillands, helicopters. Her fear of flying has flipped over into love—and isn't fear sometimes just the flip side of love, the reverse of mad desire?

And cars. She adores cars. She wishes she could collect vintage cars—but her nature is too conservative for such lavish extravagance. She has just two cars: an old Mercedes and a new—which is a silver turbo diesel with vanity plates in Middle English. QUIM slipped like butter past the Connecticut censors. The Motor Vehicle Department in Norwalk would have balked at CUNT—but QUIM, with its Chaucerian lilt, went right by the computer's scrutiny.

She drives like an ace—which, of course, she is. Isadora White Stollerman Wing Ace—Isadora Wing to the world. Growing up in Manhattan, she never learned to drive in her teens, but she has made up for that now. She accelerates out of curves like a racing-car driver, the Stirling Moss of lady novelists, the female Paul Newman of Connecticut. In her old 280SL, she's even jazzier.

Rocky Ridge and Southton coming up. Exit 43A. The exit is hard to find at night. Many times, she's missed it. She brakes, hearing the good German squeak of the Silver Nazi's strong disc brakes. She bought this car with German royalties on her first best seller—a book intensely critical of Germans. Some revenge! The Nazis had their good points, though. They build the best cars and crematoria. And what with the world being full of multinational conglomerates, who's to tell where the money goes anyway? The Germans, the Arabs, the Japanese . . . it's impossible nowadays to keep your money out of the wrong pockets the way her parents thought they could. And what *are* the wrong pockets, anyway? The world was more morally intelligible in the forties—the decade of her birth. Now it's a mess. Heroes and villains all mixed up. Who can tell the potter from the pot, or the dancer from the dance? Isadora often wishes she had been born in her parents' generation—when Nazis were Nazis and good Americans were Good Americans, when the intellectuals still thought socialism could save the world. When capitalism was seen as the only evil (rather than human, or rather inhuman, nature) and when sexual freedom hadn't yet been widely tried and was, therefore, still seen as some sort of panacea—at least by Provincetown bohemians of her parents' generation.

Sometimes, in fact, she even envied her grandparents' generation, who could call a war a name as naïve and hopeful as "The Great War," as if there could be only one. It was given to her luckless generation to know that *that* particular war was only the dress rehearsal for World War II, while the Korean War and Vietnam were mere showcases for the race's flaming talent for self-destruction—with the Main Event, of course, still to come. That her grandfather's generation could even talk about a "war to end all wars" bespoke a chasm between her and them that was almost mind-boggling.

Damn. She misses the exit, zooms down to Westport thinking how dangerous it is for her, a mother of a three-year-old daughter who is totally dependent on her, to be driving stoned. A hippie at thirty-nine—how embarrassing. Though she looks perhaps thirty-three. Far prettier than she was at thirty-three, everyone tells her. She's thinner, for one thing, and pregnancy gave her a bloom and cheekbones she never had before. Money also helps: facials at

7

Arden, sixty-dollar haircuts, health spas every winter, and designer clothes never hurt a woman's looks. She's as blond and open-eyed as in her teens, though the forehead furrows—her worry lines—keep deepening. It's Josh who looks thirty-nine—with his balding bean, his laugh lines, his eye-crinkles.

"Fuck other men, go ahead," he said last week with that maddening mock-indifference of his. And she does. She does and enjoys it mightily, too—having come to the age where, unimpeded by any pleasure inhibition, and knowing full well that she was born to die, her orgasms grasp at the emptiness of certain death with unaccustomed ferocity. But sometimes the pain of loss, the loss of family, the loss of cuddly evenings in bed reading aloud from Dickens or watching old movies (they were thus ensconced when labor began three years ago and Mandy burst forth upon the scene) is too much to bear. She remembers the couple they were when they first moved to Connecticut, he writing in one room, she in another, one bouncy dog between them (a Bichon Frisé named Chekarf); no baby, no blasted nanny invading their lives, time to fuck at odd hours of the day or night, weekend dinner parties for New York friends for whom they both cooked, both served, both cleaned up, then fell into bed bone-tired and giggled like slumber-party chums before they fell asleep, whether they fucked or not.

The house bloomed with plants, with life, with sunshine on the barnboard walls. They adopted a shaggy old mutt with mange from a local pound and cured her with their love, their life-giving sunny home, their rooms which reeked of good sex and home-baked bread, their home where typewriters clacked and unlikely people fell in love at their famous brunches, their home which danced with orgone energy, with life-force—for what else could it have been?

Now she veers around the exit, thinking of the evening she has spent in bed with her disc jockey (or Dick Jockey, as her best friend calls him). Five hours in the Ho Hum Motel (a name that always makes her think of the Seven Dwarfs)—a local hot pillow, where no one ever arrives with luggage; the desk clerk would no doubt have a heart attack if anyone ever did. "Velvet tunnels," she had muttered somewhere into the fourth stoned hour, the eighth stoned orgasm—amazing as that seems in retrospect—and he was beguiled. A poetic type. Errol Dickinson from Hartford (named for Flynn, not Emily). The sort of guy who reads *Beowulf* and Harold Robbins with equal enthusiasm. A cocksman par excellence, but also enough the *cavalier servente* to know that women

8

respond as much to sweet words as soft licks. Errol is a genius in the sack, but he can say (and maybe even mean) things like, "I'd fight off Grendel for you and go search for the Third Ring." He writes poetry, too, but thus far has had the courtesy not to bring it to their trysts. The time may come when he does. What then? Will she flee in the night? Isadora has been famous long enough to know that often when one wants simply to get laid, one gets unpublished manuscripts instead. And he is nice, poetic, decent, almost lovable—too nice to offend. She doesn't fuck mean men anymore, ever. That went out with her twenties, thank Goddess.

Errol catches on fast, too.

"Whenever I think of you, I know there's a God," he says, "and I thank Her."

What a guy.

She zooms out of the exit, home along country roads. Her headlights on high beam (there is so little traffic), she does sixty, hoping her disc brakes will come to the rescue if an animal darts out. Her car bears a sticker from the Friends of Animals, which reads: I BRAKE FOR ANIMALS. A silly slogan. Should vegetarians have I BRAKE FOR VEGETABLES on their bumpers? "Why are you a vegetarian," someone once asked our utterly deserving Nobel laureate, I. B. Singer, "for health reasons?" "The health of the animals," the wry old Jew replied. Isadora loves animals, too, and won't wear fur coats or own stock in automated farms. But last winter, it dawned on her as she snuggled smugly into her goosedown parka that they kill the geese, too. What a downer. She might as well mink it, if mink didn't make her think of Jewish grandmothers. It is an index of her middle-agedness which fast approacheth that most of her women friends have minks. Some of the men, too. Help.

Home, home, home. Her steep and curving driveway (which ices over in winter) is such a welcome sight. Never does she zoom down it without thinking of that scene in *Garp* where Garp's wife bites off her lover's penis and the kid gets killed. Literary overkill. In real life nothing is so full of ironies. (Or else the ironies take years to iron out.) Still she likes Irving, with his feisty little wrestler's style, his nice wife he went and left, his damped-down sexuality, his sat-upon violence, the Smollett of contemporary novelists. No realist—but then, is *she*? Is *anyone* in a world where three-year-old babies like her own stomp around the living room chanting "Sadat got shot! Sadat got shot!" without knowing either who Sadat is or what it means to "got shot."

QUIM, the Silver Nazi, shudders to a stop (not unlike her own most recent orgasm). The house lights are on. The replacement Bichon, Dogstoyevsky, who came into their lives when the next-to-last nanny—an insufferably bossy English girl—ran over Chekarf, yips and yaps from the rectangular stairwell window. Isadora loved Chekarf better, she's ashamed to admit. He had something of the mutt in him, and a Russian-Jewish soul. Dogstoyevsky is a Fairfield County goy, despite his hopeful name. Maybe she should have replaced Chekarf with an Airedale, or a German Shepherd, or—what Mandy wants most in all this world (except her daddy back)—a "Labradog."

She opens the huge hand-hewn door with its rustic heart-shaped hardware and Dogstoyevsky jumps on her. What do separated people *do* without dogs? "Comfort me with Bichons," she used to say to Josh in happier times.

She puts down her bag, throws off her big pink and magenta sweater (bought in Stockholm on a book tour), pulls off her purple cowboy boots, and starts her nightly ablutions. She is almost used to having the bedroom to herself, though it still spooks her sometimes, late at night. It took five weeks before she moved her evening gowns into the closet he vacated, six weeks before she moved her cosmetics to his sink, seven weeks before she dared to use the hot tub with another man (late one night when Mandy was asleep), and still she sleeps on her side of the waterbed, as if to leave room for him. She wants him back. But maybe not just yet. And not the way he is now—depressed, rejecting, seething with unspoken rage.

"*Black* soap?" Woody Allen asked in *Annie Hall*. Isadora uses it, too—Dr. Lazlo's famous formula. Sea Mud soap at thirteen dollars a cake. Thorstein Veblen must be giggling in his grave. And what in heaven's name is "Sea Mud"? Primal ooze? The muck that trapped the dinosaurs? Beauty goop from the La Brea tar pits? Whatever it is, it has certainly helped her skin. Or maybe Errol has. After a night with him, she looks so *healthy* and her nipples tingle with hickies for days after.

But Errol could get to be a problem. Already, he is starting to say "I love you," at odd moments in bed. Or does she delude herself? Errol is such a consummate cocksman that all the endearments he whispers in bed seem oddly *generalized*—as if applicable to *any*one: to wit: "You're so beautiful." "Your skin is so soft." "I love your pussy." "I love you wrapped around me." "Oooo what you do to me." "I can't get enough of you."

10

Errol is a Connecticut legend. Long, lanky, with one brown eye and one blue, and dressed like the proverbial rhinestone cowboy, Errol's fame extends from Hartford to Old Greenwich. Isadora shares him with a friend—an unlikely friend to share a cock with, but then, truth is indeed always stranger than fiction. She shares him with Lola Birk Harvey—a Connecticut heiress from Greenwich, who lives on an immense estate on the Sound with her venture-capitalist husband, a stuffed shirt named Bruce.

Lola's hobby is adultery. She is a literary agent by profession, but never has had more than a few clients because her avocation is so time-consuming. Lola grew up in New York in the neighborhood of the Madison Avenue Presbyterian Church, within shouting distance of Le Cirque and the Sailboat Pond. Her father before her was a literary agent, Foster Birk—but she has run his business nearly into the ground because she doesn't care enough about making money. (On her mother's side, she inherited a bundle—and her husband is awfully rich, too.)

What Lola cares about is the art of adultery and she *knows* things Isadora never even *dreamed* about. Like how to meet men in Merritt Parkway commuter parking lots. Like how to require that they use rented cars. Like how to keep a collection of wigs in different colors so as never to be recognized. Like how to have a handbag big enough for wine and cheese and sexy underwear. Like how to keep a corkscrew and plastic champagne glasses secreted in the car.

Lola does things with style, even sex. She knows that sex is an art, not a science. She uses her prim and proper heiress exterior to great advantage. Nobody *thinks* Lola fucks, so Lola can always stalk her prey in her own sweet time. She has a long "lead time" (as they say in the magazine biz): lunches, dinners, brunches, cocktail dates in New York or Greenwich. And then, just when the guy is beginning to wonder why this cool, angular blonde keeps calling him, just when he starts to think she wants him to write the Great American Novel (an apparently universal fantasy in this country), blue-eyed Lola (who is forty, but looks thirty-five) leans over the cocktail table, touches her hand to his, and says, "Did I ever tell you how much you turn me on?"

"The guy is always amazed," Lola reports. "Here I am—prim and proper Lola Harvey—seeming to make a *pass*. They never believe it. Never. Whereupon I continue with the line 'When can we be alone together?' And then I stroke his thigh under the table —and, if it's dark enough—take the measure of his hard-on. Listen, Isadora, if he hasn't got one by now, forget it. And if he has, then I can decide whether or not it's worth it to set up a tryst."

Isadora is amazed. Lola knows things about seducing men undreamt of in Isadora's supposedly sensual youth ("Hot Youth" as Byron called it). What on earth did she know then? Nothing. Sex at thirty-nine is better than ever. The only trouble is finding partners. Hah. Partners who aren't scared of famous women, aren't fame fuckers, or gold diggers, or daddy figures (who want to save you from yourself). How many times has Isadora heard the line "You've been my sexual fantasy for seven years—ever since I read 'that book of yours,'" and then gotten into bed only to discover the guy couldn't get it up? Who *wants* to be a sexual fantasy for seven years, Isadora thinks. How can sexual fantasy do other than disappoint?

"That book of hers" haunts her. Haunts her and blesses her both. On the one hand, *Candida Confesses* made her a "household word"—like Ajax or Vaseline. On the other, it bestowed upon her unsuspecting youth a strange sort of sexual smirch. Many people could see her only as the nymphomaniac of the literary world—when she is really (as her friends all know) a nice, *hamish* Jewish girl from Central Park West at heart.

And so she is home. She makes her reverse toilette, à la Dr. Lazlo, throws on a red flannel Lanz nightgown—a granny gown suitable only for manless nights—and tiptoes upstairs to see her daughter.

In a room as cluttered with stuffed animals (or "aminals," as Amanda still says) as a toy store, a room full of exotic unicorns and dragons and dromedaries—as well as the more normal Poohs and Paddingtons and Miss Piggys—Amanda sleeps in a bright red toddler's bed, sleeps clutching her "transitional object," a smallish stuffed camel she has named Camelia.

Camelia Camel was given to Amanda by one of Isadora's dearest friends in the world, her fairy godmother, Hope—Hope of the steel-gray hair, the voluminous tits, the melting voice, the gentle guidance in a world without guidelines. Hope, who midwifed Isadora's first book of poems almost a dozen years ago, is nearly sixty now. "It just gets better, darling," she always tells Isadora when she expresses her fear of aging. "There are presents still to unwrap under the tree. It gets less frantic, darling—and you know what?"

"What?" Isadora asks.

12

"You stop thinking about sex all the time," Hope says with a sly smile.

Somehow, Amanda knew at once that Hope was her fairy godmother, too. Given Hope's gift, she clutched the caramel-colored camel to her breast, dubbed her Camelia at once, and hasn't let go of her since. Oh, Amanda is one alliterative kid—a lover of language for language's sake just like her mom and dad, a maker of names, of portmanteau words like *Labradog*. Apparently she, too, was born under the Scribbling Star.

Goddess forbid, Isadora thinks—feeling that life is hard enough, and mother-daughter grief is grievous enough without both pursuing the same muse.

Her mother painted, still does in fact. So Isadora abandoned her brush for quill at age eighteen and never once looked back. Sometimes she longs to do a watercolor. She promises herself that when her novel-writing days are done, she'll break her pens, throw out her legal pads (no word processor for eighteenth-century Isadora, though she rents one for her secretary), and spend her dotage doing watercolors—like her old friend and mentor Kurt Hammer (once Guru of Big Sur, now mischievously haunting her from Writers' Heaven).

Amanda sleeps, Camelia in her arms. Amanda at three lives entirely in the moment, and worries not at all about whether she'll be a writer or painter—or even actress—which every actress and director Isadora knows has, in fact, predicted. She sleeps, her eyelids periwinkle blue, shading off to lavender-pink over the domes of her sight. Tendrils of red hair swirl about her cheeks; her strawberry bangs cling dewily to her high forehead; her cheeks are flushed with three-year-old dreams—dreams of dromedaries drowsily traversing dream deserts, dreams of "Labradogs" and dream dragons, of oneiric "aminals," unicorns, griffins, Eeyores, Poohs, Kermit Frogs, and Mickey Mouses.

"Goddess bless and Goddess keep," says Isadora—who, during her pregnancy became convinced that God must be a woman. She takes all dogmas—even feminist—with many grains of salt, but it does seem to her that God must certainly have a female aspect, and she, mother of an only daughter, would rather pray to Her than Him.

God, of course, has no gender, or all gender—if you will. Yin and Yang, Shiva and Kali, Great Mother and Horned God, Christ and Mary, Moses and . . . who? Alas, only the Jews have neglected

Her totally. The religion of Isadora's birth leaves out women entirely. But she will compensate—silly as she feels uttering the words "Goddess bless"—yet also somehow *safe*.

She kisses Amanda's flushed pink cheek. The child turns, lets out an unintelligible syllable, and curls into an almost fetal pose. Tenderly, as mothers do, Isadora covers up her daughter's toes. Tears spring from her eyes as she thinks of her half-fatherless little girl, the griefs of womanhood Amanda now knows nothing of, the griefs she caused her mother that Amanda doubtless will cause her, the betrayals, the abandonments by men—from father on, and the long journey to sanity a woman takes from birth to middle years.

She wishes Amanda at least that: to be saner at forty than at twenty. Some women go mad at forty, go into unending depressions, kill themselves, or wind up institutionalized for alcohol or dope, untapped talent, sealed-up rage. Isadora's gone the other way, saner now than ever, despite her grief. She has her work, her child, even though she rides her moods up and down like a see-saw, or a roller coaster. So what if she has no live-in man? No resident muse to inspire her, no best-friend-in-the-world, no constant comforter? She has a variety of part-time comforters, and right now she wants no permanent one. Maybe never. Marriage, which she has tried thrice, has thrice proved impossible. And maybe marriage *is* impossible in a world from which ceremony and convention have fled and only the great "I want, I want" is left.

Still, she weeps for Amanda, for herself, for her mother and her grandmother, for all her sisters—three by blood and millions by book—around the world. It is both blessing and curse to be born female, as Isadora knows by now. She also knows the vanity of bringing babies into a world armed to the skies with nuclear devices, a world where presidents get shot routinely on the evening news, where nobody knows what money means, whether love lasts, or how families can stay together long enough to grow up.

"Good night, Amanda. Good night, Camelia," Isadora says.

And then she tucks herself in bed.

Alone.

2

By the Light of a Jahrzeit Candle

When one subtracts from life infancy
(which is vegetation), sleep,
eating, and swilling—buttoning
and unbuttoning—how much
remains of downright existence?
The summer of a dormouse.
—BYRON
Letters & Journals

The great thing about the dead,
they make space.
—JOHN UPDIKE
Rabbit Is Rich

Patch grief with proverbs.
—MIGUEL DE CERVANTES

WHEN did their present troubles begin? Have you ever noticed that the contemporary antihero or antiheroine always asks this early in the narrative, for there can be no story without troubles.

And the troubles are always the same. Perched as we are on the very ledge of doom, two minutes on the clock before nuclear devastation, we still cry about sex and death. We still moan about loves and moneys lost. We do not cry about the coming conflagration because we cannot even comprehend it.

The wars get worse each decade. Somewhere in the world, each moment, someone is already falling off the ledge of doom. Isadora listens to eighteenth-century music while she writes so as not to think of the stopped screams in Argentina, the starving babes in Africa, the tinderbox of the Middle East, the moaning of the hordes of India, the hands and heads lopped off in Islam.

When did her present troubles begin? Did they begin with the novel she published last fall, which, at last, made even her *enemies* grudgingly admit that she was a writer to be reckoned with? Oh, she had been notorious before, noticed before, but never without condescension. She began to publish poems in the sexy sixties, was seen on the cover of *Time* in the surly seventies, but always she was seen as a dame, a broad, the Marilyn Monroe or the Barbra Streisand of the book world, not so much a creator as a *persona*, not so much an artist as a *woman* artist. Of course, she began to make her way in the world when women were all the rage—as if an entire gender could go in and out of style. She wrote a book of poems called *Vaginal Flowers* when both vaginas and flowers were "in." She was shocking when shocking was more important than anything, trendy when trendy was all there was to know, and female when female was hot. She had been good box office since the seventies—but not until her last novel (an historical epic of Venice and Venetian painters entitled *Tintoretto's Daughter*) was there anything like *respect* for the way she could write.

Did her troubles begin when that newfound success alienated

her husband, Josh (who, to his chagrin, was still publishing invisible novels), and caused him to abandon her and their daughter, Amanda, to sit za-zen in a chilly monastery in Kyoto? Did they begin when the nanny—that hearty English one with big tits—ran over her dog in her own driveway? Good old Chekarf, their beloved Bichon Frisé (named for Isadora's grandfather's favorite short-story writer—and hers), was, in a way, the first child of their marriage. When he went, so did something between Josh and Isadora. Shortly thereafter Josh departed for Japan, leaving her to contemplate her success and the chaos it had wrought, the marble urn containing Chekarf's ashes (with his old dog collar draped around the neck), and the ruins of her life. Women want work and love just like everyone else; why does having one always lead to banishing the other?

Did her troubles begin when Josh came back from Japan and proposed that the answer to all their woes was living apart three days a week, maintaining separate "spaces," fucking their brains out with other people, then telling each other about it as a turn-on? Did they begin when Isadora got involved in an affair with her investment counselor—a preppy fellow named Lowell Strathmore, with his white boxer shorts, his Turnbull and Asser shirts, his Savile Row suits, his mansion in Southport, his heiress wife with thrice the requisite number of teeth, and his fourteen-year-old daughter with the $100,000 horse? Or did they begin when she fell for a poet from Bethel—a guilt-ridden lapsed Catholic who could almost never get it up with her, but wrote her the most beautiful poems? Or did it begin the day she walked into her husband's *other* studio, just down the road—and found him—oh, cliché of clichés—fondling one of his part-time typists, a brain-damaged blonde dressed up in gold lamé Frederick's of Hollywood lingerie (for Josh was not only a Zen Buddhist, but an underwear freak)? No. She could have endured all that. Her hands shake when she contemplates Josh's abandonments, but a shaky hand may steady itself on a stout heart. She thinks her troubles really began in earnest on the day of her grandfather's funeral, when she read as the eulogy, the memoir of him she scrawled as he lay dying, and the rabbi turned green to hear such words—spoken by a woman yet—in the house of the Father God.

It was a freezing day in January. One of those days when the filth of New York is frozen in week-old snow, congealed to ice; when even the dogshit, which steams briefly before freezing, is odorless; when winds punish the corners of Riverside Drive, and the funeral directors at the Riverside are doing such a flourishing business you'd swear they had revolving walls like an old stage set.

"Pick up your coats at the elevator, not in the family room," they say as they press the mourners forward. And suddenly the bereaved relatives realize that their coatrack has been moved to the elevator alcove, so another group of mourners can now occupy the family room, murmuring and sympathizing.

Isadora arrived with Josh and her youngest sister Chloe (Randy, the oldest, being still in the Middle East, and Lahlah—who by now lived on the Last Commune in Oregon with her quintuplets—not having the bread to come east for the funeral).

"It's like a scene from *The Loved One*," Chloe said, looking around at the relatives.

And it was true. Isadora had to giggle. Her mother and aunt were saying their tentative, paranoid hellos, not having spoken for nearly thirty years prior to her grandfather's final illness. The trouble with them was that they were two peas in a pod, similar enough to be twins, though two years apart. They looked alike, talked alike, both were endowed with immense talent to paint, which the old man had sat upon—with their neurotic consent. Isadora's aunt was gay, her mother straight, but the two sisters were identical for all of that. Her aunt had a talent for being trod upon by her lovers quite as successfully as Isadora's mother was trod upon by her father. Her father, the Tsatske King, her father, the legendary Nat White, whose baffling paternal wisdom to her was: "Never follow a dog act" and "You know you're on the skids when you play yourself in the film version of your autobiography." Her father, who, all through her childhood, had wheeled and dealed, flown back and forth to Japan as some people commute to Paramus, and who now at seventy, wanted nothing more than the affection of the children he had always half ignored before. Her father, the dynamo, the seducer, the charismatic manipulator. Her father, who began life in "Bronzeville" as Nathan Weiss, translated himself to White when he hit the Catskills as a comedian in the thirties, became a band leader in Manhattan *boîtes* shortly after that, and finally gave up art for commerce in the forties, deciding that the latter was, after all, a surer thing than the former. But Isadora's being an artist was profoundly important to him. His second daughter was the arrow from his loins which hit the mark that he himself could not. He crowed over her success as if it were his own—which indeed in some ways it was.

"How are you, my lovely?" he asked, embracing Isadora like a lover and hardly looking at Chloe, as usual.

"Fine, Dad." Isadora had only recently begun calling her father "Dad" and it still felt funny to her. All through her childhood he was "Nat" and her mother "Jude." Her grandfather and grandmother, with whom they lived, were "Papa" and "Mama." *They* were the true parents; Nat and Jude were siblings of sorts—albeit strange ones.

"Let me look at you," her father said. That was what he *always* said.

"You look great. You're keeping your weight down. That's the ticket. Exercise, exercise, exercise." Isadora couldn't help thinking that if they hadn't been at a funeral, he might have begun doing calisthenics in place. Her father frequently burst into little spasms of indoor exercise. He was vain of looking fifty at seventy. By dint of regular workouts, the genetic accident of having all his hair, he looked as attractive at seventy as most men look in their prime. And *wasn't* he still in his prime? His prime went on forever, it seemed. Was this because he'd had a sauna and gym installed in his office long before such things were commonplace? Or because he had read *Prevention* magazine since the forties (so he could alternate eating sunflower seeds and yogurt with drinking triple martinis and eating beef Wellington)? He was so weight-conscious that he noticed every pound Isadora put on even before she did. Sometimes she felt she gained weight just to plague him and to thwart their oedipal connection. He adored her and at times had seemed indifferent to her sisters. That was her sisters' problem, and hers.

But Isadora was not just his fantasy lover; she was also his fantasy son. Isadora's current therapist, a bouncy grayhaired lady named Shirley Frumkin, maintained that Isadora's parents had instructed her to be "the daughter you are and the son we never had."

"No wonder you were confused," said Shirley. "Nobody can be both those things."

And it was true. Isadora knew herself as a projection of her parents' dreams. All their own thwarted artistic ambitions—her father's as a musician, her mother's as a painter—poured into her. She *had* to be a successful artist of some sort, more successful in the world outside than any son. But she also had to be a girl, a lover, a wife, a mother. Finally, with Amanda's birth, and the publication of *Tintoretto's Daughter* (a novel in which—ironically—

she imagined herself as a Renaissance painter), she had brought all these expectations together. She had it all, she thought. Whereupon her marriage cracked and Josh moved out.

A year of deaths and losses. Great success followed by unprecedented disasters. Every woman's greatest nightmare: to win success only to lose the one man she ever really loved.

Her grandfather's funeral was the turning point, his death the death knell of the marriage. Some deaths mark the end of relationships; others the beginning. The spirit of the deceased lives on to mock the living and to test their attachments. And Isadora's Grandfather Stoloff was nothing if not a mocker. Even in death, he held the whole family captive. Even in death, he set them against each other as he had done in life.

Since the old man Stoloff had not decided he wanted a rabbi at the funeral until the very last moment, he naturally knew no rabbis, or, rather, no rabbis knew him. That left Isadora's family with rent-a-rabbi: whatever sorry synagogueless specimen the funeral directors happened to have on tap. Isadora, for one, resented this —resented her grandfather both for being a devout atheist and godless Marxist most of his adult life and then for making an irritating deathbed reversion to Judaism. If only he'd had the foresight to revert a year or two *before* his death, some rabbi might have known what to say about him. But no. He decided to be a proper Jew only during his last delirium. So there they were, Isadora, her mother, father, aunt, and one sister, all squeezed into a tiny rabbi-roomlet at the Riverside, trying to tell a total stranger about their maddeningly complex patriarch, a man with more contradictions and ambiguities than his ninety-seven years, a man who could scarcely be summed up in a year of talk, let alone the five minutes allotted them before the ceremony. (O ye who are about to die—coach your clergyman!)

"What was Mr. Stoler like?" asked the rabbi, wearing a homburg, and taking notes on a three-by-five card like a schoolteacher.

"Stoloff," said Isadora's mother, looking pained. She was wearing a black Chanel suit and masses of pearls which she fingered like worry beads. Why is it always so excruciating when they mispronounce the name of someone you love when he is dead or dying?

"Ah, Stoloff," said the rabbi, looking pink and scrubbed as a pig. Couldn't they at least have provided a bearded rabbi? "Yes, where was Mr. Stoloff born?"

Blank looks all around.

"It wasn't Odessa," Isadora's mother said, "though he grew up there."

"Diatlovo, in the Government of Grodno," Isadora said.

"How do you know?" Her father was amazed.

"He told me a few days before he died."

"I never asked," her Aunt Gilda said, her Mexican silver earrings flashing. She was dressed in a black cashmere shawl and black velvet dirndl. Velvety black suede boots clung to her slender legs. She was not of that recent school of lesbians who dress grotesquely as a political statement. Rather, she harked back to the stylish days of Vita, Virginia, and Djuna. Both she and Isadora's mother looked gorgeous in their grief.

"And his Jewish name?" asked the rabbi.

"Schmuel," said her mother. "He was Samuel, but everyone called him 'Stoloff.' "

"His wife?" asked the rabbi.

"She died twelve years ago," my sister said. "Her name was Malke—Mary in English."

"And his age?"

"Ninety-seven," they all said in unison.

"Ah—a very long-lived man."

From the way he said "long-lived" (he added two syllables above the usual number like a rabbi out of Philip Roth), Isadora knew with foreboding and horror that they could all look forward to an oration upon the theme of Methuselah and the blessings of a long life. She had been to enough Jewish funerals to foretell this with horrid certainty.

Before leaving Connecticut that morning, Isadora had crammed into her handbag the scrawled remembrance of her grandfather's death and dying which she had written at a white heat, her pen propelled by the winds of his passing. While he lay expiring in a grim nursing home in Spring Valley, she was scribbling about him, as if by her scribbling she could make him stay. Now she was trembling with desire and fear—desire to read this memoir to the assembled relatives and friends, and fear that it would horribly offend them, for it was hardly a conventional eulogy. She had told her father and mother about it on the phone, and her father, as usual, sensing a good media event, wanted her to read it, while her mother wasn't sure.

"Rabbi," said her father, "this is Mr. Stoloff's granddaughter, my daughter, Isadora Wing." He waited for the aha of recognition. It never came.

"She is the well-known author," said Isadora's father, ever the promoter, ever the *tummler.* Isadora squirmed with embarrassment. Apparently her reputation had not penetrated the *shuls* of mid-Manhattan.

"You probably know her *Vaginal Flowers,* or perhaps her most recent best seller, *Tintoretto's Daughter,*" her father went on.

"*Dad,*" she squirmed. Isadora actually blushed. The word *vaginal* never sounded dirtier than it did there in that Rabbi-roomlet.

Her father charged blithely ahead. "Well, not many people know that she is a poet as well as a novelist, and it is the wish of the entire family . . ." (her mother and aunt did not seem so sure) "that she read her memoir and an elegy to Mr. Stoloff in lieu of a eulogy."

"Certainly, certainly," said the rabbi, looking a little disappointed not to be able to do his Methuselah number. "Surely a member of the family who knew and loved him is preferable to a total stranger . . ." One could not help feeling the rabbi was annoyed to be preempted.

"But we do want all the proper prayers in Hebrew, before and after," Isadora's mother said—her mother, who had probably never in her life heard Hebrew prayers except at funerals and bar mitzvahs. "He would have wanted that," she added.

"And what about the Kaddish? Who will say the Kaddish?" the rabbi asked. "I can arrange for some *yeshiva bucher* to say Kaddish."

Yes! Yes! Isadora thought. Do it right. Speed his passing. But her mother said no. Isadora was crestfallen.

"My daughter will read her memoir and a poem," Jude said resolutely, "and then you will close with a prayer."

"And *The Rubáiyát,*" said Isadora, "his favorite poem. I will read part of that."

"Of course, Miss Wing," said the rabbi, deferential to the *idea* of Fame, even if he'd never heard of the *person.* "Of course."

So it was that Isadora came to read her blasphemous memoir to an audience consisting of her sister, her mother, her father, her aunt, her cousins, her husband, two ex-husbands (one a psychiatrist, the other a psychotic), assorted friends and acquaintances— and one horrified rabbi.

"As I begin writing this, my grandfather is dying in a hospital in Spring Valley, New York, dying alone, with paid nurses to attend him, dying thousands of miles from the town in Russia where he

23

was born ninety-seven years ago—a town I do not even know the name of.

"I am writing, fast, my pen speeding over the page, writing in the hopes that if I get it all down, get it right (or as nearly right as an American granddaughter can), it will ease his passage—or mine. I know that death is a movement toward light—or so I said once in a poem—but I also know that to die by inches, and every inch alone, is neither light nor just—though it is common.

"He was a painter. He should have died the minute he could no longer paint, the minute the cataracts, the cancer, the arthritis, the exhaustion, the despair overwhelmed him. But that would be too simple, and just as we do not choose our loves or our children, we do not choose our deaths. I have known a number of men in their nineties who died by inches—Kurt Hammer, Louis Untermeyer, and my grandfather—and each at the end truly wished to die, but his wish was no command.

"I knew him only and always as Papa. My parents were Jude and Nat in that phony thirties tradition of parents-as-pals. We all lived to regret it. But Papa was the patriarch—with all the good and bad that word implies. In a house full of artists, he had the best studio, the only studio. Amongst daughter-painters he held his maulstick like a magic wand (or a bludgeon) over their heads."

Normally Isadora was a good reader. She could hold an audience captive with her incantatory poems; she could read other people's poems and novels with the conviction of a born actress. But reading this painfully self-revelatory memoir, her conviction faltered, her palms sweated. She stood at the shaky lectern, wishing she had something more to hold on to. She had nothing, not even Papa's hand. She had committed herself to this as one commits oneself to childbirth—at a moment one would commit to anything.

"When I was born, it seems he was already an old man. In fact, he was only fifty-nine. He wore round wire-rimmed glasses and painted in the witch-hatted studio that crowned the triplex apartment on Seventy-seventh Street where I grew up. That curious gothic apartment house terminates skyward in a trapezoidal roof containing a huge northern window which rattled (perhaps still rattles) in the wind that the Museum of Natural History fails to block. The window shades were dull forest green and drawn up on pulleys from below; a trapdoor separated the studio from the rest of the house. On one wall of the studio hung a death mask of Beethoven, as mute in white plaster as his ears became at the end. Only the wind penetrated those ears; and his domed eyes were sightless as well. This blind Beethoven was watched, however, by an open-eyed Voltaire, present in a bust of the same dusty white plaster.

24

"On Halloween, a sheet would be draped from Beethoven's mask, a candle placed next to a jawless skull perched on my grandfather's heavy, paint-spattered easel, and we children would gather, teeth chattering, for the tale of Dracula, told by my mother in this witchiest of settings. Here, in the heart of New York, was Transylvania— or as near to it as one could get.

"I was too little. My older sister's friends—five years older—were having the party and I was just allowed, as special grace, to creep up the studio stairs, sit upon the middle step, and listen.

"Never have I regretted any grace so much! The stake might as well have been driven through my heart; the bats might as well have flown through my skull. The nightmare galloped through my dreams for years after that fatal story hour! An evil that cannot die indeed!—but my grandfather lives on, being transfused when he wishes to die, being X-rayed when he has no lungs, being spiked through the hand and heart with tubes and needles like the living dead."

Nice, she thought. Dracula in the intensive-care unit. That was indeed how intensive-care units always made her feel.

"The skull, the death mask, the bust of Voltaire, the easel—these were my grandfather's artifacts and amulets. In the studio, there were also two damp, domed closets. One contained canvas by the roll and stretchers and tacks (my grandfather always stretched his own canvases and nearly always bashed his thumb), and another contained mysterious clothes left by mysterious sitters. A general's dress jacket, but no pants or hat; an evening gown of a style to do Mme. Vionnet proud (all paillettes and pastel chiffon); a double-breasted blazer which might have been worn to Cliveden by the Duke of Windsor.

"Papa was a portrait painter for a living (in the thirties he'd done movie posters for MGM) and his sitters were all posh, upper-class, and gentile. They rarely deigned to come, but sent instead their photographs, their clothes, a lock of hair, a swatch of fabric.

" 'Who's that?' I used to ask about the pink-faced, pinstriped, three-piece-suited man whose glowing oil-painted image (still wet) was perched on the easel.

" 'Mr. Johnson,' Papa would reply.

" 'Who's that?' I would ask the next day, when the easel bore his white-haired consort in pearls and robin's-egg blue silk.

" 'Mrs. Johnson,' Papa would say.

"I soon found out the two were no relation. Johnson was simply the most goyish name that came to mind. All the paying customers were Johnson—while the voluminous black nudes who posed at the Art Students League, or the Spanish guitarists lured in to pose for a day, all had their own particular first names. Velda or Luis or Roberto or Geneva. Only the clientele were scorned and nameless —painted for money, not love.

25

"(What I learned from this was: always write for love not money, but try to be paid for it, too.)"

Aha, thought Isadora, this is true. My whole life's lesson, gleaned from Grandpa: write for love, but do not love *merely* in order to write about it.

"He passed his legacy to me—he who painted at the top of the house (as I now write above the family roar). I was never banned from his studio; nor is my daughter banned from mine. 'I am writing a novel, Mommy,' Amanda says, at two—as I, at two, painted 'Mr. Johnson' and 'Mrs. Johnson' alongside my grandfather.

" 'Who's in your novel, Mandy?'

" 'Kermit the Frog an' Mickey Mouse, Mommy, Daddy . . . But not Lucinda.' (Lucinda is the little girl Amanda loves to hate, her best/worst friend in the world.)

Yes, thought Isadora, such relationships begin early. Catullus was right: "I hate and I love" is the essence of life.

"The smell of oil paints and turpentine so infused my childhood that I've only to pass an artist's studio to be plunged back, through the infallible offices of that Mnemosyne who lives in the nose, to my childhood."

Smells, she thought. Why do smells trigger memory so insistently? She'd read once that the olfactory lobes are the oldest parts of the brain, what we have in common with the "lower" mammals —if you considered dogs and dromedaries lower, which she didn't. Isadora was a great smeller. She had always liked gamy men, found them sexier than the overbathed variety. And as for herself, she spent fortunes on perfumes, her current favorite being Opium. "If you smell good, you can conquer the world," she used to quip. Her perfumes had "progressed" from Chanel No. 5 in high school, to Shalimar in college, Ma Griffe in graduate school, Fidji when she first met Josh, Bal à Versailles and Joy for their good years, and Opium since the birth of her daughter made her, at last, a woman. What could that possibly mean? That womanhood itself required an opiate?

"The tools of the painter's trade are as familiar to me as the tools of my own trade—and as precious. The sable brushes: Papa always washed them in the kitchen sink, at five each night, by painting them against a wet block of Ivory soap; the colors swirled in the soap, merged to become a muddy brown, then drifted away down the drain, leaving the soap white again. The turpentine: a smell of trees and forests; the primal smell of nature becoming art. The golden linseed oil: its sheen on the canvas when wet, and its strange gelatinous drops when it fell upon the easel and congealed. The Windsor and Newton paints in silvery cylindrical tubes, with their poetic names: alizarin crimson, cerulean blue, rose madder, vermilion, burnt umber, zinc white."

Reading aloud these names of paints, Isadora suddenly became comfortable—warmed, as it were, to her cold subject (like an after-dinner speaker hearing his first round of laughter, or an actor his first round of applause). The paint names had particular resonance for her. They evoked her childhood, like the smell of turpentine. What the hell, she thought, the speech was starting to flow. For better or for worse, she was into it.

" 'A good painter never uses black,' Papa would say, 'only *shmearers* use black.' Since black is all the colors put together, it was an article of Papa's faith that you made black yourself with hues of your own choosing. And you looked for the special colors in the black—the plums, the aubergines, the sea-floor greens. Black was not black, but dark violet or murky green. Nor was white white. It was ivory or eggshell or bluish or iridescent pearl. Once, when I was thirteen and already at the High School of Music and Art, Papa made me attempt a still life of eggs and onions, cut crystal and white satin, just to prove to me how many colors were in 'white.' It was a lesson I never forgot.'

"Nor was there such a thing as 'flesh color'—whatever my Crayola box might say. Flesh was pink or ocher, ivory or greenish blue, brownish gold with umber shadows. Caucasians might be pinkish, yellowish, greenish—but never white; and blacks (Papa would have objected to the term *black* not because he was a racist, but because of its color-blind inaccuracy) were brownish, creamy, even purplish where shadows were cast upon their faces. Orientals might be amber, golden, green—but never 'yellow.' The world of race was a world of multicolored shadows; Papa taught me about dapple long before I read Gerard Manley Hopkins."

Here she looked into her audience and was again seized with self-consciousness. Bennett Wing, her Chinese-American second husband, sat in the audience looking inscrutable, as usual. Seven years had elapsed since she'd seen him, but he was ageless and unchanged, immortal perhaps. Or so it seemed. More gray in his thick hair was his only sign of age; his face was as unlined as ever. Perhaps he'd die that way—the Chinese Dorian Gray. Isadora had, after all, thought her grandfather immortal and here he was mocking her with his mortality. Bennett was surely mortal, too, despite his Buddha mask. Age could not wither him. He was pickled in psychoanalysis.

The black husband of a friend of Aunt Gilda's also betrayed no flicker of emotion at her reference to race. Unfortunately, we were living at a time in history when *any* reference to race was likely to be regarded as racism and Papa was of that benighted generation which said "Negro." Though she was only his Horatio, not the protagonist of the piece, somehow she felt guilty for his sins, charged with his debts of conscience.

"If the world was truly multicolored for him, then why was it so black? For one cannot write about Papa without chronicling his depression. A chronic and contagious depressive, he spread such gloom to his children and grandchildren that often they wished to escape him. 'Life,' he said, 'was pointless' ('till the end—when his tune changed). His philosophy, often stated—until it made us furious—was that the artists and intellectuals of the world carried the 'dead weight' along. *We* made life; they ate it up. We created light; they muddied it into darkness. I had a vision of my grandfather's beautiful white cake of Ivory soap, turning to mud under the mingled paints from his brush. That was what the world did to artists; that was how *they* treated *us*.

Isadora had vowed from earliest adolescence never to be bitter like her grandfather. She would risk *everything* with her work, show the world who she was. If they liked it—fine. And if not, at least she had committed herself. She would not die wondering.

"Papa's bitterness had, like all bitternesses, a personal foundation beneath the lofty generalization: he was unsung. Through no fault of the world's, really, but only his own.

"True, he had had the ill luck to be born in the era that saw the birth of 'Modern Art.' True, he was painting figuratively when Chagall and Picasso were in the saddle. True, he emulated Rembrandt and Vandyke in a world that emulated only Picasso—but still, his very eccentricity might have been turned to advantage—had he not been so eager to stand in his own light. For he had an absolutely unerring knack for alienating anyone who might do him good. Art critics, collectors, gallery owners—he would alienate with a swift insult, like a knee to the groin! Art critics he pronounced blind, and gallery owners venal (with which many artists would heartily agree —but not to their faces). As if *this* weren't enough, Papa steadfastly and resolutely concealed the very best of his work from public view. The stiff, formal portraits he exhibited; the dream sketches (as he called them), he hid away. These sketches—done in india ink and watercolor, fountain pen and pencil—are to me his best work. They are also astoundingly original and 'modern' in a timeless, untrendy way."

How awful, Isadora thought, to have to try to convince the world of the worth of Papa's work. His work *itself* should convince the world—had he not deliberately hidden his fierce dreams away from the world's scrutiny.

"He did them on bits of paper (for he sketched constantly, everywhere) and he had masses of them, in yellowing envelopes, in stacks in closets, fluttering up like moths when the door opened.

"A few years ago, I gave him a small blank notebook and bid him fill it for me, as a gift of love. Whenever he had an idea, a dream, a vision, he would paint it in the book. His dreams must have been terrifying. The frontispiece of the little book is a staring demon such as might guard the gates of hell. (Or is it merely a Hassid staring at his wouldbe assailant on the streets of Brooklyn?) A lion falls on the neck of a terrorized horse and blood flows down the page. Two Jews in wash and india ink hold tablets heavenward. A man runs with (or from?) a pack of wild dogs. Bloody-fanged dogs howl through the forests of the book. His mother's ghost floats through the pages—green-faced, black-wimpled. People dance to expel a dybbuk. Soldiers from his youth march to the Mongol border. A man slouches through the blue-black streets by moonlight. A dark sun explodes over two prisoners who flee in the blue-washed night. An old woman kneels, begging for bread. And again the mad dogs, the mad humans metamorphosing into dogs. And so on. The vision is bleak yet there is color in all the suffering, all the skies. He rejoiced with his pen and brush even while he spoke of gloom."

A felicitous phrase, Isadora thought. Wish I'd written it. (Isadora never could identify with her own writing, quite. It was as if some spirit wrote through her and even—especially—the happiest phrases seemed somehow not to be her own.)

"But he did not die then, when I began this memoir, despite the fact that it was a night of great agitation in the spheres. I began frenziedly to write this at three A.M. on the night of December 8, 1980, because I felt him dying. I felt his soul slipping from us; but ironically enough it was John Lennon who died that night (though I did not know till the following day). Meanwhile, as the radios all over the world played Beatles tapes, Papa lingered for two weeks past his ninety-seventh birthday. Driving out to see him in the ghastly old-age 'home' in Spring Valley, listening to Beatles songs being played obsessively, *in memoriam,* I did get to ask him where he was born. 'Diatlovo, in the Government of Grodno,' he said, but

29

that was just about the last rational thing he communicated. At the end, he issued paranoid warnings to us all ('They don't know poetry, they don't know painting, they only know money'), made me promise to lock up the baby (to keep her safe from kidnappers), failed to recognize his own children and grandchildren, and finally slid into the other world on January 6, 1981, just barely two weeks after his ninety-seventh birthday. He was born on December 24, 1883 and died on January 6, 1981. (It is somehow comforting to write down these 'hard' facts. They moor us to 'reality' when all else seems shaky.)"

It was the lectern that felt especially shaky now—as if Papa were rocking it from the other world.

"Unlike those pasteboard nonagenarians of pop fiction (who are born with the century and conveniently die with it), he was eyewitness to *none* of the great tragedies of his age. During the Russian Revolution, he was in England, then in America. During the holocaust, he was painting movie posters and posh portraits in New York. When Eliot was writing *The Wasteland,* he was reading *The Rubáiyát of Omar Khayyám.* The month before he died, he was still reading it. Besides *Eugene Onegin,* it was the only poem he really loved. I think he was proud of my poems in his way (certainly he inspired them from the first), but *Omar Khayyám* he read and read —even to the end. He would not hear of my literary argument that the poems describe the Sufi process of enlightenment, masked in the conventional language of romantic love. He read *The Rubaiyat* literally and loved it no less for that. He read me this verse (perhaps for the thousandth time in my life) before he lapsed into his last incoherence.

" 'Some for the Glories of This World; and some
Sigh for the Prophet's Paradise to come;
Ah, take the Cash, and let the Credit go,
Nor heed the rumble of a distant Drum!' "

People invariably love the poetry of their adolescence, Isadora thought—just as Lin Yutang has said that patriotism is the memory of foods eaten in childhood. How funny it is that no matter how sophisticated we think ourselves, in certain areas of life we are incorrigibly nostalgic.

"At the end there were horrible things—horrible because so ordinary: the old age 'home' with no cars in the parking lot, where no one came to visit because it was so sad. The refusal to use the walker, the falling, the outbursts, the desperate mumbles of 'I have to make a living' and 'There is a law in the United States that you cannot keep someone against their will.' 'Was he a shoemaker?' the

pretty young student nurse asked, hearing him constantly mutter:
'I have to make a living.' She wore a gold Star of David, but other
than that looked quite as goyish as the Draw Me girl.
" 'He was a great painter,' I said.
" 'Oh . . .' said the nice student nurse to be polite.
"One night, his regular nurse called me in Connecticut. I had
driven hours on snowy roads to get to him and then driven back,
but he didn't even remember I had been there. He wanted me to
come at once, or to come get him—it wasn't clear which.
" 'Send a car for me,' he said.
"I promised I would.
" 'I love you, Papa,' I said.
" 'I love you *more*,' he said, competitive to the end."

That was Papa, Isadora thought—too competitive with his family, but not competitive enough with the world.

"His nurse, a lovely woman with the unforgettably ornithological
name of Lola Falcon, took the phone then.
" 'He's agitated and he can't rest. Tell him to rest.' She put Papa
back on the phone.
" 'I have to make a living,' he croaked in that fading voice that
sounded like a toy whose battery is going dead. 'I have to make a
living.' (I was reminded of how my grandmother used to say, 'make
a leeving'—her Russian accent much stronger than his). I spoke
slowly and steadily, feeling in my heart that I had to give him
permission to die.
" 'Papa, *I* will make it now,' I said. 'I will make it. You can rest
now.'
" 'Take care of the baby,' he said, trailing off to a groan.
"His nurse's voice came back on the phone. 'I think he's dropped
off now,' she said."

Isadora'a hands began to tremble fiercely reading this section of
the memoir, because she knew, on some level, that her inheritance
of the mantle of adulthood from Papa put her everlastingly beyond the reach of Josh's love and Josh's understanding. His particular tragedy was to be trapped in childhood by a father quite as
patriarchal as her grandfather.

"Paradoxically, his obscurity made my fame possible, even *compulsory*. Not only was my first real poem about him, my first novel
dedicated to him, but it was the seething sense of bitterness he had
communicated about his own lack of recognition that spurred me
on to write it. So what if the world's applause meant nothing in the
light of eternity; the lack of it could embitter the soul in the here
and now, especially when you knew you had the goods. Papa's example made me vow never to permit myself the luxury of being

31

publicly unsung but self-bemoaned. For a person who lusts desperately after fame, the getting of it may lead to growth beyond it, but the neglected artist is trapped always (if he is ambitious) in a fury of denial."

She looked for a sign on Josh's face, but none was forthcoming. His face wore an impassivity which might even have been boredom. He had never liked her grandfather much. He found Papa "depressing," he said. Ah, who could disagree? Yet, depressing or not, we all have to make sense of our progenitors in order to grow beyond them.

Isadora's mother sat in the audience weeping. For a moment, mother and daughter locked eyebeams, then disconnected.

Isadora had come to the age where she could acknowledge her mother. Since Mandy's birth, she and her mother had reached a mellow truce. She knew that her mother had done nothing less than her best for her daughters—bad as that best may have sometimes seemed to Isadora. But what, after all, does a daughter know about her mother until she bears a daughter herself? *Being* a daughter is only half the equation; bearing one is the other.

"I determined on fame at an early age, determined on it partly because of all the hugely talented people in my family who seemed determined upon self-sabotage. I saw that talent—even great talent —was not in itself enough. The world *never* wanted any new talent, however arresting; it had to be *made* to want it. It was not enough to prepare the feast; one must also create the appetite for it, cut the meat, pour the wine, butter the bread, and spoon-feed the guests.

"My grandfather's colossal vanity (as well as, perhaps, his deep terror of success) precluded this. He expected to insult the world and have it love him. He expected to scatter his paintings to the four winds and have someone *else* catalog and preserve them. He did not know that even the calculated pranksterism of a Picasso or a Dali has its own particular methodical madness, that it seeks to titillate not alienate the public (or at least that private public which constitutes the art world), that it is playing a very special public-relations game—no less ambitious for being so outwardly hostile to fame.

"Yet when I think of Picasso's children and *their* problems living with his legend, I know more than ever that the very obscurity of my grandfather made my free use of my gifts possible in a way it would not have been had he been a living legend."

Josh's father was a living legend, Isadora thought, with a shiver. He, too, sat in the audience, uncomprehending. How could he be expected to acknowledge that his curious fame had stunted his children? If ever Isadora found that her fame hurt Mandy, what would *she* do? Unwish her books? Break her magic staff and burn her quills? It was a dilemma. Bad enough for mothers and daughters, but worse, far worse, for fathers and sons. Mandy would repudiate her mother someday; that much was sure. Isadora only prayed that when that day came, she would be strong enough to love her child unswervingly just the same. To let her go—and to be there when she wended her way back.

"My family had talent to burn; and they burned it. I was the only conservationist among them. They taught me—indirectly if not directly—that talent was not a thing to waste, that wasting it was to dishonor the gods who gave it, that wasting it was to dishonor the self.

"The night I learned of Papa's death, I suddenly panicked about his obituary. What if there were no obituary in the *New York Times?*

" 'People live and die, whether or not the *Times* records it,' my sensible husband said.

"But I was obsessed with the lack of 'hard' information my grandfather had left. Art medals he had won, but lost them; clippings he had had, but lost; *Who's Who* had listed him, but he gave away the copy; his paintings he had given away to any admirer who asked, not even keeping a slide or a list of owners.

"Through a series of frenetic telephone calls, the morning after his death, I was able to assemble some sketchy data, in which the *Times* city desk seemed to have little interest. Finally, no obituary appeared."

Isadora knew that *really* important people had their obits prepared years before their deaths and that they were updated regularly, like wills. Her journalist friends had told her how they reworked obits at the very first sign that some dignitary was checking into a hospital for what was purported to be "just a routine checkup." Even in death, there was a pecking order. Even in death, the meek did not inherit.

"But my true obituary for him was a poem I wrote on his last birthday, the day before Christmas 1980. It was a day I spent away from him, unable even to pick up the phone and call his nurse. But all day, I carried him in my head and heart.

"Finally, this poem emerged, as if from the depths of a dream. Initially the inspiration for it came aslant—as beginnings of poems often do. I was trying to write the first chapter of my new novel (which I had determined would be about him) but I found myself blocked, hopelessly fidgety and upset. I listened for the doorbell, my daughter, the postman—wishing for some interruption, some distraction, to kill the working day for me. My mind wandered. I opened a book of Neruda's which lay on my desk.

" 'Dream Horse' was the title of the poem on the page it opened to. I read:

> " 'Unnecessary, seeing myself in mirrors
> with a fondness for weeks, biographers,
>   papers.
> I tear from my heart the captain of hell,
> I establish clauses indefinitely sad.'

"And then suddenly the scribbling fit overtook my right hand and I wrote, as if by dictation, this poem to Papa."

Isadora took in a great lungful of breath and chanted, as if propelled by the wind from the pit, this elegy to her grandfather (which she had not yet even titled).

> "A dream of fantastic horses
> galloping out of the sea,
> the sea itself a dream,
> a dream of green on green,
> an age of indolence
> where one-celled animals
> blossom, once more, into limbs,
> brains, pounding hooves,
> out of the terrible innocence
> of the waves.
>
> "Venice on the crest
> of hell's typhoon,
> sunami of my dreams
> when, all at once,
> I wake at three A.M.
> in a tidal wave of love & sleeplessness,
> anxiety & dread . . .
>
> "Up from the dream,
> up on the shining white
> ledge of dread—
> I dredge the deep
> for proof that we do not die,
> for proof that love
> is a seawall against despair,
> & find only
> the one-celled dreams
> dividing & dividing
> as in the primal light.
>
> "O my grandfather,
> you who painted the sea

34

so obsessively,
you who painted horses
galloping, galloping
out of the sea—
go now,
ride on the bare back
of the unsaddled horse,
who would take you
straight to hell.

"Gallop on the back
of all my nightmares;
dance in the foam
in a riot of hooves
& let the devil take you
with his sea-green brush;
let him paint you
into the waves at last,
until you fall,
chiming forever,
through the seaweed bells,
lost like the horses of San Marco,
but not for good.

"Down through the bells
of gelatinous fish,
down through the foamless foam
which coats your bones,
down through the undersea green
which changes your flesh
into pure pigment
grinding your eyes down
to the essential cobalt blue.

"Let the bones of my poems
support what is left of you—
ashes & nightmares,
canvases half-finished & fading worksheets.

"O my grandfather,
as you die,
a poem forms on my lips,
as foam forms
on the ocean's morning mouth,
& I sing in honor of the sea & you—

"the sea who defies all paintings
& all poems
& you
who defy
the sea."

She'd read this headlong, hurtling, heedless of response, not even stopping when the rabbi sucked in his breath at the mention of "hell." But now she was feeling more and more as if she had uttered a malediction, not a blessing.

"The night he died, I scrawled these words at the bottom of the page of poetry: 'Samuel Stoloff died January 6, 1981. Born in the snow, he died in the snow. He was my beloved grandfather. All those who loved him and his paintings, please pray for his soul. He was ready to die and believed that his consciousness would survive his body. It does.' "

How did she know that? She just knew.

"All this is true. Last Thanksgiving—which we spent at my husband's parents' house (with our little daughter, my grandfather, my sister Chloe and her children, my sister-in-law and her lover)— Papa assured me that he would stay around to watch Mandy.
" 'It's funny,' he said, 'all my life I have been an atheist, but now I am absolutely sure that some form of consciousness survives after death. I will watch Mandy,' he promised.
" 'Papa,' I asked, 'will you make me some sign? How will I know you're there?'
" 'I cannot do that,' he said solemnly, 'but I promise I will watch Mandy.'
"When I was moaning about the lack of information for an obituary that night Papa died, Josh said, 'One of the neatest things about your grandfather was that he did not hold on to material possessions; he did not cling to the past. He was very Zen in that.'
"And it was true. Gradually, he dispersed his paintings; gradually his world shrank from Seventy-seventh Street to Seventy-second Street, from an eight-room apartment, to a four-room apartment, to a two-room apartment, to one bare room in a 'home' for adults. He was already far away that last Thanksgiving Day. Under his jacket, he wore a pajama top by mistake and the fly in his pants was gone. His body was nearly a ruin—what with bone cancer, prostatic cancer, heart disease, cataracts—but his mind was all there.
"There should be a ritual, a blessing, something one can say to ease the passing of the flesh (while the mind endures). Papa, pass gently. I know you are at peace. I know you have entered us all, that you are part of us, that we carry you wherever we go, and that you shall seed the world with poems, with paintings, even though your eyes and voice are gone.

" 'Why, if the Soul can fling the Dust aside,
And naked on the Air of Heaven ride,
Were't not a Shame—were't not a Shame for him
In this clay carcase crippled to abide?

"From his favorite poem," Isadora said and stepped down from the podium.

By the time she found her seat again, she was covered in cold sweat as if she had a fever breaking. It wasn't just the heavy knit dress she was wearing, nor the emotion produced by reading these things about her grandfather, nor the fact that the rabbi sucked in his breath horribly when she uttered the word *hell* in the poem, nor even the unmistakable feeling that she had uttered a malediction, hastening her grandfather's passage to hell and dooming him to everlasting torment. There was more: a sense that however detailed the memoir, however accurate it sought to be, it could never sum up the man. No writing could. Life was messy, various, contradictory. Writing, which tried to impose order on experience, wound up diminishing that experience simply because so many things had to be left out. Her grandfather was gone. No poem, no memoir, not even his own paintings could hold him; no artifact could contain the multitudes within the man. What use was art if it could not deliver what it promised—respite from death? Approaching her fortieth birthday, at the crest of her career, she felt this most keenly. It was not enough merely to "make a leeving," or to win prizes, or be famous, to have a long listing in *Who's Who*, or to be assured an obit in the *Times*. There *had* to be *more* to life than what she had struggled for all her nearly four decades. But what was it? According to the *world's* estimation, she had it all. Then why was she so frightened? And what was she so frightened *of*? Ought she to sit za-Zen, like Josh? Ought she to divest herself of material possessions and become a devotee of Sai Baba—the only guru who didn't come to America and do lecture tours? No. Such enlightenment was not for a gamy girl like Isadora—a wearer of perfumes, a connoisseur of cocks. But still . . . what did this death mean to her life? Papa was, in some spiritual sense, her father, and when your father dies in you at last, he leaves you free to love another man. Then why did she feel a great tide of change overtaking her life? And why did it seem that this tide was about to sweep away everything she knew?

She sat through the closing prayers with her palms dripping and her mouth dry with grief. When the ceremony ended, neither the fact that many relatives were weeping nor that others said the most complimentary things about her eulogy, comforted her. Nor did it comfort her when her last ex-husband, Bennett Wing, the psychoanalyst, embraced her tearfully, and said how moved he'd been. Nor did it comfort her when her "little" sister Chloe dismissed her fears of malediction with: "I can assure you that the Almighty won't dispose of Papa's soul based upon your poem." Nor did it comfort her when Josh said: "Promise me that if I die before you, you'll just give me a straight Jewish funeral—with no paeans of praise to my cock, okay?" Isadora laughed. Early in their relationship she had written juicily erotic poems to Josh, which depicted the fabled organ in various stages of tumescence and detumescence. But Isadora was hardly comforted by his joking about it now. She felt that she had exposed herself in a place where only pious platitudes about the deceased were required, and all she wished was to sink six feet deeper underground than Papa was going.

Why had she read that damned memoir? It exposed her more than her grandfather! Why hadn't she let well enough alone? Papa had requested a Jewish funeral and she had desecrated it. Women were not wanted in the house of the Father-God, but if they were tolerated at all, it was as silent witnesses of generalized male devotion. To stand up and speak ugly truths about the dead was insufferable presumption. Isadora felt ill with regret. All she wanted was to undo her speech, to suck the words back in like dirt being sucked into a vacuum cleaner.

Her orgy of self-loathing was interrupted by her second cousin Abigail, a white-haired, dowdily dressed retired schoolteacher who spoke the overcareful English of one who has spent the better part of her life enunciating the unspeakable to the unteachable.

"A lovely speech, Isadora," she said. "That was truly Uncle"—her mother was Isadora's grandfather's sister—"a true portrait. He would have approved."

"Really?" Isadora asked in disbelief.

"You remember what Uncle used to say: 'Paint me as I am—warts and all'?"

"Yes—but he didn't mean that. *Nobody* ever means that." (Isadora knew this because, as a novelist, she had discovered that the people who say "please write about me" are always pissed off when you do, while the ones who make you swear *not* to, secretly lust for such dubious immortality, and are devastated if you keep your word. Nevertheless, one thing is sure: nobody wants to be painted "warts and all"—any more than "Mr. and Mrs. Johnson" did.)

"I don't know," Abigail said. "Uncle always maintained that there was no point in being an artist if you were going to lie. That was why he hated doing formal portraits. 'Liberty is the right not

38

to lie,' he often said, I think after Camus. You were faithful to that. He would be proud. Tell me, Isadora," she went on, "that painting of horses in the poem—did you ever see it?"

"No. I saw several sketches of horses and some small oil studies. Why?"

"Well, Uncle painted a huge canvas of horses galloping out of the sea—a painting perhaps thirty feet by fifty feet, to be hung as a mural somewhere in a public building. I remember it because I remember the trouble he had getting the canvas and finding space large enough to work on it. That was in the early forties, before you were born, I think. I don't even remember who commissioned it, but it was to be done for some building in the west, I think, and he was to paint it here, in sections—huge squares of canvas, then ship them out west. I remember him working on it. It was the most amazing thing he ever did—huge as the Tintorettos at the Scuola di San Rocco in Venice—and as good, to my mind. It was a stampede of wild horses galloping out of the sea. I could have sworn from that poem that you knew it."

Isadora's heart turned over at this news. "How amazing," she said. "I never even heard him talk about it." Still, she had always suspected that there was a metaphysical connection between her and Papa, something went beyond granddaughterly affection, a certain interchangeability of souls. But this notion that her poem had intuited a lost painting was eerie indeed.

"The painting was lost," Abigail went on. "The war came and the people who commissioned it never even built the building. The project was sold to another real-estate consortium, the plans were altered, and Uncle was never paid for the work. The painting was shipped out West, and disappeared. He tried to collect on the money they owed, but when the project changed hands he couldn't track down the original people. Anyway, you know Uncle: He always used to say: 'Beware of any project requiring lawyers.' He was not the sort to get into a lawsuit over it. He let it go and went on to the next work. But he was always terribly bitter about it. I think he stopped mentioning it because it pained him so. I thought it was his greatest painting, and so did he. If it could be seen and exhibited today, it would establish his reputation beyond a shadow of a doubt."

On the way to the cemetery—Chloe and Isadora drove in her silver Mercedes with the Connecticut license plate that read QUIM —Isadora thought about her various promises to her grandfather.

He had always wanted her to write his story, be his Boswell, tell it true. He had half expected that she would catalog his paintings, find him a major gallery, organize a retrospective of his work, write his biography, publish an art book of his work. And she had never done so—not for lack of *wanting* to, but because it seemed to her that all the family examples of profligacy with talent demanded her nurturing her own, even if it meant refusing to serve the patriarch.

It would have been so much easier, in a way, to become the chronicler and cataloguer of her grandfather's genius. Women are applauded for being helpmeets to the patriarchs, only denounced when they seek to trumpet their own talents. Isadora knew the joys of the good-girl role; she knew the pleasures of cataloguing, restoring, collecting anecdotes about the great man, effacing oneself in service to the Master.

Think what flak she could have avoided by being her grandfather's good granddaughter rather than the bad girl of American letters! Think of all the attacks she could have avoided, all the grief she would never have known, all the uncertainties she would have sidestepped, all the empty pages she would never have faced! And think of the garlands of praise she would have garnered, the pontifical pats on the back, the approving nods, the loving looks. No woman born in this world is immune to the pleasures of being good. We are born to goodness; it is our birthright. Only sheer grit and pigheaded obstinacy make us demand the right to be bad, for we know that only by being bad can we become ourselves— not daughters and granddaughters, but individuals and possibly artists. Being an artist demands a cut umbilicus (which often bleeds); being a daughter demands the cord intact (a bloodless but confining fate).

Josh was first and foremost a son. That was why he had trouble being a husband. At some point, he would have to jump ship— the SS *Patriarch,* Isadora called it—and swim. Until he did that, he would never write all the beautiful books that were in him. Often Isadora wished that Josh's father would die, just to release him before it was too late. But the old man hung on, unwittingly weakening his children with bribes of money and real estate, with the desperate delusion that Daddy never dies.

They drove to a cemetery in the stony wastes of Queens. For one born in Manhattan, Queens means cemeteries or a flight abroad. Papa was going on his last flight now. The earth was cold and unforgiving. Isadora thought of her grandfather—even the ruin that was left of his body—spending his first night under-ground and she began to weep. Couldn't he even take a blanket? She had the doubtless common fantasy of her grandfather discovering himself alive and pounding on the coffin lid for help. The gravesite's finality never fails to elicit blocked tears. No wonder we weep as we shovel in our modest contributions of earth.

The limousine bearing Jude and Nat, Aunt Gilda and cousin Abigail preceded them through the cemetery gates. Isadora was driving QUIM, headlights blazing. Josh had refused to go to the cemetery and had taken off for lunch with his mother and father instead. Isadora hadn't objected. "Go on, darling," she had said, not wanting to impose her grief on him. But on some level she was pissed. Why did he stubbornly refuse to see how much her grandfather's death meant to her? Was it because of his own refusal to confront his father's eventual demise?

She drove with a vengeance, thinking of her vaguely blasphemous license plate blazing through the Jewish cemetery's gates. Both Josh and Isadora were name nuts. Their dogs were named for writers; their cars for sexual organs; and their child narrowly escaped being named after the greatest woman poet of antiquity —Sappho—or else Vigée after Elisabeth Vigée-Lebrun, the infinitely skillful court painter to Marie Antonette.

Isadora's mother had also debated among the names of all the great women artists when she named her second daughter. She might have been Marietta after Marietta Robusti, Tintoretto's offspring, or Judith after Judith Leyster, Franz Hals's contemporary, or Sarah after Sarah Peale, or Constance-Marie after Constance-Marie Charpentier, or Rosa after Rosa Bonheur, or Angelica after Angelica Kauffman. Thank heavens her mother never considered Sofonisba after Sofonisba Angussola, but merely—merely!—saddled her with Isadora Zelda—after Duncan and Fitzgerald.

Actually, Isadora could sympathize with her mother's desire to name her after a great woman artist. (Her mother had also considered merely flamboyant names like Olympia—after Greece— and Justine—after Sade.) Nor would Angelica Kauffman have been a bad "role model"—to use a phrase she detested. Kauffman was a contemporary of Sir Joshua Reynolds who became one of the best and most successful painters of her time. Famous, rich, revered by the people in Rome (where she finally settled), nonetheless her story is pretty much the story of every woman artist: a life of great productivity and outward success, coupled with the inner bitterness of never being taken quite seriously; of being gossipped about as a slut for connections with male artists that would have seemed plausible and just had she been a man; the inevitable eclipse of her reputation after her death, with the concomitant attribution of the best of her oeuvre to better-known male painters of her time.

Did Isadora's mother wish this on her daughter? Hardly. No more than Isadora wished Elisabeth Vigée-Lebrun's fugitive life in revolutionary France on *her* daughter (at that time in her pregnancy when she was fixated on Vigée as the name for the baby who became, indelibly, Amanda Ace). But they had a sense of tradition, Isadora and her mother, they believed in a torch being passed, in the matriarchal, matrilineal passage of talent. Angelica Kauffman has a lovely allegorical self-portrait which shows her hesitating between the muses of painting and music. This proved prophetic, for Isadora hesitated at first between writing and painting, until writing won. (Even then, she had a sixth sense that competing directly with her mother and grandfather would have stunted her eternally.) But she wonders how Vigée (had Amanda *been* Vigée) would have taken after her namesake. Isadora did not wish on her child a wastrel husband, a reputation for seducing her subjects, or the rumors of catfights with other women artists that have plagued Elisabeth Vigée-Lebrun's posthumous reputation, but when she thought of how that woman could paint, her fear dissolved. She would have her daughter know the joy of covering a canvas with light, even if the canvas later crumbled, and with it her immortal fame.

What is immortality, after all, but vanity? In a universe that is not *itself* immortal, how dare we vainly demand the preservation of our canvases? When Isadora was sixteen, she worried about preserving her poems and drawings; she was obsessed with paper conservation, acid-free stocks, indelible inks. Now, even though her work was *really* valuable, she found all the pains artists take to preserve their papers silly and vainglorious. On the brink of blowing ourselves up, how can we worry about paper conservation? If only the human race survives, we know that some mortal will rise from her knees and paint the side of a cave with reindeer and horned dancers. That is inevitable. The urge to cover walls with our likenesses, to make image magic with brush and paint, is programmed into our genes, if only those genes survive. *Who* that artist is—or what her name may be—matters less than that she rise from her knees and wield a brush (or a stone, or a fragment of charcoal, or a bleeding berry). For our very humanity is in our urge to make magic with images. All that Isadora wishes for Sappho-Vigée-Amanda (and for herself) is a race that survives its own self-destructiveness, so that somewhere, somehow, the dance and dancers, the feast of colors, the chanting of poems, may begin again.

Then, why, as she shovels the earth over her grandfather's coffin, then why, as she embraces Chloe and weeps in her arms, then why, as she limps from the snowy grave on her father's arm, is she thinking that the only proper tribute she can pay her grandfather is to recover that lost great painting of horses, or failing that, to assemble an exhibition of his works, or failing that, to write a long novel about him, and thereby to make for him posthumously the reputation he never made for himself in life—and to make for herself the ancestor she *should* have had?

Yes, she thinks, as she leaves the cemetery—I will exhume my grandfather's bones through art, either his or mine. But she does not know what a long picaresque journey that will require or where it will take her both inside and outside herself.

3

Dangerous Acquaintances

> How characteristic of your
> perverse heart that longs only for
> what is out of reach.
> —CHODERLOS DE LACLOS
> *Les Liaisons Dangereuses*

> Marriage was regarded as an expedient,
> love as a sort of comic and
> undignified disaster, the spiritual equivalent
> of slipping on a banana skin.
> —P. W. K. STONE
> (Introduction to the Penguin edition
> of *Les Liaisons Dangereuses*)

"IF Papa hadn't died, if Chekarf hadn't died, if *Tintoretto's Daughter* hadn't been a full selection while Josh's last book wasn't even an alternate, do you think we'd still be together?" Isadora asks her therapist, mischievous, roly-poly Shirley Frumkin, who wears Norma Kamali sweatshirts, voluminous cotton knickers, and antique junk jewelry. Shirley is one of those ladies the French call *jolie laide.* The nose is bulbous, the eyes too crinkly, the figure too ample, but nonetheless she possesses an oddball kind of beauty, and sexuality so strong at seventy that it does Isadora's heart good just to be with her.

"No, no, no," says Shirley. "Stop what-iffing. Josh changed. It wasn't your fault."

Isadora has "progressed" from wild hilarity and fucking her brains out to crying almost nonstop, having migraines that last for days, blood pressure that shoots up whenever she talks to Josh on the phone. What has brought about this change? The knowledge that he's seeing another lady—a lady he spends weekends with.

"Isadora—*you* threw him out," her therapist reminds her. "You were sick to death of his rages, his attacking you all the time, his sabotaging your work, his passive-aggressive sexual manipulations."

"I know," she sobs, halfway through a box of Kleenex. (Why do therapists always have Kleenex on hand? Is it a hint that they want nothing less than the homage of our tears?)

Shirley's apartment faces east and the little heliport in the East Thirties is right below them. From time to time, a chopper takes off, leaving Isadora feeling as leaden as a dead body dangling from a helicopter in a body bag (her private image of the Viet Nam War).

"Why does another lady change anything? You have at least a dozen other men," Shirley reminds her.

"I know," Isadora says, "but mine don't count. They're just office temps. His do."

"Isadora," scolds Shirley in her funny Brooklyn accent, her

huge antique amethyst earrings shaking. "I want you to talk about your father now. I want you to figure out why this 'other lady' matters so. Because if I know Joshua Ace—and I *do*—I'd stake my life on the fact that she's mousy, uninteresting, no great shakes, and that the only real value she has to him is that he knows she makes you crazy."

Shirley certainly did know Josh. Josh and Isadora had, in fact, consulted Shirley for "marital therapy." Josh had gone into a deep depression just around the time Isadora's book was coming out. He had plunged into despair—despair over his work, his trapped feeling in the marriage, his sense that he was playing house husband to Isadora's career, his anger at being younger, "second fiddle" (as he put it), and constantly upstaged by her.

Never mind that they had both signed on for all of this seven years ago. Never mind that he had met her at the very height of her fame, that he had *convinced* her—over *her* misgivings—that he "could handle it"; that he wanted desperately to be with her despite all this; that he claimed to love baking bread and playing with the baby; that nobody ever made him do the house-husband number full time anyway (there were nannies and housekeepers galore); and that he claimed to share her dreams for her work as if they were his own. But all of that proved to be a trendy delusion. The dream of the "new sensitive male" of the seventies had given way to the old insensitive male of the eighties, and Josh now wanted for *himself* the career Isadora had built. The contract had changed, as marital therapists say, and Isadora was left reeling.

"I married him and had a baby and now he simply says: 'I've changed.' How *dare* he?" Isadora says. "There's Mandy to think about. He can't just 'change.'"

"That's life, kiddo," says Shirley. "Do you think you're the first woman in history to be left with a child to raise? Do you think you're the first woman in history to have a husband who throws tantrums like a three-year-old? Do you want to torment yourself about it for the next seven years or do you want to get on with the only life you've got?" A sobering thought. "The only trouble with you, Isadora, is that you never get angry at Josh—you turn all your rage against yourself. If you'd only rage a little at baby Josh, you'd feel a hell of a lot better."

What could Isadora say to counter that? That their love had been so special, their rapport so great that for the first five years they felt they could solve any problem? What did it matter that Isadora was older, more successful? Josh was a free spirit; he was

48

beyond mere money matters, beyond conventional morality. He and Isadora often used to talk about the fact that most people lived their lives like lemmings racing to the sea. They did what their neighbors did. They shunned what their neighbors shunned. They justified their slavery with talk of duty. They claimed that economic necessity enforced their conformity, or that the fragility of wives impelled them to chronic lying. Or that the jealousy of husbands made secrecy and deception necessary. In fact, they did not know that secrecy and deception excited them; that lying came more naturally than telling the truth; that economic necessity and duty were abstractions invented by humankind for the express purpose of not enjoying life.

"People are more afraid of happiness than of anything," Josh had said to Isadora that first night in bed at the Beverly Hills Hotel. "They will give up anything sooner than they will give up their suffering. All the great sages have known this. They have said it again and again—in Chinese, Greek, Hindi, English, Hebrew, Arabic, Egyptian . . . but no one listens."

Here at last was a man after her own heart, a man dedicated to art and happiness, a real hedonist. How could she know that a scant seven years later, they would be mired in the same jealousies and resentments as the rest of the lemmings, that they would be suffering from all the predictable miseries: sexual jealousy, professional jealousy, lust, avarice, greed, and all those other boring deadly sins?

They began as sinlessly as anyone. They wanted nothing but each other because neither of them had ever had it so good. Great sex, immediate understanding with a look, a glance, a word. They could go to a dull dinner party, listen to some fatuous speech by the host, merely glance at each other, and understand at once what the other thought, because it was the same as what the first one thought. They were that similar—or so they believed. It was Plato's dream, the two halves reunited, the cosmic joke undone, the wholeness reasserted, the potter and the pot made one (and who was who?—ah, both were potters and both were pots!)

In most loves, there is a lover and a beloved. The lover creates the beloved as the potter creates the pot—out of his own clay. But here they were *both* creators and creations. It was impossible to say who loved the more. Except. Except. She was the older, the better known, the twice married. He was twenty-six when she met him, and his whole life had been plagued by being the younger brother. His older sister was her age exactly—and she looked like her— blond and small. Moreover, he was the son of a legendary father, a screenwriter father who had faced down the blacklist, gone to jail, and come away a martyr, forever wearing a crown of thorns, surmounted by a slightly tarnished halo.

Like Isadora's father, he was a man who had almost forgotten he had children when he was young, but who now required that they be the succor of his old age. But unlike Isadora's father, he could not let his children go. When Josh hooked up with Isadora he got the older sister and the father in one, at first alluring, package—a living legend, an older sister, the works. In time, as the allure faded, the package seemed more and more tightly wrapped and he seemed to be wrapped within it.

The pounding on the coffin lid was slow to start. At first, he adored her, looked up to her age, her fame, her work, like a loving disciple. (And we know that one out of twelve disciples is a Judas.) Nothing she did on paper was less than a miracle. Nothing she said was less than brilliant, witty, and wise. She's here to testify that one can get very used to that—especially a person as mercilessly self-critical as she. It helps to have a good friend in court when one is constantly sentencing oneself to death.

But then, as their problems progressed, as his reputation remained modest and hers exploded, he began, bit by bit, to believe that she was the one and only problem in his life. (Why do people blame the ones they love when things go wrong in their lives? This is the serpent in the garden of Eden: the propensity to blame the one you claim to love.)

Josh's books were always reviewed under the rubric "husband of" or "son of." "It's hard to live one's life in a parenthesis," a friend of Isadora's sagely said. Moreover, they were rarely left alone to love each other. Journalists picked at their relationship as if it were a scab, and eventually it grew infected. Were they competitive? Did they think—at breakfast—about who was more famous? Did they criticize each other's work? If so, what did they say? Was she afraid he'd leave her as she aged? Was he afraid she'd find a rich old man? And so on, and so on, prying, picking, praying to discover that their evident delight in each other was only an illusion, that they were as wretched as everyone else and as unforgiving—and eventually, the prophecy came true.

Does "open" marriage kill a relationship? Or do people determine upon "open" marriage when they know their relationship is dying? It is the chicken/egg dilemma writ in bloodstains on bed-sheets. "What is the worst year of a marriage?" some wag once asked. "The last year," another wag replied.

They only started screwing around in the seventh year. A natural itch, more natural still to scratch. They had never sworn fidelity; whoever, in honesty, could? But, except for two wholly irrelevant flying fucks in the first year (one his, one hers), they never took the freedom the other granted.

They didn't want it. Life was complicated enough without that. Isadora would not have so much as looked at another man because she felt that a fellow who is unfortunate enough to have a famous wife cannot take another single blow to his self-esteem; and he would not have looked at another woman because he was too honorable, and too honest to lie, and too kind and considerate to tell the truth.

So they had a Mexican standoff. They always suspected the problem would rear its head, but they couldn't plan for its solution, so why think about it? When it rose up and whinnied, it did not look like a horse at all; it looked instead like their dear friend Sophia Kurtzweiler Washington. Sophia, the *second* most famous feminist of the sixties (but for Gloria, Germaine, Kate, Phyllis, and Betty), Sophia with her shaggy bangs, her astounding Amazonian stature (nearly six feet), and her trademark black harlequin glasses —Sophia the six-foot-tall operatic, big-breasted, histrionic mama of sexual politics.

She was in love with Isadora. Josh was in love with her tits. (How simple these postmortems are—because the body is already dead and doesn't move.)

She came to spend a weekend with them when her own marriage—to a famous black activist—was dying, and like the good comforters they were, they took her to bed.

Sophia had a generous nature. She could never be brief about anything. If you asked her how she was, she'd heave a long Semitic sigh (in which the history of the race was told) and say: "Where can I begin? The world is crumbling to its ruin. I have no money, no lovers, no nursemaid for my twins, no contract for my new book—and where is it written the human condition should be any better?"

If you had asked her about the weather, she would have doubt-less heaved the same sigh and said: "Some astronomers believe we are on the verge of a new ice age, and some that we are on the verge of a tropical period, hospitable only to dinosaurs and giant reptiles—but as for me, I'd be happy if I could find someone to fuck me regularly, watch the babies, and pay the rent."

Sophia believed the world owed her a living. In 1970 she'd written a trendy best seller, a sort of feminist *Greening of America* called *The Feminization of America,* which theorized that all our social woes came from maleness, and that all we needed to do to turn the world back into Eden was to put women in charge of everything.

The book was badly written, but brilliantly timed. It made a small fortune, of which Sophia spent half and lost the rest—most of it in a disorganized but idealistic attempt to set up the first all-female film studio. Sophia became a celebrity (someone who, as Isadora's mother says, "is famous for being famous")—a rough-rider on the talk-show circuit, a video Voltaire, a radio La Roche-foucauld, and an interview junkie. Unless some humble journalist was kneeling before her plugging in a Sony cassette recorder, she felt unheard and unheeded. Her natural mode of speech was the polemic. Unfortunately, after *The Feminization of America,* she had nothing much left to say. Perhaps as a desperate publicity ploy, she married her black activist (they'd met on the Phil Donahue show) and promptly had not one but two mulatto babies: Martin Luther King Washington and Billie Holiday Washington. Both the marriage and the babies got her another round of talk shows and new "issues" to talk about. Now she was not only an expert on women, but also on blacks, interracial marriages, and the rearing of twins. Publicity, alas, did not prove a lasting marital glue and the union fell apart.

Left with these two adorable moppets to raise, Sophia became more hysterical than ever. Times changed, but Sophia still had to eat. She owed books to half a dozen publishers, and grew outraged when they asked for their money back. She hosted her own late-night interview show, but quit the network because they refused to bend FCC regulations for her and let her use four-letter words on the air.

Sophia was an unforgettable weekend guest. She would arrive at your house with bags of special organic foods, sprawl on the couch waiting for you to cook them, leave you to diaper both babies, wash their clothes, change their sheets, then disappear into your bathroom to use up all your Opium bath silk, deposit her wet towels on the floor, and borrow all your cosmetics. After having Sophia for a weekend, the novel you were in the midst of reading was missing from your nightstand, your favorite shawl departed in her suitcase, and your bathtub was ringed with her dirt.

Isadora thought that perhaps *she* had an even more generous nature than Sophia—because she invited her back several times. On the weekend in question, somewhere toward the beginning of the end of Josh and Isadora, Sophia arrived sans babies. She was baby enough. Taking care of Sophia would have been a full-time job for a saint. (She had, however, brought her favorite cat—Mary Wollstonecraft Washington, who roamed the property killing shrews and field mice.)

After dinner, Sophia, Josh, and Isadora were all three bemoaning the state of the world and smoking a little dope. From which they progressed into one of those discussions of "open" marriage which is clearly a come-on. Since Isadora could see Josh eyeing Sophia's tits with undisguised yearning, and since Josh was in a deep depression following the publication of a book that was ignored, and since Isadora believed she could sooner keep him by holding him loosely than by trying to bind to herself his joy (to steal a metaphor from Blake), she didn't protest when Josh maneuvered them all to the waterbed.

"Let's watch TV in bed," he said. (There was a big projection TV in the bedroom opposite the waterbed.)

With many giggles, Sophia got in the middle (her famous black harlequin glasses perched on her nose) and they all cuddled, watching *Tale of Two Cities* on TV. (Why were they always involved in *that* epic at critical moments in their lives?) Inevitably, Josh began fondling Sophia's tits. Inevitably, Sophia began fondling Isadora's. Before long, they were into one of those curious tangles of limbs, in which it is impossible to tell whose are whose.

"It is a far, far better thing that I do than I have ever done," came the booming voice from the video tape machine, but they were all too far gone to care. Josh was eating Sophia's generous cunt; Isadora was sucking at her generous tits; and that fourth person in the room, who always watches when we break a sexual taboo, was sitting back amazed that she was not even mildly shocked.

That fourth person was Isadora, too, of course. That fourth person believed that since Josh had the multiple handicaps of famous father, famous wife, a book that had not gone as well as he hoped, a lifework that was not going as well as he hoped, she should make it up to him by letting him screw her friends. Better that than have him screw her enemies out of spite. As she watched Josh pump away at Sophia, trying vainly to make her come, Isadora thought how noble she was, how unjealous, how generous, how *mature*, to understand his needs like that. (Was it portent that when these three ill-assorted lovers awoke in the morning, they discovered that Mary Wollstonecraft Washington had left a bloody trophy—a dead shrew—at the foot of the waterbed? It was, but they all preferred to ignore it.)

Perhaps Isadora insulted Josh more by coddling him like this than she might have done by telling him to get his own girl friends —and get out. For the more she gave him, the more depressed he became, yet the more powerless she was to stop giving. It was as if she were desperate to make up the disparity between them—the disparity in ages, incomes, and power.

Because, here is the problem when the woman has more power in the marriage than the man. He doesn't like it, and neither does she. She feels guilty about it, and he feels cheated, and sooner or later the truth comes out in bed.

But they didn't know that then. They talked a lot after that evening with Sophia and both declared that it had brought them closer. Closer to the end, Isadora now knows. At the time, they thought they'd struck a blow for honesty.

Fuck honesty. More relationships founder on the shoals of honesty than sink in the depths of mendacity—a word Isadora can never use without thinking of Big Daddy in *Cat on a Hot Tin Roof*. A phony word—phony to the core, and so too is the concept of saving marriage through sexual confession. Is lying better? Isadora wonders. Lying also corrodes the heart. Perhaps the answer is to make no marriage until one is past forty and ready for moderation, or else to be wheeled up to the mate of one's dreams in an old-age home, when one is ready to consummate it bodilessly, as the angels do. (But how then would we get our children, who, after all, give us more undiluted joy than romantic love ever does?)

Sophia and Josh soon began an intermittent affair—although neither really wanted the other. They both wanted Isadora— either to have her or to get her riled. Sophia wanted her fame, her calm (compared to Sophia, *any*one is calm), her income, and Josh wanted to make her miserable—though he was too nice a person to *think* he did. Whenever he was feeling particularly depressed, particularly dissatisfied, he'd announce to Isadora that he was going off to see Sophia (*and* the twins *and* the sixteen cats), and she would stay home seething with jealousy. (The only thing worse than jealousy, she discovered, is pretending not to be jealous when you are.)

"I wish you'd screw other men, too," Josh would say (departing

54

for the East Village, where Sophia lived, in sixties style hippie squalor). "It turns me on, it really does." Why was it Isadora could never believe that? Oh, maybe she was as guilty as he for all these banal attempts at *Liaisons Dangereuses*. She had often complained to Josh that she was a member of the transitional generation—too old to screw around without guilt, too young not to envy those who had. Josh graduated from college in 'seventy—the class for whom sex was more available even than dope (and often simultaneous)—and before he graduated, he had screwed more women than had ever attended the entire Ivy League before the advent of coeducation.

Isadora tried, in fact, to tell Josh about sex with other men (for she was finally driven into the arms of Lowell Strathmore, her investment guy, and those of Wilson Donohue, a hapless Connecticut poet). But here was the rub: she didn't *believe* Josh wanted to know all the physical details. He wanted to make sure that the guy was neither more famous than he (fame made him jealous) nor a friend of his (a perfectly reasonable request). Other than that he wanted to know all—and to fuck Isadora while she told.

Now, it is absolutely impossible to describe sex without describing the person in question. Sex, after all, is a bore from the strictly plumbing point of view. Nor does the plumbing differ that much from person to person. What differs is the talk, the texture, the train of thought, the passion, the poetry. What differs is not so much the fucking as the fantasy.

Isadora had known Lowell Strathmore for about four years. One of the most amazing things about him was how much he looked like Josh. But a preppy version of Josh. (Isadora has a theory, by the way, that when one is pushed to adultery by sheer misery, cosmic loneliness, and the irrefutable sixth sense that tells you your beloved is pulling away from you—you always pick someone who *looks* like your beloved. Perhaps it seems less adulterous that way, or perhaps you really want only one lover and are being driven to two by your partner's restlessness, not yours. Since every long-standing relationship is, in part, a *folie à deux,* how are you to know whether it is *his* lust or your own that drives you?)

Lowell Strathmore was big and hairy like Josh. He was, in truth, a little taller (six foot four while Josh was six foot one). He was as clean-cut as Josh was shaggy: the Savile Row suits; the boxer shorts; the pink, scrubbed cheeks to Josh's red beard and balding bean; the thinning red hair parted amidships in the Wall Street manner (Isadora has often noticed that Wall Street men are either

55

drapeheads—concealing bald spots—or middle-parters, and she wonders whether some French philosopher—or even Susan Sontag trailing them in her Swedish sneakers—could write a phenomenological essay on this); and little tortoiseshell Ben Franklin glasses to make you trust him with your money.

He wore midnight-blue pinstriped suits and all his shirts were baby blue. His socks were silk and had clocks up the side. He had no ties that weren't from Turnbull and Asser (while Josh had no ties at all).

Isadora had met him in 1978 when she was heavily pregnant with Sappho-Vigée-Mandy. They were immediately attracted, but it seemed obscene to do anything about it then, and besides, she was happily married. Anyway, he was only after her money. Despite the fact that Isadora had a bouncy Jewish business manager named Mel Botkin who did most of this stuff for her, Lowell wanted to put together a portfolio of investments for her kid— and right after Mandy's birth, she gave him the chance. She set aside a hunk of money in her daughter's name, and established a trust for Mandy which Lowell invested.

He had done well with it before the market bottomed in eighty-one—buying her high-technology stocks (she wanted no oil, no radioactive minerals, no companies with assets in South Africa, no animal factories, and no environmental blights—so she was not an easy client. But still, despite these limitations, he managed to do a fairly respectable job).

She ran into him in Europe the fall before her grandfather died. Josh was depressed, was screwing Sophia in desperation, and Isadora was in desperation, too. She knew Josh didn't love Sophia and *did* love *her;* she knew he was trying to drive her away, as if that would solve his problems, and she refused to let herself be driven away. The trouble was: she loved Josh and she knew he was terribly unhappy. She did not really blame him. Trapped, desperate, trying to outrun his shadow, he was screwing Sophia because he didn't know what else to do (except to rage at Isadora, which he did often enough). There is an old French proverb, "Don't fart above your asshole." *(Il ne faut pas peter plus haut de son cul.)* And that was more Josh's problem than sex.

Pretty soon a new request surfaced:

"I don't want to be treated like a second-class writer in this house," Josh announced. "I want dinner on the table; I want my work to be as important in this house as yours; I want you to take care of Mandy full-time on the nanny's day off."

"But Josh, your work *is* important. Whoever doubts it? Surely, I don't."

"You do. You act like I'm the hack and you're the artiste."

"But I *don't*." Or did she? Was she guilty of this without even knowing?

"Then why don't you cook my dinner?"

"Josh—I *never* cooked your dinner. We cook together or we go out. Or the housekeeper cooks. It's been like that for *years*."

"I want you to cook for me. It turns me on." (This—from the "new sensitive man" of the 'seventies!)

So, she'd cook for him—gorgeous gourmet meals—but it didn't seem to help much. *Nothing* she did seemed to help much. He was as depressed as ever, only now Isadora was resentful. She had a baby, a household to run, books to write. She could cook with the best of them when she wanted to, but cooking was never fun if it was compulsory. And she felt she was burdened enough without having to pretend to be Pollyanna-housewife to assuage Josh's ego.

Shortly thereafter she was in Munich alone on a book tour. She had almost forgotten that she'd told Lowell Strathmore about it at lunch one day—but, astonishingly enough, there he was at the same hotel. (He had to be in Munich on business, and with his photographic memory—he could quote stock prices and dates the way little boys can quote batting averages—he'd recalled the hotel she'd booked and even the dates of her stay.)

The German publishers were throwing a cocktail party for her one night in the ballroom of the Goldener Hirsch. God, Lowell looked good to her in that smoky room full of German avant-garde types in leather jackets. Three hundred hip-looking Nazis putting the make on her and she goes home with Mr. Prep from her own home state. It was only to be expected. Whenever she's in Germany, she expects deportation to Auschwitz momentarily—and Lowell made her feel intensely *safe*.

Since he was even staying at the same hotel, what could be more convenient than to hit the sack? Except that they were both terribly nervous. They had to consume two bottles of Liebfraumilch before they could get into bed—and after that, they kept getting up to pee.

(Sex is God's joke on the human race, Isadora thinks: if we didn't have sex to make us ridiculous, She would have had to think up something else instead.)

Lowell was hardly the smoothest of adulterers. Before he

hopped between the sheets, he called his wife. It was midnight in Munich and dinnertime in Southport; predictably enough, his wife was out.

"There's an etiquette even of the one-night stand," Isadora said. "It doesn't include calling one's spouse as foreplay."

"I know," he sighed mournfully, "please forgive me." He put his hand over the mouthpiece of the phone to muffle her, but only the answering service was there after all.

So he checked his messages and sent lots of love for Leona—his rich wife with far too many teeth. He was so unhappy with her that he was bound to her forever. Joy makes a light linkage; but misery is the most unbreakable of shackles.

"Your wife terrifies me," Isadora said. "It isn't just her teeth, but her nickname. How can you find a woman named Pixie less than daunting?"

"It's true," he said, hanging his head. "She terrifies me, too. I'm a slave—and not even a happy slave, but a grumbling, complaining one."

"Then why do you stay?"

"I've often thought of leaving. Life is too short to spend it in such acrimony. But I love her. Underneath her harshness is a poor, insecure little girl who'd be devastated if I left."

Isadora looked at him mockingly.

"It's true," he declared. "She'd fall apart. Everyone sees Leona as tough and determined, the sort of woman who could organize the Balkans—but I know how vulnerable she is."

"Come to bed," Isadora said. She was thinking of pixieish Leona, whom she knew as a neighbor—Leona of the jet-black Dutch-girl coif, the china-blue eyes, the nose with a razor's edge, and hipbones to match. A man could be impaled on Leona's hips; a woman on her merciless tongue. She was the sort of person who never invited you to dinner, let alone telephoned you, unless she wanted something: a contribution to her favorite charity, a free speech at the Hunt Club Ladies' Auxiliary Lunch, an original manuscript to raffle off, an old hat for her "celebrity auction," other famous people's unlisted phone numbers, the name of your caterer, or your cleaning lady. How many marriages survive because "she'd fall apart"? Leona would no sooner fall apart than Mt. Rushmore. She was in truth a beautiful woman, but the hardness of her face made you forget it.

Lowell Strathmore finally came to bed. And Lowell Strathmore was such a *surprise* in bed. You'd have thought—if you were a late-fifties Music and Arter like Isadora—that a WASP stockbroker, a hunt-club member, a person who managed discretionary accounts measuring in the tens of millions, would make love like a stiff—or an Englishman—but no: this seemed to be the one area of his life where he could really be free. Jews have been sold a bill of goods about WASPs, Isadora often thinks. According to Jewish myth, made up, naturally, by Jewish men, to keep their women out of the clutches of WASP men, WASP men are supposed to be bloodless and passionless. The truth about WASPs, Isadora now knows, is that they can be absolute priapic maniacs in bed—freer in the sack for all their starchiness out of it.

This was certainly the case with Lowell. He nibbled and licked and giggled. He talked dirty. He whispered things like "titties" and "pussy" and other words parents did not particularly send their children to Andover to learn. Like his language, his whole face softened during sex. Perhaps it was just the effect of taking off those glasses—those glasses that seemed to organize his lumbering tallness and give it point—or maybe it was true relaxation. This poor, slouching giant of a man—who lived his life in an ill-fitting straightjacket, sewn for him by a wife he feared, lined with her money, tied with his fears—could only relax when he had fucked a woman he wasn't wedded to. For one halcyon hour, he unmasked, and then, the anxiety, the fear, the straightjacket, the horse shows of his daughter returned.

Isadora notices that it isn't fashionable to write too much about sex anymore. In the seventies, post-Portnoy, you couldn't pick up a novel, it seemed, without getting sperm on your hands. Not only the hacksters and fucksters, but *literary* writers, good writers, had to chart the interiors of vaginas as if they were the caves of Lascaux (and all primordial truth were writ therein). Women were discovering the poetry of penises; men were unmasking before the Great Goddess Cunt.

But then the hacksters got hold of sex and ruined it for everyone—like condominium developers ruining Florida. They took the license to explore Lascaux as a license to kill little girls; they turned the poetry of the penis into stag films so loathsome they made you want to become a nun. Before long, the puritans were howling—"See! We told you how awful sex is! You should have listened to us! We were right about censorship! Put the mask back on!"

And all the poetry of the penis, the sweet sexuality that peeked out of the fly of the Brooks Brothers pants for a brief decade, was in danger of being covered up again.

Even Philip Roth has recently published a book in which he cuts away from every sex scene. And Isadora's old buddies, the feminists, are passing out leaflets on street corners protesting pornography, trying to make the world believe that people molest little girls *because* of pornography (rather than that pornography flourishes because people want to molest little girls), and in general doing their best to blur the distinction between sex and rage.

"There is no sex without rage!" they rage. Except sex between women, which is supposed to be pure and perfect, nonexploitive, as heavenly as heterosex is hellish. You'd think they'd never heard lesbians yell at each other, or seen them strike each other in bars. You'd think they had never known a lesbian relationship (like Isadora's Aunt Gilda's) where the femme is as oppressed as any fifties wife—and the butch is a female chauvinist pig. Of course, feminists don't *mean* to come out on the same side as the Moral Majority when they denounce pornography, but alas they do. And sweet sex, the great unmasker, is dragged in the gutter again. If this trend continues, Isadora thinks, Mandy's generation will have to unearth sex all over again, like a buried Sphinx.

She really resents this confusion of sex and rage. For her, what is great about sex is precisely the momentary *respite* from rage it grants. When even Lowell Strathmore can shed his mask, something constructive is surely at work.

O sweet sex, Lawrentian waterfalls, Joycean rivers, Millerian springs (so black they are blue, too)—it's *you* that Isadora longs for! The whole humid earth opening like the Great Mother's thighs, the cock rising pinkly, a crystal tear at its tip, the breasts swaying as if to a ballet by Ravel—*this* is what she tried to write about in her notorious *Vaginal Flowers*. But the feminists who picketed, and the critics who sneered, and the public who bought to be turned on (but then to disown the sexuality that stirred), preferred to see it all as smut, and keep their masks on still.

"One does not choose one's subject matter," says wise old Flaubert (who apparently said everything), "one submits to it." Amen.

How could Isadora describe sex with Lowell to Josh without describing Lowell himself? How could she ever get the *flavor* of it right? The cock itself was unremarkable—though ample and indefatigable enough. It was the contrast between the straightjacket and the freedom that was so amazing (and so oddly erotic). It was the whole thing—the boyish calling of the wife, the unsexy underwear, the Ben Franklin glasses coming off, the use of the word *titties*, the nervousness, the fear, the dropping of the mask.

Back in the States, they met from time to time. Never enough to satisfy Isadora, and never without the most elaborate plans. You'd think they were planning the invasion of Normandy rather than two hours in Fort Lee. Because the fact was that Lowell was so nervous about Discovery that they had to go to a *third* state. Neither Connecticut, where they both lived, nor New York, where he worked, but New Jersey—where, he maintained, his wife had never been.

"Not even across the bridge to attend some charity function or a horse show?" Isadora asked.

"My wife is not interested in anything that goes on outside Manhattan or Fairfield County—unless it happens in the Hamptons!"

Isadora had to laugh—because she knew it was quite true. She and Lowell would have to be safe at the Fort Lee Motel. Who on earth would think of looking for them there? Except that on one occasion, as they were fucking their brains out at that very same motel, there came a pounding at the door, as if the Hulk himself were loose.

"Where's my wife?" came an enraged voice. "I want my wife or I'll break down all the doors!"

Lowell and Isadora jumped apart. They raced to the door—but the madman was already gone. They heard him pounding on the next door with the same, and then the next, and the next, and the one after that. They looked at each other and collapsed on the floor with laughter.

"Are you thinking what I'm thinking?" he said.

"Yes," said Isadora between giggles.

"There probably isn't a man in this place who hasn't lost his erection," Lowell said, having lost his own.

How could Isadora relate such stuff to Josh? He would have loved the story, but it was basically meaningless without imagining Lowell's reaction, and Isadora couldn't describe Lowell because Josh knew him slightly and would have guessed who he was. The rules for revealing their *"liaisons dangereuses"* were impossible rules. Because sex is hardly amusing if the man remains masked. The whole point of sex is dropping the mask. This may not be true for what men want of women, but it is certainly what women want of men.

Ah, men—the inscrutable sex. What do men want? Freud should have asked, because what women want is so pathetically clear—they want unmasked men! Isadora has finally come to the conclusion that she has never really understood men. Not that she doesn't like them, only that they are hidden from her—as if they were all wearing iron masks. Whenever she fantasizes about what her work would be like if she had become a painter instead of a writer, she imagines a whole exhibition called simply "Men." It would be a series of paintings of masked men. In each, the man would be wearing a different *kind* of mask. One would have an iron mask, like the hero of the same name; another a diving helmet; another a black silk mask like one of Guardi's Venetian gentlemen; another a wet white silk handkerchief which clung to his face, making him look (oddly) like the death mask of Keats; another a gorilla mask; another a Mickey Mouse mask; and so on.

The fantasy of the masked-men exhibition is elaborate. It extends to the opening itself—which, like *Vaginal Flowers*, gets a vast amount of ambivalent publicity, both very bad and very good. Scandal clings to Isadora even in her fantasy of herself as painter. In the days following the opening, Isadora-the-Artist lurks around the gallery in dark glasses and a babushka so she can see the reactions of her audience.

Women come into the gallery with a perplexed look on their faces and then—after they have examined three or four of the canvases—a sly smile begins to manifest at the corners of their mouths, the aha of recognition, followed usually by a gasp or a chuckle.

If they are with female companions, there is much elbowing, pointing, and conspiratorial laughter. But if they are with men, they look sheepish or else become soberly expository, desperately trying to explain to their escorts why the paintings are funny, but encountering the very same mask the paintings seek to unmask. Men visitors, on the other hand, shrug, not knowing why the paintings "matter"; some are openly hostile; some drag their ladies bodily from the gallery and shout at them on Madison Avenue.

This whole fantasy of her secret life as an artist pleases Isadora immensely. Never does she feel more truly "successful" as a writer than when she sees what passions her works arouse in people. One writes alone in blissful, or paranoid, solitude. One feels vaguely masturbatory about one's work; and if one is a woman, the whole world conspires to reinforce that notion, calling one "narcissistic," "self-absorbed," "self-obsessed" (as if Picasso were not, as if James Joyce were not, as if all artists were not maddened narcissi falling into their own reflections—the drowning in self being one of the conditions for transcending the self). So one always feels guilty, somehow, about closing the door to work. There are: the child that needs mothering, the nanny that needs scolding, the petty-cash box that needs filling, the husband or lover who needs care and feeding lest he sulk and run off to fuck one's friends, the dogs that need heartworm pills, cuddling, brushing, dinner! One fights so hard for a bit of narcissistic reflection. So, to see actual fellow humans being moved to laughter, tears, and argument by one's work—that is the true vindication. One is a good social being after all—a good *woman*. That solitary paranoia has a function. What a relief! One can return to one's reflecting pool restored, one's face validated by the eyes of others.

An exhibition of masked men—what a fantasy! Isadora has by now been a professional writer so long that in her fantasy life, she chooses other roles: painter, actress, rock singer. In *Tintoretto's Daughter*, she imagined herself as a 15th century lady painter. Her grandfather became Tintoretto; her mother and father, aunts and uncles masqueraded as courtesans and doges. But whatever profession Isadora chooses for herself, one thing remains the same: her sexuality. It is the sap that through the green fuse drives the flower, the cosmic juice of her being.

One reason Isadora has always loved sex (once she can get past her awful transitional-generation shyness about enunciating her yeses too clearly) is that during sex one has a man's undivided attention. For a little while, at least, he drops the mask along with his pants. Of course he is usually pretty quick to put it back on. Just as there are men who are mad showerers, and Keystone Cops dressers, there are men who can put the mask back on within a half-hour of orgasm. But usually there's that half-hour of grace, that honeymoon period (like the first hundred days of a presidency), that blessed interval of naked face.

Lowell Strathmore was the swiftest dresser Isadora ever bedded down with. He could shower and throw on his preppy white boxer shorts faster than you could say Dow-Jones (let alone Standard and Poor). But there was always that enchanted hour or so (longer if he had come more than once) when he shed the mansion in Southport, the membership in the hunt club, his wife's teeth, his daughter's horse, his paranoia about Discovery—and behaved as if he were actually human (as if he were a woman, that is).

It was never easy to meet Lowell. Weeks would go by between phone calls and months between trysts. (In the intervals, they used to have strangely formal, strained conversations about Isadora's portfolio—which, in his guilt about not screwing her, he was managing better and better all the time.) Whenever they finally met in

Fort Lee, he'd say: "I don't think I'm very sexy," and then he'd take her in his arms.

"Well, I do, and I'm supposed to be the expert," she'd say. They'd screw like mad for an hour, he'd drop his mask for an hour, and then he'd disappear for months at a time.

It was hardly what anyone would call a satisfying affair. Between his elusiveness and Josh's, Isadora often felt she had less than no one—two men adding up to minus two.

This was the state things were in when Isadora's grandfather died. She and Josh were together, yet not together. Her beloved dog had died. (Why do our dogs always die when relationships are ending?) Lowell had not called in weeks. Isadora felt empty, desperate, and devoid of ideas following her last successful book. (That it had been praised was somehow more daunting than the attacks and pickets she had braved at the start of her career.) Papa's deterioration in the waning months of his life had done her in. She felt that her marriage had died as her grandfather had died. She was depressed, unable to work, unable to pick up the phone and call for help; she was at wit's end.

"And still," said Shirley, after Isadora had filled up her whole session with these musings over the end of her marriage, "you haven't really talked about your father and you haven't raged *at all* at Josh. If you did, your headaches would magically disappear."

"I hate the fuckin' shithead bastard!" Isadora pretends to scream, watching a helicopter take off over the East River. But she lacks conviction. Somewhere deep inside, she still believes that the ending of the marriage was "her fault." That if only she'd been more giving, more patient, and less successful, everything would be okay.

"Don't you know there was *nothing* at all you could have done?" Shirley shouts. "Oh, Isadora—I'd dearly like to shake you. If you treated another person as badly as you treat yourself, you'd think yourself a horrible sadist; your heart would *bleed* for the poor victim. So will you please show a little *rachmones* toward *yourself*? Will you please? Boy—do we still have a lot of work to do on *your* head!"

And then—as usual—the hour was up.

4

Megrims & Miseries

A dream of well-filled hose.
—JAMES JOYCE
Ulysses

ISADORA drives up to Columbia to meet her medical student. She parks at a meter on Broadway and 105th, wondering whether her car will be towed or the tires slashed while she is with Roland Rabinowitz, who has the dubious distinction of being the very youngest of her lovers.

She started to screw Roland as a lark, or for revenge—she's not sure which. Roland is the same age Josh was when she met him—twenty-six—and his mother is also Isadora's friend (as Josh's parents were when she met and fell in love with Josh). Roland's redoubtable mother, Sylvia Sydenheim-Rabinowitz, is a sex therapist —one of the most famous sex therapists in America (but for Masters and Johnson). She's a tiny, platinum-blond, green-eyed woman with a professorial air, a Zsa Zsa Gabor nose (and accent to match), a penchant for spike-heeled designer shoes, Chanel suits, and enormous diamond earrings (bought for her by her many lovers—most of whom are rich, vulgar, and former patients). Once she has cured them of premature ejaculation, she lets them practice their newfound skills on her.

Sylvia is a curious combination of shrewdness and vulnerability, a lady who escaped the Nazis in Hungary an indeterminate number of years ago, a savvy Hungarian temptress (with gorgeous skin), a power broker, and a horny woman—not exactly in that order.

Isadora adores her, admires her, and mistrusts her. Or rather, she mistrusts her motives. Though Sylvia has always been very good to Isadora, Isadora wonders whether Sylvia loves her for her fame or her own sweet self. Sylvia is also something of a voyeur; she delights in arranging sexual scenes (allegedly for therapeutic purposes). Since Isadora and Josh have parted, Sylvia has fixed Josh up with various ladies, and has fixed Isadora up with her Rolls-Royce illiterate antiques dealer—"I don't have to read your books, I can *smell* them," said he—a drapehead par excellence, who not only draped his bald spot, but actually *sprayed* the hair (this must be a new subcategory, Isadora thinks, the sprayed drapehead) so that when Isadora mussed it in bed—that was during her early fuck-everyone phase—it felt tacky to the touch, just like its owner.

But more to the point, mischievous, blond Sylvia has fixed Isadora up with her very own son, Roland, of the huge cock, and the equally huge pharmacopoeia.

"It vud be good for you to go to bed viz Isadora *vunce*," Sylvia instructed her son, "but no more zan zat. She vudn't be good for you." (Sylvia not only wants to matchmake, she wants to control the *duration* of the match, and Isadora rather resents this.) Roland, instructed to fuck her once, promptly rebelled against his mother and fell in love with Isadora—although with Roland, it's hard to tell about love because he expresses himself in bed like something out of one of his mother's best-selling sex manuals. To wit: "Are you tumescent enough or shall I give you more head?" "Should I assume the missionary position, or would you rather assume the female superior position?" "Do you require more foreplay, or shall I enter you?"

An expert and diligent lover, Roland makes love like a robot programmed by Alex Comfort. He is of that curious generation (born in the fifties, coming to adolescence in the late sixties) for whom sex was not only encouraged, but almost compulsory—yet also oddly mechanistic. Reaching puberty at the Elm-Tweedsley School (where Isadora once went herself, before Music and Art claimed her), with the children of movie stars and famous writers, Roland learned fucking at fourteen, but he never learned sensuality. That, Isadora means to teach him. She has taken him on as a little *hommage* to Colette, one of her favorite writers. And the bargain she and Roland have struck is this: he will supply her with sex and drugs, and she will give him polish and sensuality as if he were Gérard Philipe in *Devil in The Flesh*. (She is busy teaching him how to manage maître d's, soft lights, sweet music and how to say something in bed other than "Will you assume the female superior position?")

Alas, Roland doesn't look like Gérard Philipe—though he does have beautiful hazel eyes, an amazing cock, and a nice body (if only he wouldn't slouch). The number of drugs he takes simultaneously astounds Isadora. Any ordinary person would be comatose. Roland takes antidepressants, Valium, quaaludes, and smokes pot so resinous and red-haired, it smells like hash. His freezer contains psilocybin mushrooms; his breast pocket a little vial of coke. Not surprisingly, Roland's speech is slurred, his coordination (everywhere but in bed) not too dependable. He's afraid to drive, for example—in any weather. But his brain—*mirabile dictu*—still functions. He is trying to figure out a way to poison cancer cells, and he can also splice genes and do all sorts of other things that Isadora finds astonishing.

"Hello?" he says through the intercom. Roland phrases nearly everything (not having to do with cell nuclei) as an interrogative.

"It's me," says ungrammatical Isadora (who, despite her nearly constant migraine, is still superficially chipper). She must wait for Roland to come down, since the buzzer doesn't work. And when he appears—wearing a blue oxford-cloth shirt, baggy jeans, and his lank brown hair in a late-sixties ponytail—she is once again amazed. Roland is twenty-six, but looks perhaps sixteen. He also has the demeanor and the poise (or lack of it) of a sixteen-year-old (with the brain and the cock of a grown man). Isadora, who has no son—but rather wishes she had—wonders whether *this* is what it's like. Many of her contemporaries have sons in their teens. If, in fact, she had done what most of the class of 'sixty-three at Barnard did, she too would have a son in his teens. But Isadora was a late breeder. She had books to gestate, places to go, men to marry, a whole odyssey to shlep through before she could go home and get knocked up.

"Hi, Roland," says she.

"Hello?" says Roland, shaking the ponytail. "You look great?"

Up they go in the creaky old elevator—a very slow one whose smells and claustrophobic slowness remind Isadora of her Columbia graduate-school days. This separation from Josh keeps hurtling her back in time. She is an adolescent again, a college student, a graduate student—except that she has the uncanny sense she sees it all through the semitransparent scrims of her age and experience. She knows too much. Knows and understands. Roland is, in some ways, like herself as a college student. She feels incredible empathy for him—the empathy she never felt for her own young self. Is this what middle age means? Mellowness? Self-forgiveness? Seeing the world through eyes grown wise with experience? Roland is brilliant about cancer cells but stupid about life (just as she, at the same age, was learned about literature and a moron about life). Roland's "moronitude" (a word Isadora and Josh made up in a giggling fit a few years ago) takes the form of always wanting to pin everything down—as if life could ever be made secure. (Ah—the chief delusion of youth!) "Will you see me next week?" he always asks, and "What time?" "What day?" Unless the next date is pinned down, he has an anxiety attack. Isadora vainly explains that by next week they could all be dead, or in a bomb shelter or a DP camp. The Jews and intellectuals might be rounded up; the Bomb might fall; biological warfare might intervene. Isadora knows the folly of planning too far ahead—which also gives her a healthy sense that one must seize the day. *Carpe diem* cannot, she thinks, be understood by anyone under thirty-five.

"How's your headache?" asks Roland, unlocking his two-room apartment, with its mingled smells of sinsemilla and mildew. Roland's apartment faces a court or a stone wall—she's not sure which, because he never opens the curtains—and it reminds Isadora of the Columbia apartment where she lost her virginity some twenty-two years ago. Oh, one of the joys of middle age is seeing everything come full circle! Here she is again in the old Columbia neighborhood to get laid. Nostalgia of the loins, perhaps (as Sartre called it), or is it rather *la nostalgie de la boue?*

"The headache is fine," says Isadora. "I'm *awful.*"

"You *look* great," says Roland.

"Oh, Roland—my fate is always to look great, strong, brave, and fearless when, in fact, I feel like shit."

"Nonsense," says he, "you're the healthiest person I know."

"Which isn't saying much," says Isadora.

She flops down on the couch, sheds her handwoven shawl—it's late October and not yet really cold—takes off her gold boots ('tis the season of metallic shoes, bags, belts, even underwear, for god's sake) and puts her feet up on Roland's couch.

"Sorry to lay my headache on you," she says.

"*Lay* it on me? Isadora, I'm *honored* that you feel free enough to come here when you have a headache. I want to be some solace for you. I think that Josh Ace is the dumbest, meanest shit in America. You're the pearls, he's the swine."

"That seems to be the common report," says Isadora. "But I feel sorry for Josh. Think of how tough it must have been for him, being the salami in the sandwich—his father on one side, me on the other."

"But he's treating you so *horribly*," Roland says, "and I'd give anything to trade places with the guy."

Isadora's headaches had begun on the very weekend it became abundantly clear that Josh was probably never coming back. Not only had he, seemingly, found another lady, but he withdrew totally from marital therapy with Isadora, saying that it was useless,

70

no change was possible, the marriage was kaput, he wanted out. Up until then, she had nursed the hope that the whole split was merely a sabbatical—a sort of rabbit-running separation, after which the fates would reunite them, for they were fated, or so she believed.

The first two months of their separation, he shuttled back and forth, appearing at the house constantly, putting Mandy to bed, hanging around to check on whether or not Isadora was going out, being lured into her office for the occasional blow job, or quickie, and then leaving as if she were nothing but the most casual one-night stand. This pattern grew unbearable after a time. After their zipless encounters in her studio, Isadora, of course, wanted him to stay, and he was always going. It was better to break off relations entirely and ritualize their visitations more rigidly than keep enduring these constant comings together followed by wrenching partings. He told Isadora he was off sex, that his libido was gone, that there were no other ladies at this point. After a while, it emerged that he was lying—albeit to try to save her feelings. There was still the typist, and the mother of one of Mandy's three-year-old friends. (The number of divorced women in Connecticut requiring sexual services was endless, apparently.)

The headaches began innocently enough. Faced with the fact that Josh was through with marital therapy, that his weekends were filled with this mysterious other lady—Wendy or Wanda, Isadora wasn't sure which—that Mandy was coming home with reports of "Wendy's cookies," and "Wanda's doggie," and "Wendy's ice-skating lessons," Isadora had a major recurrence of insomnia—the sort of insomnia she had suffered during the last year of their marriage—waking at four, never to be able to get back to sleep. She called Sylvia Sydenheim-Rabinowitz asking for an anodyne—and Sylvia, ever the purveyor of "scripts" (as her son calls them) gave her Dalmane. The Dalmane knocked her out, all right, but it must have also knocked out her ability to dream—REM sleep, as they call it—and so she would wake up every morning, more zonky and depressed than ever, her rage at Josh now having nowhere at all to go—since she could neither express it awake or asleep! 'Twas then that the headaches began—began at first merely when she talked to him on the phone, and then proceeded to grip her whenever she had an orgasm. It was an almost Dantean punishment. No sooner would she be on the verge of an earth-shattering climax with Errol or Roland than she would develop blinding pain—a steel band around her forehead, a throbbing in her temples—that made her whole body tense with agony, threw her orgasm off, and left her teeth chattering with pain so intense she was sure it portended a brain tumor or an aneurysm.

It was then that she began her tour of doctors, her quest for the holy grail of Cure. Whereupon she discovered with a vengeance that she lived in a whole society of legal addicts. A neurologist friend put her on an antidepressant called Limbitrol, which not only didn't ease the headaches, but made her so uncoordinated she couldn't walk, drive, or pour juice, and left her mouth so dry she couldn't talk, let alone give head—her one creative solace, since she couldn't write. Five days later, feeling for all the world like a state-hospital patient, she tossed the Limbitrol in the garbage.

Next, her internist (a charming young man—also recently divorced) prescribed a different antidepressant—one called Norpramin—which she was to take with Librium, when needed. Roland, at that point, was her psychopharmacology expert, and he approved of neither prescription, although he took vast quantities of antidepressants and tranquilizers himself.

"When the headache strikes, I'd opt for a simple fifties remedy —like codeine or caffergot instead of these fancy seventies-style tricyclic antidepressants," said Roland. "Drugs go in and out of fashion—just like hemlines. The old drugs of the fifties were perfectly okay."

So Isadora threw out the Norpramin, saving the Librium for anxiety emergencies, and took caffergot or codeine when a headache came on, but neither seemed to work. She felt like a character in the seventh circle of Dante's *Inferno,* or like Prometheus, chained to a rock, doomed to have his heart eaten out at regular intervals. Josh brought on headaches; orgasms brought on headaches. The two things in life that had once given her the most joy now gave her incredible pain—pain that neither ice packs, nor tranquilizers, nor antidepressants could assuage. As for aspirin, it had long since become useless. And the drug called Midrin (Isadora thought these names of drugs terribly funny, really) did little or nothing at all. Percodan, Darvon, Elavil, Haldol, Mellaril, Paxipam, Surmontil, Asendin, Tofranil, Talwin, Tylox, *bibbity bobbity boo.* Lombotriol, Perkupitrol, Nadanil, Highatril, Climaxine, Overcomitol, Hylox, Isadora countered. She could spend her sleepless nights making up names of drugs with the best of them, but still her headache did not abate. What a punishment for sexuality! The obviousness of the symbolism was pathetic. Talk about pleasure inhibition, the dreaded anhedonia—Isadora (who, two weeks ago, had thought herself so liberated) was now a walking testament to self-inflicted pain. She had finally freed herself from guilt, it seemed, whereupon the Great Migraine in the Sky had come to claim her.

Only Valium worked, Valium and dope (preferably the Sonoma County stuff that Roland supplied). Moreover, Swedish massages were good—and Shiatsu—if only for a few hours. She was on the verge of trying acupuncture, T.M., levitation—even a trip to Sai Baba's ashram in Puttaparthi, India, to get some of his famed Vibhuthi . . .

"Nonsense," said Roland. "Take the Valium, if it works, and wait. You'll be fine in no time at all."

Whereupon he laid upon her heaps of pills—yellow ones, green ones—and his own two trembling hands. He gave her odoriferous buds of gorgeous dope, freshly picked by hippies in the blessed counties of Sonoma and Humboldt.

The dope was rare. The hands she could teach not to tremble so much. But the Valium, she discovered, was available nearly *everywhere.* Every pharmacist was a legal dope vendor. Connecticut was full of druggists who'd refill you endlessly. And so was New York. The whole world was on Valium—the main drug in the Divorce Pharmacopoeia, it seemed—Valium, booze, coke, and dope. No, not quite true. Three-quarters of the world was on Valium, booze, coke, and dope—the other quarter was "at a meeting." The number of friends she had who were "in the program" astounded her. A.A.-niks were everywhere. Sometimes she went to meetings herself just to be inspired—but alas, they did not cure her headaches.

"Do you want to do something sexual?" Roland asks, sitting across from the sprawling Isadora, rolling a joint, and producing little green shield-shaped pills.

"Roland, how about some soft lights, sweet music, a jug of wine, a loaf of bread, you know?"

"I thought wine gave you a headache."

"It does. God—don't be so literal."

"I'm sorry," Roland says, looking rebuked.

"Sure, we can do something sexual," Isadora says languidly. "But first, you ought to get me in the mood."

"Well, what would get you in the mood?"

Isadora laughs.

"Do you want me to make you a list on my *Things to Do* pad?"

"Really, Isadora," he says stiffly, "I'm not nearly as *experienced* as you. I'm not good at the dressing and undressing, the soft lights, the sweet music . . ."

"But you'd be irresistible if you'd only *learn* to be good at it. Isn't that why I'm here?"

"I don't know. What can I say? I've never gotten into that stuff."

"So, get into it now."

"First, *you* take a Valium and relax."

Which Isadora does. She takes two, in fact. Then they smoke dope. That marvelous, odoriferous stuff from northern California, America's greatest contribution to agriculture (not to mention agribusiness) since the Big Boy tomato.

Isadora's temples are still throbbing. The back of her neck is still somewhat tense, but she's starting to unwind. As the resinous smoke enters her lungs, she becomes, predictably, amorous. This stuff *really* dissolves the superego—if she has any left. Once all superego, she is now, it appears endless id. Endless, meaningless id. What the fuck, she thinks, beckoning to Roland to come to her.

After she and Josh split, she had endured a period of such intense horniness that she found herself gazing at crotches in supermarkets, crotches at Connecticut tag sales, crotches at vegetable auctions at county fairs (now, *there's* a zucchini), crotches on airplanes. Once, early in the separation, she had necked throughout a transatlantic flight with a total stranger—a Swedish real-estate developer, who was a great kisser, but an equally great liar —and who turned out to be just another boring, mendacious married man. They took over the upstairs lounge of the SAS 747 and hugged and kissed from somewhere over Goose Bay to somewhere over Oslo—where he departed (deplaned, as they say, her phone number in his bulging pocket). In New York a month later, he proved an utter boob, so hopeless at dinner she never even groped him. The entire beguiling story of his life he'd told her on the plane proved a monstrous lie. He was married, with three kids —not the young *bon vivant* with a tragic history of an alcoholic teen-age ex-wife he'd presented himself to be. Isadora hardly cared that he was *married* (she wasn't looking for marriage, after all, but just diversion from her pain over Josh), but she did care that he had lied. She hated liars more than anything. She knew that sometimes one had to lie by omission to spare another human's feelings—but conscious, useless lies infuriated her. This Nordic fool had pretended to open up the entire story of his life

74

there in the upper lounge of the 747, when, in truth, the whole spiel was bullshit—and not even amusing bullshit at that—but aimless bullshit, pillow talk that doesn't quite make it, like cowflop on a satin pillowcase.

"Are you relaxed?" Roland asks, getting up to put on a record. "Would early Beatles be appropriate?"

"Most appropriate," Isadora says.

"Then you're getting relaxed?" he repeats.

"Mmm," says Isadora.

"Shall we commence something erotic?"

Whereupon Isadora commences a fit of the giggles.

"Yes," says Isadora between giggles, "let us commence something erotic."

"A kiss?" asks Roland.

"*Do* it, Roland, don't *say* it." Which he comes back to administer —inspecting her mouth with his tongue, like the sort of boy she and her friend Pia used to call a "tooth inspector" when they were in high school. (God—she had gone from drapeheads back to tooth inspectors in one short month!)

"Sweet kisses, soft kisses," says Isadora, assuming her role as mother-teacher, Roland's perfect oedipal object—since his real mother is also a famous lady, a lady famous for being sexy.

Roland dutifully kisses her with attempted tenderness. He begins to fondle her nipples with soft little tweaks.

"Shall we remove our clothes?" he asks formally.

"Shall I reply by engraved reply card?" Isadora mocks him.

Roland is so busy concentrating, he doesn't even realize he's being mocked.

Isadora loves to tease him, for Roland is as humorless about sex as a stud dog. Sex is a serious business—no laughing matter. Roland goes about it like work, or college boards. It's a performance, and he, as the son of the chief auteur-director, had damn better perform well.

The first night they had been together (at the Carlyle, where Isadora was staying for a week of TV shows for the paperback edition of *Tintoretto's Daughter*), Roland had *not* performed well. He had kept losing his erection. This bothered him so much more than it bothered her that he kept badgering her to give him "another chance." (It had amused her hugely that upon exiting the hotel that morning, she had seen none other eminence than Philip Roth sitting in the lobby, engrossed in the *New York Times*. It was all she could do to keep from telling him the story of last night's adventure. But she knew better. It was important not to confuse writers with their books. So she tiptoed past Philip, leaving his privacy inviolate.) As for Roland, she gave him another chance, and another, and another after that—whether out of kindness or horniness or revenge, she didn't quite know. She liked Roland's mind. She liked the fact that he was infatuated with her. And he was undeniably well hung. In the absence of "one true love," those things would have to do.

In sex, as in life's other activities, the participants are not often after the same things. They come together for a time because certain of their needs mesh, but in a short while it becomes painfully obvious that not *enough* of those needs mesh for the connection to endure. Isadora had known many kinds of connections in her time—a marriage of passionate adolescent puppy love (Brian Stollermann), a marriage of convenience and the Delusion of Rescue (Bennett Wing), a demonic affair with an Unsuitable Object (Adrian Goodlove), a marriage of True Minds—and bodies— (Josh Ace). When even *that* had not worked, she felt all loved out, dry as a bone in the love department, spent.

"Spare me from love," she told Hope in the bitter days after Josh moved out, when they were still having screaming fights on the phone at midnight, and all their love seemed to have festered into hate.

"You'll find it again," Hope said. "But a different kind of love, a better kind of love."

"Never," said Isadora. "After Josh, never." For she was truly disillusioned. She had almost begun to believe the polemics of her novelist friend Regina Lynch, who wrote bitter best sellers about the impossibility of love between the sexes, and who, on the occasion of Isadora's splitting with Josh, had sent her a case of Perrier-Jouet Fleur de Champagne with a card that read: "I congratulate those who aren't, not those who are." (Oh only the greatest of romantics can possibly become so bitterly cynical of love!)

But Isadora, alas, couldn't fully share Regina's cynicism—even in her bitterest moments. Isadora *liked* men. She liked their saltiness—the tang of yang on yin, their smells, their hairiness, their bulk. What a bore the world would be without two opposing sexes. Besides, Isadora saw men's vulnerabilities so clearly. She knew they worried about their erections, their prostates, their performances, their bank accounts, their tax audits, their hearts. She also knew that a lot of them were big babies—as immature at forty as they had been at four—but she couldn't find it in her heart to hate the whole sex. It was just as it had been in grade school. The girls were more mature than the boys. She remembered sixth-grade graduation at P.S. 87—the girls with their budding breasts and "training" bras, the boys still apple-cheeked and peach-fuzzed.

Things were tougher now, however, because the girls had more things to do, heavier responsibilities. Babies to raise *and* incomes to provide. Isadora's generation of affluent Jewish girls from Central Park West had liberated themselves, she often thought, right into being as burdened as the black women who took care of them in Central Park when they were kids. They had to earn the bread, bear the babies, and at the same time pretend to their wandering studs that they were merely courtesans, hungry for love. The songs of Billie Holiday took on new meaning. The men hopped from flower to flower, and the women, having insisted on their right to be superwoman, now had that right firmly thrust up their asses (or upon their breaking backs). How much smarter their mother's generation was—playing canasta, and having their nails done while their husbands brought home the bacon—though Isadora's mother hardly fit the description.

I am just like Yolanda Worthington now, Isadora often thought during the last couple of years of her marriage to Josh. She was thinking of the wiry West Indian woman who took care of her and her three sisters when they were little—a tough Trinidadian with six children of her own and an errant, erring husband she both adored and raged against. Now all the white men were free to do the same—wander from woman to woman—while Isadora's generation turned as matriarchal as the black women who'd raised them.

Was Yolanda Worthington my role model? Isadora often wondered. For Yolanda was hardly a bad role model. She was a survivor, a worker, full of guts and spirit. Was that, after all, better than being a dependent wife, shopping at Bergdorf's to appease one's sense of powerlessness? Maybe. At least Isadora knew how strong she was—as Yolanda had also known. The gift of strength is a great gift, though the price is eternal exhaustion.

"Let me undress you," Roland says, trying to be sensual for Isadora's sake.

"I've worn my sexy underwear for you," Isadora says. And, indeed, since the separation, she had not only gone to exercise class regularly, but she'd laid in a lavish supply of silk teddies, bikini underwear, lacy bras, silk slips, and lacy body suits. Josh liked these things—and maybe Isadora was still, on some level, hoping for his return (on the underwear level?). But consciously, she was merely playing courtesan.

In *La Naissance du Jour*, Colette writes, "Love, one of the great commonplaces of existence, is slowly leaving mine. The maternal instinct is another great commonplace. Once we've left these behind, we find that all the rest is gay and varied, and that there is plenty of it." So she wrote, and then hooked up with a man sixteen years her junior. But Isadora *really* plans to give up love anon— and before she does, she means to do it right: silk underwear, vintage champagne, rare dope, young lovers. And then? And then? Then she will become—what?—a nun, and devote the remainder of her life to literature alone. "*Hah*. Not so fast, Abernathy," Isadora can almost imagine Hope saying.

Roland begins unbuttoning her white silk blouse, then unzips her black velvet jeans. He is clumsy but determined. Underneath everything he finds a white lace teddy, with white embroidery coyly covering pubic bush and nipples.

He pulls down one strap, then the other, and takes her right breast in his mouth, sucking on it, like the baby he is. Isadora's mind, time-tripping on sinsemilla, wanders, while her cunt grows, undeniably, wet. She remembers what Sylvia Sydenheim-Rabinowitz said to her shortly after Josh moved out. "He's haffing a veening tantrum, Isadora—merely zat. Baby chimps haff it ven ze're taken off za breast. At sree, Roland used to pee in za fruit bowl, to try to stop me from zeeing patients. I used to tell him, 'Roland, pee all you like, I'm still vurking. He ztopped peeing zoon enough."

And now, here was baby Roland, sucking her nipple. Thrown out by one mommy, another takes him in—the story of the male sex.

"Are you lubricating yet?" Roland asks.

"If I was, a remark like that sure would stop it."

"I don't know what you mean, Isadora."

"God, Roland, sometimes I think you've never made love to a woman who said anything to you other than—'a little higher, a little lower, no not there, *there* . . .' Can't you whisper sweet nothings?"

"I think such things are absurd," Roland says.

"So do I—but they work better than 'are you lubricating.' "

"What words would be appropriate under the circumstances?" asks Roland.

78

Isadora suddenly recalls her disc jockey with great fondness.

"How about, 'I'd fight off Grendel for you and go search for the Third Ring'?"

"I don't know the literary allusion," says Roland, unzipping to reveal a tall, thick, erect cock, which he has already told her is "an inch longer than the national average." Ever the scientist, Roland has measured it in all stages of tumescence and detumescence. Roland should be a "member" (as it were) of the Star Studs, an arcane sex club in California whose "President-at-Very-Large" often writes to Isadora describing the cocks of his colleagues (not to mention his own) and inviting Isadora to orgies. (Her secretary puts letters like these in a box marked "Crazy Mail." Isadora long ago discovered that it is perilous to answer them.)

"You have a great cock, Roland," says Isadora.

"It's an inch longer than the national average," he says humorlessly.

"I know—you've already told me," Isadora says.

"You have a great cock" is not exactly a line she hasn't used before either—though Isadora reserves the compliment for special cocks—not the common or garden-variety zucchini. Roland is exceptionally well endowed; indeed, it is his chief charm other than his hypertrophied brain.

Now Roland begins to make love to Isadora in the slow, deliberate manner made famous by Masters and Johnson (and his mother). Sensate Focus is the name of the game. One is supposed to pleasure (and be pleasured by) one's partner with no concern for performance. The touching, the feel of skin on skin is supposed to be an end in itself. For the truth is, that even when sex is supposedly "free," we wily humans have ways of fettering it with our fettered minds.

Roland, however, has not quite got the Masters and Johnson message. He bends to Isadora's body as if to his microscope or exam bluebook. She feels as if he has outlined the erogenous zones of her body with eyebrow pencil, so that he can find them more easily. First he stimulates her nipples with his fingertips, then he proceeds to her thighs. Then he sucks on her nipples while he grazes her clitoris with his practiced fingers. She responds (she nearly *always* responds) but her overwhelming impulse is to giggle. She thinks of that early Brian de Palma movie, *Greetings*, in which a Kennedy-assassination nut of the late sixties is drawing entry and exit wounds on his girl friend's naked body. Roland's lovemaking seems oddly cerebral—despite the pot, the music, the excellent technique. What is sex when feeling is removed? *This*, thinks Isadora. Even Errol with his corny poetry has more of the *idea* of sex than Roland.

Meanwhile, Isadora is playing with Roland's cock, teasing it with her fingers, contemplating its bigness filling her up. She takes it in her mouth eventually, twirling and tonguing it, feeling pride in her own skill at this, and in his moans and sighs. How delicious for a woman of thirty-nine to have a twenty-six-year-old lover; no wonder men did this for so many years—still do, in fact. The delights of playing mentor, the ego trip of being wanted by youth itself ("I am youth, I am joy!" cries Peter Pan), the pleasures of playing Pygmalion—all these are not inconsiderable—and they can be enjoyed if one knows enough not to take the liaison too seriously.

"Why don't you come inside me?" says Isadora.

"Not yet," Roland demurs. "I want to give you a few orgasms through cunnilingus first." And he bends to her cunt, licking her clitoris with a clever tongue, flicking the right side, then the left, playing trills down the middle. He looks up momentarily, shakes his ponytail, and asks: "Do you prefer the right side of your clitoris to be licked, or the left?"

"I never thought about it before," says Isadora, who, in the last two months has experienced refinements in lovemaking unknown to her during the long winter's night of marriage. It was, sexually, a very gratifying marriage—but still, what variety there is out here in the brave new world of sex!

"Roland, really, you *can* come inside me."

"Not yet," he says, "I can only come once—so I want to wait until you've come five or six times and then we can climax together the last time."

"What makes you think you can only come once?" says Isadora, rising, as it were, to the challenge.

"I know," says Roland. "I know my own capacity."

"Your capacity is only what you *think* your capacity is."

"Nonsense," says Roland. "Even when I was fifteen, I could only come once."

That's all Isadora needs to hear.

"You must have had very uninspired partners," she says. Then as the music throbs, as the sinsemilla turns her brain to flowering fireworks, memories, dreams, reflections, she turns on all her charm and sexual determination for an amazed Roland Rabinowitz, playing acrobat on the high wire of his cock, astounding him by making him come once, twice, three times, in a night that seems endless because they are both so stoned.

"This is amazing," Roland keeps saying, with slurred tongue. "I've never done this before. I never imagined . . ." And Isadora feels wonderful, smug almost, to be the tutor to his innocence, the mentor to this *idiot savant* of sex who thought he knew everything (and *did* know it—but only by the book). She is his *practicum,* his lab course, the frog he must dissect to pass the test.

Oh, Isadora's brain is full of the most irreverent recollections: her own truncated medical career, quashed when she could not dissect a frog in Zoo:1–2 without shredding its internal organs; the Mt. Sinai gynecologist a friend of hers is fucking—a student of the famous crazy twins—who screws around a lot but always takes a smear from his cock after making it with a new woman. Does he have slides by the bed and a magnifying glass secreted in the bathroom linen closet? What insane sexual habits people have nowadays! Who would ever dream . . . In two months as a single woman she's discovered that one longtime friend is, astoundingly, into rubber diving suits; another into "Greek culture"; and still another into voyeurism. He wants to take her to Las Vegas and watch her get fucked by three black studs. If he's a voyeur, is the other a *diveur?* And what of the third? *Assineur?*

Everybody does *something* with his genitals, a shrink friend of Bennett's once said—if only the old flying fist. Sex is a great commonplace. Considering how common, why such secrecy? Might as well be secret about our livers or our noses. We all have them. Sex can be merely hydraulic; or an ego trip; or a cosmic merging with the other—as, oh god, it sometimes was with Josh, her husband, the father of her child, her love, her love. She begins to come, thinking how like Josh's cock Roland's is, and now her attraction to Roland is suddenly explained, as the spasms start and just at the crucial moment, she sees Josh's face, sweet as in the first days of their love (before his mouth turned cruel), and she is suddenly blinded by pain between the eyes—as if Cupid himself had shot his arrows there.

"Damn, damn, damn," she says as the steel band tightens around her head, and the imaginary drill bit enters the fontanel, and the arrows behind the eyes seem to sharpen themselves on her bony sockets.

"Damn."

"What?" asks Roland (who is beneath her, moaning in pleasure as she rotates herself on the maypole of his prick).

"The headache has come back," she says, slumping into his arms.

"I love you, Isadora," he says, weeping with the wonder of his own three orgasms, and her pain, which she has entrusted to him.

"I love you. I love you. I love you. I'd fight off cancer for you and search out cell nuclei in the dark . . . Is that better?"

"Much better, darling boy," she says, through her blinding pain.

5

Deciphering the Fire

A thing is not necessarily true
because a man dies for it.
—Oscar Wilde

Facing me from the other side
of the looking glass, in that mysterious
reflected room, is the image of
'a woman of letters who has turned
out badly.' . . . That is what I
must remain for everyone, I who
no longer write, who deny myself
the pleasure, the luxury of writing.
—Colette

NOVEMBER in Connecticut. The flaming leaves of October are just beginning to succumb to the bareness of winter. Orange and yellow and nutmeg brown (this is, after all, "the Nutmeg State"—though who knows why?)—they line the gutters of the winding country roads, slippery as greased lightning after a heavy rain and just as lethal.

Isadora is once again driving QUIM, rushing away from her house so as not to be there when Josh and his girl friend come to pick up Amanda. Let the nanny open the door and deliver Mandy. Isadora finds she can't bear the sight of the other woman in Josh's car even though Josh parks so that she can only see the back of her head.

The girl is definitely called Wendy, or Wanda, but Josh won't tell her which it is. Though Josh wants Isadora to confide in him about *her* love life, the formerly hang-loose, free-spirit Josh has suddenly become cagy as hell about *his*. Wanda or Wendy No-Name. Wanda-Wendy Emanon is how Isadora thinks of her. Nor is Isadora allowed to have her phone number—though Josh spends several nights each week with her in New York and Isadora would like to know where he is in the unlikely event that some emergency should arise with Mandy.

Wanda-Wendy E. is a computer programmer and an old high school classmate of Josh's. She has dirty blond hair which straggles down her back, and a pug nose. (Isadora has seen her profile in the car and to the untrained eye she seems like a homely version of Isadora.) Josh never goes very far afield to get laid. After all, his parents actually delivered Isadora into his arms, and the other ladies in his life either worked in the health-food store he frequented, typed for him, or were found at yoga classes, Zen meditation sessions, or class reunions. Josh wants everything delivered straight to his lap—UPS, as it were.

So Isadora is racing away from her own home to avoid him. She is so fragile and shaky these days that it never occurs to her to just brazen it out. Why should she be driven out of her own house?

She doesn't even think to ask the question. Somewhere deep inside she believes that if she is "nice" to Josh, if she atones for her power and success by annihilating herself in some way, then he will come back. It is the old female love-work dilemma, the dilemma Isadora thought she'd solved years ago, now come back to haunt her in a new form. (It is Isadora's conviction that we never shed our neurotic dilemmas totally. We merely solve them in one guise, but they return to bedevil us in another.)

She races QUIM's motor. Up the hill she goes and around the serpentine curve that gives its name to the road she lives on: Serpentine Hill Road. She remembers how much the name meant to her when she bought the house, she a lover of S-shaped curves, an aficionado of Hogarth's theory that the S-curve is the essence of beauty. She remembers how lucky she thought the address—11 Serpentine Hill Road—lucky eleven and the Hogarthian ring of "serpentine." Not to mention the Serpentine in London, one of Isadora's favorite haunts.

Then, later, when Isadora became a devotee of the Great Mother Goddess, she realized that the snake was the Mother's symbol, the embodiment of the Great Goddess' power in the ancient world, transformed into a devilish serpent by the misogynistic patriarchs who wrote the Old Testament. The address seemed doubly lucky then—like the double serpents the Cretan priestess holds aloft in beautiful blue Knossos (or is it the Heracleon Museum?). At any rate, serpents were lucky. Serpents were powerful. Serpents represented Goddess power. Serpents represented the power Isadora has felt utterly stripped of since Josh moved out.

She is scattered in a million different pieces. Her head is like a phrenologist's chart of worries and stresses. In one box, there is Mandy and "Worry About Motherhood." In another box, Men and "Worry About Getting Laid." In another box, Money and "Worry About Making Money." And nowhere does there seem to be any room at all for writing—for the kind of full-blast concentration that writing requires and that has always been Isadora's center, her salvation, her solace, even her livelihood.

The funny part of it all is that Isadora really knows of no other way to make money than to write her heart out. And to write she must find her center. But her center is so drowned in worries that she cannot locate it. She is rushing around madly instead of staying home and waiting for her calm center to claim her. The meditative peace she has always found in her yellow legal pads now eludes her totally and she is looking everywhere for solace outside

86

herself when she knows perfectly well that solace can only be found within. "Happiness is difficult to find within, impossible to find elsewhere," said someone called Sebastién Chamfort, who knew.

So she rushes down Serpentine Hill Road, taking the S-curve much too fast, and, as she does, some demon within causes her to look down at her odometer to set the mileage (suddenly she feels she *must* know the mileage from her house to town)—whereupon the car veers into the leaf-choked shoulder of the road, hits the skiddy mass of wet leaves—orange, yellow, red, and brown as the owls of Dylan Thomas—screeches out of control madly, and seems to fly across forty feet of leaf-greased macadam until it climbs a little Robert Frost stone fence (allegedly making for good New England neighbors) and stops dead, with a heart-contracting shudder, its three-pointed Nazi star looking heavenward, its grille unscathed, but its undercarriage hooked, locked, barnacled upon the three-foot stone wall.

It has all happened so fast—the curve, the odometer, the skid, the wall—that Isadora, who is wearing no seat belt and yet is utterly unscathed and unscarred, can only sit bolt upright in the car shaking like the autumn leaves above her and rerun the accident again and again in her brain. Her hands sweat on the steering wheel; the blood has drained from her face; she is amazed her bowels have not let go. Quaking, she opens the door on the driver's side, astounded that she can still remember how to manipulate the latch. Every motion her body makes seems astonishing and new as if she were a toddler learning these simple operations for the first time. How to open a door. How to step out of a car. How to remove an ignition key. It is as though she is new-made by the accident, suddenly aware that her nerves and eyes and ears function, that the world, so lately in danger of being annihilated, is still present, and her muse, her guardian, her Goddess, holds her in the palm of her ample hand, saying: Not yet, the time is not yet ripe to go.

The car is perched three feet above the sodden, leafy ground, like a sloop run upon rocks. Shaking as if after an orgasm, Isadora hops down into the leaf mulch, blessing the wet of it, blessing the world, the stone fence, herself—but blessing and blaming both. For she has nearly annihilated the wet, wonderful, leafy world merely for the lack of love of one man—and her politics rebel though her heart (for one hideous minute) did not want to beat without Josh's.

What to do? QUIM is hooked on the stone wall. Isadora looks madly around for help, slams the car door, runs into the road, leaving handbag, keys, coat in the car. No one in sight. Just the leaves falling and the road gleaming with an almost sexual wetness. Sex and death—the twin poles of our being, and somehow allied. She thinks of animals killed in the road, of her own dog, Chekarf, not yet one year gone, of her grandfather eating the earth, of her own hungry mouth so voracious that it would rather do the same than close around air. The air she swallows is redolent of Josh's absence. Without a man's tongue in her mouth, would she rather eat earth? *No,* she says. But her heart betrays her. Why did she look down at that odometer, and why was that stone wall there? Why did she walk away unscathed? Saved by the Silver Nazi? Oh, the Jews' revenge on Hitler! To be saved by one's own Mercedes—bought with the royalties of books castigating the whole Teutonic race? How astounding to be thirty-nine and to see the curious circles that life completes.

Her parents wouldn't drive a Mercedes and only bought Cadillacs (until just lately when Nat indulged himself in a huge Lincoln Continental, as if to spite the gas crisis. Spite or deny it.) Yet if she had been in one of those American deathtraps, she'd probably be a goner or a cripple by now.

How many times has Isadora nearly done herself in and been saved by the protection of the Goddess? Or whomever. She won't insist on the gender. It's the protection she's sure of. The leg she broke in Zürs following Bennett Wing down an icy slope. The riding accident at Fort Sam Houston which could easily have made her a paraplegic (her spine thrown against an outcropping of rock). The car accident on a corniche road in Sicily (between Palermo and Messina). And so on. Isadora used to think she could read her life story in her scars as accurately as in her poems. Each scar was, in fact, a sort of poem. But this accident would be different. No scars at all. Only the blinding recognition that she had nearly killed herself for want of Josh. And that sooner or later this stuff would have to stop.

She runs down the road to a white colonial farmhouse which bears a plaque on the side: ETHAN WHEATWORTH HOUSE, 1701. The hills are full of 'em. Old colonial WASP shrines. What is a Jewish girl like Isadora White Stollerman Wing Ace—though now estranged from husband number three—doing in this WASPy historic part of the world? And driving a Silver Nazi? Should she have stayed on West Seventy-seventh Street where her kind belongs? Are the dangers fewer there? Merely muggings and murders and suffocation by immersion in trendy boutiques selling art deco *tsatskes?*

She rings the bell of Wheatworth's old manse. Commotion within. The sounds of kids and slippers. Typically enough, old Ethan's house is now inhabited by an *echt* Connecticut "family"— new style. The husband—a nice-looking fortyish blond—is called "Murph" by the kids, who are clearly not his biological kin (except possibly the youngest). The wife, a toothsome brunette whose babes these three urchins are, comes down the stairs wrapped in a pink towel, with another pink towel turban-wise on her head.

"We heard the screech," she says, glistening with drops of water from her shower. "What happened?"

And Isadora, still trembling, and having almost lost the use of her voice, says in a voice gone three octaves above the usual level, "I hit the leaf mulch and skidded. I'm terribly shaken. May I use the phone to call AAA? My car's hooked on a stone wall. I can't believe I'm still alive."

Again she has that very odd sensation of a world new-made and she a sort of female Adam, bearing witness. This is the New Family. Mom and kids and lover man (or new husband). At any rate, only the mom and kids are surely linked. The men come and go. Or is she projecting?

"Come have some coffee," says the wife, who now introduces herself as Lena Browning-Murphy. So this is New Husband— "Murph." Still, it may not last.

The wet, newly hatched, newly married Lena glides across the floor in bare feet to get coffee from her redone colonial kitchen. The kids, perhaps disappointed that no one has been killed, disperse.

Murph offers to go outside and assess the car damage. A man's job. That's what men are still for, even in the New Eden, though the players change from decade to decade.

"No," says Isadora, "just let me collect myself. I'll go, too."

"It's no trouble," says Murph.

"Oh, *thank* you," says Isadora, apologetically, "but there's no need—really." She truly *does* feel like a troublemaker—she with no husband of her own to assess the damage.

At some point in this exchange, the Murphys recognize her. Isadora knows just when this happens, for their voices change audibly, and their friendliness, honest enough before, now becomes truly cloying. Isadora can always tell the very moment when this happens. The gazes penetrate deeper. The voices become more lyrical and somehow higher. Like her own voice, filled with the fear of having come so near to self-destruction.

The amazing thing about being a well-known writer is that your name is well known, but your face, reinterpreted through so many distorting book-jacket photos, is not. (In Italy the publicity photos make you look Italian; in Japan, vaguely Japanese; in France, French; in Germany, German; *und so weiter*.) But when people see the name—exactly like in those American Express ads, they gasp. "You? The writer? I read your book." "Which one?" you ask at first, chip on shoulder about the other seven. But, after a while you mellow. How lucky, after all, to have even one book like a shot fired around the world, a guided missile, a contagion, a whisper round a whispering gallery, a shared dream, a chain letter, a fable told and told again in different tongues. "Thank you," you learn to say simply. "Thank you."

Which Isadora does. The Browning-Murphys stare, as if she were an extraterrestrial dropped from an orbiting saucer. This shaken woman—so small and vulnerable-looking—is really a Famous Personage. They can't make sense of it, and Isadora is too agitated to help them make sense of it; she wants someone to help her make sense of her life—which is suddenly so unmanageable, so insane, so inexplicable: to have all that the world desires, yet also to have nothing, and to be able to think of nothing but to call Josh.

But Josh is not home; he's on his way to Isadora's. She tries and tries, getting only the chilly recorded message on the answering machine she bought him last Christmas.

"Who are you calling?" asks Lena Browning-Murphy.

"My ex-husband," says Isadora, feeling the word strange on her tongue, for he is still more husband than ex. "Now I'll try AAA."

She does, gives them the site of the accident, meanwhile replaying the tape of it again and again in her head. Her limbs still tremble as if with the aftershock of an earthquake. She keeps dialing Josh's number, then her own, spasmodically. Finally, she reaches Josh at her own house.

"I crashed the car," she says, half apologetically, half defiantly, still apparently thinking he will feel guilty enough to say: "I'm coming back; all is forgiven." But does she really *want* that? She doesn't know.

She knows, however, that Josh's reaction makes her feel more abandoned than ever. He is, frankly, pissed off. His voice is cold, unforgiving, furious to be disturbed in his plans by her boring suicidal impulses. His mandate to protect her has lapsed. She had too much—success, a baby, all the womanly things as well as the manly ones—and now, by god, she'll have to give up something. She'll have to pay. She'll pay with the loss of her lover, the father of her child. ("You have everything"—he'd said on the phone one night after they'd separated—"except me." Except my life, she thought, except my life.)

Josh arrives alone in his Toyota Land Cruiser. He is furious. Furious at Isadora for nearly killing herself and furious for having been called in to witness it. The neediness and panic in Isadora run deep. Will I never get over this? she wonders. Will nothing appease it—not fame, nor money, nor a child? She longs for Josh to cradle her in his arms and protect her—but he is merely outraged. His mouth looks cruel. He has cut his hair very short, in a sort of Teutonic style. His beard is close-cropped, and through it one can see that he has a smallish chin. A wen has grown on the back of his neck—and in his characteristic stubbornness, he will do nothing about it. Still, she desires him. His arrival brings a tumult to her innards. Her heart races; her cunt moistens. What funny creatures women are, to fixate as we do, upon particular cocks. No one else Isadora has slept with since Josh feels quite right to her. The bodies are unfamiliar, the cocks strange; she can never bear to spend the whole night. She wants the man astrally transported out of her arms by three A.M.—so she allows no one to stay with her all night, no one. She has even made men leave through the dog run at three A.M. Her home is her castle, her body still Josh's garden. Why does he refuse to understand?

"The car is fine," Josh says gruffly. "At least I mean it goes. I drove it off the wall. The undercarriage may be wrecked—but it can be driven to the Mercedes place. Okay? I'm leaving."

"Wait a minute," says Isadora.

"Why?" barks Josh. (Is he compelled to cruelty by residual love for her? Was Oscar Wilde right in saying that "each man kills the thing he loves"?)

The Browning-Murphys stare. But Isadora is too gone with grief to give a damn. She races out the door after Josh, who has pulled the Silver Nazi up to the Browning-Murphys' door and is now climbing back into the Land Cruiser.

"Don't go," she pleads. The Silver Nazi trails wires and metal wreckage from underneath like a disemboweled warrior, but clearly Josh had driven it to where it now stands, so the damage cannot be lethal. Not so with her heart, which aches like a mortally wounded thing.

She runs to the Toyota as Josh slams the door. She opens it.

"Please stay," she whimpers.

"I have to meet Wendy," he says, twisting the knife. (Well, at least she knows the girl's name now.)

"Please," she begs.

"*No*—" he thunders, starting the motor.

Suddenly, and with no thought at all, Isadora runs in front of the Land Cruiser and throws herself down on the pavement. Whereupon Josh swerves around her and begins to drive off.

"Have you no pride?" he screams out the window—and with a roar and screech of tires, he is gone.

None, she thinks, lying on the cool pavement, none at all. The Browning-Murphys have watched this scene from their colonial driveway, but Isadora doesn't care at all. She's like a crazy person, the madwoman of Rocky Ridge, Connecticut, a beast that wants reason, pride, self-consciousness.

Why do men always mention pride? she thinks, still lying on the pavement. What is pride compared to love? What is pride compared to motherhood? What is pride compared to poetry? Pride is an invention of the devil, of the male ego, of the male demons. "Pride goeth before destruction, and an haughty spirit before a fall," it says in Proverbs. "From pride, vainglory, and hypocrisy; from envy, hatred, and malice, and all uncharitableness, good Lord deliver us," it says in *The Book of Common Prayer*. And yet men always speak of pride when a love affair is ending. Christ and Buddha were not concerned with pride. Women are not concerned with pride. Demeter and Persephone were not concerned with pride. Nor am I, Nor am I, Nor am I, thinks Isadora.

Just then Murph comes out of his house and helps her up.

"Thanks," says Isadora. "Thanks a lot." She wonders why she cares so little at having humbled her supposedly famous self before these total strangers, but truly, she does not give a damn. There are times in life—great illness and pain, childbirth, the end of love, madness—when one simply does not give a hoot how the outside world perceives one.

Let them think me insane, Isadora muses. They probably do anyway. If people think writers crazy, might as well not disappoint. Besides, there is some freedom, after all, in having a scandalous reputation, no matter how ill deserved. "If your reputation is ruined—might as well have fun," goes an old German proverb.

If you can call throwing yourself in front of your ex-husband's car fun!

For years Isadora used to anguish about the disequilibrium between her reputation and her life. Now she's come to see a bizarre sort of liberty in it. Where is it written that we are meant to be understood in this world, except perhaps by a few close friends? Where is it written that true interpretation of our characters is our birthright? If we can count even half a dozen people who love and understand us, then we are truly blessed. For seven years Isadora had thought Josh to be chief among this half-dozen. She thought he knew that her extraordinary *mazel* still did not make her immune to pain; she thought he knew how much she needed him and the intimacy of family life—especially in the light of being notorious to the outside world. But alas, it turned out that even *he* envied her and saw her as invulnerable. She wanted the protection of his love, and he thought she needed no protection. Now, with a child to raise, she needed it more than ever. And now was when he elected to cop out for good.

(Had he *always* been this way—or had he changed? Had the birth of the baby made him petulant and perverse, moody and melancholic? She no longer knew. She no longer knew anything it seemed.)

Isadora climbs into her wounded QUIM, waves good-bye to the Browning-Murphys, and starts the car. The shattered chariot coughs and shudders as it starts up, but it runs. The Germans build amazingly invulnerable machines. If only they'd built *her*. I could use a little more invulnerability, Isadora thinks, driving back up Serpentine Hill Road to her house, passing Josh and Wendy and little carrot-topped Amanda on one of the curves.

"There's Mama!" Mandy shouts out the window as the cars pass each other.

Amanda is sitting on Wendy's lap, and Wendy is indeed a homely (and skinny) version of Isadora.

Isadora's heart contracts again. To be left for one's lesser, not one's better, is indeed a strange form of tribute. And to see one's child fondled by one's husband's girl friend is the final *coup de grâce*. Isadora had thought the child would forge a final and unbreakable link between them. Having delayed bearing for so long, she put a great symbolic weight upon that act. It was Isadora's proof of commitment, her proof of love, her statement of faith in family, her statement of faith in continuance. Now here was Josh, not even two whole seasons gone from the nest, mocking her with

93

a pallid clone of herself: another small-nosed blonde, but this one not—thank god—a writer, nor notorious, nor even very pretty.

It always comes as a shock to accomplished women that their men leave them for *un*accomplished ones. They assume—wrongly —that what holds true for men will also hold true for them: that accomplishment will bring with it fame, fortune, and beautiful lovers (to paraphrase Freud). But alas, we often get just the reverse. All our accomplishment buys us in the love department is threatened men, soft cocks, abandonment. And we reel backward wondering why we worked so hard for professional glory, when personal happiness is the forfeiture we have to pay.

Isadora parks QUIM in her driveway, and goes into her house to cancel the tow truck. She is still shaking with fear and the accident still keeps replaying in her brain. After calling AAA again, she gives in to her tremors and pops a Valium from her much-reduced Divorce Pharmacopoeia. She'd smoke a joint if she had one—but Errol and Roland are her sources of supply and she'd just as soon contact neither of them. With all the men in her life, there isn't even one she'd really like to talk to now. But dope— dope is what she'd like to have. Instead, she goes to the fridge and pours herself a big glass of California white wine—a lovely Freemark Abbey chardonnay she buys by the case.

Isadora hardly remembers a time in her life when she did so much drugs and booze. It seems her head is always a bit scrambled from dope, a bit woozy with booze. She seems to live in a time-trip of drugs, booze, and sex—in which she can hardly remember what she actually did, what she dreamed, and what she wrote once in a book. If I don't stop this, I'm going to become an alcoholic, Isadora thinks, gulping, not sipping, the white wine. (She can gulp the wine without a disapproving audience, because the nanny, having delivered Amanda to Josh, has been given the night off.)

Isadora herself disapproves of the drinking and drugs she's been doing—she who hitherto seemed to live long stretches of her life only to write—she, the arch-workaholic of the Western world. Many mornings, since splitting from Josh, Isadora has awakened after a motel night with Errol, or a random fuck with some man she had to get rid of at three A.M., and felt she was in the wrong novel—a novel not written by her, but by her friend Lola Benson, who has chronicled her own alcohol and drug addiction in several of her books.

"Christ—I'm in the wrong novel!" she'd say to herself, waking up. "I'm a Lola Benson character—not even one of my *own!*"

And then she'd wonder whether this constant intoxication was to blot out the pain of divorce, or was a sort of midlife crisis she was having, a midcareer mind-fart, or else some insidious loss of drive triggered by the fact that her two greatest successes in life— Mandy's birth and the publication of *Tintoretto's Daughter* (a far better book than the one that had made her a "household word") —had brought her, inexorably, the loss of Josh's love. Why bother to write beautiful books if you will only have to pay by losing the man you love? Oh, she was really in a bad way—turning forty, losing Josh, and having to face writing a book about her grandfather—all in the same rotten year.

To write, she thinks, oh to write. To cover a page with memories and dreams—even with scribble scrabble—*that* would bring a temporary truce between body and soul. To dream upon a page is in some sense to steel oneself against the blows the world deals. It is its own reward, and brings the blessings of peace even to the most troubled spirit. So upstairs she goes to her beautiful tree-house writing studio—the one she designed herself and had built with the royalties from *Tintoretto's Daughter*—and sits down at her immense oak desk to contemplate the mess of papers that litters it.

"Writing a novel does not become easier with practice," Graham Greene says somewhere in his prefaces. And nothing could be more true. With each passing year, with each book and with growing reputation, comes greater and greater inhibition, not greater and greater freedom. One becomes more perfectionistic—and perfectionism is the enemy of art. Since art is essentially divine play, not dogged work, it often happens that as one becomes more professionally driven one also becomes less capriciously playful. Also, one becomes more cynical about the capacity of art to effect change. In hot youth, every writer believes that the word changes the world, but as the writer grows older, it becomes apparent that the world sometimes fails even to read the word, or if it reads, it deliberately fails to understand. Young writers believe that writing is a form of communication, but the middle-aged ones know that writing is merely a catalyst for people's reactions, and that these reactions, like reactions to drugs, are often paradoxical—not at all what one intended. Books *do* change the world, but in an indirect, not direct way. The whole creative process comes to seem more and more complex as the writer continues on her journey. One no longer writes with the gusto born of *"I'll show them!"* One writes instead for one's own intimate pleasures: the pleasure of getting some subtle state of mind on paper, the pleasure of using one's gifts with language, the pleasure of finding a shape for the amorphousness of life.

Isadora's desk appeared a random mess, but, like a novel-in-progress, it had an inner logic apparent only to its begetter. Stacks of books stood upon it, unfinished poems, notes and jottings about the various and sundry men she'd bedded and their peculiarities in speech or in the sack. Buried somewhere in this morass was the book Isadora had begun about her grandfather, the book she'd promised herself to write next, the book she'd been working on ever since Papa died, the book she was working on when the crisis between her and Josh stopped all work cold. This book haunted her, like an unpleasant dream. This book blocked her way. She knew she had to write it to get to the next book, and the next, and the next. She knew it was the labyrinth she had to first traverse to lay to rest—once and for all—that Minotaur, her grandfather. Oh, there were other books she'd *rather* write next—many, many of them. Her notebook was full of ideas, outlines, and false starts (for Isadora usually started three novels for every one she brought to completion). But contrary to what most people think, writers do not choose their subjects; their subjects choose them. Just as God (or Goddess) picks us out to parent some babe, who is never the child we *dreamed* we'd raise, so too the Muse chooses us to parent some book and we become Her conduit.

The grandfather book was next. That much Isadora knew. The pile of papers which formed the compost heap out of which this novel would—not so miraculously—spring was labeled *Dreamwork* or "Papa novel." If *Candida Confesses* was her "Mama novel," this was her "Papa novel." Yet the voice for the book stuck in her craw. She didn't really want to write it. She wasn't sure, she really knew *how* to write it. And that was a great pity, too, because the book already had an arresting beginning:

Dreamwork

He walked across Europe at a time when Europe was much larger than it is now. I can see him carrying a knapsack all the way from Russia—a knapsack filled to bursting with paints, books, all the grandchildren and great-grandchildren he would have, all their houses and apartments, their toys, sleds, cars, their lovers, husbands, wives.

But of course it was not like that. He was a boy of fifteen, unencumbered by great-grandchildren, hardly thinking of children—and with virtually no possessions. What he carried in his head and his groin would seed my life. His dreams, his protoplasm are still the very marrow of my bones, the juice between the tissues, and the tissues themselves.

He walked and walked. He raced toward this moment as if in seven-league boots; he raced there, not realizing until the end that he was racing toward his death.

These paragraphs were to be set in italics. They were to represent dream material, which the novel itself would later flesh out. Below them in the pile of stuff for "Papa novel" was the memoir she'd read at the funeral, all the poems she'd written about him through the years (including the elegy that had caused her such grief at the funeral), and rough notes and jottings for the novel's plot.

Isadora looked through this mass of material and wondered. Was she ready to write the Papa novel? What did she really know about her grandfather's life? The chasm between a poor Jewish man born in Russia in 1883 and an affluent American girl born in New York in 1942 was enormous. Could one bridge it? To imagine 16th-century Venice seemed somehow easier. Would it help to *go* to Russia? She had a friend who was fluent in Russian and who might accompany her. But the more she tried to imagine her grandfather, at fourteen, leaving Odessa to walk across Europe, the more astounding it seemed to her. The details of daily life in Russia circa 1890 she could re-create through research—that she knew. Having written one historical novel, she knew that it was not so hard to reconstruct a vanished world—if you were a diligent researcher—and she was. She loved the *process* of research. She adored reading and adored wallowing in library stacks. She had done all her own research for *Tintoretto's Daughter* and had enjoyed it immensely.

But it was Papa's *consciousness* she was not sure she could recreate. The paradox of his fearful Jewishness, his evil-eye mentality—yet the astounding gut courage of a fourteen-year-old boy who was driven to leave home and family without a kopeck in his pocket—seemed like the toughest task she had ever contemplated as a novelist. Could she capture his mind-set, his point of view? That was the dilemma. Isadora knew that it was relatively easy to discover the clothes people wore in different periods, the way they took a crap, how they rode (or walked) to work—but it was the *Zeitgeist* that was so hard to evoke. Because people's minds *do* change from era to era and when they do, they leave imperfect prints of themselves, partial residues—in books, in music, in paintings.

The phone rang. Saved by the bell—that enemy and yet great reliever of writers—the telephone!

Oy, it was the rabbi.

"Isadora—Ronald Gutweiler here. How *are* you?"

"Terrible. I just nearly killed myself."

"Should I drive right up? I have the car this weekend." (Ronald-the-ex-rabbi shared a car with his ex-wife, Sheila-the-ex-rebbitsin, and they alternated weekends with it, since their seven daughters were too grown to alternate weekends. Oh, the strange divorce arrangements people had nowadays!)

"No, thank you, Ronald sweetie," said Isadora. "I'm writing."

"Are you sure?"

"No writer is ever sure she's writing."

"I mean are you sure I shouldn't come up?"

"I'm sure," said Isadora. (The rabbi was about as good in bed as a knish—a cold knish at that. Oh certainly there were other things in life than sex, but the rabbi seemed to think he was devastating to women, and the prospect of having to fight him off did not cheer Isadora. It was Isadora's curse—or blessing—that nearly all her one-night stands fell in love and proposed permanence. Where *were* these divorced men who were fearful of commitment? Isadora seemed to meet nothing but desperate lonelies who couldn't wait to get hitched again—and hitched to her. Was that only because she wanted none of them, because her heart still belonged to Josh? Or was it because men nowadays took sex far more seriously than women did? At least older men seemed to. They now seemed for all the world like the vanished good girls of the fifties where sex was concerned. After one fuck, they proposed!)

"What happened? How did you nearly kill yourself?"

"Oh, I crashed the car on Serpentine Road. My whole body is still shaking from it."

"Stay right there—I'm coming," said Ronald. "I won't take no for an answer!"

"Ronald—you're a darling—but I really, really want to work. I just have to center myself with work right now—much as I'd love to see you."

"Are you sure you're okay?"

"Absolutely. I'll call you later, when I've done ten pages, okay? If you're still home, maybe we'll have supper."

"If you insist—but I really think I ought to come . . ." his voice trailed off. (Deliver me, Oh Lord God, from rabbis, Isadora thought.)

Lonely as she was, the prospect of Ronald's comfort did not assuage her pain. But he was impenetrable, it seemed.

"Some day, you'll come to your senses and marry me," the rabbi said, rabbinically. And Isadora, though wretched, could hardly hold back a guffaw. The rabbi was a nice-looking, balding, mustachioed man who wore English suits and sported bow ties and red silk handkerchiefs; he doused himself in Penhaligon cologne—yet somehow the thought of more than a brief lunch with him seemed like a life sentence. Chicago-born like some Saul Bellow hero, educated in Israel and England, he was a dandy with his bow ties and boutonnieres, and he could not see what a figure of fun he was. (Why do men who wear bow ties have so little self-knowledge?) He came to her house and criticized her gin ("You must buy Bombay, not Beefeaters"), her vodka ("Polska, not Finlandia"), her daughter's manners (which, admittedly, were those of a well-entrenched South American dictator), and then he expected to be adored in return.

"Thanks so much for calling, Ronald," Isadora said. "I'll call you back anon. Okay?"

"Okay—if you insist . . ."

Just then, the other line rang. Isadora hurriedly said good-bye to Ronald and pressed the button for the other number.

"Hello?" came the voice at the end of the line. It was a very slurry Roland, a Roland who had apparently done so much sinsemilla, Valium, and various combinations of antidepressants that his tongue emerged from the bottom of his mouth like a frog from a quagmire.

"Hi, Roland," said Isadora, sipping her wine. "How goes it, sweetheart?" Isadora liked Roland a lot better than she liked the rabbi and not only because he was better in bed. In his flat-footed, naïve way, Roland was good-hearted and loving, while the rabbi was a con man. (Isadora had learned from knowing the rabbi that perhaps the secret of being a clergyman—of any faith—was being a con man, and also that rabbis, as a group, definitely did not believe in God.)

"How are *you*, Isadora?" Roland asked with genuine, if slurred, concern. And Isadora had to relate the whole story of the accident again—embellishing the details somewhat to make it more lurid. (This was one of the problems with having so many lovers—having to tell the daily events of your life over and over again, and never remembering what you had told *whom.*)

"Shall I come right up and stay with you?" Roland asked. Isadora didn't think Roland could even negotiate Grand Central Station and find Conrail, let alone drive a car, so she thanked him for his concern, promised to call him later (Roland was terrific at marathon midnight conversations—like a teen-ager)—and buzzed off.

Now, the other line rang.

"How are you, lovely lady?" came the husky DJ's voice of Errol Dickinson.

Isadora didn't want another offer of physical solace, so she said, weakly, "Fine" and neglected to mention the accident.

"You're a goddess to me, earthling Isadora," said Errol, and Isadora could almost feel his soft touch on her nipples, his lovely tongue on her cunt, and see his huge, unmatched eyes that would face down mythical monsters for her—Grendel, the Gorgon, basilisks, the lot.

Why do men with high-school-equivalency degrees make love so much better than intellectuals? Is it because "failures" have devoted all their time to learning lovemaking? Or because they are freer and less cerebral? Isadora fucked her "blue-collar stud" (as she thought of him) the way intellectual men, for centuries, fucked bimbos. She enjoyed the hell out of him, but she then heard herself saying things like: "I can't make any permanent commitments right now" or "I can only see you Wednesdays because I'm afraid I'll get too involved" or "of course, I adore you, but I'm deep into my book." She kept Errol away from her friends, her kid, her parents. If he ever came to her house, he arrived after ten P.M. and left before six A.M., when Amanda stirred. He had never ever laid eyes on Amanda, except in photographs—though he adored her by proxy and sent her tickets to circuses and kiddie films, and plied her with Barbie dolls!

Isadora knew that Errol was much nicer than most of the high-class men she knew, not to mention much better in bed. But he embarrassed her in public (because he so stirred her sexually?) and if pressed for an escort, she'd sooner take Roland, "her psychopharmacology expert"—or the rabbi, with his bow ties, boutonnieres, and references to Roland Barthes. Why was that? Errol was smooth enough in public—though he possessed no dress pants that weren't polyester.

"Lady, I love you," he now said on the phone—and much as

Isadora longed for him, she was determined to stick this night out alone with her book and the ghost of her grandfather. So, she thanked him for his concern and went back to her compost heap of pages, leafing through it dully, and sipping her large glass of wine.

But the phone wasn't through with her; it kept ringing, as if possessed. Now it was—amazingly enough—the antiques dealer, the Rolls-Roycer, the sprayed drapehead—whose name was Ralph Plotkin. Ralph, Roland, Ronald, Errol. The Plotkin curse without the Plotkin diamond, thinks Isadora, hugely amused by her almost adolescent popularity—even though none of the suitors satisfies.

"Whaddya get when you cross an octopus with a nigger?" whispers Ralph Plotkin in his nasal New York accent. (Ralph is in the habit of starting phone calls without any intro, and Isadora has begun to recognize his voice).

"What?" she asks.

"A terrific shoeshine," says Ralph, laughing uproariously.

"That's the most racist joke I've ever heard in my life," says Isadora.

"Oh, all you parlor pinkies are alike," says Ralph. "Ya like that —'parlor pinkies.' I made it up."

"You truly have the gift of gab, Ralph," says Isadora, with an irony utterly lost on him. (Isadora has observed through the years that men named Ralph are almost always assholes. Why is that? Does the name *create* the assholery or does the assholery create the name? Do men named Ralph have mothers who unconsciously— or even consciously—*want* their sons to be assholes so no other woman will ever claim them? A big question.) Sylvia Sydenheim-Rabinowitz, Roland's redoubtable mother, has pronounced Ralph Plotkin "terribly vulnerable and zensitive," but then, she finds anyone with twenty million dollars "zensitive."

Ralph is perhaps the least sensitive and vulnerable person Isadora has ever met. Also, he hardly seems about to share his money with anyone. The single time he took Isadora to dinner, he plied her with booze, hamburgers, and fries at a railway-station joint in Westport. Oh, he parked his Rolls ostentatiously in front of her house, but then proposed the cheapest eateries in the area. Rich men are generally so paranoid about divorced women wanting their money that they take them to dives and hint on the first date that *if* they ever remarry, they will require elaborate antenuptial agreements. So why, Isadora wonders, does anyone bother with them—unless they're charming, which few are—the full-time pursuit of Mammon never making for much charm in either sex. No sir. Liberty for men may be the right not to lie, but for women it is an ample bankroll, earned with one's own hand, skill, art, craft. If pressed to the wall for a husband or live-in lover, Isadora would sooner take Errol, her blue-collar stud, who would at least be grateful and loving. For a while.

"How about dinner, doll?" says Ralph.

"I can't," says Isadora. "A previous engagement." The engagement with her dead grandfather, of course.

"Don't say I never asked," says Ralph, clearly offended.

"Ralph, I'd *love* to see you—but I just can't tonight."

"Okay, babe, catch you again."

When this phone call is over, Isadora is thrown back on her own resources. She reads the beginning of her book over and over, but through the white sheet all she can see is the accident. Here she is, alone—but for Dogstoyevsky—in the house she and Josh bought to be their ivory tower, their retreat from the world, their castle. It is a beautiful house, but haunted.

The sky has changed from the blinding blue of October to the grayish autumnal color of November. The light begins to fade by four. Having decided to go it alone tonight and devote herself to her book and her ghosts, Isadora is suddenly devastated by loneliness. Her child is with Josh and his girl friend. Her sweet Bichon Frisé only seems to remind her of the other dog she lost. In her heart, there is an emptiness so deep, it seems bottomless.

What a damnably lonely profession writing is! In order to do it, one must banish the world, and having banished it, one feels cosmically alone. Unless there is a mate who comes home at nightfall, a fellow artist to struggle with, a café to commingle in, one is alone with one's house and one's ghosts and the treacherous feeling that one does not really exist at all.

When the work goes well, one straddles the stars, leaps around the house as if the very lines of poetry or prose were tightropes and the writer a sort of rope dancer, a clown, an acrobat, working without a net and loving it. But when the work stops dead, there is only this loneliness. The writer is a vessel for the muse, and when nothing fills the vessel, the vessel wonders whether it exists at all.

Unable to write, Isadora polishes off the white wine. This only plummets her further into despair. She wanders around her own home like a lost soul, feeling abandoned, unwanted, unloved. Ten men could call her and she would still feel unloved when she put down the phone. Why is she so needy and lost? Can't she get through a night alone without a man? Or is it the country dusk, the wan autumnal light? Or is it the house she used to share with Josh?

Suddenly the phone rings again, and Isadora races to it, as if it were a life raft.

"I had a feelin' about you, lady," says Errol, "a feelin' that you shouldn't be alone." Damn, thinks Isadora—that Errol. A poet in his soul, which links with hers. Belatedly, she blurts out the whole story of the accident, and Errol, as sensitive to human needs as anyone she knows, insists that he will come over to hold her hand. This time Isadora is too spooked to resist.

She leaves the study, turning over the sheaf of scrawled pages, goes downstairs to let Dogstoyevsky into the dog run, and then wanders into her own bathroom to make her pre-erotic ablutions. They are elaborate: a diaphragm and jelly *over* the IUD she now wears (the former being a herpes and VD preventative; the latter having been installed after Mandy's birth in the hopes that it would be removed a year or so later so that the little one could have a sibling—but then, of course, the marriage was in the process of self-destructing). After putting in the diaphragm and jelly, she runs a bath with Opium bath silk and soaks in it to remove all taste of the jelly, and scent her thighs and cunt and breasts (Josh had, for years, refused to go down on her unless she'd washed elaborately and Isadora is still undoing Josh's various bad magicks). After that, she douses herself with Opium—thighs, knees, elbows, neck, even the mundane dab-behind-the-ears, creams her legs with more Erno Lazlo goo, and makes up her face meticulously. Oh, let the diehards say that makeup is a compromise with feminist truth—Isadora loves it anyway. She's a born vagabond, a performer, a believer in appearance as well as essence—and even though she's never longed to strut the boards, she knows she's the star in the play of her life—that tragic-comedy, that mock epick, that *meiseh*.

She dresses carefully—black lace underwear up—everything is designed to be ripped off later. For Errol's sake she wears a black T-shirt with rhinestones, black jeans, black cowboy boots with silver studs, black fringed cowboy jacket. She switches on the hot tub, puts more white wine in the fridge, tequila (his favorite booze) in the freezer, and bowls of taco chips on the dining-room table. (Her nod to his plebeian tastes.) Then she lights a fire in the dining-room fireplace, puts scented French candles around the

living room and bedroom and goes to make a bowl of guacamole
—his favorite hors d'oeuvre.

These preparations delight her, as writing today did not. She
feels womanly, erotic, wise, as if she were doing what nature intended, while, when she is writing, she is doing something vaguely
sinful—not servicing men, but merely ("merely"!) her soul. This
is another of Josh's legacies. When their love went bad, her writing, which he had previously adored, became the target of his
rage. How unkind! He fell in love with her in part because she
was a writer, but then he began to punish her for it. And all the
years that Isadora has spent, pre-Josh, unlearning the female
brainwashing that one must serve men above the muse, suddenly
for nought. If I, with my success, with a child to support and raise,
still feel that I must choose between writing and love—then what
the hell must *other* women feel? Isadora wonders. Will we never be
free, never? Is the wound to the self-esteem *that* deep? And yet
these "womanly" tasks delight her. Preparing for a man's arrival
proves one *has* a man. Isadora has several men—and yet in her
center she is shaky as an unfledged sparrow in a windy nest,
mouth open wide for the fat worm.

Dogstoyevsky barks. In the steep driveway, there's the sound of
Errol's car. Isadora's heart leaps at his arrival—which suddenly
banishes the autumnal spooks, the ghostly dusk, the lonelies, the
grungies, the sads. People weren't meant to live alone, she thinks.
Even in caves, they huddled. And she alone in her fifteen-room
house, with all its extra wings for Josh's work, Josh's hobbies,
Josh's offspring.

Errol appears, wearing pale-blue polyester jeans (his "dress"
jeans—they are "western" stitched), a beige ten-gallon Stetson
(with feathers in the band), and a pale-blue polyester "leisure"
jacket with "western" stitching. The tips of his pointy cowboy boots
curl sexually skyward from under his polyester jeans. He is tall—
six foot six—stoops a bit in the manner of very tall men, and his
myopic eyes (one blue, one brown) seem dilated behind amber-
tinted aviator glasses. Errol is a doper. He could well be stoned,
but tonight he seems less stoned than usual. He is so in love with
Isadora that he makes little pacts with her not to use dope between
their encounters, hoping to cure one addiction with another. Isadora understands this well, being an addictive type herself. Love,
junk, booze, food, sex, sex, sex. "I'm a love junkie," Isadora says
to her best friends. "That's all there is to it."

"Hello, lovely lady," says lanky Errol. "I've missed you."

And when he puts his arms around her to hug hello, Isadora can feel that his hands are shaking. Can he be afraid of me? she wonders. Of *me*, who is afraid of *everything* right now? It astounds Isadora that other people think of her as formidable and famous —when she feels so frightened inside.

"You're a goddess to me," Errol says, looking down at five-foot-three-inch Isadora from the height of his six foot, six inches.

There is always an awkward moment with Errol when Isadora wonders what she, with her Phi Beta Kappa key, is doing with Errol and his high-school-equivalency degree—but not for long. Because pretty soon they are smoking dope, drinking tequila, and loading up a tray with guacamole, taco chips, tequila, lemon, salt and climbing the spiral stairs to Isadora's tree-house study.

There, on the pearl-gray carpeted floor, they tear off each other's clothes and begin to make love with a passion born as much of desperation and dope as of true conviction—though there is that, too. While Isadora's Papa novel lies abandoned on the desk, while foreign editions of *Tintoretto's Daughter*, *Candida Confesses*, and Isadora's other books glare gaudily down from the bookshelves that reach all the way to the thirty-foot ceiling, Errol buries his head between Isadora's legs and eats her as if all primordial truth and wisdom lay therein.

Isadora's brain, as usual, races. The accident, Josh, Amanda, her own efforts to write today, her grandfather's death, her uncertain future—all these things shift and glitter in her brain as if they were bits of glass in a shaken kaleidoscope. She sees herself making love to Errol as if from the top of the shelves where her books crouch, stalking her, predicting a future when this whole scene will *itself* be committed to a book and translated into various languages, bound in gaudy colors and sold for pesos, rupees, shekels, kroner, guilders, francs, pounds sterling, American dollars, Canadian dollars, yen, or lire. O book within a book! O self-begetting (as one scholar calls it) novel!

And yet that is not why she is here, nor yet why she is here with Errol. Isadora never does things specifically to write about them —nor does she write only about what she had done. The equation between her life and her art is far more subtle. It is as if she is constantly driven to desperate situations so as to have to prove her mettle again and again and again. *Look—I can work without a net—* her whole life seems to say. Here I am, a woman who has never grown scar tissue over her wound, and I exist to display the wound of womanness, or maybe just the wound of humanness, for all to see.

Let go, let go, let go, she commands herself now. Stop thinking. And as she does, she starts to come, weeping tears of gratitude to Errol for having taken her away from her book, her loneliness, her wound, at least for a little while.

He holds her in his arms.

"I love you, earthling Isadora," Errol says; "on whatever level you want it, I can handle it."

He says this last guilt-relieving sentence because he knows that she has always balked at his "I love yous"—being too wounded by Josh, too done in, too wary of love to ever say "I love you" back. And yet, in a way, she *does* love him, loves his straightforward love of her, loves his lack of pretense, his blue-collar macho, his assumption of female strength, his idealization of her motherhood. Working-class men often paradoxically seem less chauvinistic to Isadora than intellectuals, the bourgeoisie, the Wall Street middle-parters with their Ben Franklin glasses, the WASPocracy with their racquet clubs and their genteel racketeering. And why? Because blue-collar men are frankly matriarchal; they honor babes and moms; they know that women work and work damned hard; they do not *pretend* to be anything but cavemen. A blue-collar man never says to his woman: "Go ahead, fuck other men. It turns me on." He says instead: "I'll kill anyone who touches you." And there is more truth to human nature in that threat than in all the games intellectuals play. If Isadora has learned anything from this split with Josh, it is that lying to oneself about jealousy does not eradicate jealousy; it merely drives it underground, where it does more damage.

Now, in a sudden burst of playfulness, a desire to banish the ghost of Josh, the ghost of her grandfather, and the ghost of her unwritten book about him, she sticks her mischievous fingers into the guacamole bowl, covers Errol's cock with it, and begins, tantalizingly, to lick it off. Erroll moans and arches, groaning words of love and gratitude. Despite the dope, giving him head is one way Isadora can get him almost entirely hard.

"I love you, I love you, I love you," he moans, and Isadora, relieved of having to speak sweet nothings in return by having a mouth full of cock and avocado, wonders what, in truth, she is doing here. *Does* she really love giving head, or does she better love the sense of power over a man giving great head provides?

Does she want to win the Academy Award for blow jobs? Or is she linked to Errol in some special way that even she does not understand? All of the above. The sense of skin on skin, the intimacy of genitals in each other's mouths does ease the pain of divorce, does affirm her being alive, after having come today so close to willful death. I fuck, therefore I am, thinks Isadora. I blow, therefore I am. It used to be: I write, therefore I am. But now it seems that writing only eradicates the self, and sex restores it. In midcareer, eight books on the shelf of her life, Isadora feels that each volume has been a sort of eraser that rubbed out a portion of her life. Sex brings it back; sex proves that she's palpitatingly alive; sex is, for the moment, what she exists for—giving and receiving pleasure in this most ephemeral of ways.

Errol is getting really hard now—Errol who has a back injury which he thinks prevents him from getting really hard, Errol who smokes so much dope that he should never be really hard—is getting hard as a rock.

"I want to be inside you," he moans. "I *have* to be inside you." And he climbs on top of her, all six foot, six inches of him, and thrusts away at her wet cunt until she weeps with pleasure. She comes once, twice, three times, says she's done, then comes again, realizing as she does that something is missing as a result of the accident—her headache! Perhaps it is her gratitude for the absence of pain that makes her gasp, "I love you" to Errol for the first, maybe the last, time. This brings tears to his eyes and such passion to his pelvis that he goes nearly wild fucking her, groans, trembles, shakes, and comes with a scream that would wake the household—if anyone were there but Dogstoyevsky, who through an oversight has been left in the dog run for over an hour and now barks mournfully asking to be let in. In all her satiated nakedness, Isadora gets up and does this now and the little dog scampers merrily after her into her studio, where Errol still lies on the gray carpet, utterly blissed out, utterly stoned. With a mischievousness that seems to mirror his mistress, the little Bichon (who resembles nothing so much as a dust mop crossed with a poodle) scampers playfully over to her lover, sniffs his cock, and, without hesitating, licks the remainder of the avocado off it. Errol groans, sighs, and thrashes his lanky legs.

"Earthling Isadora, my goddess," he moans, with closed eyes.

6

Isadora's Shwantz-Song or What If the Prince Doesn't Come?

I hope you have not been
leading a double life, pretending
to be wicked and really being good
all the time. That would be hypocrisy.
—OSCAR WILDE
The Importance of Being Earnest

Do we not say: "Go get yourself a fuck!"
Strange locution. As if one could
possibly get a fuck without giving one.
Even in this basic realm of
communion, the notion prevails
that a fuck is to get, not give.
—HENRY MILLER

Every woman is at heart a rake.
—ALEXANDER POPE

IN the month that followed the accident, Isadora disproved Oscar Wilde's maxim that "anybody can be good in the country." Despite the fact that she lived deep in the country, that she was the most concerned and responsible of mothers, that she had a book to write, a house to run—Isadora devoted herself, dedicated herself, to being bad.

Novel-writing was impossibly lonely for someone as fragile and as fragmented as she found herself at this juncture of her life. She admitted it and abandoned the Papa novel—at least for the moment. Her life as a celebrity and public figure whirled on, almost as it had begun, without her. It was a communal creation, a fiction born of all the half-truths and untruths published about her; it was in most ways more fiction than her fictions. It did not really require that she be a writer or even a real person; it only required that she impersonate someone called "Isadora Wing"—whoever she was. This personage, construct, fiction—for she was hardly human—was fearless, unflappable, indefatigably sexual. An artist must be first a *mensh,* a person of integrity, a human being of substance, before she can have anything to say to the rest of the world, but a celebrity must be just the reverse: a hollow core. The suggestion that there are contradictions beneath the skin only confuses that lowly sector of the press that feeds off celebrities. Celebrities must be one- or two-dimensional, while the best artists, the best humans, the true *menshes* of the human race, exist in at least three dimensions—preferably four or five. But such five-dimensional living takes guts, courage, grit. To dream on the page, one must be grounded in real life, in real nurturance, real love. Isadora had lost her grounding. Her whole life was a dream of sex and booze and dope—so how could she dream on the page? Her grounding was gone. Her days were more packed with more improbable incident and excess than those of any of her heroines. So she abandoned herself to the sordid novel of her life which featured someone called "Isadora Wing"—a blond lady nearly out of her fourth decade, who somehow (perhaps because she had never lost the damnable vulnerability of girlhood) had the bounciness and succulence of youth.

Isadora discovered that she was indeed what Hope had once dubbed her: "the universal honeypot." Once the word was truly out that she was at liberty, calls began pouring in from everywhere. Every recently separated man in Fairfield County tried to date (and bed) her. In fact many married men of the ridiculous region—some toying with the idea of divorce and some just toying with the idea of diversion—put in their calls for "lunch," "brunch," "dinner" (i.e., help, rescue, head).

Isadora's secretary—a serenely wise and beautiful gray-haired lady in her fifties (who, before Isadora, had organized the life and opus of a famous female gossip columnist)—ceased almost entirely to be a literary secretary and became, as she and Isadora both quipped, "a sexual secretary." For all three phone lines buzzed, bleated, and brrred continuously with social invitations, veiled sexual offers, offers to "speak," offers to "read," offers to "guest-host" or merely just "guest" on TV shows, offers to sit at New York dinner tables beside "eligible" single men.

The "eligible" men were the worst, Isadora soon found out. "Eligible" meant simply that in a world gone increasingly "gay"— if you believed the conundrum that people were either "gay" or "straight" (which Isadora didn't)—this particular dinner partner was a *bona fide* heterosexual. *Bona fide* by whom? Isadora often wondered. The hostess? Had she sampled him? Even if she had, that did not mean he did not have *other* problems—far worse than the dark compulsion to pork males. Oh, no. The "eligible" man at a swell New York dinner party was likely to be a terminal neurotic, so wounded by one, two, three, or four ex-wives that he was unlikely to ever trust a person of the female persuasion again; and so burdened with insouciant adolescents, outrageous debts, or labyrinthine legal and tax problems, that he had little time for the "ideal woman" he claimed to be seeking even in the unlikely event that she might cross his path. Or else he was apt to be another Ralph Plotkin, rich as Croesus and paranoid as Macbeth and Lady Macbeth put together.

Isadora's secretary had, comfortingly enough, been through all this once herself, having been divorced years ago, and she found it hugely amusing. Renata Loomis—for that was the lady's name —had never, by definite choice, remarried, but she knew far better than the much-married Isadora how to negotiate the treacherous shoals of the suddenly single.

"We should write *The Divorced Woman's Book of Etiquette*," Isadora often said when phone number one, phone number two, and phone number three all began fervently ringing at (nearly) the same time. For the dating mores of the divorced person of the eighties were far more complicated than anything Isadora had known in her adolescence. First of all, everyone seemed to be balancing the complexities of children on alternate weekends, city homes, country homes, elaborate careers, and at least two, three, or more liaisons. Most of the divorced men Isadora dated seemed to have various other ladies to fall back on—as if, having been wounded in the wars of marriage and of divorce, they would never again put all their eggs in one basket. This meant that everyone was always shooting for the main chance, juggling lovers, and hoping eternally to "trade up." Isadora sometimes had the sense that when she accepted a date, two other ladies were displaced and rearranged; similarly, she herself—though normally scrupulously honest—got very good at social white-lying, canceling dates at the drop of a hat if something better came along. Of course, it also worked the other way. There were men she knew who were never free on, say, Wednesday and Friday nights—but only on Thursdays and Saturdays. Obviously there was a regular Wednesday or Friday lady or perhaps a Wednesday *and* Friday lady— though the man, of course, never admitted to her existence. Sometimes, when Isadora suspected a regular Wednesday night lady, she deliberately claimed only to be free on Wednesdays, just to "test" the man in question and see if he'd cancel the other lady for her. How wicked!

All these complexities were dealt with through numerous phone calls. To her amazement, Isadora got good at hastily making excuses if a juicier invitation was proffered. It was dog eat dog, every man for himself, all's fair in love and war. It was also completely out of character for mostly monogamous Isadora. But it did, at least, distract her from her pain over Josh. Fortunately, one had enough real excuses—what with a child, a career, a home to run —to rearrange dates with impunity. The basic law of divorced dating seemed to be "no strings," and if you made an excuse, however flimsy, it was never questioned.

The worst dates, Isadora soon found out, were the "fix-ups." Isadora's well-meaning friends had decided that the problem with Josh and Isadora was their age difference and their difference in status—so they all tried to fix Isadora up with "substantial" men in their forties and fifties—"eligibles," in short. Thus it happened that one evening in late November, Isadora found herself dining out at an overpriced East Side Chinese restaurant in New York with a swarthy little lawyer named Melvin Lebow—a kind of anti-semite's parody of a Jew—who had deliberately requested that Isadora meet him at his home so she could witness his Central Park South apartment (with its wraparound terrace and pano-ramic views), his eight-year-old daughter-in-the-Brearley-School-uniform, his Scottish nanny, his Puerto Rican housekeeper, and his selection of vintage wines.

The preliminary conversation over wine, in the drearily over-decorated flat (it had black walls and spotlights on fuchsia silk furniture), was punctuated by little Clarissa Lebow's endearing hops upon Daddy's lap while Daddy discoursed on her education, her nanny's qualifications, her charming sayings of the last week. (Clarissa—little minx—preened and pranced while Daddy quoted her, angling for toys and treats, if she suitably impressed his "date.") Father and daughter appeared to have done this whole routine many, many times before—and their *folie à deux* did not seem to admit the intrusion of a third party. *They* were the mar-riage—Daddy with his proud "custody" and daughter with Daddy securely wrapped around her little finger.

Later, at the restaurant, Isadora had the impression that she was being interviewed preliminary to a merger rather than being looked upon as a future lover. Melvin Lebow, whose nose seemed fixed and whose chin seemed lifted, fixed Isadora in his shit-brown gaze, and asked (almost as if taking a deposition) how many acres her house had around it, how many cars she possessed, who managed her investments, where she summered, where she win-tered, and where her daughter went to school. Isadora's daughter, at that time, went to an "alternative" nursery school in Westport called the Blue Tree School, where the male teachers had shoul-der-length hair, the female teachers sometimes married other fe-male teachers, and the main course of study seemed to be the baking of granola cookies. This was hardly "sandbox chic."

"How's your separation," Melvin then wanted to know, "is it amicable?"

Now, Isadora feels, felt even then, that no sooner do you con-fess over dinner that your separation is "amicable" than your ex-husband immediately calls and begins screaming insults in the night. It seems to be an unwritten law of separation and divorce that just as a plane is a comfortable living room that can turn into

114

a blazing inferno at a moment's notice, so too is an "amicable separation."

"What's 'amicable'?" Isadora asks.

Melvin finds this very funny. In fact, Melvin seems to find everything Isadora says very funny. He gazes into her eyes and confesses that she's been his sexual fantasy for seven years—ever since he read "that book of hers." Apparently she has enough acreage and enough assets to be a take-over prospect worthy of his attentions. She feels she's just become what investment analysts term "a special situation."

But Isadora has heard the magic words—"my sexual fantasy for seven years"—the magic words that almost infallibly predict impotence, premature ejaculation, and other sorts of sexual disaster too smarmy to contemplate. So Isadora excuses herself from the Szechuan beef with scallions and the scampi with garlic and she sprints to the telephone to call her daughter's nanny and check in on the home front. The baby is fine, she learns. The house is fine. The dog is fine.

She returns to the table and with many apologies announces to Melvin:

"I'm going to have to head back to Connecticut early because, alas, my daughter seems to be getting a cold."

This is real desperation. Isadora has broken the ultimate parental taboo. Lying about your kid being sick almost invariably *causes* the kid to *get* horribly sick. All the gods and goddesses of wrath frown upon this sort of lying; the chthonic deities would not be pleased. But suddenly the prospect of finishing dinner with Melvin, and having to make small talk through liqueurs and the obligatory pass, fills Isadora with dread. Earlier in the separation, Isadora would have picked up the dinner check in order to avert the obligatory pass. Now she has "progressed" to lying about her kid's health—albeit with a sinking heart, feeling for all the world that she will, for her lies, return to Connecticut to find her daughter dead of a sudden nineteenth-century "chill," or an eighteenth-century attack of the "vapours."

So much for "fix-ups"—the doctors, the lawyers, the Indian chiefs, the "appropriate," the "eligible," divorced "older" men. Among these Isadora encountered an elderly academic flasher— a professor of political science—who, during drinks in his elderly, roach-ridden West Side kitchen, whipped out his cock and discoursed to her of its thickness, its length, its propensity for satisfying pussy. (This was *another* bad sign Isadora had learned; whenever a man said: "I *worship* pussy"—the odds were excellent that he didn't. Those who can, do; those who can't, talk about it.)

After the academic flasher came a white-bearded Nobel Prize-winning biochemist who spoke English as if it were a second language (or as if he were reading from a bad translation—like the English instructions to some Japanese electronic toy).

When they met, he pronounced her his "adequate protagonist" —meaning that her fame and fortune made them equals. Then, when he wished to express lust, he told her she was "a vivid woman," "a woman of great clarity," or "a sharply etched woman." Finally, when they bedded, he pronounced her "a woman of warmth and nuance"—perhaps because she came so readily and seemed to have so few hang-ups about sex. This was Isadora's blessing, as her extreme vulnerability was her curse. She could respond sexually to almost *anyone*—but her mind, her blasted mind, just went on racing.

She abandoned the fix-ups and the blind dates, but soon she discovered that if you were hungry enough, needy enough, and emotionally open enough, men were to be met *everywhere*. She could go nowhere, it seemed, without meeting *someone*. Since she had no preference for the eligible, since she almost instinctively preferred men who *weren't* seeking mergers, she found that the world was suddenly *full* of men—hot-tub men, gardeners, blue-collar studs, sons of friends, graduate students, young journalists, the starving, the poor, the restless. The romantic readiness of younger men more than made up for their inability to pick up the dinner tab.

"Shall I do an article for *Cosmo* called 'The Lady Chatterley Complex'?" Isadora asked Renata Loomis, when they were arranging weekend plans one Tuesday morning.

"I think what you have is the Stella Kowalski Complex," Renata said drolly. And it was true. Sometimes weeks went by without Isadora going out with anyone who could pick up the dinner tab —or who even *owned* a suit. She listened patiently to other divorced women tell her tales of woe about how they never met any men, and she tried to explain to them that they *did,* they did meet *plenty* of men, but they just weren't *looking*. Or they were looking in the wrong place—at the man's wallet, when they should have been looking steadily and only at his cock (and of course at his heart—for a big cock is no good without a generous heart).

It was Isadora's theory that given the fact that men were not going to support women anymore (since women had opted to support themselves, and quite often their kids), women might as well get the one thing men were really good for—sex. Or perhaps the two things they were really good for: sex and protectiveness.

"We'll all become like lionesses eventually," Isadora theorized to Renata. "We'll feed the cubs and take care of the lair and basically choose our lions for their potency and their fierceness in defending the pride."

"Then liberation leads right back to the cave?" Renata asked. "I think you have an article there."

"Yeah, for the *National Review*," said Isadora.

Renata laughed. "No, it's more one of those self-righteous Lance Morrow fulminations for *Time* magazine—the kind with a portentous title like 'Does Liberation Lead Back to the Cave?' and a scolding tone which implies that the author has cornered the market on morality."

"Let's write it," Isadora said, and then, in pear-shaped tones, she chanted: " *'Women today are facing a terrible truth. Having liberated themselves right off their pedestals and out of the Küche and Kirche, they now wonder who will support the Kinder?'* Of course, the article will imply that it serves us all right, that if only we obeyed our biological imperative to stay home and crochet doilies, none of this would ever have happened."

"So who's the lucky man this weekend?" Renata asked.

Isadora was perplexed. Errol was the most *gemütlich* stud of all —but she could hardly stand Errol for a whole weekend. Roland would get her so stoned, her brain cells would atrophy forever (he had psilocybin mushrooms "on hold" in his freezer awaiting some catatonic country weekend), and the rabbi would just depress the hell out of her with his bow ties and bon mots. Maybe she should leave the weekend open and see what turned up (to coin a phrase). Or maybe she should make an insurance date that could be hastily canceled if something better came along. The one thing to be avoided like the plague was being alone after the sun went down. Oh, she could stand her house in the daylight hours, but at night it was horrendously lonely.

"I don't know, Renata, maybe we should put off the weekend decision 'til Wednesday . . ." (Was it true—or did it only seem so, that separated and divorced people spent ninety percent of their time arranging to get laid, while coupled people had time to work?)

Just then, little red-headed Mandy skipped into Renata's office.

Mandy was three; a drop of drool still trembled on her lower lip, though her vocabulary sometimes made you think she was five. At that point, Mandy was entranced with the myth of Sleeping Beauty. She had Isadora read it over and over again, night after night. Against all Isadora's feminist wishes, Mandy loved best of all the place in the story where the Prince kisses the sleeping girl and she awakens.

"Read 'Sleeping Beauty,' Mama, read 'Sleeping Beauty,' read 'Sleeping Beauty' . . ." Mandy said, unable, like her mother, to say anything just once.

"Darling—we're working," Isadora said. (She said this because she and Renata were in the office, though she knew perfectly well they were not really working at all. What *were* they doing? Trying to tread water emotionally, trying to preserve Isadora's sanity until the next book came along, trying to banish the headaches, the fears, the loneliness, while Isadora waited to become a functioning professional writer again?)

"Read 'Sleeping Beauty,' Mama," Amanda insisted, in that insistent way three-year-olds have—and Isadora, knowing she wasn't really working, and probably wouldn't today—and adoring her daughter above all others, allowed the little girl to drag her by the hand into her playroom, where she produced, in her fat little hands, the gorgeously illustrated Walt Disney version of Sleeping Beauty.

Dutifully, Isadora read. She read of the spinning wheel, the curse, the slumber.

"Where are the dwarfs?" Mandy asked, having confused the legend of Sleeping Beauty with the legend of Snow White and the Seven Dwarfs. (Isadora confused them herself—for the elements in both stories were astonishingly similar: hexed by an aging hag in one case—and an aging beauty in another—the lovely, pubescent innocent slumbered, awaiting release by a prince who recognized her dormant charms. Are women most beautiful when they are asleep—like children?)

Mandy listened, rapt, while her mother read this most ancient of tales. The girl slept, in all her unconscious beauty—as a three-year-old, her lip trembling with spittle, is unconscious of her own transcendent mauve-lidded splendor. Mandy sucked on one dawn-colored finger. Her eyes downcast beneath those opalescent lids, she dreamed of that absent prince—Daddy?—who would come to her and awaken her passions. Ah—the absent male! How we women, three and thirty, five and fifty, long for him to come and make all things right! As Isadora read, she thought of her sexual escapades of the last few months—the yearning for the Prince underlying all that random promiscuity. And who is that Prince? Daddy? For we know that no one will come and make the world all right. Princes are temporary; we have ourselves and our own souls for good and all.

And so she had reached the final paragraph:

"The Prince ran up the steps of the tower, two at a time, past all the sleeping courtiers, until he reached the chamber where Princess Aurora—his beloved Briar Rose—lay. Gently he kissed her. The Princess awakened, smiled at Phillip, and the whole room lit up. The fountains in the courtyard started to play again, candles flamed once more, the court awoke, and trumpets sounded from the balcony as the Prince and Princess walked down the Grand Stairway hand in hand."

Mandy absorbed it and sat and thought. Her purple eyelids flickered as the intelligent blue-gray eyes moved beneath them. She took in the myth, the memories, the mother-daughter flashes that passed between them. Isadora had the sense that she would like to impart to Mandy all that she had learned about men and herself in four decades—but she knew it was impossible. Even if she *herself* had been clear about her life—and her life, it sometimes seemed, had never been more murky—she knew that she could not impart that putative clarity to Mandy. "A woman of great clarity," the Laureate had called her. Hah. She was as ruled by her cunt as she'd ever been, as subject to the whims of the chthonic deities as Medea. Oh, to be Athena, not Aphrodite! Oh, to be cool and passionless, mathematical, not ruled by her raging blood.

Mandy looks up, fixes her mother in her blue-gray gaze and says, with perfect clarity:

"Mama—what if the Prince *doesn't* come?"

Isadora thought and thought. She knew that this line would be her mother-daughter epitaph. Mandy would remember it on the analyst's couch—if they still had those in 1998—and she herself would remember it forever and ever, even perhaps in the afterlife to come.

"Well then, darling, she just kisses herself and wakes *herself* up."

Mandy seems astonished, but she believes.

"That's right, my darling. If no one's there to hug her, she hugs herself, and then she gets up and goes back to work."

Whereupon Isadora hugged her daughter and went back to

work—or at least back into her office to arrange the rest of her princeless week.

If there were no princes, then Isadora would just sop up her princelessness with sex. She would try every spindle in the kingdom! She would try and try until, at last, she found the magic one or the lethal one, or the one that caused forgetfulness, unless perhaps those three were all really the same.

Why is there no fairy tale about the search for the magic spindle? Isadora lived that quest during the month following the accident. She would vow to work, vow to put nose to grindstone, pen to paper—but as dusk fell over Serpentine Hill Road, she found the melancholy overwhelming and she found herself flipping through her datebook for even the most hastily scrawled male phone numbers. Inevitably, she'd invite someone for drinks, or dinner, or she would drive on out, down the winding country road, to meet some swain at a dive in Westport, a diner in Norwalk, or a railway-depot joint somewhere along Conrail's bumpy, unreliable route.

Quite often these encounters led to bed, bed in some fusty motel along the Post Road, or bed, once Mandy was safely asleep, in Isadora's king-size waterbed, with a man who'd be asked to leave before dawn dyed the Connecticut hills the color of fuchsined water in some recollected apothecary jar, standing in the window of some recollected Madison Avenue pharmacy of the fifties— these were now mostly vanished in the high-priced Madison Avenue of the eighties—where there were marvelous marble lunch counters, gaudy high-gloss Revlon lipstick posters, and the most luscious BLTs on earth. The hemlocks outside the picture windows seemed dark cutouts against the magenta dawn when a rather stoned and shaky Isadora got up to let the swain in question —or the questionable swain—out. *Exeunt omnes* through the sliding glass door that led from Isadora's bedroom to the redwood decks that surrounded her rustic Connecticut home. "Lanai doors," they call them in California—which sounds for all the world like an obscene anagram.

She was always glad when the gentleman left (on the pretext, of course, of Mandy's mental health). She would run upstairs in her bare feet to check on her sleeping daughter—sleeping beauty—as if somehow the sexuality downstairs might have penetrated the girl's dream, corrupting her virginity. Then she would mutter her little prayer to the Mother Goddess—"Goddess bless and Goddess keep"—and run back downstairs to luxuriate alone in her big bed until it was time to get up and make breakfast for the sleeping princess.

During the first months of the separation, breakfast was always hot oatmeal (Irish oatmeal, if possible) and there was always a fire in the dining-room fireplace. Isadora felt that if somehow she could just hold on—keep the homefires burning, hot oatmeal in the pot, and no visible (or audible) gentlemen callers in her bedroom, then she and Mandy would make it through the winter.

Some mornings, she stomped out to the woodpile in flannel nightgown, snow boots, down parka, to shlep wood into the house before her kid and the nanny stirred. This seemed essential somehow—the fire in the hearth, the oatmeal in the pot, the dining-room table bare of any traces of the swain the night before. (No scumbled crumbs of weed, no white powder, no single-edged razor blades, no Zig-Zag nor Big Bambu.) Womanhood suddenly seemed simpler to Isadora than ever before: it was merely a matter of keeping the flame, of keeping the oatmeal hot, of toting the wood (even, on occasion, of chopping it), while her daughter slumbered serene as Princess Aurora, aka Briar Rose. (Aurora for the color of her cheeks—and briar for the hedge she would need around her roses to get through this man's world unscathed.)

And what did Isadora learn of magic spindles during this period of her life? She learned that very few provide magic or even forgetfulness, except for the littlest of whiles. She learned that not only is the Prince not coming—but often he can't even get it up. She learned that cocks differ widely from man to man—some curl seductively forward; some lean reticently back; some take the world by storm; others insinuate themselves gradually like counterspies. Some are pink, some red, some yellow, some brown, some black. Some are veined like lunar maps; some are smooth as pink marzipan pigs; some leak before they spout, and some refuse to spout at all (because their owners are so preoccupied with the presumed demandingness of feminist pussy that they cannot squirt at all—but, alas, must stay painfully priapic forever). But despite all the variations in cock, one thing remains constant: you cannot love a cock if you do not like its owner.

Oh, you can like it well enough—well enough to spasm once or twice, before rolling over and wishing the man astrally transported out of your bedroom, but you cannot clutch it, love it, trust it with your pussy, squeeze it between your labia like a miser squeezing a gold coin, rub it against your clit like a lump of butter against a bumpy bundt pan. No—you cannot really love a cock if its owner is about to speak up momentarily and say something dumb, if he is about to dub you "a woman of warmth and nuance," or "an adequate protagonist," or "a woman of great clarity." Isadora found, finally, that she could not love a cock that did not have a sense of humor, that had not read Shakespeare, that regarded pussy as a creature to be humbled—or still worse, a creature to be feared. The sorts of sexual disaster endemic to the age of (supposed) sexual liberation were far worse than any of the disasters Isadora had known in the fumbling fifties—a decade that, thanks to the absence of reliable birth control and the prevalence of puritanical social mores, had brought the art of mutual masturbation to a degree of sophistication and ingenuity unequalled in any decade since. One almost felt that kids today were *missing* something in not having to fumble so ingeniously, being, as they were, allowed to fuck fiercely from the first.

So big deal. You could fuck anyone. But you did not really feel like *fusing* with just anyone. You did not necessarily *like* just anyone's smell. Nor his voice, nor his touch. Everyone of the male persuasion had by now figured out that the clitoris was top priority, but not one man in ten knew how to touch it—neither flailingly nor ticklishly, neither too hard, nor too soft. The over-fifties were the worst, usually. Raised in an age when the mere maintenance of an erection was presumed to be enough, they now made random feints at the clitoris, thanks to the consciousness-raising of feminist literature—or more likely thanks to the charge of the sex-therapy brigade (led, of course, by Roland's warrior mother). They flicked, but they did not caress. They licked, but they did not really *mean* it—and Isadora could tell. The poor rabbi was a perfect example of this. He went down on Isadora as if he were sampling a veritable thousand-year-old egg at a banquet on the Great Wall of China, attended, perhaps, by Henry Kissinger. He went down in a spastic panic—as if he were about to enter a world devoid of oxygen; you wanted to proffer a scuba-diving suit and oxygen tanks—that was how panicky he seemed.

Eyes closed in dread, tongue stuck out in a point (as if hoping to avoid hair), he took the plunge, licked a little (thirty seconds' worth, by some imaginary stopwatch), and hastily came up for air, opening his eyes, and asking: "Was that enough?"

There should have been a *broche* one could say before eating pussy, or a pertinent quote from the Talmud—for Isadora would have quoted them both. *Baruch, atoi, adonai,* pussy *melech Hair'lochim.* In the name of the mother, the son, and the holy sepulcher. By the Rock of Ages (which was really a phallic symbol), I now pronounce you sexually liberated.

Well, at least Isadora had learned not to let herself be defrocked ever again by clergymen—whether frocked or de-, clergymen are lecherous all right, but they haven't had much practice. Like psychiatrists, they can so intimidate by their robes that they *need* no technique—until, of course, the frocks come off and the fucking begins.

The Nobel Laureate was just as bad—though superficially his technique was more studied. He had this charming habit of dropping the names of other famous women he'd fucked just before he and Isadora went to bed, but in bed he was doggedly determined and inclined to the use of the most clinical verbiage. Now, the English language is curiously limited where sex is concerned. It seems to be divided between latinate, medical terms like *vagina* or *cunnilingus* and Anglo-Saxonisms. Sure, there are people whose puritanical brainwashing makes them wince at the mere mention of such four-letter words—but at least these words represent the language of *feeling*, the language of powerful emotion, while the latinate words smell of disinfectant. If—as a certain German writer maintains—language is the universal whore that has to be made into a virgin, then *fuck* and *cunt* can be virginified (or perhaps one should say "gentrified") by an able writer, an able talker. Besides, if these words were good enough for Chaucer and Shakespeare and Joyce, then they're *certainly* good enough for Isadora.

But not for the Laureate. A little ferret-faced man with a long white beard, twinkly gray eyes, rosy cheeks, a mop of woolly white hair (which he sought, vainly, to drape over a bright pink bald pate), the Laureate embarked on foreplay as if he expected to win the Nobel Prize for that, too. Ah, but he lacked dynamite! His kisses were premeditated; his touch lacking in spontaneity; his fingers fumbling. He approached a female body as if it were a scholarly paper to be annotated and the footnotes festooned with *vides, ibids,* and *op. cits.* Even Roland Rabinowitz, clinical as he was, seemed touched with the spirit of Venus compared to the Laureate.

The Laureate was five foot two and like the rabbi, a fop. But his foppishness was of a different order: flowing scarves rather than bow ties, collarless shirts rather than elegant English ones, and (astoundingly) red bikini underwear—his one concession to stylishness and sex. Watching the Laureate undress, Isadora wondered if a girl friend or an ex-wife had bought this rubicund underwear. "My mother," the Laureate declared. Oh, what oedipal depths lurked in that confession! The Laureate (whose actual name was Gower Grodofsky) had a barrel chest covered with white fuzz, and legs that were bowed and simian. His cock was pink and a perfectly ordinary *Homo sapiens* specimen.

When intellectuals copulate without love, they still must think of intellectual things to say afterward. And the Laureate was a big summer-upper. "That was a most satisfactory ejaculation," he would say, to our heroine's utter astonishment. Or, on the one occasion when she gave him a great blow job, he complimented her by saying, "What a memorable arpeggio—or shall I say cadenza?"

"Why not just call it a blow job?" Isadora asked, irreverently. "A blow job by any other name is still a blow job."

Gower looked at her as if she were the crudest of vulgarians, raised his bushy white eyebrows, pulled his white beard, and said: "You certainly are an amazing woman, a woman of warmth and nuance."

"Let's just say I'm a good lay," Isadora said, "and leave it at that." And that, in fact was where they left it for all time.

No—there were certainly not many magic spindles to be had around. Sleeping Beauty would slumber for a whole millennium if she had to depend on the supply of princes available in America in the eighties. The courtiers would snore forever, the fountains dry up, the candles stand cold and unmelted, the trumpets remain silent, and the Prince and Princess never join hands to descend the grand staircase.

Merry-go-round dating and lottery sex had become so depressing that it was inevitable that nostalgia for the marriage would assert itself from time to time, despite Josh's unwarranted, and perhaps unwitting, cruelty to Isadora. After all, Josh was still the person to whom she felt bonded, the person who shared Amanda, the person with whom she had gone through labor and birth, eight years of crises, joys, and private jokes. There had been happy banter between them once, such happy banter that it seemed nothing could ever destroy it. They had talked about everything so openly, it seemed, that nothing could sever them. Now they had joined the divorce Olympics—that crazy state of running, running, running, burning torch in bleeding hand, from lover to lover, listening to all the brokenhearted songs on the radio late at night as if the lyrics had been written by Keats, Shakespeare, and Donne rolled into one; keeping the music going at all costs; and the fire blazing and the oatmeal hot.

Josh still came over from time to time on the pretext of needing to see Amanda, and Isadora let him tamper with the visitation schedule (though less and less as time went on), because it still seemed like his home, too, because she still somehow felt that only he could fix things around the house, because—she had to admit it—she wanted to see him.

She would dress and make up elaborately before he came, and then he would march in, eyes glazed, or averted, and go right to the fridge to help himself to a snack before running upstairs to Amanda's room.

"Daddy! Daddy!" the little girl would shout, thinking the separation was all a bad dream and Daddy was coming home for good.

Isadora felt that way too. Somehow his presence in the house obliterated all the random one-night stands, the stoned night drives, the depression, the suicidal thoughts. If only he would stay, she would find ways to make it all right, she thought. She would demand less of him, let him drift more, forgive him the typist, the computer programmer, the mother of Mandy's friend. She would cook for him, devote herself to him, not ever write unless he was writing too, never go off on another book tour and leave him with the baby and the sitter, never succumb to another hotel-room romp on the road, never ask him for anything at all. She would just give and give and give and give—with no return expected. After all, hadn't Josh's own father said (once when Isadora wept on the phone about missing Josh) that she should "woo him back"? But how on earth could she woo him any more than she already *had*? True, she had "kicked him out," after years of listening to his complaints about his supposed lack of freedom, his playing "second fiddle," his being "house husband." But then she had immediately repented and invited him back, and he had stubbornly maintained that he was *never* coming back, had refused to continue marital therapy, had loaded on the insults and rejections until the rift was so large it had begun to resemble the Grand Canyon. She was left playing the heavy, the kicker-outer, the decision maker, the homewrecker. He was self-righteously absolved of any responsibility for the split, when of course, as in any divorce, they had both contributed to the "decision."

Now he was here in the house again, putting Mandy to bed. She paced outside the child's room, waiting to have him to herself. She heard the sweet little girl/Daddy chatter, that delicious diction of a three-year-old who is chirping because Daddy has come home and made her universe complete.

"Are you got a penis?" Mandy used to say to all men at that point in her life. "Are you a mommy or a daddy?" Those were the questions asked because that was all she needed to know about people, all that mattered in her three-year-old world.

Daddy was whom she wanted, Daddy was *it*—all the more because he came and went.

"Go to sleep, cupcake," Josh said to Mandy, with a tenderness Isadora coveted for herself. Her daughter had replaced her in Josh's affections. Her daughter got the protectiveness she would have wished for herself.

"Don't go, Daddy," Mandy said. "Read in my room, please, please, please." Mandy had the habit of saying "please" as if the word had two syllables—so that it came out "ple-ase." All Mandy's funny pronunciations endeared her to Isadora. Having had a child so late in her odyssey, she knew that these charming quirks of toddlerhood and little-girldom were fleeting, fleeting, fleeting —and that before she knew it, Mandy would be speaking like a grown-up and waltzing out of her life.

Josh emerged from Mandy's room, still averting his eyes.

"We made a good one," he said, smiling.

Isadora laughed. Their shared pride in their joint creation still bonded them, perhaps it always would. She thought of Donne's lovers in "The Ecstasy," whose hands were cemented by a "balm" —sweaty palms—never to be severed. Perhaps a child could also be such a "balm"—a natural effluence, which would cement two people and make them one.

"Would you come into my office and talk to me?" Isadora asked.

"Okay," said Josh, clearly not wishing to. Still, he followed her into her sanctuary, with its pale-gray carpeting and purple velvet sofas, with its memorabilia from Isadora's literary career—framed magazine covers, book jackets, and posters used to advertise her work in different countries. Just coming in here was an assault on Josh's own modest career. Isadora felt guilty and apologetic for his lack of success—almost as if she had caused it and created it. But she was not *that* powerful. She did not even feel responsible for *her* success. The muse had chosen her as a medium—that was all. True, she had worked terribly hard, but all the hard work in the world did not create talent where none existed, and often Isadora felt that her best ideas, her funniest lines came aslant, came unwilled—as if the "nigger in the basement" (as Joyce called the unconscious) were working and not she herself. Being an artist is more a matter of calling than of willing. Why, then, did she feel guilty toward Josh? Perhaps because he was her man and she had been blessed (and also strangely cursed) with more success? But what was the answer to that? She needed her work *and* she needed her man—she was, after all, a woman, not a freak of nature. She merely carried her talent around in a woman's body. Why did that condemn one to eternal punishment?

Isadora sat down on one of the purple couches and looked at her man. He still averted his eyes.

"Why can't we try again?" she asked him, her gut roiling, her head beginning to ache.

"Because I don't want to," Josh said.

Well—that was simple enough—and as sharp as he could make it. She felt his words like an arrow through her temples—like that silly arrow Steve Martin used to use in his comedy routines.

"But we can go back into marital therapy," she said, knowing it was in vain. "We can try again—for Mandy's sake."

"It won't work," Josh said, as if he were God and totally omniscient. "I know it. Besides, I refuse to live my life for Mandy. My needs come first."

Now the arrow had moved from Isadora's head into the back of her neck and she was in a rage.

"They certainly do," Isadora said. "They certainly do." She was beside herself with anger; she didn't know where to put it. Mandy *did* come first, *had* to come first—that was the way of nature, of the species, of the cycle of life. Isadora had put Mandy before everything, before her writing, before her earning a living, before her own sanity. How *dare* Josh do otherwise? She exploded with her fury.

"You can't just have a child and *then* decide that your own needs come first! You can't!" She got up now and walked to the window, turning her back so as not to be tempted to strike him.

"That's why we can't get back together,"—he said angrily—"because you never stop hocking me!"

"Hocking you? *Hocking* you! I merely remind you of your responsibilities and you call that hocking you! What the fuck do you want? You expect me to support Mandy, support the household, write, and never ask a thing of you—and if I ever point out that Mandy has needs or that I have needs, you call it hocking. What about *my* needs? What *about* them?"

Josh stood up, looking as cold and impassive as he could, his eyes glassy.

"Your needs are no longer my problem," he said, "Your needs are your own problem now. We are no longer a couple." And he strode out of the room, leaving Isadora in the study filled with her success trophies and able to do nothing but crumble in a heap on the floor, and cry her eyes out on the very same carpet where she had, not so long ago, made love to Errol.

Dimly, through her sobs, she heard Josh's car pull out of her driveway.

"We are no longer a couple," echoed again and again in her head. The very phrase seemed more piercing to her flesh than if he had shot her with arrows throughout her whole body like St. Sebastian.

"Better get used to it, girl," she muttered to herself as she lay on the floor. But the fact was that she no longer wanted to live. If it were not for Mandy, she would have found a way to check out. Ah, children, she thought, they eat up our lives, but they also sustain them—a paradox, like most things that are true in this world. Amen.

7

The Aroma of Birth

The strong odor of sex is . . . really
the aroma of birth; it is disagreeable
or repulsive only to those who
fail to recognize its significance.
—HENRY MILLER

What would happen if one woman
told the truth about her life?
The world would split open
—MURIEL RUKEYSER

MANDY was born when Isadora was thirty-six. She was born after protracted labor, protracted ambivalence about getting pregnant, and protracted worry about whether or not having a baby would interfere with writing. Well—of course it did. And of course it didn't. What on earth would you write about if you insulated yourself from all of life? And if you had the good fortune (and in some ways the bad fortune) to be born in a woman's body, having a baby was one of the experiences you simply had to have.

Isadora goes back in her mind to the self that became pregnant with Mandy. It seems she was a different person then—before pregnancy doubled her, birth halved her, and motherhood turned her into Everywoman. Without that experience, who would she be? Another literary lady who thought literature would always come before life? Another neurasthenic Emily or Virginia —barren yet womb-ridden, moon-ridden. No—Isadora is convinced that though there are indeed women who know for sure they don't want children (and therefore ought not to have them) those who long for children—even ambivalently—have to do the dirty deed and be done with it.

For her it was a necessary metamorphosis—like tadpole into frog—to go from maiden into mother; not that Isadora had been a maiden for years; her maidenhood had succumbed to finger-fucking at age thirteen. But in some ways, she felt she had been a maiden up until the time of Mandy's birth. She had lived for literature, not life. She had not confronted her own mortality. All these metamorphoses children bring about, and then, when they have taught us to put them before all else, they moor us to life when our will to live gets shaky.

Josh and Isadora were in Paris on a book tour when the sperm and egg that were meant to be Mandy met. In retrospect, it seems fated. At the time, the event was far from certain. Isadora and Josh had been trying to get pregnant for a year, had been at any rate toying with the idea. They had stopped using contraception —which at that juncture was Isadora's diaphragm. But Isadora was just uncertain enough about the decision to do this ambivalently, too. She would leave off the diaphragm for days and days and days—and then suddenly use it again once or twice, and then be crestfallen (and also oddly relieved) when her period came yet again. Sometimes she would use the diaphragm without jelly and then take it right out much too soon. Sometimes she would leave it off altogether, and on odd occasions, she would leave it in. It was as if she felt that this was a decision for God to make, not she, a decision beyond her humble human powers, a decision for that Demeter-Persephone who dwells in the diaphragm.

By the time Isadora and Josh got to Paris, this shilly-shallying had been abandoned. Isadora quite definitely left her diaphragm in a bathroom drawer in Connecticut, and departed for Paris with the intention of doing a week of interviews and getting pregnant at the same time.

She remembers the night it happened, remembers it as if she were the heroine of *The Rose Tattoo*, it was that dramatic an occurrence. She and Josh were staying in a little hotel on the Left Bank, not far from the boulevard St. Germain. The hotel was a refurbished town house—a real *hôtel* in the French sense of the term. Their suite had been decorated so that it had a sleeping platform above the living room.

They had made love, made love twice in a row in that frenzied, not entirely pleasurable way couples do when they are trying to make a baby. They had done it wordlessly, tired as they were after a day of interviews and overfeeding—fancy publishers' lunches and dinners having bloated their guts and too much wine having made their temples throb.

The first fuck was an ordinary one—missionary position, deep penetration, a decent enough orgasm for each. But then, oddly, the flesh had stirred again, and they turned to each other with desperate need, like two strangers who had just met in a bar or like a sixteenth-century witch copulating with the Grandmaster she believes to be the devil—the mating was that passionate and charged. And then, as Josh came and his semen pumped deep into her still-pulsing cunt, Isadora had the sense that her orgasm began again, or that it had, in fact, never stopped, and she had an image, an image out of *2001*, an image such as portends great earth-shaking changes, comets or meteorite showers, or even whole solar systems being sucked into black holes in space. She saw a giant, glowing planet surrounded by wriggling tadpolelike sperms. And one of these tadpoles pierced the planet, making it glow all the brighter—and Isadora knew, knew beyond any doubt that she had just become pregnant.

She and Josh were not married then. They had procured a wedding license two months earlier, procured it because Isadora blamed her "bourgeois ovaries" for her inability to get pregnant. She felt terribly insecure about getting pregnant without being married—although, now she wonders whether she did not just feel insecure about getting pregnant with Josh, knowing what a baby he was. Once, on a previous trip to Paris, she had dreamed about herself and Josh, dreamed a dream that predicted all this present grief with him. Oddly enough, Isadora had written it all down, too, though despite her years and years of analysis, she did not usually write down her dreams.

It was July of 'seventy-six and Josh and Isadora were in Paris, staying in the boulevard St. Germain apartment of two sex-therapist friends named Hans and Kirstin—those amiable orgy-organizers and erotic-art collectors, those writers of books on the subject of sex and society. They had introduced Isadora and Josh to the art of orgy once, a long time ago, and their apartment in Paris seemed to be designed, above all, for the conduct of same— the chairs, the tables, the hassocks, all turned into fuck furniture at the flick of a finger.

Isadora and Josh were there alone—Hans and Kirstin having departed for the States to visit friends—and Isadora was profoundly spooked. She was spooked by the fuck furniture, spooked by the plethora of Parisian roaches, who actively shared the apartment with them, and spooked by the fact that her idyll with Josh seemed to be curdling into grief. (Had she fallen in love with Josh just to leave Bennett? There is always that danger when one falls passionately in love with fresh flesh in order to leave a rotting marriage.) As so often is the case in life, the dream said to the sleeping Isadora all the things the waking Isadora could not say to herself.

I am with Josh. I have Chekarf on a leash. We are in a marble hallway high above the main floor (5ième étage). Chekarf goes to the edge, looks over, walks too far, falls, smashes on marble floor way below, his tiny body shattered; blood, white fur. I cry inconsolably, long choking sobs. My mother's voice (coming, it seems, from nowhere) says: "See, you did it. You can't be trusted even with a dog."

Feeling, in the dream: That I have failed. I experience real loss —as if Chekarf is indeed dead and there will never be another dog just like him. I have failed as a mother, failed to protect this puppy, and I am worthless. How can I support myself and Josh and a baby if I cannot even keep Chekarf alive? I lie awake all night feeling a worthlessness and brokenness so deep I think I will never recover. I am nothing. A middle-aged woman with no child, a dead dog, a child-lover, and even he will leave me.

I wake up weeping. Josh holds me. The ceiling spins. It seems I am on a ship rocking—some ghastly, fog-bound ocean liner stranded in the North Atlantic. When morning comes, I can barely walk. The floor rears up at me. Everything appears as if through a fisheye lens. The croissant at the café glares at me. The table tilts. Sunlight fails to banish the demons.

I dream about Chekarf a lot—dream about losing him. In these dreams, is the dog me? Or a baby? Or is the dog an aspect of myself?

That was the dream and accompanying journal notation from the year before Isadora became pregnant with Mandy—her thirty-fifth year, when the urge to make a baby was growing stronger and stronger within her and she was trying to sort out all the complexities of the decision.

She knows now that there is no proper way, perhaps no conscious way, to make that awesome decision. In a sense it is all in the hands of the Goddess. Isadora vacillated and vacillated about becoming pregnant. When the pregnancy was finally confirmed, she tortured herself by toying with the idea of an abortion—though she had very negative feelings about abortion and in fact had never let herself become pregnant accidentally so as never to be faced with the horrible "choice" of killing a part of herself. (Politically, she was *for* reproductive freedom; personally, she would have found abortion akin to the amputation of a hand or an eye.)

She remembers the day she discovered she was pregnant as if it were today. She had gone into New York on the train to see an ob-gyn man—a certain Dr. Remsen, a small, white-haired, pink-cheeked man who had an office on Fifth Avenue in the Sixties. She had gone to him after not having had a pelvic exam for at least a year, because a friend recommended him. She was newly settled in Connecticut and knew no doctors there.

As she spread her legs in the stirrups for this elfin, white-haired doctor, Isadora had a flash that she had always deliberately distanced pelvic exams from sexual feelings, but that *if* she were to submit to her sense of arousal, she could, in fact, become aroused even here with those cold, gloved fingers probing her.

"Your uterus is slightly enlarged," the doctor said.

Her heart leapt at these words—leapt with fear and excitement both. Then the doctor drew a blood sample from her arm, and so as to let her have the answer to her question on that very day, he suggested that she carry the blood to the lab herself and call later to see what the verdict was.

It was a very cold day in early January. (Isadora and Josh had finally succumbed to "bourgeois ovaries" and married secretly on Christmas Eve.) Now, as she trudged up Madison Avenue, clutching her test tube of blood, she thought how strange it was not knowing whether she was pregnant, even though she had the answer in her pocket.

Blood into blood, flesh into flesh, dust into dust. She had not bled that month, and she suspected she knew the reason. Yet even as she wished for this phallic-shaped phial of blood to tell her she was indeed with child, she also wished for her period to begin so that her life would not, could not, change.

Oh, how we fear the metamorphoses through which we become truly fledged humans, real *menshes* of the species *Homo sapiens*. Yet even if we do not willingly undergo them, changes pursue us just the same. The woman who never bears a child metamorphoses in different ways. We may dig our heels in and dare life never to change, but, all the same it changes under our feet like sand under the heels of a sea gazer as the tide runs out. Life is forever undermining us. Life is forever washing away our castles, reminding us they were, after all, only sand and seawater.

Sand and seawater. Seawater and blood. Salty both and the stuff of life—the nutrient stew from which the world began. Isadora clutched her little phial of blood and trudged up the cold avenue —past art galleries and designer boutiques, past the Whitney Museum and the Carlyle with its Bemelmans Bar. She hardly suspected that four years hence she would be reading *Madeline* (a book she loved as a child) to a little girl whose only present trace was in this phial of blood in her pocket.

Change, change, change. Change in the blood portending pregnancy or cancer. Change in the air; change in the ozone layer; change in everything we say or do. We think our families are immutable, or our pasts—but even as we watch them they transform themselves like backlighted scrims in a play, changing as the lights change. The mother we knew at twenty is not the mother we know at forty. Has *she* changed or have we? And the womb:

even if it never bears, it changes. Bears cysts, bears fibroids; sheds blood month after month; sheds invisible eggs whose loss the mind mourns—if only in dreams.

Isadora dropped off the phial of blood at the lab. She dropped it off almost nonchalantly, as if it did not portend her entire future. The Puerto Rican girl at the reception desk there checked off "pregnancy test" as if it were a matter of the slightest indifference to her that the whole galaxy was about to shift a little when Isadora gave birth. And of course it *was* a matter of indifference to her. It was not *her* galaxy. But Isadora was glad to give up that phial of hot blood which had seemed to be burning a hole in her pocket as she trudged down the cold street. It was almost too torrid to handle—contraband of sorts. Cosmic come—an explosive substance no mortal should carry.

She took off to spend the day shopping and walking. At Bergdorf's, she bought a beautiful brown silk smock dress (with a ruffled neck) that could well be used as a maternity dress. Isadora already knew the answer the blood told. And yet, when she called the lab from Grand Central later in the day (the doctor had authorized them to give her the answer directly), she was appalled and shocked and not a little panic-stricken when the answer was "positive."

"Are you sure?" Isadora said.

"It says here 'positive,' " said the bored lab receptionist, whose belly was not going to swell, whose feet were not going to ache, whose clothes were not going to grow tight.

"It says here 'positive.' "

Isadora next called Josh in Connecticut. She was standing in one of those carousellike phone pods in Grand Central, watching the gray-faced commuters come and go, the men she thought of as Cheever people, all the Lowell Strathmores of the world, with their Ben Franklin glasses, their passionless mouths, and their dormant cocks that longed to dance in the night but knew not for whom.

She called collect. And just as Josh said: "Yes, I'll pay," Isadora said, "You certainly will—I'm pregnant!"

A pause.

"Cookie—that's wonderful. How do you feel?"

"Utterly terrified," Isadora said.

Her honesty at that moment (she later learned) Josh never ceased to hold against her. He took wholly personally the fact that

136

she might have some ambivalence about this momentous change in state.

"Don't worry, cookie," he said, "we'll do it together. I'll help you with *everything*, I swear it. I'll never let you down. There's no reason to be nervous."

Having stated her fear, she was now free to experience elation. On the train home, she looked at all the gray-faced commuters and exulted. She was the only one carrying life within; they carried death. She was the one bearing the race onward as it hurtled through the cosmos. She was the cupbearer, the good-news bearer, the genetic messenger. She found, to her astonishment, that she liked that role very much. Having always borne life forward through sheer acts of thinking and willing, she now found that her cells themselves were propelling life, that the mystery printed in the DNA was doing all the work. For an intellectual woman who feels that nothing is but thinking makes it so, the very will-lessness of pregnancy is immensely appealing. The cosmos comes through you without your conscious thought. You give up control and thereby gain the greatest control. You open your palm to the skies and the stars kiss it. You open your belly to a shower of golden rain and your wealth multiplies.

On that dour, urine- and disinfectant-scented commuter train, Isadora felt smug in her secret knowledge that she was pushing life forward into the future. She remembered that as a prepubescent girl, she used to sit on buses in New York and think (with utter amazement) that every man, in his gray gabardine suit, had one of those tubular things called a "penis" dangling between his grayish legs. She was both fascinated and repelled. What an awful thing to have to dangle there! If repressed envy was concealed in her fantasy, she could not find it. All she knew was that *she* would have felt horribly embarrassed if she always had to shift her thighs from side to side to accommodate that dingling dangling thingling.

When Isadora got back to Westport station, she discovered that a light dusting of snow had covered the region, making even the grim bars opposite the train station look cheery.

Josh was not waiting in the Mercedes. She called home.

"The driveway isn't plowed yet, cookie," he said. "I can't get up it." (Their driveway was impassable even in the lightest of snows.) "Why don't you take a cab home, and I'll walk up to the top of the driveway and escort you down."

"Okay," she said, not really registering the disappointment and anger she must have felt. What an ungallant way to greet a newly pregnant bride!

She looked everywhere for a taxi, and not finding a free one, was almost about to call Josh back, when a woman who had been staring at her on the train recognized her and called to her by name.

"Ms. Wing," she said. "I just *had* to tell you how I love your books."

Now this took Isadora aback; it always took her aback when people recognized her (since she always forgot she was famous). She thanked the woman heartily. (She was secretly pleased—if overtly somewhat abashed by such praise—who among us can accept compliments graciously?) But on this occasion, she took her heart in her hand and asked the woman if she would do her the special favor of driving her home.

"Of course, I'd be honored," the woman said. She was a fortyish, brown-eyed, bleached blonde, who wore a dress-for-success suit and "sensible" midheel pumps.

"I'm Louise Mooring," the woman said. "By coincidence, I live right near you in Rocky Ridge."

As they drove home from Westport into higher and higher, snowier and snowier terrain, Louise poured out the sad story of her divorce, the grimness of raising children alone in Rocky Ridge (and commuting to New York to work in an ad agency), and the grimness of divorced dating in Connecticut. "That could be me," Isadora thought, Isadora always thought, though the warmth in her belly obliterated all present doubts and dire premonitions.

When they reached Serpentine Hill Road, they found that, as always, the snow was deeper than anywhere else. On the most treacherous curve (where four years later Isadora was to skid and climb a stone wall) the car would go no more. It slid sideways and spun its wheels uselessly in the snow.

After numerous attempts to negotiate the curve, Louise turned to Isadora and said:

"Would you horribly mind walking the rest of the way? I have no snow tires and my two kids are waiting for a hot dinner. I live right here."

She pointed to a white colonial house with a plaque on it—the eighteenth-century Ethan Wheatworth House, Isadora noted. How could she know that just a few years later that house would have again changed hands and would again figure in her life?

138

"Not at all," said Isadora, feeling glad to have been driven even this far by a total stranger.

"Thanks for all your kind words about my work," she said, stepping out of the car into the slippery snow and starting up the hill on foot.

It was ungodly quiet here in the snow, and the trees, weighted as they were by wet snow and icy droplets, seemed to droop their branches. Her thin suede boots gave her a poor foothold and became soaked almost immediately. It was too dark to see icy patches in the road and every little step slid her somewhat backward even as it propelled her forward.

Although her house was perhaps only half a mile up the hill, the hill was steep and the road was dark. No moon shone to guide her, and she knew that if she fell and sprained an ankle, no one might find her for quite a while. She cursed herself for not having called Josh again before leaving the station—but in some way, she must have wished that she *would* fall and flounder in the snow so that his lack of gallantry would be underlined. What pointless masochism! Better to choose a man who was loving and protective than to choose a child-lover and then try to punish him for being what he always was, perhaps always would be—a child.

Ten minutes or so further in her climb, Isadora heard a crackle of branches behind her and her heart raced. She turned around to see a doe walk delicately out of the underbrush, cross the road on dark, sure-footed hooves, stop for a millisecond to fix her in her wide-eyed brown gaze, and disappear into the underbrush on the other side with another crackle of dead wood and leaf mulch. This was one of the joys of living in Connecticut, and also one of the sadnesses—for often the animals one saw in the road were dead animals, oozing blood, or already furiously moving with maggots. "God bless the souls of the animals," Isadora would say whenever she saw the road-kill. But now, peered at by another female, albeit a female of another species, she felt a surge of identification. Two females trudging through snow with no males to protect them. Who would weather the winter better—she or the doe?

On up the road she went, her stockings soaked, her boots making squishing noises as they slid backward with every step. Isadora was tired from a day in the city, drained from that grim hour or so on the commuter train. She wanted to be home in bed; she wanted to absorb the news of her pregnancy and try to make sense of it all. Never had the half-mile to her house seemed so long. She had walked it many times in the summer, jogged it even in good weather, but in the dark and snow, it seemed forbidding.

Christmas lights were still up in some of the houses and they winked and twinkled through the branches. The Bradleys had electric candles, one in each window, and the Grimshaws still had their hemlock trees draped with ugly neon-green lights. Who had the key to whose bomb-shelter? Isadora wondered—for she could never walk this terrain without thinking of Cheever, who had chronicled it all so well long before she had moved to this bleak New England landscape. True, he had written about Ossining, or his fictional Shady Hill—but it was all the same desiccated WASP terrain, the same forbidding antisemitic woods. She hardly belonged here, but then, had she ever lived *anywhere* she felt she belonged? Never. She hadn't belonged in Heidelberg or in Malibu, or even in New York City, where she was born, bred, and educated. Perhaps *other* people felt they belonged. Isadora always felt like an alien. Or maybe everyone else felt like an alien, too. Maybe that was why poets and artists were needed by the human race: because *everyone* felt like an alien, but poets were the ones who knew how to express it in words.

When she came to her driveway, she saw Josh waiting with a large flashlight in his hand; he was wearing snow boots and a ski cap. He had a long scarf draped around his neck and icicles trembled from his red beard. Seeing him, she felt warmed and happy, suddenly ready to forgive everything. She ran to him and threw her arms around him.

"Cookie," he said, "that's *wonderful,* about your being pregnant!"

They walked down the driveway arm in arm, Isadora's boots slipping in the wet snow, Josh's flashlight beaming on the large wet flakes whose myriad crystals, no two alike, reminded her of the blastula—or was it already a fetus?—in her belly.

They walked into their house, and Chekarf, his coat all matted and wet from earlier romps in the snow, jumped on her. Their big red mutt, Virginia Woof, sulked in a corner, as if she already knew she was about to be replaced in their affections by a baby. These two animals had *been* their babies ever since they came to Connecticut. The animals bonded them; Josh and Isadora spoke a whole secret language about the dogs—each of whom, like an Eliotesque cat, had several names. Virginia Woof was also "Ginny" and "Woofly,"and "Dame Dog." Chekarf was also "Arf," and "The Teller of Tales," and "Russki." Many things are lost in the process of divorce, but the loss of the secret marital language (which comes with the division of the animals) is perhaps the most crushing.

"What happened with the test?" Josh asked.

And Isadora related, as best she could, the whole story of slogging up Madison Avenue with the phial of blood in her pocket. She tried to communicate what she had felt at the moment of being told she was pregnant, but there seemed to be no way to say it right.

"I was suddenly terrified," she said. "I feel like too much of a baby myself to *have* a baby. But I also feel terrific somehow—as if for the first time in my life I am doing something without my bloody *mind* controlling it. I seem to swing back and forth between these two feelings—terror and elation."

Josh didn't want to hear this; he had his own ambivalence to deal with and he didn't want to hear about Isadora's. He went into the kitchen and began making cocoa. It was carob cocoa from the health-food store. Josh had, not so long ago, given up meat, fish, caffeine, and all alcoholic beverages. He had been a serious doper in college, and virtually, as he once said, "majored in LSD," but now, like a number of members of his generation—refugees of the sixties—he was into pure foods, Zen meditation, and yoga. He had replaced one obsession with another, like so many of us do.

Isadora and Josh sat down at their dining-room table to drink the cocoa. A fire roared in the large fieldstone fireplace; outside the snow kept falling.

"What do you feel about having a baby?" Isadora asked Josh.

"Great—I've wanted it for years," he said, staring impassively. He didn't *look* happy. *Stunned* was more the word.

"Don't you have any mixed feelings about it?" Isadora asked. "Most people do."

At the utterance of that phrase, Josh stood up suddenly and pounded the table with his fist so hard that the carob drinks splashed all over the wormy-chestnut veneer.

"God damn it, Isadora! I'm *not* like you!" he shrieked. "I *know* what I feel! I *don't* feel ambivalent about everything the way you do and I hate your goddamned Freudian, psychological way of looking at everything!" He stamped out of the dining room and into the bedroom, slamming the door behind him.

Isadora sat there in stunned silence. Whenever anyone screamed at her, she crumbled, felt utterly wrong, utterly wronged. She joined in the accusing, attacking voices and began

141

to destroy herself. He was right; she was nothing but a psychologizing Freudian fink, a character out of a Jules Feiffer cartoon, a silly goose, a vacillator, unable to feel totally glad about anything. The voices in her head joined his attack on her until she began to tremble, as she had in childhood when her mother screamed at her. Finally, she broke down in tears and buried her head in her hands.

The bedroom door flew open and Josh ran in.

"God damn it to hell!" he screamed. "Can't you ever be happy about anything? Can't you ever stop nitpicking and noodling? We wanted this baby, wanted it so badly we've been trying for a year, and now all you can do is say how ambivalent you feel!" He screamed so loudly that even the dogs ran into the guest room to cower under the brass bed.

Isadora trembled, pursed her lips, wanted to strike out at him, or yell, or fight back—but she didn't know how. As the clown of family, the second sister, the conciliator (not the gladiator), she only knew how to dance and sing and backpedal, how to be charming, or how to compress and contain her anger until it glowed like a hot coal in her gut that gave off wisecracks like sparks.

"I want an abortion," she said, lips thin, arms folded. Totally untrue, it was simply the most hurtful thing she could think of to say.

Josh looked at her, incredulous. Then he fell to his knees, weeping. He put his head in her lap. "Please don't kill our baby," he cried.

They went to bed, hugging, kissing, and crying. In a flood of tears they made peace, imagining their unformed baby suspended like a helium balloon above their heads. Delicate pink, it hovered in the room before losing the lightness that kept it up and falling to earth as if into the realm of consciousness.

After Josh fell asleep, Isadora lay awake trying to imagine the baby-to-be. She could no more abort it than she could gouge out an eye or cut off a leg, but she had grave doubts about Josh—particularly his random rages, his denial of all ambivalence, yet his quickness to blame her. How to convey a woman's feeling of terror at carrying the baby of a man she feels will betray her? A baby is an unbreakable bond, a bond of flesh, a pulsing umbilicus between a man and a woman. Isadora knew full well that this baby would moor her to Josh as she had never been moored to any of her previous husbands. She wondered at herself for having chosen a mate so capriciously—for his jokes, his smell, and his furry belly.

Yet the truth was that most women probably chose their mates just as capriciously. The decision was made in the pheromones, not in the conscious mind. Maybe Nature had a greater scheme, was threading helical strands of DNA according to Her own omniscient plan, was juggling chromosomes according to some divine design. Maybe we were just bearers of the chromosomes, as poets were the bearers of the Voice; maybe we were cups, not the wine itself. *There* was a sobering-intoxicating thought.

Isadora slept. In her dream, she was already nursing her baby. Both breasts were full and ached. The milk (how could she know this, not having yet given birth?) squirted across the room when she squeezed her nipple between two fingers.

But when she looked down at the baby, it was Chekarf who suckled her, not a human infant. In the dream, this seemed quite natural. The little Bichon lay on its back, its vestigial nipples turned heavenward, its shiny black eyes open, its little black mouth sucking away at her pink nipple as if he were the most ordinary and healthy of infants. She felt proud of him, as if he were her child—proud of his excellent sucking, proud of his sweet little wet black olives of eyes. Isadora had often wished to suckle Chekarf when he was a puppy. She had looked at the tiny furry white thing and wanted to give it her breast, even to suck its diminutive penis (with its one yellow drop of urine trembling at the end of that delicate strand of white fur). She loved the dog *that* much; she felt she and it were one flesh. Small, helpless creatures still brought out such responses in her—baby raccoons, skunks, field mice. She and Josh had lived with a family of field mice during their first winter in Connecticut, had lived with them simply because Isadora would not consent to their being poisoned. They tolerated the field mice, even welcomed them until Isadora, finding mouse droppings everywhere—in the silverware drawers, in the dishwasher, in the stove, in the canisters of oatmeal, flour, bran, granola—began to worry about a possible health hazard.

"What would Swami Satchidinanda say?"

"Mouse droppings not verry sannitary," Josh said, doing his Indian swami accent.

"Butt, Mahster, can we kill any livving thing?" Isadora queried in *her* corresponding Indian accent.

"Better to kill *them* before they kill *you*," Josh riposted guruishly. Whereupon he undertook to poison them with a poison whose death he claimed was painless. Isadora doubted that any death was painless, but she looked away. The furry gray bodies of the mice seemed to haunt the corners of her vision after the poisoning. Whenever she walked into the kitchen, she seemed to see little gray blurs scurrying at the edges of her sight.

The beginning of Isadora's pregnancy was emotionally shaky—like the beginnings of all pregnancies. But once the little heart was firmly entrenched, once they went to the gynecologist and *heard* it beating, she took on a sureness, a beatitude she never had known before.

The worry lines smoothed out of her face; she smiled always. The mood swings, the depressions she had known all her life evened out and she became serene, well tempered, cheerful. She was suddenly so pretty she marveled at her face in the mirror. Always used to being *told* she was pretty, she had never really believed it before; now, she looked at herself and *saw* the prettiness—a radiant pink-cheeked blonde, with gray-blue eyes and enough life-force for three women. Could that person really be *me?* she wondered.

She ate and ate and ate and never gained much weight. At full term she had put on only twenty-two pounds. She gorged on ice cream, on milkshakes, on yogurt with fruit. Pregnant in early winter, she lived through her queasy period in January and February (she found she could not bear the smell of certain heavy perfumes she had previously loved, Bal à Versailles and Joy, and could not drink coffee, but other than that, she was fine) but then she bloomed into midpregnancy in the spring. By her thirty-sixth birthday, she was flying around the country promoting a new book—with a smile on her face and billowing silk paisley blouses disguising her belly. She was even lucky that that year's fashion was a return to smocklike dresses with ruffled necks and full sleeves. All seemed right with the world, and she seemed born to bear. Her fear of pregnancy had turned to sheer exuberance; her panic to peace. Never had she known such mindless certainty.

She researched and wrote and wrote, wrote and researched *Tintoretto's Daughter,* even flying to Venice when she needed to see the Scuola di San Rocco again, and smell the canals and *feel* the history in her pores and nostrils.

The summer she came to term was like one long house party. She wrote in her warm, brown-carpeted attic studio, and downstairs it seemed guests were always assembling to meet her when she descended—publishers from overseas, friends from everywhere, family. Her grandfather was ninety-four that year and he came up from time to time to regale Isadora (and her blooming belly) with stories about his childhood in Odessa—almost as if he were trying to communicate with the baby-to-be about his past (and her future). Isadora only hoped that he would live to see this great-grandchild, and he did! He was still mentally sharp that summer—and full of black irony and bitter wit, though his body was more and more a ruin.

As the summer progressed, Isadora grew increasingly sure of herself, and sure of her coming maternity, and Josh grew increasingly nervous. He taped a map of the hospital environs to the inside windshield of the car; he started to be afraid to fuck her for fear of hurting the baby. Isadora often thought that hard as it was for *women* to adjust to the idea of a new person in their lives, it was doubly hard for men because *they* did not have the nine months of physical preparation. By the time the baby was due to be born, it was so much a human being to her, so clear a personality, that she and it did not have to be formally introduced. As her pregnancy wore on, she grew happier and happier; Josh, for his part, often withdrew into a state of anxiety bordering on panic.

By the beginning of August, her belly was huge. She posed in the nude for Josh's camera on the redwood deck outside their bedroom. The pictures show a rosy Rubensian figure with legs far too long and thin to support it—sort of like an artichoke on toothpicks. But the smile on the lady's face is one Isadora has not known the like of since. She looks blissfully unworried. Why on earth was she so happy? Was it just such a blessed relief to be bearing with her belly rather than with her brain? Was it the freedom of having fulfilled some biological mission and now being released to continue with her life? Or was it the joy of discovering that one could create with one's body and with one's brain at the very same time? Shaw may have pronounced it impossible. Nietzsche may have pronounced it impossible. But she was writing better than ever and she was also carrying—she was sure—the world's most astounding baby.

One hot afternoon in August, Isadora was working in the airless crypt of the Beinecke Library at Yale. She was wearing a loose pink cotton dress Josh had bought for her birthday and she was researching one of the things she loved most to research—some detail of sixteenth-century costume, a particular sort of bodice worn by sixteenth-century Venetian ladies. She had that wonderful sense of floating concentration one sometimes gets during research or writing: the world had gone away; nothing remained but herself and the book.

Then, all at once she felt a surprising wetness under her. She stood up and looked over her shoulder to discover that a large circle of moisture had formed on the back of her dress. With no alarm whatsoever, it occurred to her that she must find a public phone to call Josh. As she ascended through the stacks in the elevator, she had an image of herself—her blooming pink belly under the full pink dress, rising up through layers of old books and manuscripts, rising up through the climatically controlled environment, through the windowless white marble crypt that is the Beinecke Library, rising like a balloon whose string a child has let go of, the baby in her belly triumphing over all those dusty books.

She called Josh at home in Rocky Ridge.

"I think I'm leaking amniotic fluid," she said.

"Come home right away," he blurted out in a panic. "I'll call the doctor and tell him."

She drove down the hot, dusty Merritt Parkway as if on a cloud of cherubim, painted by Tiepolo. Never had she been so calm. All the pregnancy fears she had known before becoming pregnant; all the midpregnancy dreams of monsters, of Frankenstein babies, half beast, half human, were banished by the imminent reality. She had known for several months that the baby she carried was a girl, known it because of the amniocentesis she had undergone in her third month, but she had no vision of the baby at all—only that it was a version of her little-girl self.

She drove down her toboggan-run driveway feeling utterly regal. Josh was waiting anxiously by the door of their house, waiting for her to return and bring their baby to him. She got out of the car slowly, walking deliberately (in her flat white sandals) down the flagstone path that led to the door.

"What happened?" Josh asked when she walked in.

She merely turned around and showed him the wet spot on her dress.

"What did the doctor say?" she asked.

"That we should come in right away."

"First let me pee," she said—since peeing is to pregnancy as heat is to summer: endemic.

They got back into the Silver Nazi, with the map of the hospital environs taped to the inside of the windshield and they drove to the doctor's office in Stamford.

146

In the car, they chattered happily—of Venetian bodices, of names for the baby, of the incumbent miracle—so ordinary, yet also so transcendent. Josh had gone with Isadora to every gynecologist's appointment, from the first hearing of the heartbeat, to the strangely frightening amniocentesis (a needle piercing her belly in the whitest and most vulnerable of places), to the Lamaze classes that were so baffling to both of them—but now they were entering a phase of the process that only she alone could do. She wasn't sure whether she felt exuberant about that or terrified. A little of both. Never had she been quite as proud to be a woman.

It was curious, wasn't it? Curiouser and curiouser, as Alice would say. For years, she had feared pregnancy and birth, yet now that birth was almost upon her, it seemed like the single most important, the pivotal experience of her life.

At the gynecologist's—a sweet Stamford gynecologist who had supplanted the elfin New York doctor who'd diagnosed her pregnancy—Isadora was measured and probed.

"Only two centimeters dilated," said Steve Lowenstein, her pedantic but gentle ob-gyn man. He was a nice Jewish boy, exactly her age—the sort of boy who'd gone to medical school when she'd gone to graduate school at Columbia. The sort of boy Jewish princesses hope to marry, but then grow hideously bored with at thirty and seek to deceive. He had brown eyes, brown hair, and looked at her with longing. Not sexual longing maybe, but longing for all that was exotic. Her ovaries were not exotic, but her life-style (to use that awful word) was. To Steve Lowenstein, she represented the forbidden female—much-married, sexual, seemingly free. They were about to share, with an intimacy perhaps even greater than the conception of this baby, one of the most astonishing experiences of life.

Steve sent Josh and Isadora home, admonishing them to wait for contractions to begin, then call him back. Since the amniotic sac was punctured, Steve would have to induce labor if it did not begin that day or the next. So Isadora and Josh went home to wait.

It was hot and sunny, a beatific blue-skied August afternoon when Connecticut seems the loveliest place to be in the whole world. They went home to wait and prepare, but how do you prepare for an event that is, by its very nature, utterly unique? Birth is common enough, but it is also absolutely individual. Every birth is different; every baby is different.

Waiting for the contractions to begin, they read poetry—Whitman, D. H. Lawrence, and Thomas Hardy—and they sat on the waterbed trying to fathom how this experience was going to change them.

Isadora had the sense of being on the brink of transcendence. She remembered how Papa had spoken of her grandmother's death—an event that occurred while she was in Heidelberg. "She looked off into space," he had said, "and her face became more beautiful than it ever was before. She was suddenly peaceful; when she died, that transcendent expression remained."

Isadora felt somehow that she was joining her grandmother, joining her mother, joining that long chain of women giving birth to women, transcending death. How unexpected this feeling was! How utterly without precedent in her life!

Dusk came over the ridge on which their house stood. Isadora and Josh got into the waterbed, cuddled together, and watched the film of *Tale of Two Cities* on their videotape machine. At about eight in the evening, in the midst of the French Revolution (as retold by Dickens), Mandy decided to make her appearance in the sublunary world.

Oh, she had been present before, present for years in dreams and for nine months she had breathed (though she had not breathed air), but now she was ready to join them in the world of air breathers, the world of mammals, the world of milk drinkers.

The contractions began coming closer and closer together. Josh was timing them with his stopwatch, and Isadora was practicing her pant-pant-blow. At first, it was all a lark. The pain was not severe, and Isadora was elated that she was about to have this famous rite of passage, was about to join the multitudes of women —alive and ghostly—who had made this trek up the Mountain of Motherhood before her.

They got into the Silver Nazi and roared along I-95 to Stamford. The contractions got more and more severe and closer and closer together, and Josh ran the Norwalk toll booth, hoping to pick up a police escort. Not a police car in sight—now that they needed one.

The doctor had been called. He was to meet them at the hospital. Both Isadora and Josh had the feeling that they were rushing to an appointment with Destiny, but when they left the highway in Stamford, Josh got lost.

"God damn it," he said, "I knew we'd never find the hospital."

"Relax," said Isadora. "First babies never come all that fast."

"How are you, cookie?" he asked.

"Darling—I'm fine," she said. And she felt fine, too. Though usually inclined to panic about physical pain, on this occasion, she was serene. Why was she so goddamned serene? It blew her mind to realize how ruled by her hormones she was, how much the Great Mother—Demeter, Persephone, or whoever—had imbued her with the strength of the species to face this coming ordeal.

Once they found the hospital, she was transferred to a wheel-chair, while Josh was dispatched to park the car. Riding along the corridors of Stamford Hospital, starting to feel stronger and stronger contractions, she felt how central her role was and how vestigial his. She felt the unbridgeable chasm between the two sexes.

If I had had a baby earlier, she wondered, would I ever have written *any* of those books?

Yes, she thought—but what different books they would have been! Books that celebrated rather than bemoaned womanhood, books that knew the miracle of woman's strength.

In the labor room, the nurses come and go, talking—if not of Michelangelo—then of last night's pickup. Isadora was relieved of her clothes, given a green gown, and hooked up to a fetal heart monitor. She was watching the needle draw peaks and valleys on the graph paper, taking mental notes on this strange experience, when Josh appeared, camera in hand to snap pictures of her in labor. They got through just two pictures before the contractions became so strong that it seemed in bad taste to continue.

Isadora was suddenly lost in the pain, overwhelmed by it—as if the peaks and valleys on the graph had become blood-red mountains and she was climbing them, climbing from one surge of pain to the next. The Lamaze breathing was next to useless. As long as the pain was mild, it was sufficient distraction, but when the pain became really severe, it was all she could do to *remember* to breathe.

Josh breathed with her; but even through her pain, she could tell he was freaked out by his helplessness. This experience was dividing them somehow, as much as it was bringing them together. She remembers his hazel eyes, very spaced-out and fearful. She remembers Steve Lowenstein arriving, examining her, and declaring after barely two hours of labor, that she will need a cesarean. She remembers pleading with him to let her deliver the baby "naturally"—though what can be "natural" about this process, she does not know. She's amazed that any human being ever arrived on the planet before her—so inefficient, painful, and pointless the process seems. The pain goes on and on and on. Steve and Josh try to labor with her—panting and blowing—but she is still only three centimeters dilated and she's been laboring three hours already. The minutes crawl by on bloody feet. When she is given an injection of pitocin, the contractions get so close together that the pain is unbearable. Then she is given pain-killers and the contractions slow again. Then more pitocin, more pain. Then more pain-killer.

The whole cycle seems absurd—and the two men—doctor and husband—so utterly useless. They want to help, but don't seem to know how. They are as insubstantial as clouds reflected in a puddle of rainwater; and only she and her baby, she and her pain, finally exist at all.

She labors for hours. The clock on the wall, the peaks and valleys on the chart, and Josh's spacy eyes are all that she remembers.

"You are going to need a cesarean," Steve keeps saying, at intervals, but he is too nice, too respectful of her desire to deliver "naturally" to press her. Only when the baby's heartbeat falters does he insist. And by then she is too exhausted by the pain to protest.

All systems go. They ready the operating room, call for a litter, and Steve himself pushes her along the neon-lit halls of the hospital. They find the elevator. He pushes her into it, pushes the button—and somewhere in the middle of a contraction, the elevator gets stuck!

She and her obstetrician stuck in an elevator at Stamford Hospital and her baby fighting for its life! Her heart sinks. She always knew she'd die in childbirth, always knew she'd die in some absurd situation like this. A stuck elevator and her nice gynecologist helplessly fiddling with the buttons. He presses the alarm. Through her excruciating pain, she hears a siren screech.

"Please don't let me die!" Isadora screams. "I'm writing the best book of my life!" She thinks of Charlotte Brontë, of Mary Wollstonecraft, of Paula Modersohn-Becker—all the women artists of the world felled by their own biology. The very protagonist of the historical novel she is writing—Marietta Robusti, La Tintoretta, daughter of the great Jacopo Tintoretto, died, in fact, in childbirth.

"Don't worry," Steve says. Don't worry, they always say—but then, *they* don't have to worry, since women have the babies for them.

Isadora looks up. A black orderly in a green suit is climbing down the elevator trapdoor above her and his foot (in white crepe-soled shoe) hangs suspended directly above her enormous throbbing belly. Suddenly she thinks that all men have to do is build reasonably foolproof elevators, while women do the really *tough* work of the human race—bringing the next generation to birth.

"Excuse me, ma'am," says the orderly, jeté-ing away from her belly, as if trained for some minstrel version of a Harold Lloyd film. Even in her madness and agony, Isadora can see the humor in this situation. The nightmare of the stuck elevator—and she in labor, needing a cesarean.

"Don't worry, don't worry," Steve Lowenstein keeps saying, as much to allay his own fears as hers. Meanwhile, the orderly is fiddling with the buttons, trying to get the elevator to work.

In the best of times, Isadora loathes stuck elevators with a passion bordering on panic. But in labor, when your whole life is flashing before you, when you are sure you'll die from the pain—all you really need is a stuck elevator to flip you over the brink into madness.

Lying on the litter, watching the men toy ineffectually with the elevator buttons, hearing the screaming sirens, Isadora flies back in her mind through all the days of her life. She is growing younger and younger—until she herself is this throbbing in her belly, longing to be born.

"Get me out of here!" she screams. "Get me and my baby out of here!" And just at that moment the elevator starts to move again, as if powered by her voice. They are all in motion now. The elevator ascends, the doors open, the litter flies along a hall leading to the O.R.

Nurses are waiting; an anesthesiologist with a long needle; lights; no camera; action!

There is a moment, before the needle pierces her back, when she remembers tales of women paralyzed by "spinals," but then the blessed relief from pain floods through her and she is glad to be numb from neck to toes.

A sheet blocks her view of her belly, but down below, Steve is cutting, cutting.

Suddenly he lifts aloft a bloody bundle, cuts again, wraps the object in a towel, and lays it down in Isadora's arms.

"Is it the placenta?" she inquires—so bloody is the little mortal lump.

"It's your daughter!" he says with great delight.

151

Isadora does not remember a first cry, nor a first breath—but she does remember her first look at the baby who became her own Amanda.

The little moon face wore a crust of blood as if she were a planet rich in iron ore. The little eyelids fluttered on the little cheeks as if in greeting, a mat of auburn hair clung to the little dome of skull. The softness of the skull spoke of mortality.

"Hello, my darling, my daughter, my familiar stranger," Isadora said, weeping. She and her daughter had come apart that they might come together.

Steve Lowenstein apologized for all his sewing.

"It takes longer to sew you up than to cut you open," he said. "So many layers of skin and muscle." So many layers. The baby, the book, the stuck elevator, the fear of childbirth, and triumphal reality. Her heroine would die, yet she would live, baby at her breast, to finish her book. She would have it all. Was that fair to all the women who had died? Was life ever really fair?

Josh was waiting in the hall outside the O.R. as a drained, tired, but ecstatic Isadora and a newly washed, newly named Amanda, exited on wheels through the double doors of that amazing room where her whole life had metamorphosed into something new. No longer would she be merely a woman, or a writer, or a lover. Before all else, she would be a mother: a mother-who-wrote, a mother-who-loved, a mother-who-mothered. Even if her baby were—O unthinkable thought!—to die, she would be a bereaved mother. The identity was unbreakable, unshakable.

"Hi," she said with parched throat. "Here she is."

Josh came over to the litter, and with wonder and delight, viewed the baby. Little miracle, she opened her opaque deep sea-blue, unseeing eyes.

"I love you, little one," he said, the tears streaming down his face.

At home, everything changed. No longer were Josh and Isadora ever alone. There was a baby nurse. There was a cook. There were all these people supposedly to help, but every one of them was as much a hindrance as a help.

The baby nurse ate and ate and ate. She resented Isadora for breast-feeding and she retaliated in the classic baby-nurse manner: "Mrs. Ace," she would say nasally whenever the baby cried, "your milk's not rich enough—your baby is starving to death."

The baby nurse was an immense bewigged woman from Waterbury called Mary Hogg—which she pronounced to rhyme not with "log" but with "rogue." No one was fooled. Hog it was—however much she might wish us to believe it Hogue. No Dickens character could have been more aptly named. Mary Hogg ate for herself, for the baby, and for Isadora, who wasn't exactly dieting, but who refused to eat ice cream and cookies—a fact which piqued Mary Hogg because it then became evident how much *she* was eating. She did little, in fact, besides change the baby and eat Isadora and Josh out of house and home. But the new parents were so anxious about their baby, so mystified by its habits, that they were almost afraid to touch it without an intermediary. Mary Hogg knew this and seized the upper hand. She had apparently taken up baby nursing as a means of feeding herself incessantly, almost as though she were compensating for the mothering she never had. An enormous bulk of a woman with black polyester hair and a snub face covered with wens, she cradled little Amanda in her huge arms, speaking for her, eating for her, interpreting her moods for the two bewildered new parents.

The little girl was beautiful but mysterious. Her sleep patterns, her bowels, her watchfulness—all of these seemed utterly without precedent. When the baby cried, Isadora's breasts leaked. When the baby was brought into the room by the nurse, Isadora roused herself out of a dead sleep and sat up in the waterbed to take the little bundle into her arms. The little rosebud lips latched onto her nipple with a prodigious force—the primal force of the universe, it seemed. And Isadora would look down on the suckling baby, feeling her womb contract and her eyes fill with tears—but tears for what, she did not know. Tears for Mandy's future, or her own? Tears for the unknowability of any baby's destiny? Tears for her own changed state? For never again would she go anywhere without thinking of her child; it was almost as if that cut umbilicus, now useless and dried, had ceased to be a physical object and had become a powerful moral one, a matrix in which her whole life was bound—so that never again would she make any decision just for herself. Every decision would include Mandy. Every thought that flitted through her mind would have Mandy lurking somewhere behind it. Every dream, every motion, every fantasy would mirror Mandy as the human blood mirrors the salt content of the seas in which we first received the gift of life.

Mandy was not just a suckling infant; she had become a climate, a landscape, a planet. And Isadora now walked this planet, this planet called maternity, which was larger than her consciousness, larger than her writing, larger than her life.

Mary Hogg—with her excess avoirdupois, her wens, her warts, her wigs, her little gold granny glasses, and her polyester uniforms —was the physical embodiment of the change in Isadora's life. Not the baby. The baby was lovely, healthy, pink-cheeked—a joy, even when she woke up to feed at three in the morning. But the baby came with such impedimenta! Not only the nurse, but the playpen, the baby carrier, the diaper bag, the changes of clothes. It was no longer possible for Josh or Isadora to stir out of the house without looking like the Foreign Legion on the move, or a gypsy caravan in full regalia. Spontaneity was gone from their lives. They dared not go anywhere without the most elaborate plans. Everything was now so complicated. Where to put the baby in the car, what sort of baby seat to use, how the baby's schedule would be affected, what foods and blankets to take, which porta-crib, which basket, which toys. The baby seemed dwarfed by all her equipment, all her attendants.

In addition to Mary Hogg, the redoutable baby nurse—whose tenure was, in the light of history, brief, but seemed at the time interminable—there was also an aged black cook named Lilyanne.

She had been hired by Josh while Isadora was in the hospital recuperating from her cesarean, and she had glowing, if tattered, references. She seemed at first the embodiment of all those motherly black servants played by Hattie McDaniel—every Jewish girl's dream: a black mammy out of a forties movie to mother her, as her own mother, her pallid white mother, never could, never would.

Lilyanne was old. (*How* old was not ascertainable.) She had worked for the great and the near-great. From Gypsy Rose Lee to a relation of the Rockefellers (*which* Rockefellers was also not ascertainable), to the judge who wrote the *Ulysses* decision. Her teeth were not quite her own, nor was her hair, but her eyes were kind and sparkling and she could still cook up a storm.

Storm was also the word for the condition in which she left the kitchen—flour everywhere (as if a contingent of eighteenth-century dandies had powdered their wigs there), pots unwashed, onions and potatoes rolling along the floor, appliances spattered with sauce.

But oh, how that woman could cook! Poached salmon with dill

sauce; filets of fish in white wine; divine fried chicken; baked potatoes taken out of their jackets, mixed with cheddar cheese and sour cream, and stuffed back in; trifles and soufflés for dessert.

"Is this all health food?" Josh would say as they sat down to an absolutely scrumptious meal.

"Yes, Mr. Ace," Lilyanne would swear.

"Amazing . . ." Josh would say. "The cakes are so light, and the fried chicken so crispy. I've never tasted such delicate cakes made with whole-wheat flour, and I've never had such great fried chicken."

"It's my secret recipe," Lilyanne would say coyly.

Lilyanne was a great cook, but she needed a pit crew to follow behind her, picking up pieces of kitchen equipment, mopping up, and even retrieving her wire-rimmed glasses when they flew off her nose.

For Lilyanne was terribly unsteady on her feet. She wore Minnie Mouse shoes that appeared to be three sizes too large, and her legs were pitifully thin and frail. Though she was a small woman, her legs still seemed insufficient to support her, and since Josh and Isadora's house was full of steps, half-steps, balconies, and decks, Lilyanne always seemed in mortal danger. She saw none too well, her shoes gaped, and her knees buckled. Many a time, Isadora came flying down from her attic studio (clutching her cesarean scar) because she heard pots crashing and glasses shattering in the kitchen.

"Now you take care of that belly of yours," Lilyanne would say perfectly calmly, as she picked herself up from the floor and began sweeping up the rubble. She never broke anything important, but Isadora thought she might break her legs—for wherever Lilyanne was in the house great clashing and clattering followed. On one occasion she fell down a full flight of stairs with a breakfast tray, then miraculously, rose among the rubble, pronounced it "nothin'," and began sweeping up. Isadora loved her, but she finally had to let her go because she required an additional cleaning woman just to clean up the kitchen after her great gourmet achievements. One day Isadora came downstairs to the kitchen and saw Mary Hogg, Lilyanne, and Rowena (the cleaning lady) all eating together while the baby screamed from the English pram on the kitchen deck.

"How long has she been crying?" Isadora asked, breasts leaking at the sound.

"Oh, it's *good* for her to cry, Miz Ace," Mary Hogg professed in her irritatingly nasal voice. And the other two *fressers* nodded in unison as they stuffed their faces.

With that, Isadora strode in the kitchen, slid open the glass door that led to the deck, seized Amanda in her arms, and stomped off to her own bedroom, kicking the door shut behind her. She was outraged at all these people who were feeding off her, living off her, while she wrote to support them, and her baby cried. Her heroine was dying in childbirth (she was in the midst of writing the very death scene), but she had survived into a more complex destiny: to be writing of a dying heroine while nursing a living child. She was angry at the "help" (misnomer though that was), but whenever she had the baby in her arms, she marveled: marveled at how the crying stopped with the warmth of her body, marveled at the efficiency with which Amanda sucked, sucked, sucked, as if sucking were all there was to do in the world, marveled at the shell-pink eyelids, the pink toes that had never touched the ground, the impenetrable sea-blue of the infant eyes.

Isadora was cruelly tugged between the book and baby: when she was with her baby, she wanted never to return to her book, and when she was with her book, she resented the baby's cry that made her breasts leak. And yet, with her daughter in her arms, she felt she was passing on a legacy of working women—all mothers are working women—who go from one sort of labor to another, with never enough time for either, and yet with undiminished goodwill toward their children.

Who can say which labor is more important? The two should be reciprocal—one to bring the next generation into the world and one to sustain it when it arrives. But society has arranged that both these labors be unduly hard for women because they are largely unrecognized and because this world is still arranged for the benefit of men, for the benefit of men's lives.

Isadora nursed Mandy, first at one breast, then at the other. While she nursed, she thought of Marietta Robusti, La Tintoretta, dying in childbirth upstairs on a yellow legal pad in her study. Breasts leaking with milk, alive with anger and with love, Isadora chronicled the death of another woman artist. She had to invent the scene totally—for only the barest of facts of La Tintoretta's life were known. Favorite of her father, considered as good a painter as Jacopo, she was so indispensable in his atelier (or else he was so in love with her) that the great Tintoretto allowed her to marry only upon the condition that she remain part of his household, not of her husband's. What a classic patriarch maneuver! To keep the married daughter castled in his studio, to keep the matron a virgin, to defeat the rival lover by holding close his beloved little girl.

But the ploy did not work. The worm got into Eden anyway— the worm in the form of an errant, wriggling sperm. Childbirth was a matter of life and death in sixteenth-century Venice—and death won. The story had everything: life, death, art, history, feminism, the oedipal myth—and Isadora seized the theme as her own, inventing the details where none were known. The best subjects for historical novels are those characters about whom just a little is known, but much remains to be invented, for then the imagination flies free.

Marietta lay dying. Amanda was sucking. Amanda literally took in with her mother's milk the fate of all women, of all women artists: from La Tintoretta to her own mother. If she knew any of this she did not say. She only closed those mauve eyelids in perfect satiation, fluttered the long auburn lashes on the shell-pink cheeks, gave a ferocious intestinal gurgle and released a hot wad of yellowish-green breast-fed baby shit into her infant-size Pamper. Isadora changed her, wiping the rosy little anus with oil and lotion, putting on a new Pamper, then letting her own mind wander back to the deathbed scene on her desk.

"Is the baby through yet?" came the nasal voice of Mary Hogg.

"She's fed and changed," Isadora answered through the closed door.

Amanda slept. Isadora got up and carefully handed the bundle to Mary Hogg. Then she went back upstairs to complete Marietta's death.

In due time, both Mary Hogg and Lilyanne were fired—the former without, the latter with, regrets. When Lilyanne went, Josh and Isadora themselves cleaned the kitchen from top to bottom. In the pantry closet they found, secreted behind the whole-wheat flour and safflower oil and bran, boxes of Swansdown cake flour, confectioners' sugar, and cans of Crisco.

"I'll be damned," Josh said. "No wonder the 'health food' tasted so good."

8

The Naked Nanny or Amanda's Side of the Story

> The little world of childhood with
> its familiar surroundings is a model
> of the greater world. The more
> intensively the family has stamped
> its character upon the child,
> the more it will tend to feel
> and see its earlier miniature world
> again in the bigger world of
> adult life. Naturally, this is not
> a conscious, intellectual process.
> —C. G. JUNG

> A child's among you takin' notes,
> And faith he'll prent it.
> —*On the late Capt. Grose's*
> *Peregrinations through Scotland 1793*

THE current nanny was Alva Libbey, also known as Nurse Librium—she was that slow. Before her there had been Rae-from-Santa-Fe, a vague vegetarian, and before her Cicely from Stoke-on-Trent, the insufferably bossy English girl who had run over Isadora's beloved Chekarf, and then run off with the carpenter who'd built Isadora's new studio. Before that, there had been dolorous Olive (who hated her name and consequently asked that she be called Livi).

Olive was a ruddy-faced, sullen, overgrown adolescent of twenty-eight or so whose fondest wish was to earn enough money to be "audited" by the Church of Scientology so that she could become a "clear." While Isadora was away on a book tour (Mandy was then two), Olive fell in love (by telephone) with Isadora's one and only totally deranged fan—a woman Isadora had been eluding for years because of her conviction that she was Isadora's long-lost daughter (born when Isadora was fourteen). Somehow, this woman—who previously had only written long, rambling letters —managed to secure Isadora's unlisted phone number. (This fan was, in fact, the reason Isadora no longer answered "crazy mail.") Not only did Olive talk to her, but she encouraged her to the point of seduction, so that soon the two women were fantasizing together and engaging in mutual masturbation by telephone.

Josh and Isadora were in Chicago one night when Isadora called home to ask how the baby was.

"The baby's fine," Olive said, "but I'm in love."

"Oh, that's nice," said Isadora. "With whom?"

"With Beryl Springer, your daughter."

"Oh god—" Isadora said, "how did she ever *find* you?"

"She just called one night, desperate for her mother—and since you weren't here, I thought I'd talk to her. She was terribly lonely. Well, one thing led to another and we fell in love. We've consummated it by telephone. Isadora, it's something you haven't written about in any of your books—but it *is* possible."

"Spare me the details. Just take care of the baby until I get home."

Olive, of course, had to be fired. The phone line had to be changed—and Beryl, a *bona fide* psychotic who had somehow managed to find out everything about Isadora's life—including her credit-card numbers—went on a shopping spree and charged thousands of dollars of merchandise and hotel bills to Isadora's American Express number. Had Olive given her the number as a token of love? The whole situation was so bizarre that you couldn't even use it in a novel, Isadora thought—but it was true, truth being, as everyone knows, stranger than fiction.

Before Olive, there had been Bertha-Belle, an elderly black lady from Georgia who was not only taking care of Amanda but all of South Norwalk, and who managed to inflate the food bills to triple the usual, although there was never anything to eat in the house. Bertha-Belle was loving with the baby though, and she was motherly and protective toward Isadora. Or did Isadora keep her only because she claimed she had the power to pray books up the bestseller list? Writers are strange creatures who will put up with almost any interruption in their lives if the promise of a great character or magic in helping them write are also proffered. And Bertha-Belle was a great character who promised such magic. A hefty *café au lait* lady who wore white turbans and white polyester uniforms, Bertha-Belle was by her own admission a former numbers runner and a drunk who had been converted to the Way of the Lord.

She rocked that baby in her powerful arms—and she was a fount of misinformation on health matters. She'd grease Amanda when her nose was stuffed because she averred that "colds hate grease." She warned of drinking too much grapefruit juice because "grapefruit thin de blood." Her favorite food, she said—with no antisemitism whatever—was "Jew food," by which she meant the greasiest of chopped liver, and Nova Scotia on bagels absolutely encrusted with cream cheese.

But Bertha-Belle's most endearing trait was her ability to communicate with the Lord as if by walkie-talkie. She knew what God was thinking at any given moment. She knew His will. She knew what He wanted her to earn, what days off He had ordained for her, what sort of car He meant for her to drive (a white Cadillac), what sort of coat He meant for her to wear (white mink), what sort of seats He intended her to have in airplanes (first class). God was her auto mechanic, too; when the car stalled on the road, Bertha-

162

Belle prayed it back to health. She could also heal headaches (by sending the pain "back to the pit where it come from"), and occasionally read minds. She was undeniably psychic—though often in a most self-serving manner.

Next to her, Alva Libbey was a bore. (Next to Bertha-Belle, *everyone* was a bore.) Bertha was a black queen and Alva was white trash. She pronounced tomatoes "tomatehs." She walked like a puppet held up by a string at the small of her back. Her face was long and thin and her nose was hooked. Despite her obvious unattractiveness, she primped and preened before the mirror like a starlet about to make her debut on the "Tonight" show. She was also mad about perfumes like Evening in Paris, which on her smelled like Night in Norwalk.

Nurse Librium mixed up the names of Isadora's boyfriends— which, admittedly, wasn't hard to do—and when she didn't mix them up, she neglected to give messages at all. Weeks later, she would say, when queried, "Oh, *that's* right, I *do* remember someone calling that night—but what*ever* was his name?"

Alva's habits in the kitchen were also bizarre. She bought foods in odd quantities: three juice oranges, one grapefruit, two dozen chicken legs. She filled the freezer with tiny beef patties she spelled "hambergers," and every night of the week she made one for herself and one for Amanda till the child would *eat* nothing but hamberger. (Isadora even ventured the thought that she'd only eat it if it was *spelled* that way.)

Alva's idea of vegetables was sweet potato and white potato, or peas and sweet potato. Isadora could never get it across to her that two starches did not make for a nutritionally balanced meal. But what did it really *matter* what Alva cooked? She cooked it for so many hours that no nourishment whatever remained anyway. Sometimes she'd put suppers on the stove at two P.M. and serve them at 5:30. She covered all her own food with A-1 sauce, tabasco, ketchup, and chutney; Isadora would have done the same if she'd had to eat Alva's cooking.

Isadora was traumatized enough by all these nannies, but what about Amanda? People kept disappearing from her life. She'd no sooner build an attachment than some catastrophe would intervene—whether true love or Scientology—and she and her mother would be alone again. The hot-and-cold-running nannies had been bad enough when Josh was there, but now that he wasn't, poor Amanda was making do as best she could. She held on to her rituals: the bath, the Muppets, the bedtime recital of the day's activities. She was a happy child—full of bounce and joy—but she was also angry about all these changes in her life and she expressed her anger by bossing people around—as if that way she could control an increasingly uncontrollable world. Isadora knew damn well that she and her friends rationalized to themselves about divorce and what it was doing or not doing to their kids. Outwardly the kids got used to the alternate weekends, never seeing Daddy and Mommy together unless they were fighting, and negotiating the treacherous shoals of boyfriends and girlfriends appearing on weekends to woo them with undeserved toys. But there was no denying that these precious children of divorce received a notion of themselves that was inappropriate to their tender years. Alternately fought over and treated like burdens, how could they not feel somehow self-accusatory, and self-doubting?

From time to time Isadora would call Josh and plead with him about what the separation was doing to Amanda.

"Can't we try again—for her sake?" she'd say.

"For your sake, you mean."

"I don't know why we have to put Amanda through this," she'd say.

"Because we have to."

"But do we?"

"I care about Amanda just as much as you do. I love her as much as you do and *I* have to do this," Josh would say.

"Why?" Isadora would say.

"Because," Josh would say, "I don't have to account to you anymore."

"You're a selfish goddamned bastard!" Isadora would scream as the whole conversation degenerated into a shouting match. He'd hang up. Then she'd call him back. She'd scream and hang up. Then he'd call her back. He'd apologize. She'd apologize. And they'd both hobble away clutching their vitals.

Isadora couldn't understand why they were doing this. They both *did* love Amanda. They had made Amanda as a bond of flesh between them. Amanda knew this intuitively as children somehow always do, and she lost no opportunity in reminding them.

When Daddy came to the house, she tried to get them to hug each other as they had when she was a baby.

"Hug Mommy, hug Mommy," Amanda would say.

And, sheepishly, Josh would hug his two ladies, then quickly draw away. It was excruciating. Sometimes Isadora had the sense that Josh had to reject her, the way an adolescent has to reject a parent. It was an exercise, a phase he had to go through—but when he emerged from it, would he be sorry? Isadora didn't know. She supposed a time would come when Josh would understand all that he had thrown away and be sorry, but when that time came, would she still want him back? Probably not. The orbits would have shifted, some suns would have waned and died, and the whole galaxy would appear quite different. Relationships between men and women seemed, if left to themselves, to go through metamorphoses rather like cosmic creations. They flamed at birth, then cooled, then began the long trek toward entropy. That was why families could not be built upon the vagaries of passion alone. Passion was too unpredictable a force. Passion was too unreliable.

Isadora didn't know what she thought about passion anymore. She was *for* it—clearly it was the pulse of the universe—but how could you indulge your passions and also raise children? Sometimes she thought that the reason her generation was forever committed to alternate weekends was that only *that* emolument of divorce returned romantic passion to domestic life.

Had they not been prepared for children—any of them? Having waited so long to have kids and having grown up in such small families themselves (with no little brothers or sisters to raise), had the demands of child-rearing hit them squarely between the eyes and made them blame each other—rather than Mother Nature, whose "fault" it all was?

And yet what gave life more joy, more meaning, more pleasure, than children?

Putting Amanda to bed each night, Isadora reviewed the day with her.

"Let's talk about my birthday, Mommy," Amanda would say. And then they would make elaborate plans involving animals and presents, balloons and cakes, musical accompaniments, clowns, costumes, and flowers.

Sometimes these bedtime conversations turned eschatological, and Amanda would ask whether God was a boy or a girl, whether dead people could still see us, and whether Grandpa Stoloff was in heaven.

Isadora opted for God as a woman, but she told Amanda, in all fairness, that not everyone believed God to be a woman. Amanda claimed to remember the time before she was born, which Isadora, as a good Wordsworthian Romantic, thoroughly understood.

165

"Before I was born, Mommy, I was up on the cloud with all the other babies. Then I got born. You were on that cloud before you were born, too, Mommy."

"Did we know each other on that cloud?"

"Sure. God wouldn't have had us born as mother and daughter if we didn't know each other on that cloud."

What had the little redhead done to deserve two parents who battled and split before she could even get her feet off that cloud and onto the ground? She was still trailing clouds of glory. Sometimes it seemed that Isadora's generation had babies as a *prelude* to splitting. Seized by the biological imperative in their early or mid-thirties, they grabbed a suitable partner and reproduced; then, when the troubles came, they went their separate ways, resuming their truncated adolescent lives, but now, with the impediments of children, nannies, school bills, houses. Were they perennially adolescents—Josh's generation, those flower children of the sixties, and Isadora's, those baby-boomers? What would *their* children think of them? Amanda's college class, the class of 2000, the alternate-weekend kids, the children of nuclear fear—what on earth would they think of their parents (assuming, as you really *couldn't* anymore, that the world and all its apparatus—college graduations, etc.—would still be there for them in twenty years or so)? These little children had been forced to grow up too early—just as their parents had been kept in adolescence too long. Would they get ulcers at twenty, or revert to some philosphy that would make John Calvin seem liberal? They were wise little souls, Amanda's contemporaries. They talked about divorces the way Isadora's generation had talked about Howdy Doody. But underneath all that precocity, they were just little kids. They adjusted to the alternate weekends, to the divorces, to the girlfriends and boyfriends, but when all was said and done, they were being given a curious preparation for life.

One day, Isadora wandered out of her study and down to the kitchen (to get yet another cup of coffee) and she overheard Mandy and Ishmael playing in the guest room downstairs.

Ishmael was a tough little tank of a kid, rough-and-tumble, and the son of the lady friend of Josh's who had caused Isadora such grief in the first days of their separation. He and Mandy had become friends because his mother was Josh's lover, but nonetheless the kids had hit it off terrifically. (This was another of the vagaries of divorce—do the kids get along? In adolescence you only had to worry about your *own* feelings; in second adolescence, you also had to worry about your kid's.)

"Now, you be the daddy," Mandy said, "and let's pretend we're getting divorced. I'll be the mommy. I'll cry on the telephone."

Mandy picked up an imaginary telephone.

"Boo-hoo, boo-hoo," she cried into it. "Now you cry, too," she instructed Ishmael.

"Boo-hoo," he cried, obligingly.

"Now, you call your lawyer," Amanda said.

"What's a lawyer?" asked Ishmael.

"Someone that puts bad guys in jail, like a policeman," Amanda said.

"Oh," said Ishmael.

Isadora passed the guest room without appearing to eavesdrop. Tears were in her eyes. She brushed them away. Mandy often brought tears to her eyes. She had cried nursing her, had cried when she bought her the first pair of white Bonnie-Doon ankle socks, had cried when she bought her her first English Chesterfield coat with black velvet collar.

Mandy looked so much like Isadora, had such similar verbal abilities, such similar precocity and energy, that it was dangerous how much Isadora identified with her.

"Boo-hoo, boo-hoo-boo-hoo," she heard again. Apparently Ishmael had fallen in love with his own boo-hooing and had resumed it in very loud tones, almost as if he were imitating a police siren.

"You can stop crying now," she heard Mandy ordering. "Only cry when I *tell* you to cry. That's how it will be a *real* pretend divorce."

"Oh well, Isadora thought, climbing the stairs to her study, maybe Mandy is better prepared for life than I thought.

Mandy had no trouble ordering little boys around. She was absolutely clear on the fact that *her* needs came first. Isadora, on the other hand, *still* had trouble with this. To her own detriment, she tended to put everyone's needs ahead of her own: Josh's when they had lived together, Mandy's—now that Mandy was here— not to mention the needs of her various crazy boyfriends.

Suddenly, walking upstairs to her studio, she thought again of her grandfather and the novel she had wanted to write about him. She thought of the three generations of Russian-Jewish-Americans: Mandy, playing Divorce in Fairfield County, Connecticut; Isadora and her sisters playing Running Away from the Nazis on the Upper West Side of Manhattan; and Grandpa Stoloff as a child in Odessa, dreaming of America and escape as he stuffed a dried pea into the spigot of the family samovar.

He was only three and a half or so—Mandy's age—when, in the story he had so loved to tell over and over, he took a dried split pea (one that had somehow eluded the soup) and worked it up in that aimless way children have, into the spigot of the samovar. His elder sisters all arrived for tea—and lo and behold, the samovar did not work. His mother tried. His father tried. His sisters tried. But the samovar was mysteriously dry. Little Schmuel shuffled around in the corner, wearing his worn high-button shoes, and a guilty look on his baby face.

What could have happened? the grown-ups all wondered. What on earth could have happened?

"Maybe a pea got in," Schmuel averred. Whereupon the adults rained blows upon his poor bewildered child's shoulders.

"How the devil did they know it was me?" he always asked, mischievously, when he told this story. "How the devil did they know?"

What would Amanda remember for *her* grandchildren—assuming that she (and the planet) got past graduation in 2000 and continued well into the twenty-first century—to 2040, say—by which time her progeny would have their own progeny. She wouldn't have the memories her mother had—the giant balloons being blown up on Seventy-seventh Street on the eve of Thanksgiving, the game of eluding the Nazis which Isadora and her sisters played in the linen closet—but she would have her own set of haunting images.

Would she remember Daddy coming to visit on Serpentine Hill Road and then leaving again and again? Would she remember her ancient great-grandfather Stoloff—who, just a wink of time before, had been a baby himself—painting her portrait when she was only a tiny child? Would she remember the divorce Olympics —the crying on the telephones, the shouting in the bedroom, Mommy and Daddy screaming behind locked doors? Would she remember the nannies—from Mary Hogg to Bertha-Belle to Nurse Librium? Isadora was reasonably sure she would remember Cicely from Stoke-on-Trent. She had stayed the longest: the others' tenure had been very brief.

Cicely had arrived when Mandy was just past two, and had stayed until she was just past three—departing, in fact, a little while after her parents split. That was a real trauma—for Cicely was Amanda's Mary Poppins, the nanny you dream of and idealize when you are grown—and she had had the bad faith to leave two months after Josh and Isadora broke up.

Isadora had found Cicely in London. It was not long after Bertha-Belle's food-buying habits had been discovered, and not long after dolorous Olive had tied the knot with Beryl Springer. Isadora had had to go to London to negotiate a prospective film deal (a BBC producer wanted to make a miniseries about Marietta Robusti and Isadora was to write it), and since she and Josh were currently sans nanny, she figured she would give the famed NNEBs of England a tumble. (NNEB was short for National Nursery Education Board—for only in England was nannying still considered an honorific profession.)

Isadora got a list of nanny agencies from a British friend, and one day, sitting in a splendid mirrored suite at the Savoy, before a cart of gorgeous crustless Oscar Wildean cucumber-and-butter sandwiches, she interviewed a motley parade of English girls, who all came equipped with a National Nursery Education Board degree, and were all dying to go to the New World.

One was a timorous blonde with albino eyelashes (who also looked distinctly pregnant). Her name was Arabella and she squeaked like a mouse. One was an Irish wench who confessed under duress that she had a boyfriend in America who studied at NYU—but that she had absolutely no intention of getting married. One was a well-born lass from Oxfordshire named Sophie who appeared to be fleeing a lecherous stepfather (as in some eighteenth-century saga). And one was Cicely from Stoke-on-Trent.

Cicely was red-haired, buxom and sloe-eyed. She had what appeared to be a Heidelberg dueling scar on her cheek from some mysterious accident, but this somehow only made her sexier. She wore spike heels, a frilly white blouse, and a black flannel skirt that seemed to have been shrunk onto her body.

"How do you feel about marriage?" Isadora asked. That was the first question she always asked.

"Oh, I don't think I want to get married until I'm thirty or so," Cicely said, tossing her marmalade mane.

Famous last words.

A few weeks later, Cicely arrived in America on a Laker flight, with a temporary visa in her pocket. She took to the baby immediately, bringing Amanda puppets she had sewn with her own hands. She cooked steak-and-kidney pies, onion tarts, and blood puddings, and she assembled fabulous trifles out of ladyfingers, clotted cream, and strawberry jam. She was Brisk, British, and Organized. She made Isadora think of the glories of the British Empire, and of course she won Amanda's heart at once.

Isadora and Josh breathed a great, shared sigh of relief. They had found Mary Poppins. But Mary Poppins is notorious for appearing and disappearing at will.

Cicely did a brilliant job for the first six months. ("Brill," as the Sloane Rangers say.) Amanda adored her, adored her brisk British discipline, adored her cooking, her accent, her elaborate way of making up her face. And Cicely was devoted to Amanda, too. Baby and Nanny were clearly in love. But then construction began on Isadora's new studio and into their island paradise came Carl the Carpenter. You could almost see Cicely suck in her breath and mutter, "O Brave New World that has such people in't," when Carl first crossed their threshold.

He was the sort of dumb California beachboy hunk an English girl adores—handlebar mustache, platinum-blond surfer hair, loutish male chauvinist ways. In his hand, he carried a six-pack. In his head, visions of big English tits. He would hang from the rafters wielding his great big hammer, and Cicely would flounce in, wearing her flannel nightgown, tits abounce underneath, and she would say, "Coffee anyone?"

Carl would salivate and smile: "Please."

"Black or white?" Cicely would sing. "One lump or two?"

This mating dance went on morning after morning as the office was framed, floored, roofed, outfitted with bookshelves, built-in desks, library ladders, balconies, and decks. Hammers rang in the house all day and hammers must have been ringing in Cicely's thighs too.

Carl hailed from Canoga Park and he was married (to a wife he did not love, Cicely informed Isadora), but he seemed to have a glad eye for the girls. Cicely was clearly mooning over him, but Isadora did not think things had got past the mooning stage— which only goes to show how wrong she can be.

Oh yes—there *was* the time that Cicely had asked Isadora whether she had ever been in love with a married man—but Isadora did not make the appropriate connection. She could be quite dense and naïve in her way. Her head was always so full of her own fantasies that she sometimes failed to see what was happening around her, in her own house. Anyway, things did not really come to a head until one ghastly day—the first day of spring it was, and just slightly before Isadora's birthday—when Cicely's love intersected with Chekarf's life.

Isadora was putting on her makeup—listening to the sounds of hammers ringing above her in the half-built studio—when she heard anguished barking, the unmistakable sound of tragedy in the driveway.

She ran out of the bathroom, a lipstick in hand, and at the front door collided with Cicely, who was sobbing uncontrollably.

"I wouldn't have hurt him for the world," she choked.

"Where *is* he?" Isadora demanded.

"There!" she cried, running past her into the house.

In the driveway, sat Chekarf, wearing a stunned expression on his wholly trustful face. He was a small, quizzical ball of white fur, oozing blood onto the asphalt of the driveway.

Isadora scooped him up in her arms, screaming for Josh to come, to come quickly, so that they could rush him to the vet's. At that very moment, Isadora saw her other baby, Amanda, sitting in the back of the same black Datsun that had just run over Chekarf. Amanda witnessed this mayhem calmly as two-year-olds tend to do. The significance dawns later.

"Where Cee gone?" she asked in her two-year-old cadences. Cee, being her name for Cicely.

Where indeed? Cee was having hysterics in the secretary's office, while the baby was stranded in the car, the dog was dying, and Isadora was realizing to her horror that she could not both hold Chekarf and rescue Amanda from her infant seat. The mortally wounded took precedence over the healthy.

"Wait a minute, darling," Isadora said, "Cee will come to get you."

"No—*you* get me, Mommy," Amanda said.

"I can't, darling. Chekarf is hurt."

"Chekarf *not* hurt," Isadora's daughter said, sweeping away death with a wave of her small pink hand.

Just then, Carl the carpenter appeared in the driveway.

"Carl—get the baby, will you? We have to rush to the vet's."

Carl opened the Datsun door and took Amanda in his arms; Josh emerged with the keys to the other car and they began their maddening trip through the winding Connecticut roads to the vet's—getting stuck behind trucks, behind cars that seemed driven by the lame, the halt, and the brain-damaged, behind earth-moving equipment, tractors, school buses.

"Oh God, God, God, let him be okay," Isadora said, looking down at Chekarf, her first baby, now six years old. Was she holding him right? Did he have internal injuries? Had he been run over, or only broken in a mendable way like a chipped cup?

"Let it be a broken paw," Isadora pleaded with the deity, "please only a broken paw." And she almost convinced herself, despite the blood that flowed over her brown leather jacket, despite the stunned expression in those eyes like wet Greek olives, despite the anguished howls and growls he uttered periodically before he lay still again, still again, still again.

"It will be okay, Chekarf my love," Isadora said. "It will be okay."

Josh swerved around a garbage truck, nearly colliding with an oncoming car. Isadora's own death seemed less important to her at that moment than Chekarf's.

That dog represented *her*—he was her alter ego—a bouncy little ball of fluff—cocky, yet vulnerable—sensitive, almost psychic, yet childlike in his willingness to trust. He was the Don Quixote of dogs, the Candide of canines, simultaneously the Portnoy of pooches—always jerking off on the sofa cushions until they were stiff. He was the first animal Isadora wholly loved, the first animal she trained (if you could call it that), the first animal who taught her about the bond between humans and other species.

Because of Chekarf, Isadora gave money to animal rights' groups, and picketed outside furriers' conventions. Because of Chekarf, Isadora wrote letters to congressmen deploring the baby seal slaughter, the dolphin slaughter, the slaughter of calves, and the confining of chickens to brightly lit coops where they laid eggs, day and night, until they dropped.

Because of Chekarf, Isadora knew that the souls of dogs and the souls of people partook of a great communal soul, that we were, on some level, all one being. Because of Chekarf, Isadora understood certain mysteries of the universe she had always scoffed at before.

Chekarf was her familiar, her friend, her reflection. Were she a witch, he would do her bidding. Was that why he had to be killed?

At the vet's, Chekarf let out another mournful howl, and then he was taken into the inner sanctum of the operating room. The vet, a nice, plain-faced young woman with ash-blond hair, advised Isadora and Josh to take a walk. They did.

Arm in arm, both trembling, they ambled down the Post Road, where the traffic was roaring by. Isadora thought of all the times they had brought Chekarf here and how happy he always was to go home. Would he this time? She thought of their big red mutt, Virginia Woof, who had come to them from the pound, almost dead from her various canine diseases, but who now stood an excellent chance of outliving Chekarf.

"Our first baby," Josh said. "I hope he makes it."

"God—I hope so."

Like Mandy, Chekarf was a pulsing flesh-and-blood link between them. They had not conceived him, perhaps, but they had raised him, trained him, loved him, slept with him. He had guarded their homes, slept between them in bed, watched them fuck, amused them with his antics, prompted them to invent a whole language of intimacy, jokes, songs, games. They had driven out in search of him at night when he strayed on the road; they had offered to get the bitch an abortion when he knocked up a neighbor's pet. (The offer was declined.) They had cuddled him, brushed him, bathed with him, picked off his ticks, powdered his fleas.

They walked mournfully back to the vet's office, both praying. When they came in, the vet was there to greet them.

"He died on the table," she said. "I think he was in deep shock when you brought him, but I had to probe his internal organs just to be sure. He had massive internal injuries. When I inserted a tube in his throat, it filled with blood. I'm sorry. There was nothing I could do to save him. Thank goodness it was so quick. I don't think he felt much after he was hit. He was in shock."

Isadora remembered the wide, staring eyes on the way to the vet's. Those pupils were a sure sign of shock. But if he had felt nothing, why those hideous howls and yelps? Chekarf had felt pain—not only pain, but betrayal—the betrayal of a small creature who depends on big creatures for life.

"What should we do with the body?" Isadora asked, feeling her heart go cold as a stone.

"We can send it to be cremated, if you wish."

Isadora looked at Josh.

"Yes," they both said in unison—because they could not bear looking at that broken body again. Isadora felt as she might have if it were her baby's broken body—the finality of rended flesh. How difficult to believe in spirit at such a time. What an abstraction spirit seems at that moment. And yet, what a lottery it was— flesh. Had the tires of the car swerved slightly, they would be taking their beloved bundle home.

They drove back to the house silenced by grief. Isadora's brown leather jacket was crusted with blood and bits of white fur clung to it. She vowed never to clean it. It smelled of Chekarf. She loved his smell as she loved the smell of Josh's armpits, the smell of Amanda's pee, the smell of the sweaty back of her baby's neck, all moist and pink. If flesh is merely a lesson, a way of learning spirit, why does it mark us so, why do we love it so? Why do we grow so attached to flesh if it is only a way station? And where is that world of pure spirit in which we do not grieve over mere flesh?

At home, Cicely was still sobbing and Amanda was toddling about, pursuing Virginia Woof. She did not instantly notice the absence of the other animal.

"I wouldn't have hurt him for the world," Cicely sobbed again, "not for the world."

Isadora wanted to murder the girl with her bare hands. She wanted to thrash her with a broom, or bring down a hot poker upon her head. Yet it was difficult to commit mayhem against somebody who sniveled so. At the very least, she wanted to take Amanda out of her care lest she kill *her,* too.

"If it weren't for Carl's wife," she sniveled, "Carl's wife."

"What on earth are you talking about?" Isadora demanded.

"She won't give him a divorce," Cicely whimpered. "She won't."

Was this her explanation for running over Chekarf? Dear God and Goddess—was Chekarf the sacrificial lamb to propitiate Cicely's prospective nuptials?

"What are you talking about?" Isadora asked again—but of course she knew.

"Carl and I are lovers," Cicely said primly, "and we wish to be married. We thought you'd disapprove."

So you ran over my dog, Isadora thought, but she was too kind, however, to actually say this to the miserable girl. After all, *anyone* can run over a small dog—or can they? Especially when a marriage is coming apart. Oh, especially then. That is when the animals always get it.

That night, it poured. A huge March rainstorm with sheets of water cascading down the plate-glass windows, drumming on the roof. It was the sort of night Chekarf hated to be out in, and Isadora thought she heard him scratching at the doors, as was his habit, streaking across the redwood decks from door to door until somebody heard his scratching and let him in.

"Poor Chekarf," she said to Josh as they drifted off that night.

"Chekarf's gone to a better place," said Josh. "Poor us."

And it was true that the death of the dog was the harbinger of the death of the marriage. Could they already have known it then? It was in the air like fallout; it was in the wind.

All that weekend, as they mourned their dog, they seemed to see him in all his favorite corners of the house. They went to a movie to get their minds off their grief and happened to pick a movie in which a dog died. They left in tears. They both felt haunted, spooked. First Papa, then Chekarf. Would God take Amanda next? No—just her parents' marriage. That was death enough.

Josh moved out in late July, but Cicely stayed on, taking ever greater and greater liberties with Carl in Isadora's house. In those days, Isadora was not wise to the importance of disciplining nannies and keeping aloof from "the help." In her disorder and sadness, she let Carl and Cicely take over as if they were the master and mistress of the house. And they moved right in. They began using the hot tub and sauna while Isadora was out for dinner, and even at times when she was home. Perhaps they were even fucking in the playroom when Mandy was asleep. If she lives to be a hundred, Isadora will never forget the sight of red-headed Cicely flouncing sauna-ward through the house wearing nothing but one of Isadora's own monogrammed bath sheets (*IWA* they all said in red letters). *The Naked Nanny,* Isadora thought. What a title for a porno film.

Every night Cicely made Carl dinner and set it before him in the dining room, and Isadora skulked off to her bedroom, dispossessed by her own "help." It was as if, having punished herself once by losing Josh, she was now punishing herself over and over again in various ways. Having shed Josh, she now had Carl as a pseudo-husband.

He was no prize. He stomped into the house smoking a cigar and carrying a six-pack. He sat down to his special meals of sirloin steak and french fries (he would not eat the veggies and brown rice that prevailed in the Wing-Ace household). Cicely waited on him, wearing the same flannel nightgown she had worn while wooing him with coffee. Better take off that nightgown, girl, Isadora thought. It was cute once, when it was novel, but now that you're an unwed wife, he'll tire of blue flannel.

Carl was already criticizing Cicely's cooking, criticizing her clothes and her figure, and thinking up new reasons daily why he needed money (to fix his truck, to pay for his kids' teeth, to take a room somewhere, and move out of the wife's). Cicely, who had no green card yet (it was being obtained, at great expense, by an immigration lawyer Isadora had hired), was paid in cold cash. Since she had no social-security number, she couldn't even put it in a bank account, so all her money was literally in her shoe box—where it was ever more and more available to Carl.

He spent it freely enough. He also amused himself on the construction site by singing the praises of Cicely in bed. Once, while Cee was at the beach with the baby, Isadora wandered into the half-built studio just in time to hear Carl boasting to his young assistant that he couldn't wait to "pump a load into" his "bitch" that night.

"Her tits stand way up—like marshmallows," the poetic fellow said. "Ya know when they stand up like that—even when the bitch is lyin' down?"

"Excuse me," Isadora said, as if she'd heard nothing, but Carl looked at her and his eyes said he knew she knew.

Carl could see that Isadora was distraught now that Josh was gone, and that she needed Cee more than ever. Instead of responding to the situation with kindness, Carl and Cee became ever more surly and demanding.

Every morning, Cee would peremptorily demand of Isadora: "Are you going to be in or out tonight?" Often Isadora didn't know—the vagaries of her social life were such that she couldn't really plan ahead—but it soon became a battle between Isadora and the nanny as to who was going out that night. Cicely pressured constantly for more nights off and Isadora, stranded far out in the country, without a husband or a support system of mothers, friends, acquaintances, was afraid to lose yet another nanny—so she gave in. She knew the girl was tyrannizing her, but she was too vulnerable at that point to draw the line, and Cicely moved right in to press her advantage. Oh, the vulnerability one has to people who take care of one's child even in the best of times! Oh, the hazards of being a single parent!

The showdown came one night when Cicely had been promised an extra weekend off. She was to leave on a Saturday after putting the baby to bed and return on the following Monday night. Her precious Carl from Canoga Park wanted to go hunting in the back woods of Vermont (Amanda called it "Termont") so he could kill animals with some of his loutish friends.

He arrived at Isadora's house about an hour early, parking his truck assertively in the driveway (making sure that it blocked all

176

the other cars). He sauntered into the kitchen clutching a six-pack, smoking a foul cigarillo, and muttering that he wanted his "bitch."

"Where's that fat English girl?" he said angrily to Isadora. "Where the hell is she! We're supposed to leave for Vermont."

"She's supposed to get the baby in bed before she goes," Isadora said. "That was the deal we made."

"Oh yeah?" said Carl. "Well, you work that girl to death and I'm *sick* of it—sick of it—do you hear?"

He strode to the stairwell and called up it.

"Cicely! Cicely! If you don't come this minute, I'm leaving without you!"

Now, Cicely had the baby in the bath, but she had heard her master's voice, so she ran to the stair railing and called down, in her sweetest and most English tones.

"I'm coming, darling. Just give me a moment, darling."

"God damn it," Carl said. "If you don't come now, I'm coming after you."

Carl climbed the stairs, stomped into the bathroom, and demanded that Cicely come at once.

Amanda sat there stunned, as the nanny begged and pleaded for more time and the boyfriend insisted that she go at once.

"I promised Isadora I'd get the baby ready for bed," she said.

"God damn it to hell," Carl said. "I'm sick of hearing what you promised Isadora. I'm sick of Isadora. I'm going without you."

And Cicely, torn between her hormones and her British sense of duty, got up, left the baby in the bathwater, and ran downstairs behind Carl (as Mary Poppins would *never* have done).

Seeing them come down, Isadora bolted upstairs to rescue her baby. Halfway there, she turned and said to them (with controlled fury):

"If you leave now, you can bloody well never come back."

"My pleasure, *Ms.* Wing," Carl said, with melodramatic irony. "I don't want to return to a house built with the royalties on dirty books."

So, he was a literary critic, too—this total illiterate. Isadora did not dignify his attack with a response. She merely continued up the stairs to find her daughter.

Amanda sat in the bath looking for all the world as Chekarf had when he waited on the pavement for Isadora to scoop him up.

"Where Cee gone? Where Cee gone?" Amanda asked.

"Cee has gone on her day off, darling," Isadora said, choking

177

on the words. Although she would have dearly loved to cry and scream, she put the whole effort of her being, all her concentration, into staying in one piece for Amanda, drying her, powdering her, reading her a story, doing the whole bedtime ritual. But Amanda was bewildered. "Where Cee gone?" she kept saying.

"Cee had a fight with Mommy and she left," Isadora said.

"Like Daddy?" asked Amanda.

Isadora didn't know how to answer that one. She never wanted to lie to Amanda, but she did conceive it to be her duty to soften the blows.

"Darling, Cee had to go hunting with Carl. She misses you a lot, I know."

"Like Daddy?" Amanda asked again.

"Yes," Isadora said. "Daddy misses you, too."

"Is Daddy hunting, too?" Amanda asked.

"I suppose he is," Isadora said sadly, realizing this was Saturday night and Josh probably *was* "hunting."

"Why do grown-ups always fight?" Amanda asked.

"I don't know," Isadora said. "Maybe they're not really grown-ups yet."

"But they *have* to be grown-ups," Amanda insisted.

"I know, darling," Isadora said.

"Because I'm the kid," said Amanda. "I'm the kid—right, Mommy?"

Cicely and Carl, plighted their troth that weekend. (Had the wife suddenly given her consent?) Now that Cicely had hopes of becoming a citizen and no longer needed Isadora to get her a green card, she never apologized—though she came back, briefly, to get her shoe box of money.

In the battle between hormones and duty, Isadora sadly reflected, hormones nowadays always won. It also never failed to occur to her that she *herself* had helped to aid and abet this great validation of the female hormones. But once children arrived on the scene, the battle between hormones and duty became more intense than ever—and more imponderable. It was a true conundrum, an insoluble mystery: raging hormones sometimes led to children, and children, like it or not, led to duty.

After Cicely abdicated the Nanny-for-a-year throne, Rae-from-Santa Fe arrived. She was a disaster, leaving pots to boil over on the stove and bathtubs to overflow. She was so absentminded that Isadora feared leaving the baby with her and eventually she, too, had to be fired.

Then came Alva Libbey, the current treasure. At least Amanda knew that her mother was always there. And Isadora knew that she was Amanda's forever and ever. Whether on earth or on that cloud full of babies, Isadora and Amanda were linked forever. That was all Isadora knew. Was it enough?

And what would Amanda remember for her grandchildren? Would she remember the nannies quitting? Daddy leaving? Or would she have some totally different random stray memory—something equivalent to Grandpa Stoloff's samovar that maybe a pea got in? If so, what would it be? How could a mere mother know?

9

My Old Flame

My old flame,
I can't even think
of his name.
—*popular song*

I will be good.
—QUEEN VICTORIA

SOMETIME before Christmas of that ghastly year, Isadora met an old friend. She met him at a party in what was, that year, New York's trendiest disco—a place called Hades—whose decor featured caverns, artificial flames, and waiters dressed as lurking demons. The occasion was a party in honor of a friend's book. *The Demon Lover*, it was called, but the title evoked more dignity than the book deserved, for it was merely a trashy "Hollywood novel," that sort of *roman à clef* in which all the noble Romans are shown to have feet of clay (or more likely, penises of clay, not to mention other glaring defects).

The party was very posh and "A" list. Lurking in the dark caverns of the disco were some of the people presumed to be in the book (who presumably wished they weren't) and other people presumed *not* to be in the book (who presumably wished they *were*).

Isadora wore what was required by the invitation—"demonic attire"—though not all the other guests complied. Consequently, she was looking bewitching (and haunted) in a black velvet hooded cape, a high-necked black velvet gown with leg-o'-mutton sleeves, and a high peaked witch's hat. She felt a little silly in this getup, but then she always felt a little silly these days because she was brokenhearted and on the prowl. She went to *everything*—all the parties she had previously refused—because it was common wisdom that a lady bereft of spouse did not stay home and mope. So she went out and glittered. But in her heart, she moped; and those who were not insensitive to paradox could tell. In her eyes was a look as stunned and betrayed as Chekarf's, as he sat on the black asphalt of the driveway. For the truth was that Isadora had given her whole heart to Josh, as fully as a little dog gives his whole heart to his mistress (she finally knew the meaning of that old canard—to love "not wisely but too well"), and when it turned out that Josh had held back a piece of himself, many pieces of himself, in fact, she was as stunned as a struck dog. Her eyes bore the kind of pained and hunted look which only a rabbi or a Nobel laureate would be dumb enough to confuse with unbridled lust—although, it is true, there is a kind of lust which is born mainly of broken-heartedness.

Isadora was mildly besieged at this party, despite the dim lights and the demonic trappings. A young journalist made lascivious advances; then an old mogul; then a middle-aged lawyer. Broken-hearted promiscuity breeds brokenhearted promiscuity. During this brief (yet seemingly interminable) period of her life, Isadora was so promiscuous that she had a why-the-hell-not attitude toward every male she met—and boy, could they tell! She'd try almost anyone *once*. But she was likely not to return their calls after that. She went through men as if she were going through the yellow pages, trying everyone's number, then hanging up without concluding a deal, so to speak. She thought herself fickle, heartless. Not true at all. She was merely heartsick, heart-weary, heartworn. She wanted her heart never to get involved in fucking again—merely her cunt—though she knew in her sane moments that the best fucking comes when heart and cunt are one.

The old friend was the antidote to all this poisonous promiscuity. He approached her through a crowd of would-be suitors and he said, without novelty:

"Do you remember me?"

She did. Remembered the face, but not the name. It was a nice face, the face of an androgynous angel painted by Bronzino: golden skin, soulful hazel eyes, tousled salt-and-pepper hair which boyishly covered his forehead. He was small and wiry, and nattily dressed in a white tux of the thirties, and on his head he wore a pair of devilish red horns. They were made of long, slender extrusions of foam rubber and were attached to his forehead with spirit gum. From under his white tuxedo jacket projected a wicked red velvet tail. The outfit was riveting. The horns swayed in the breeze.

"My name is Kevin Karnofsky," he said. "We went to high school together. I took you to hear Leadbelly in the Village during Christmas vacation in 1958.

Suddenly, she remembered. She remembered a slight fellow who used to hang around her parents' living room, never daring to make a pass. She remembered a guy who took her out several times and never even kissed her. She remembered no fumbling in the dark.

Now, even in the fifties, dear younger readers, there *was* sex. But Kevin had not discovered it. Or else he could only "do it" with low-class girls from the outlying boroughs. Isadora was too posh a princess, too much the Marjorie Morningstar in her family's triplex full of Oriental antiques and family art to be fumbled (or fumble-able) by the likes of Kevin Karnofsky from Brooklyn.

"Do you remember?" he asked again.

"I certainly do," Isadora said, as hundreds of high-school memories flooded her brain. What a comforting idea—to go back to high school! To start all over, as it were, with a boy who represented a path not taken. To start all over and maybe get it right this time.

Banished were her first husband, her second husband, her third husband. Gone were all the fumblers in the dark of her parents' living room. Gone was Steve Applebaum who, when she was thirteen, had taught her the subtle art of mutual masturbation and unwittingly induced a massive case of *anorexia nervosa*. Gone was Ron Perkoff (whom she and her best friend, Pia, naturally called Jerkoff). Gone were the assorted Florentines of her twenty-third summer. Gone was Charlie Fielding, the conductor who loved his baton. Gone was Adrian Goodlove, the demonic lover of her Viennese summer (who had proved not only callous and cruel but impotent). Gone were the analysts she messed around with during her analytic phase. Gone was the despairing promiscuity of this past year. She would start again. She would, like Queen Victoria, be good.

"I remember that concert well," Isadora said, "as if it were yesterday."

He looked at her intently with those hazel eyes and something in her melted. What she had missed most that fall was a sense of family, a *mishpocheh*—and Kevin, though dimly remembered, represented that. No more strange beds, strange locutions, strange smells. She would go back to Music and Art and start again.

Ah, high school, when all possibility is trembling on the brink! Isadora remembered herself in high school—brash, talented, dying to stand out in a crowd, but also terrified and covering her terror with bravado—just like today! (Do we never grow up—not even at thirty-nine?) She suddenly felt an irrepressible desire to leave the party with Kevin, to drive him up to Connecticut and pamper him all weekend. Once on her own home turf, she was an expert seductress, but making the initial move still scared her. Besides, she had already committed herself to go home (or at least *out*) with the lascivious young journalist. What the hell, she thought. Life's too short to be ruined by such casual commitments. She excused herself from the crowd of would-be suitors, signaled to Kevin that she would return momentarily, and headed for the ladies' room.

It was a demonic ladies' room, done in smoked mirrors and flame-red silken drapes. In it, several hardworking ladies from the publishing world were powdering their shiny noses. This party was work, not fun, for most of the invitees—perhaps for Isadora, too.

After peeing and washing up, reapplying makeup and brushing her mane of blond hair, Isadora extracted one of her business cards from her purse (they were engraved Tiffany ones—ordered shortly after Isadora had made the fatal error of going to Tokyo on a lecture tour *without* business cards) and wrote upon it:

"Kevin, dear—if you can possibly have a drink with me after this fiasco, please stay and I'll try to shake the goon I'm promised to. If not, please swear you'll call me tomorrow? Love, Isadora White." (She deliberately used her maiden name to trigger his nostalgia.)

Then she scrawled her phone number across the bottom of the card (which only bore her name and address), and hastened out of the ladies' lair to look for Kevin in the demonic gloom.

Since her metamorphosis into a "free woman," these business cards had come in handier than they would have *even* in Tokyo. She would often go to a party with one man, meet someone else who interested her, and leave a little note for the new man on her engraved card. She had become brazen about it, scrawling such things as "You are beautiful—call me!" or "You, of all people, must have my unlisted number" or "Let's collaborate." In her younger days, Isadora never would have dared so brash a stratagem. But by now she had a clear sense that her notoriety might be off-putting to men, and thirty-nine years of wooing and warring with the opposite sex had taught her so much about their vulnerabilities that she knew there wasn't a man in the world who didn't need encouragement—and plenty of it. If you could live without men—fine. You need never stoop to stratagems like this. You could be haughty and pure as you went to the movies with women friends and hugged your vibrator at night. But Isadora liked men, found them indispensable in the sack, and at thirty-nine she was resigned to treating them like the fragile sex—because she knew what all wise women know: they *are*.

She spotted Kevin, sidled up to him, and slipped the scrawled card in his breast pocket.

186

This maneuver delighted her, titillated her, even amazed her, almost as though she were a character in one of those old romantic comedies where Cary Grant dispatches the waiter across the restaurant with a rose and a note and a magnum of vintage champagne.

Kevin was delighted, too. (Any guy who wore a "retro" tux would *have* to be.) He extracted the note from his pocket, perused it, looked at her, and beamed. His horns quaked.

He stuck one thumb up and gestured to her in that ancient Roman signal meaning: "Spare the gladiator." She nodded, smiled, and went off to inform the young journalist about a sudden medical emergency that had arisen (her dog? her kid?) in frozen Connecticut.

She and Kevin met at the cloakroom and beat a hasty retreat. While they were walking down windy Third Avenue, in their black, white, and red getups, he turned to her and said:

"You're as beautiful as you were in high school—and you don't look much older either."

Then he touched her cheek with the flat of his hand—in a gesture that was halfway between pat and stroke.

She felt protected, taken care of—all the things she had not felt with any of the men she had known this past fall.

"Do you want to pretend to deliberate by having a drink?" she asked. "Or do you want to come right home with me?"

"How do you suppose I'd answer that question?" Kevin asked. "My old love from high school inviting me home . . . do you suppose I'd say no?"

"Well, good—because my kid is with her father this weekend . . ."

"And my kid happens to be with his mother . . ."

"So our weekends are already synchronized," Isadora said. "Do you suppose that's an omen?" For she had often wondered at what point in a relationship between two divorced people they decided to synchronize their alternate weekends. What a great statement of commitment that was! She and Kevin would never have to make that awesome decision. They were *already* synchronized.

Isadora led the way to the stygian New York garage where she had QUIM parked.

She cashed in her ticket and was told "Twenny dollars" by a rather stoned-looking black garage attendant with one hoop earring in his left ear and a large scythe-shaped scar on his left cheek.

187

"Is that for the whole car, or just the hubcaps?" she asked.

"You funny, mama," the dude said, not without a hint of menace.

Kevin laughed.

"You were always the funniest girl in high school," he said.

"Was I?" Isadora asked incredulously. She remembered being so conscious of her various pubescent angsts that she hardly remembered her ability to make all her dates (and her girl friends) laugh uproariously. But Kevin reflected back to her all the nice things about herself that she had forgotten. The wanton humor, the emotional openhandedness. Even then she was too much of the naïf, trusting that her generosity would inspire the same in others—which it did not always accomplish. She gave and gave and gave—and often got socked in the teeth for it, but that did not make her stop giving. Was she a masochist or a poet? Or were the two interchangeable, perhaps?

"You were hilarious," Kevin was saying just at the moment QUIM, the Silver Nazi, arrived above ground from the pit. Isadora saw Kevin's expression change slightly as he took in the fact that she drove this expensive German vehicle with vanity plates.

"Wow," he said.

"Merely the official car of the S.S.," she said. "Wait till you see my house. I even have crematoria."

He laughed.

"No, not really, but I *do* have a sauna."

They drove up to Connecticut. Or rather, Kevin drove. Isadora was still too acutely conscious of all the things Josh had accused her of—second fiddle, house husband, her supposed "domination" of him—to allow *herself* to drive a new man up to Connecticut, though she loved to drive.

Kevin drove very slowly. (Why have all the men in my life driven either too slowly or too fast? Isadora wondered. Is there no happy medium?) He also delighted in working the windows, the radio, delighted in switching the speakers from back to front, front to back, delighted in playing the tape deck.

Isadora navigated, reminisced about high school, and took in Kevin's profile and mannerisms of speech. She liked what she saw. A lovely aquiline nose with slightly flared nostrils, and a Brooklyn brogue that had a whiff of Damon Runyon about it.

Would she like sleeping with him? She didn't know. She had really taken a terrible chance inviting an unknown quantity like Kevin up for a whole weekend. How on earth would she get rid

188

of him if he proved to be a total disaster? But somehow she wasn't worried. In the car with him, she felt rather as if they had been married for the last twenty-five years. She felt that they could move right in together and never feel the least discomfort.

"What are you thinking?" Kevin asked.

"I feel that we've been together for the last twenty-five years," Isadora said.

"That's funny I do, too," said Kevin.

When, an hour and a half later, they arrived at the house in Connecticut, the calm feeling evaporated. There they were, alone (but for Dogstoyevsky, and one poor lonely goldfish) in Isadora's cavernous Connecticut house. There were no excuses. The kid was gone. The nanny was gone. Only Dogstoyevsky was there to express his disapproval by lifting his leg against the cedar barn-board molding and barking ferociously.

"He doesn't like new men," Isadora said, running to get a paper towel to mop up the mess.

"How about the fish?" asked Kevin. "Does he like men?"

"Oh, yes,", Isadora said, blotting up the floor, then getting up to feed the impossible wall-eyed creature. "But I hate him. I call him the guilt fish because he makes me feel so guilty. The damned animals are forever dying and having to be replaced before the kid gets back from school. . . . This fish is the legacy of the next-to-last nanny, Cicely—the same one who ran over my dog."

"You should write a poem," Kevin proposed, "like Browning: 'My Last Nanny,' with apologies to Robert Browning."

Isadora was charmed. Literary references always won her heart. Now, could he fuck?

Isadora had turned on the hot tub before leaving the house at four P.M. She also turned on the stereo now—choosing an old Nat "King" Cole record of the same vintage as her high-school years. She had actually planned to shanghai *some*one to come home with her—or else maybe even to come home alone. It was not unheard of. From time to time, she stayed alone in the isolated house, never really fearing robbers or ax murderers, but merely her own ghosts. This was her home, after all, and she felt physically safe here. Psychologically was another matter. The only danger was that the ghost of Chekarf might come to call, or the ghost of Grandpa Stoloff, or even the ghost of Josh (accompanied by the ghost of Virginia Woof, who had moved out with him).

"Would you like a drink?" Isadora asked Kevin. "Then possibly a hot tub?"

"First let's dance," said Kevin, gathering her into his arms and singing along with "Nat," who was halfway through "Mona Lisa."

"Mona Lisa, Mona Lisa,
Men have named you.
Are you just the lady with the secret smile . . ."

Sweet Kevin had a nice voice and an even nicer touch.

"Am I the lady with the secret smile?" Isadora asked.

"Not so secret," Kevin said.

They drank, smoked dope, tubbed, and went, predictably, to bed. The stars had been very clear above the hot tub, and the hemlock branches swayed to reveal a gibbous moon. In the hot tub, Kevin revealed a prodigious erection. They were already nude and stoned, so why not go to bed? That was why dope and divorce went together so invariably. You never knew who you'd have to sleep with—so it was good to have dope on hand lest he proved unappealing. Oh, this was a world we could not have predicted in high school!

Once in bed, Isadora panicked slightly about the possibility of having a relapse of her pounding headaches, or of discovering Kevin to be, like so many of her early suitors, impotent.

He was nervous, too. Whoever supposed that the so-called "sexual revolution" would so change human nature as to eliminate nervousness?

"Do you like my body?" he suddenly asked.

She wondered if he was joking—the vulnerability of the remark was so unexpected.

"Of course," she said. He had a nice body—hairy, muscular, with a long thin cock that stood up at a respectable angle. "Your body is lovely," she said.

He made love slowly and gently, trying desperately to satisfy her —but not enough to satisfy himself. His mind appeared to be working overtime as well as his body. And in fact that was his problem, for he seemed, after hours of fucking, to be unable to come. She had the distinct feeling that he was laboring over her rather than pleasuring her.

Vaguely, because she was so stoned, Isadora wondered if *she* was doing something wrong. Going to bed with new men was never quite what it was touted to be.

190

"It's not you," Kevin said, shaking that silvery mop of hair. "I just can't give myself the pleasure of coming."

"Are you sure I'm not doing anything that upsets you?" she asked.

"No, no. I promise you. It's *my* problem."

So they fucked and fucked and Isadora came and came, but Kevin seemed to arrive just at the point of coming and then stop himself.

"Next time will be better," she said, reassuringly, like a man comforting a girl who can't come.

Well, add this one to *The Divorced Woman's Book of Etiquette,* Isadora thought. What's the proper thing to say to a man who can't come? What do you say, for that matter, to a man who can't get it up (but whom you wish to encourage)? This was certainly Isadora's year for learning about strange situations that required an entire new lexicon of social behavior. Actually it intrigued her. Always, because of the books she had written, people had presumed her to be extremely knowledgeable about men, but, in truth, her experiences, prior to this *Wanderjahr,* had been rather limited. (Or else they were the experiences of adolescent and young womanhood rather than the experiences of womanhood). At long last she was *really* beginning to understand the varieties of sexual experiences, the fears of the male sex, the way that every man sees his daddy's penis, looming, as it were, over his head as he goes to bed with a new woman.

"You're a wonderful lover, Kevin," she said to the gentle face in the waterbed next to her, and she meant it. "You care so much. Maybe you care too much . . . that's the trouble. You should just let go and be an *animal.*"

"Grr," he growled, but with far too much restraint.

"Grrrrrrrrr," she growled emphatically. "Really let it out and *growl.*"

"Grrrr . . ." he went.

"Louder," she urged.

"Grrrrrrr," Kevin growled.

"You're holding back."

"Grrrrr."

"You know what the trouble with you is, Kevin?"

"No, what?"

"If you *really* let out all the growls in you, women all over the isle of Manhattan would keel over from sheer ecstasy."

Kevin laughed. "Do you really think so?"

"I *know* it. Just let it all out and *growl*."

"Grr. Grr. Grrr," Kevin went spasmodically.

"You know what, Kevin?"

"What?"

"You should be a male chauvinist pig and just fuck your brains out for your own pleasure. Don't worry about me. Be *in*considerate. Make love like a gorilla. Like John Wayne. Like Superman before he had his consciousness raised. Forget about my pleasure and just be a *beast*."

"I'm going to report you to *Ms.* magazine," he said.

Kevin didn't manage to let out all his grrs that weekend, but they had a wonderful time anyway. They danced to old Nat "King" Cole records, reminisced about the fatal fifties, drove verbal stakes through their ex-spouses' hearts.

There was something so *cozy* about their budding relationship. They made eggs together in the kitchen as though they had been doing it for decades. They were so considerate of each other. Both wounded by the divorce Olympics, both wondering how on earth they got to be adolescents again at nearly forty, they handled each other with overabundant generosity and kindness.

Isadora had come to believe, anyway, that kindness was the oil that made the gears of life move smoothly: that every human thing that went well in this world did so only because of kindness, that kindness prevailed and conquered where psychoanalytic interpretations were just irritants.

Of course, it was important to *know thyself* (to know one's friends and lovers, too), but, when all was said and done, kindness went much farther than anything in keeping the human race civilized. "Do unto others as you would have others do unto you" seemed as good a way to run your life as any.

Were these the lessons of middle age? Probably. Mellowness was the great unexpected blessing of middle age. Not that Isadora was *always* mellow. She still suffered from superabundant *spilkes*. (She often thought, in fact, that she would call her autobiography *Spilkes: The Story of My Life*.) She could never leave well enough alone. If she was happy, she wondered *why;* if she was unhappy, she sought to blame and change and rearrange. She sometimes thought she didn't so much live as *gobble* her way through the world. She could do nothing by halves. She loved desperately and hated desperately. She was wildly horny, wildly hungry, wildly extravagant, wildly workaholic. She loved her child to distraction, her men to the point of obsession. When she wrote, she wanted to write all the time. When she fucked, she wanted to fuck all the time. Moderation was the only thing she couldn't seem to master.

But from time to time, she would have an inkling of the moderation middle age brings with it, and she loved this feeling. From time to time, she would stand back from herself and laugh. She would count her blessings instead of her curses. She would glimpse true detachment as the Zen masters know it.

Kevin inspired this feeling in her more than anyone. He seemed to have the power to make her feel calm. Oh, clearly he had his own problems. He was stalled in his life, stalled in his career. He was jack-of-all-trades, master-of-none—now doing voiceovers for commercials, now selling advertising time, now trying to promote his own paintings, now giving up painting and wanting to start an art gallery. But, though his life had its setbacks, he was able to nurture other people's lives to an extraordinary degree. He was generous; he was kind—with everybody but himself—and Isadora was determined (like that Mailer hero in "The Time of Her Time") to make him come. We certainly have come a long way since the fifties, Isadora thought—a longer way than just three decades would seem to justify. In the fifties, the women couldn't come; in the eighties—Goddess help us—it's the *men!*

Almost immediately, Isadora and Kevin fell into a comfortable relationship. They talked on the phone every night before bed. They compared notes about the atrocities of their ex-es. They commiserated about fights over childcare, over money, over the division of property. They supported each other. They analyzed and rationalized. They felt almost married, yet clearly they were not married. They were friends and they also were lovers. The lovely thing about middle age was that you could easily be both.

The following weekend, Kevin arrived with his son. This was the acid test—bringing the kids together.

Isadora was really nervous as she drove to the Westport station on Friday evening with Amanda in the backseat of the Mercedes. Amanda had insisted on going to the train station; she was curious about the weekend guests. She clearly knew something was up, because Isadora had never *had* weekend guests with Amanda around before.

It was Christmas time—the loneliest time of the year for divorced people. Main Street in Westport was strung with tacky lights. The bars near the railroad station were full of weary wassailers who dreaded going home. What a town this was to be divorced in! The men went to the city all day and the women shopped. Alcoholism and genteel drug addiction were rampant. People were too idle, too rich, and yet at the same time much too pressured. They lived their lives under hideous stress. But not the stress of fighting saber-toothed tigers or slaying fire-breathing dragons. Rather, it was the stress of having not *enough* dragons to slay—or else the dragons of tax audits and adulterous discoveries, the dragons of anorexic children, alcoholic wives—modern dragons lacking in any kind of magic.

Isadora pulled up at the train station about ten minutes before the train came in. She had always loved this Friday-night ritual, loved watching people come off the train and trying to figure out who belonged to whom and what their stories were. That young man—was he the son of that woman, or her lover? That gray-faced, jowly older party—was he in deep shit with the IRS or merely suffering from "gasid indigestion" as the admen so charmingly put it. That lady with too much rouge and spike heels she can hardly walk in—is she somebody's sluttish maiden aunt, the Blanche du Bois of Darien, or is she the new nanny, who will soon be found to have a drinking habit and will have to go?

But this time, as Isadora circled the station, she saw a sight that made her blood run cold: she saw Josh in his Datsun waiting for the same train.

Fortunately, she spotted him before Amanda did (or before he spotted her, for that matter). She stepped on the gas and floored it, then tore away to the very end of the railroad platform, where she screeched on the brakes and sat trembling, waiting for the train to come.

The sight of Josh still made her quake all over—with longing and with rage. She was that connected to him, that connected to the marriage. Their little bundle of DNA sat babbling in the backseat—and there they were in different cars, waiting for different lovers. It made no sense. They were man and wife, one flesh, one dream. What on earth were they doing this for? What were they trying to prove? What contemporary myth were they enacting? What contemporary torment?

The commuter train arrived like a noisy cyclops, lancing the station with its beam. It stopped and began disgorging passengers onto the platform. Isadora was waiting so far down that she couldn't see *her* passengers because she was so intent on not seeing

Josh's. It was probably the old school friend—Ms. Emanon—but Isadora wanted to neither see nor be seen.

The station ritual is a brief one: the cars draw up for a little while, hover expectantly, then drive off one by one carrying their human cargoes. The cargoes are pink in this part of the world and wear trenchcoats. In other continents they are black, or ocher or yellow or brown. But probably the ritual is the same. Waiting for the train, one wonders. One wonders about the person one is waiting for. Is he *worth* waiting for? Is he as nice-looking as one remembers, or is he a beast? Is he really good-hearted, or only pretending to be? Could one be better spending one's time doing something else?

The cars had pulled away by now and Isadora was still down at the very end of the platform. She swung QUIM around and headed back, sure that the black Datsun must be gone by now.

Suddenly she saw Kevin waving his arms and followed by a very small boy of seven or eight who had a hateful expression on his face and carried a fluorescent backpack and a *Star Wars* sleeping bag.

"Oh, those must be your new friends, Andrew and Kevin," Isadora said to Amanda, pointing out the little boy and his father. Amanda didn't seem convinced. Neither was Isadora.

You could tell at almost first glance that the kid was, as Bemelmans' Madeline so quaintly puts it: a bad hat. He had a sour expression and his face was sallow and mean. He looked like the kind of kid who tears the wings off dragonflies and the limbs off daddy longlegses. His father's face was as smily as his face was sour. Kevin looked as if he were sunnier than usual to compensate for the sullenness of Andrew.

"Hello! Hello!" he said, waving a brown Borsalino hat and carrying an attaché case which bulged with extra shirts and extra socks. "This must be Amanda."

"I hate him," Amanda said, at once, pointing to Kevin. "He's *not* my daddy."

That was how the weekend began and that was how the weekend progressed. The kids hated each other at first sight. Andrew greeted Amanda by bashing her on the head with his fluorescent backpack, and Amanda responded, appropriately, by saying, "I hate you."

Kevin smiled apologetically, but did not restrain his kid. Instead, he flapped his jacket lapels open and closed in a compulsive gesture and cleared his throat.

"Andrew," he said unconvincingly, "If you don't stop that, I'm going to *make* you stop."

"No you won't," Andrew said. "Mommy says you're a wimp."

Ah, divorce! One of its great unsung joys belongs to the kids alone—the joy of manipulating each parent in perfect freedom from the other's scrutiny!

Kevin looked as if he were about to cry when his kid said that, but he quickly mastered himself and scowled.

"Mommy never said that," he said.

"Oh, yes she does. She says you are a wimp in business and a wimp in bed."

The air inside the car suddenly fell silent. How to redeem this situation, Isadora wondered, or was it even her responsibility *to* redeem the situation? Fortunately, Amanda didn't understand what was going on—or did she?

When in doubt, say nothing at all, Isadora thought. Learn from the WASPs, dummy; if you've learned nothing else from living in Fairfield County, it should at least be that: the best response is frozen silence.

Isadora drove home to Rocky Ridge seemingly ignorant of the fact that in the backseat of the car Andrew and Amanda were still bashing each other cordially and calling each other "Knockhead." Amanda was three, so you really couldn't expect otherwise, but Andrew should have known better.

"How are you, pussycat?" Kevin asked Isadora, all mellowness. How could *any*one be so mellow with kids screaming?

"Oh, I'm fine," said Isadora, her neck beginning to go into spasm and her head beginning to pound.

"How *lovely* to have you both up for the weekend," said Isadora mechanically.

"Yes," said Kevin. "How lovely."

Well, it was another one for *The Divorced Woman's Book of Etiquette*, all right. What to do when his kid and your kid detest each other? Do you stop seeing the man? Kill both kids, or kill yourself?

Once home, Isadora began fussing like a maniac, hoping to get the kids settled, finding fresh sheets for all and sundry, fixing martinis for Kevin, and dispatching Nurse Librium to bathe Andrew and Amanda and get them, if only momentarily, out of Kevin's hair—and hers.

"Oh, don't worry, Miz Izzydorry, I'll take care of the kids,"

Nurse Librium said, attempting to herd this ill-mated pair of juveniles upstairs. "Now you kids be nice and go along upstairs fer yer bath," Nurse Librium said, shuffling along behind them.

"She's a *baby;* I don't want to play with her," screamed Andrew.

"I *hate* boys that I don't know," said Amanda.

"Well—which boys *do* you like?" asked Kevin, trying to conciliate.

"My *daddy* is the only boy I like," Amanda said.

"Well, of course," said Kevin, "of course you love your daddy."

"I hate you," Amanda spat again. "You're *not* my daddy."

"Take them away!" Isadora directed Nurse Librium.

"Oh, I'll take care of them, Miz Izzydorry, don't let it bother youse none." And she laughed her nervous laugh which concealed god only knows what sort of malice.

"Maybe this wasn't such a good idea," said Kevin, as the shrieks and shouts issued from upstairs while they attempted to drink their martinis.

"Maybe not," conceded Isadora, her mind a million miles away. She wished she were in Venice, being rowed along the Grand Canal with a handsome young lover. She wished she were anywhere but here.

Instead, she fussed over Kevin. The parting from Josh had left her in some ways so insecure about men that she did what she had never really done before in her life: she became overwhelmingly domestic. She cooked for them, she mixed drinks fastidiously, she made sure they never had to lift a finger. Men loved it—but Isadora was left wondering about herself. Is *this* where liberation leads? To be doing a man's job and a woman's job and wearing black lace underwear (or white lace underwear) through it all?

There was not much Nat "King" Cole that weekend. Every time Kevin and Isadora would get slightly mellow, and slightly looped, the kids would scream from upstairs or come tearing down with some new dispute. If it wasn't the kids, it was Dogstoyevsky fleeing Andrew in terror. Had Andrew hit him, put toothpicks under his claws, poisoned him? Isadora could tolerate a great many things in life but dog abuse was not among them. Not being Andrew's mother (but only Amanda's and Dogstoyevsky's), she couldn't really discipline Andrew correctly. What was she to say? "Lay one more finger on that dog and I'll kill you?" No. She was stuck with palliatives like: "Andrew, we must not hurt animals," and "Andrew, Dogstoyevsky is as human as you are." He was more human, of course, but Isadora couldn't really say that.

The kids took seemingly forever to go to bed. Kevin, who, like all divorced fathers, longed for his kid and missed him all week long, had to sit with Andrew for hours before Andrew would even pretend to go to bed (Amanda had long since dropped off). When Kevin finally came down from the attic playroom, where Andrew was laid out in his *Star Wars* sleeping bag, he was exhausted.

"What a pussycat that boy is," Kevin said. "I love him so." And his eyes filled with sensitive paternal tears.

Isadora was thinking that the kid was a pussycat in snake's clothing, but she could say nothing because criticizing your new lover's kid is something no sane woman would do.

"A pussycat? Well, yes, I guess he just covers it up with rambunctiousness." *Rambunctiousness* was certainly a neutral enough word here. She was thinking that other words would be far more appropriate. Like *beastliness,* for example—though most beasts she knew were sweeter than Andrew.

"He's suffered so over the divorce," Kevin went on, "and his mother bad-mouths me to him all the time—which puts the kid in a tough spot."

Isadora was sympathetic. Her separation was still new enough so that sometimes she had all she could do to keep herself from bad-mouthing Josh to Mandy. Instead she tended to be overly supportive. "Oh, Daddy will *love* that picture you drew," she would say to Amanda. Or, "Aren't you looking forward to seeing Daddy this weekend?" In her heart, she still had black malice toward Josh —and yet, and yet, she also still loved him. "I love and I hate," says Catullus, and in no life situation is that more true than in a divorce with a young child involved. You may despise the way your ex-spouse is treating you, but still you know in your sane mind that your child must love her father to love herself—and you *do* want your child to love herself. The ambivalence of emotions is painful and exhausting. Sometimes it seems your whole body is a battleground on which conflicting emotions clash by night. Besides, there is no way to stop loving someone with whom you have shared pregnancy, birth, the first frantic nights of parenthood. Experiences like that bond two people forever. The bond remains, however you may wish to break it. It may not be as strong as the bond you have with your child, but it is almost as strong, almost as unbreakable. Isadora knew that a piece of her heart would always belong to Josh—and that it would bleed from time to time, whatever she did to cauterize it.

"Well," said Kevin, "the kids are in bed; shall we be going, too?"

He walked over to where Isadora sat on the couch, took her in his arms, and began to kiss her with great gentleness. She felt herself responding to him as she had not responded to any man since Josh left. The passion was not demonic, maybe, but there was such a sense of comfort and familiarity that she was warmed to the very bottom of her being. They stood up and hugged for a long time, feeling their bodies fit together in the friendliest of ways. Isadora could feel Kevin's erection against her (they were almost exactly the same height) and she could feel herself quickening—her cunt moistening, her heart racing. They went into the bedroom and began undressing each other. Then they fell back on the velvet patchwork spread of the waterbed and wrapped their arms around each other. Isadora felt, for the first time in ages, that she could go to bed without pot, without wine, without anything. Half undressed, wearing only an unbuttoned dress shirt and no trousers, Kevin fondled her until they both became so excited that they could hardly restrain themselves. He entered her and began to move gently inside her. She felt a sensation she had not known with any of the random lotharios of the past few months: trust. And as her cunt warmed to him and her spirit warmed as well, she began to come, rather more quickly than usual, pulsing rhythmically around him and saying, "Thank you, thank you, thank you."

The choice of words was strange. She had never chosen those particular words before. But she *was* grateful—for the warmth, for the trust, for restoring her belief that sex could have sentiment in it once again.

Kevin was really turned on now, turned on by her responsiveness, her gratitude. He began to move quickly, thrusting his penis in on an angle, managing somehow to touch her clitoris and her cunt at once—so that she began to come again and again, and as she cried out in pleasure, he began to come, too—very silently, but with an expression of utter bliss on his face.

"Daddy!" came a scream from the staircase. "Daddy!" Then there was the thud of not so little feet—and Andrew was suddenly there banging on the door and shrieking.

The expression on Kevin's face turned dismal—as if he had been interrupted midcome (which apparently he had been).

"What is it, Andrew, pussycat?" he called.

"Open up!" yelled the little tyrant.

"One minute, darling," said Kevin.

Isadora just lay there in bed amazed. Kevin should have killed the kid, and instead he was placating him.

"Coming," said Kevin. He threw on a bathrobe (a Japanese cotton Yukata—which, to tell the truth, had already been worn by a host of different men that fall) and flung the door open to the imperious child.

"Well . . ." said Andrew challengingly.

"What happened?" asked Kevin.

"The zipper on my *Star Wars* sleeping bag got stuck! Will you fix it for me, Daddy?"

What an astounding dialogue! No wonder Kevin had trouble claiming his own pleasure. No wonder! She knew that Kevin was guilty about the divorce, felt he had abandoned his wife and child and was plagued with fantasies of losing his child forever (if his wife married her current boyfriend and moved to Hawaii)—but she truly could not believe that he would fail to discipline Andrew for so obvious a stratagem. Instead, she heard him dutifully following the kid upstairs to fix the sleeping bag's zipper—which probably wasn't even broken anyway.

After Kevin disappeared, Isadora got up, put on a velvet caftan, brushed her hair, perfumed herself, and went into the kitchen to get a bottle of wine. She prepared a beautiful polished brass tray with crystal wine goblets, a frosty bottle of Trefethen chardonnay, large strawberries still glistening with water droplets (and wearing their fey green caps), and a slice of very ripe brie. She carried this feast into the bedroom and put the gleaming tray in the middle of the waterbed. Then she climbed onto the bed herself, eating strawberries, drinking wine, and waiting for Kevin to appear.

He was gone for about a half-hour, during which time she mulled and brooded about the strange changes that had occurred in her life in the last few months. She was living an inner picaresque—episodic, farcical, with overtones of great melancholy if not true tragedy. Perhaps a woman with a child could not hit the road as easily as a real picaresque heroine—like Candida—the horny heroine for whose sake she had become so peculiarly famous, but the picaresque continued even as one was rooted to hearth and home and woodpile. Sometimes it seemed that so many things went on in her head at once that she had the sense of a dozen movies being run simultaneously on the same screen. One was the movie of her childhood and adolescence; another the movie of her first marriage; another the movie of her second marriage; another the movie of her marriage to Josh and the birth of her daughter; another the movie of the various lovers in her life; another her family's saga; another her grandfather's life as she saw its trajectory superimposed over her own; another the life of Tintoretto's daughter as it paralleled and diverged from her own life . . . All these lives were running concurrently with her own life, and her own life was composed of all these lives, commented upon all these lives; was an *exemplum,* a parable, a myth.

She had not meant it to be this way. She had not meant to lead one of those specimen lives that becomes an *exemplum* to people who read about it, but the times she was born into, the fact that relations between men and women were changing drastically in these times (and that everyone was confused about what to do with these changes), had made her fumblings with fate (which she had mischievously chronicled) assume a significance beyond themselves. Fans wrote her and said, "I am waiting for your new book so I know what step to take next in my life." And there *she* was, so confused about what to do next, yet somehow saddled with the responsibility of being a guru to others.

"I fumble, therefore I am," she wanted to say. "I stumble, therefore I am."

This strange inner picaresque that she was now leading (in her post-separation year)—would this become a sort of parable, too, when she was done with it? For it did seem that she was going through what many women she knew were going through—a time of total insanity following the breakup of a marriage.

Kevin came back into the bedroom full of apologies.

"Don't apologize to me," Isadora said. "Apologize to yourself. You're the injured party. Poor baby—Andrew got you right in the middle of a great come. Here—have a glass of wine."

And she poured for him, then fed him a luscious strawberry to go with it.

Kevin took the wine, sipped it, and joined her on the bed.

"Kill the kid, I say," Isadora laughed, but even as she made this comment, she worried if she was right to risk it.

Aha. Kevin looked slightly offended.

"Of course I'm kidding," she said. "But *really,* darling, you shouldn't let him gobble up your life like that; it's not even good for him."

"But I love him *so* much," Kevin said, "and I see how he's suffering."

"He'd suffer much less if you'd take less shit from him," Isadora said. "I mean, who the hell am I to advise anyone about child-rearing? I'm scarcely what you'd call an infallible mother—but I *do* know from my own experience that we all tend to spoil the hell out of them because we're guilty about the divorces—and our guilt doesn't do them a damned bit of good."

They didn't get into sex again that night, but they slept peacefully in each other's arms. They slept an almost marital sleep—without benefit of any anodyne other than a little wine.

They had left the bedroom curtains open, and in the morning Isadora opened her eyes to see the hemlock branches peacefully rustling at the windows in the dazzling sunlight. Isadora had always loved her house, had felt it a refuge from all the things in life she could not deal with—her notoriety, her detractors, fans who thought she was a long-lost mother—and now with Kevin there in bed with her, that feeling was restored. Not that she had not felt peaceful, at times, without the presence of a man. She had lain in bed on many mornings and been grateful for her solitude, grateful that the swain of the night before had left at dawn (or even that there had not *been* a swain of the night before)—but on this particular morning, the sense of coziness and peace was so great that Isadora could have given the sleeping man a kiss and gone upstairs to her office to confront the demons of her troublesome Papa novel.

She did, in fact, kiss him, and he stirred and wrapped his arms around her. And his legs. She could feel his erection against her, nudging her navel, seeking lower to find her cunt, and it seemed to her that he was more turned on than he had ever been, and so, suddenly, was she.

"My old flame," he muttered. "Do you have any idea how I worshiped you in high school?"

"Worship me now," she whispered.

"I do, I will," he said, entering her.

They began to fuck slowly and gently with a kind of rocking motion that echoed through the waterbed. It was such sweet fucking—lacking in violence, but not in passion.

"You're yummy," Isadora said, holding him.

"So are you," said Kevin, giving himself totally to what was happening.

Suddenly, there was a crash in one of the rooms above them and the sounds of shrieking children.

"What's that?" Isadora asked, rolling out of Kevin's arms and leaping out of bed.

"Your daughter murdering my son," said Kevin automatically. Isadora really resented that. She saw blood behind her eyeballs. But, for the moment, she said nothing. Instead, she threw on her caftan, threw open the bedroom door, and charged up the stairs. There on the first landing she saw a sight she would never forget. She saw her little three-year-old Mandy sitting on bad-hat Andrew and trying to pummel him with her tiny fists.

Andrew was half amused by this, half annoyed. But Mandy was shrieking with real anger—and Mandy was not an angry child.

"What happened?" Isadora asked. "What on earth happened?"

"He hurted my camel," Amanda screamed.

"I did not touch her camel," yelled Andrew.

"Camelia—he hurted Camelia," Mandy cried. Whereupon she ran into her mother's arms.

"Did you take Mandy's camel?" Isadora asked.

"I did not!" shouted Andrews.

"He taked it! He taked it!" protested Amanda.

"Did you, Andrew?"

"I did not!" the kid screamed.

Now Isadora was really livid. Of all the "aminals" Amanda possessed, Camelia was the most meaningful. She was the toy Amanda carried back and forth to Daddy's house, the toy she slept with, the toy whose job it was to get her through the divorce. She was her amulet (her camulet?), her guardian, her protector.

Isadora began a panicky search for Camelia, with a whimpering Amanda trailing behind her. While Andrew ran downstairs to seek refuge in his daddy, Isadora searched Mandy's room, finding four Paddington Bears (all sizes), two Miss Piggies, a Pooh Bear, a Garfield the Cat, a Tigger, a Piglet, a Basic Brown Bear, a giant Steif lion from F.A.O. Schwartz, any number of white mice, yellow chicks, pink pigs; a variety of unicorns in all sizes (dressed in doll clothes, for that was the way Amanda loved to play with them), a vast collection of Barbies—*The World According to Barbie,* Isadora called it—and horses for all the Barbies to ride—but absolutely no Camelia.

"Let's go up to the playroom," Isadora said to Mandy.

"Carry me, Mama, carry me," cried Mandy.

Isadora scooped the little girl up in her arms, covered her face with kisses, and started up the narrow steps to the playroom.

The playroom was a very special room to Isadora because when she had first bought the house, it had been her study. It was where she had written *Tintoretto's Daughter* while she was pregnant with

Mandy, and it had low sloping eaves, punctured with bubble sky-lights, large picture windows at the sides, built-in desks and book-shelves, and carpeted platforms to sprawl on. All Isadora's books on sixteenth-century Venice were still up there—as were her old poetry books from college, her collection of Shakespeare, Chaucer, Marlowe, Donne, Ben Jonson, Shelley, Keats, and her very favorite nineteenth-century muse, that classical romanticist, that contradiction in terms—Byron. But scattered all over the floor were Mandy's toys, and Isadora's former desk was now covered with finger paints, oaktag, crayons, watercolors, and gaudy stickers of every sort imaginable. Isadora had long since moved to her tree-house studio. But she still liked this room better—its warmth, its coziness, the sweet memories of what she now considered the very best time in her life—the time she was carrying *Tintoretto's Daughter* in her brain and Amanda in her belly.

She looked down at the whimpering child in her arms. Amanda's beautiful face was contorted with grief as if she already knew the story of what had happened to Camelia.

"He hurted Camelia, Mommy. He hurted Camelia."

"Where is Camelia, Amanda? Do you know?"

The child shook her head.

"Do you know, Amanda—answer me?" Isadora said this with all the urgency she might have felt if it were Chekarf who lay bleeding in a corner somewhere and he had to be found and rushed to the vet's.

"The playhouse," Amanda conceded.

A yellow plastic playhouse stood in the middle of the room. It had clear vinyl windows, a green flap for a front door, and green vines climbing its plastic sides. Pink morning glories ascended to an imaginary sky above them. Inside the playhouse was a veritable Babi Yar of stuffed animals, thrown in at random as if into a mass grave. This was not Andrew's doing—but clearly what Isadora's eyes next beheld *was* his doing. Camelia had been disemboweled and now lay on the top of the pile of animals, spilling stuffing from her belly.

Isadora clutched the wounded Camelia to her bosom, feeling as wronged and as vulnerable as she had when she carried the mortally wounded Chekarf. Mandy was sobbing.

"Darling—we can sew Camelia up," said Isadora. "We really can." It occurred to her that this was something she could not have done for Chekarf.

"Let's go get the sewing box and sew Camelia up."

Andrew and Kevin appeared in the playroom.

"Did you do this, Andrew?" Isadora asked.

The kid shifted from foot to foot and did not deny it.

"Say you're sorry, Andrew," Kevin directed.

"I'm sorry," said Andrew—but somehow that scarcely sufficed.

Isadora led the parade downstairs to the guest room, where the sewing box reposed, and sitting on the big brass guest bed (with Amanda beside her) she carefully put Camelia's innards back in place and began to stitch up her belly. Isadora was thinking of that recurrent scene in *Catch-22* where Yossarian discovers the dark secret of the spilling guts, and she felt a little godlike to be able to make such magic for Amanda.

"See," she said, "good as new."

She was not an expert seamstress but Amanda didn't seem to care.

Kevin applauded as Isadora presented the amazingly healed camel to Amanda, but even as he did so, he and Isadora exchanged a look that said: *no more weekends with kids.*

Andrew just stamped a sneakered foot and looked unrepentant. (There was still all of Sunday to be endured.)

Sunday proved exhausting but mayhem-free, and later that night, when Isadora and Mandy had driven Kevin and Andrew to the station for the end-of-weekend train back to the city, they had a bath, a story, and then their bedtime chat in Mandy's room.

"Do you have any sad thoughts or glad thoughts you want to share with me before you go to bed?" Isadora asked Amanda, who was clutching the miraculously healed Camelia.

Amanda lifted her hands to her eyes and said, "Bad dreams on both channels, Mommy."

This was Amanda's shorthand for communicating fear when she woke up with scary dreams in the night.

"I know it, honey bunny," her mother said. "But I think the bad dreams are going to go away now. And after all, you have Camelia to protect you."

There was a long pause..

"I hate Kevin," Amanda finally said, "he's *not* my daddy."

"Of course, he's not your daddy," Isadora said, "And you don't have to love him—but you cannot say you hate him to his face, because it hurts his feelings."

"He hurted *my* feelings," said Amanda. Then she paused a minute, thought, clutched her camel, and said, "Can I say I hate him when he's not in the room?"

Isadora didn't know what to answer to that one. "I guess you can, darling, but not to his face."

"Oh," said Amanda, "I see."

Isadora was not quite sure *she* did. But if Amanda understood this Alice-in-Wonderland logic, she supposed she understood it, too.

"I love you, I love you, I love you," Isadora said.

"Leave my door cracked, Mommy," said Amanda, clutching her camel.

"Okay," said Isadora, getting up and starting to leave. "I'll be in my office working, darling. Call if you need me. I'll come back and kiss you when you're asleep."

But Amanda's shallow breathing revealed that she was already dropping off to sleep, so Isadora went back and kissed her right away.

The little girl, half into a dream, rolled her eyeballs upward under purplish lids and muttered, "Mommy." Then she turned, kicked off her blankets, stuck her tush up into the air, and settled into a deep sleep. Isadora covered her again. She kicked off the blankets again. Isadora kissed her on her upraised tush, murmured her prayer to the Mother Goddess, and left the room. "Goddess bless and Goddess keep," she said again. Then she added: "Help us make it through the winter and I promise I'll never ask for anything again."

No answer was forthcoming from that moon-faced Mommy wearing her white wimple up above. She just sailed through the Connecticut skies in her eerie radiance, smiling benignly or sinisterly—depending on your point of view.

"I take that back," Isadora said, walking down the hall to her study. "I probably *will* ask for lots of things."

Oh, she could tell she was definitely getting better.

10

Adrift

Where are the snows of yester-year?
—FRANÇOIS VILLON
"Ballad of Old-Time Ladies"

The way a crow
Shook down on me
The dust of snow
From a hemlock tree

Has given my heart
A change of mood
And saved some part
Of a day I had rued.
—ROBERT FROST
"Dust of Snow"

BY Christmas, they had already had three major blizzards that year. Pipes froze. The driveway iced over. Many mornings, Isadora would look out at the deck and find the hot-tub lid piled high with snow and the hemlock branches dangling icicles. Great gobs of snow slid off the skylights. The furnace conked out and the telephones went on the blink with great regularity.

It was a tribute to the depths of connection between Isadora and Kevin that they kept on seeing each other through this siege. Sometimes he would come up on a Friday night despite the fact that the trains were late or canceled, and Isadora had to call the local driver service to get a jeep to fetch him at the train because she could not get up her driveway.

Her driveway was, anyway, a nightmare. It seemed to have a life (and a *Geist*) of its own. It was possessed. It had, after all, taken Chekarf's life. And it seemed to want more blood. Whenever Nurse Librium drove Mandy to school, Isadora worried that the driveway, not being content with Chekarf as a sacrifice, would try to take Mandy, too. She had suffered so many losses in the last year—Papa, Chekarf, Josh—that she could not believe there were not more to come. If she had been a horror novelist, she would have written a novel about her driveway and how it got to be so bloodthirsty. Was it something in the asphalt perhaps, some dark ingredient—like the bones of an unavenged murdered innocent? Was it the karmic legacy of the builder, who had had the poor judgment to perch this house on a ledge of rock overlooking a beautiful river valley, but then had not even bothered to face the upper-story windows onto the view? Only the lower floors faced the view, and Isadora was always dreaming of building picture windows in the playroom and transforming it into her bedroom.

The builder—a spacy young fellow who had become a friend of Isadora's—had built the driveway with maximum perversity. It went down from Serpentine Hill Road at a sixty-degree angle, took a hairpin turn (which was badly drained and therefore always iced over), and then went up a little rise, right after whatever car you were driving had already gone into a skid. It was the property's most eccentric and impossible feature. The Mercedes—with its wide wheelbase and skiddy rear wheels—often could not make it up the driveway in winter. And now that Josh had gone off and taken both the Land Cruiser and the Datsun, Isadora had to buy a new front-wheel-drive car for the nanny, simply to get Amanda back and forth to nursery school. But sometimes the snow was so deep and the plow so late in coming that even the new Saab could not get up the road. On such mornings, Isadora would just sit dismally staring out her window, waiting for the plow to come, and hoping that the furnace did not go again. There were so many fuel deliveries that winter that sludge on the bottom of the oil tank was always being stirred up to foul the works, and the house would suddenly go cold as one of those haunted houses in the sort of horror novel Isadora wished she could write. (Oh, *anything* would be better than the Papa novel at this point, and anything would be better than having to digest and transform her own life before she could get on with the next book.)

For a New York girl, whose habitual response to domestic fuck-up was to phone the super, Isadora got amazingly good at finding the reset button on the furnace. She would throw on her ski parka over her jeans, climb into moon boots and stomp out through the snow, cram herself through the tiny Alice-in-Wonderland door that led to the crawl space under her house (there was no basement—for the house was built on rock ledge), and grope around in the darkness for the reset button. When she found it, it meant far more to her than just that her furnace would run again. It meant that she could live without a man, that Josh's departure had not done her in, that she could set an example to her daughter about how to be—that contradiction in terms—"a free woman." For that was freedom, wasn't it?—finding the reset button on the furnace? Now, if she could only trade in the Mercedes for a jeep with a snowplow attached, and learn to plow her own driveway, she would *really* be a free woman! Until that time came, she would pick her men, she decided, for their skill in plowing and sanding driveways and in chopping wood, but how much better it would all be if she could learn to operate her *own* plow!

She had a fantasy of herself giving up men altogether and becoming one of those stalwart Connecticut ladies (in boots from L.L. Bean) who raises dogs, plows her own property, fixes her own boiler, and lives happily without a resident male (or even a nonresident male). Could this be what Isadora's odyssey had in store? Well, not yet—but perhaps *one* day. Would it finally be a relief to be free from the *Sturm und Drang* of relationships and just live happily alone? Perhaps. For the first time in her life, Isadora saw the appeal of such solitude.

What a sense of self-reliance she had when the furnace kicked over and started to run again! If she remembered this winter for nothing else, it would be for the discovery that she could make it in the woods alone.

Still, Kevin came up on weekends to temper the loneliness. And there were a variety of other swains. None of them meant much to Isadora compared to Kevin, but Isadora had enough reservations about Kevin (partly because he had sired such a monster and partly because Kevin had another girl friend whom he juggled with Isadora) that she didn't feel the impulse to give herself to him totally. This was fine with him, since the one thing Kevin feared most in life was making some sort of commitment. Kevin sometimes reminded Isadora of that joke about the guy in the singles bar of whom a pretty young woman asks "What time is it?" "I'm not ready to make a commitment yet," he replies.

As Christmas drew ever nearer, Isadora wondered whether she and Mandy might have to spend the holiday alone. Perhaps Kevin's other girl friend had seniority over holidays. Isadora was afraid to ask. But the thought of a solitary Christmas panicked her, so a few days before the holiday, she called up all the friends and family she knew who might be alone that year and invited them to a Christmas Open House. Mandy was hers that Christmas; next year she would be Josh's (lawyers had already begun dickering over a separation agreement, and Mandy's life was being divvied up). Josh planned to go to Las Vegas with Ms. Emanon—and unfortunately, he chose to take his leave a week or so before Christmas, during the worst blizzard yet.

The power was gone, the furnace had blown, and the telephones were ringing erratically (threatening imminent loss of communication with the outside world) on that dark and foreboding night in December when Josh came to say goodbye to Mandy.

It was about five in the evening, but already dark as midnight. Nurse Librium was giving Mandy a bath by lantern light, making use of the tub of water she had run before the power went (lest the water pump not work for the next day or so). Isadora was dashing around madly, lighting candles, finding lantern batteries, filling pots with water, trying to phone the fuel-oil service line before the phones went dead (all the things you do in Connecticut during a blizzard), and suddenly Josh drives down the snowy driveway in the Land Cruiser, stomps to the door, and rings the bell.

The house is spooky by candlelight, it almost seems haunted. Candles flicker in the living room and dining room. Fires are lit in all the fireplaces, but they seem oddly lonely in the darkness and silence. Seemingly oblivious of the emergency situation around them, Josh walks into the house and demands to see Mandy.

"She's upstairs, having a bath," says Isadora.

Josh takes off his red ski cap, his green down parka (which Isadora had bought for him the year before), gives not so much as a nod to Isadora, and clumps upstairs to Mandy's bathroom.

"Daddy!" she cries in ecstasy, as he enters her lantern-lit bathroom.

Daddy! Isadora wants to scream. Where are all the daddies who promised to take care of us if we were only good girls and always, *always* put them before our own self-esteem? Nowhere to be found. Daddy is dead—or else in hibernation—like God. It's the Mother Goddess who will answer our prayers now—or no one.

Josh spends not more than ten minutes with Mandy, comes back downstairs, and starts putting on his parka again.

Isadora has not been able to reach the furnace people or the snow-plow people or *any*one. The phones are still ringing on and off in that way they do in Connecticut before they conk out altogether. She is getting hysterical.

"Josh," she says, "isn't there a number where I can reach you in case of an emergency?"

Very funny. Doesn't she realize that this is *already* an emergency? What on earth would she do if the kid had an accident and had to be rushed to the emergency room? She couldn't even get up the driveway.

"I don't want you to bother me on vacation," Josh says coldly.

"But what about Amanda? What if there's an emergency with Amanda?"

"There won't be—but if there is, you can call my parents—or my sister. They can reach me."

"But what am I going to do? How can I get out of here if there's an accident or anything?"

"It's not my problem, Isadora," he says, "I told you we were no longer a couple."

"You bastard!" Isadora spits out. "You don't support your kid.

212

You don't even leave phone numbers. I don't have a word low enough to describe what I think of you!"

"I know what you think of me," says Josh. "And I don't care."

"Can't I at least borrow the Land Cruiser? You'll hardly need it in Las Vegas!"

"I'm lending it to Ishmael's mother," Josh said, cruelly. "She needs it more than you do."

"Get out of here, you fucking bastard!" Isadora screams, and she flings out one arm to strike him, but he dodges her, taking off into the blizzard and leaving his house, his child, his wife, again, again, again. Were they doomed to repeat that scene for all eternity.

Isadora lets out a scream that could have pierced hell itself. Then she goes to the fridge, fixes herself a very stiff vodka-and-grapefruit-juice, and returns to her frantic telephoning.

Fortunately, the power was restored before long, and the phones never blew, but the snowplow did not come for two days, and during that snowbound time, Isadora had plenty of hours to reflect on Josh's treatment of her. He needed so to punish her, he'd even subject the person he loved most in the world—Mandy—to discomfort, if not outright danger. Why? It made no sense at all. Was the need for vengeance that strong, or was he simply oblivious of the hurt he inflicted on Mandy and Isadora?

"I never want to depend on him for anything again," Isadora told Kevin on the phone later, when they commiserated about Josh's ungentlemanly departure. "If he calms down and wants to be a human being again—great. I hope so for Mandy's sake. But I never want to count on him for anything. Never. It just hurts too much when I get kicked in the teeth."

This was a turning point of sorts. Up until then, Isadora was playing the Penelope game, waiting for her errant Odysseus to come home. Although she led her life as if she were on her own, there was a part of her that never really embraced independence. She would learn to reset her own furnace, haul her own wood, plow her own driveway—but after that, Josh would come home and kiss her on the forehead for being so independent. Daddy would reward her after all—reward her for her self-reliance.

It was a paradox, wasn't it? The more she took pride in her independence, the more she had fantasies of his applauding her for it. She knew this was inconsistent and absurd. She should love her independence for its own sweet self, enjoy it because it gave her choices, not because it would please Josh—who might or might not ever come home. But she had not quite reached that point in her self-transformation. Would she ever? She wanted to come to that lovely moment of inner-directedness where she delighted in her strength without wondering whether a male (or female) audience would be there to give her a standing ovation for it. She had won all the other battles most women never win—her own professsion, her own money, her own autonomy from both father and husband. But in her heart, she still had Daddy installed as censor, judge, arbiter of her achievements. And if she, with all her freedom, was so unfree, what did that bode for other women?

It snowed, it snowed, it snowed. The snow drifted over the hot tub and filled the walkways and the driveway. The snow swirled mistily in the houselights that beamed out into the hemlock branches, and the snow outlined Mandy's wooden climbing frame and the branches of the vulnerable little fruit trees that Josh and Isadora had planted during their last spring together—most of which had died. The sky was pink with snow, almost a fleshy pink, not at all the clear white of a blizzard in a paperweight.

After Mandy was safely tucked off to bed, and Nurse Librium had retired to her rerun heaven, Isadora pulled on her moon boots and her parka and walked out onto the deck to survey the blizzard. The valley below her house was virtually obscured by the swirling snow, but each of the multitudinous hemlock tops she gazed down upon endured its own diminutive blizzard. Every treetop was like a little universe in which snow swirled, then caught on the needles and was stopped in midflight. What an amazing substance snow was! It had the power to suggest eternity and mortality at the same time. Its crystals celebrated the amazingly protean powers of creation, but its evanescence reflected the fragility of that creation. And here we all were, poised on the nuclear brink, as Isadora was poised over her own invisible Connecticut Valley. After the holocaust, there would be no more snowflakes, no more hemlocks, no more beautiful dawn-cheeked babies with purplish lids. How silly and unimportant her divorce from Josh Ace was in the light of that possible nuclear extinction. How minor it was even in the light of her own brief odyssey on the planet—which was as brief in its way as the life of a snowflake.

The redwood lounge chairs had never been put away in the

garage that fall (in times of crisis one forgets such autumn rituals), and a thick layer of snow had formed on each one, as if a snowy overstuffed cushion had been tailored to each chaise. The contours of the snow cushions were almost cloudlike—making this deck seem a foretaste of heaven with Isadora poised on a heavenly balcony above the mortal coil.

The snow had trapped her in her own house, in her own thoughts, yet it had also, oddly, released her. She lay down on one of the snowy chaises, looked up into the swirling pink sky, and opened her mouth to receive the snow crystals as a sacrament. Lines from her favorite story by Joyce came back to her, but they came back to her only in snatches. Something "swooned" as the snow kept "falling faintly on through the universe . . . over all the living and all the dead."

Drat. Why couldn't she remember the whole quote? She had taught "The Dead" many times during her years as a college English instructor, and the story had never failed to amaze her with its richness. She could quote other beloved works by heart—great chunks of prose and poetry—but this one somehow eluded her.

Did the snow swoon or did someone's soul? Did the snow cover Ireland or the whole universe? She flipped through her mind as if it were a book whose pages she was turning. She did not want to get up, go inside, and look up the quote, but she knew she would have to before long. Remembering the Joyce quote made her suddenly taste the blood of wanting to write again. That was what Josh had robbed her of more than anything—the lust to write—which had always been her center, her soul.

Reluctantly, she got up from her snow-chaise, admired the wingless angel print her body had left in the snow, and went inside to find a copy of *Dubliners*.

She turned to the last paragraph of "The Dead" and read that dazzling concluding passage.

. . . snow was general all over Ireland. It was falling on every part of the dark central plain, on the treeless hills, falling softly upon the Bog of Allen and, farther westward, softly falling into the dark mutinous Shannon waves. It was falling, too, upon every part of the lonely churchyard on the hill where Michael Furey lay buried. It lay thickly drifted on the crooked crosses and headstones, on the spears of the little gate, on the barren thorns. His soul swooned slowly as he heard the snow falling faintly through the universe and faintly falling, like the descent of their last end, upon all the living and the dead.

She felt her scalp prickle as the White Goddess passed over her head, and she felt her heart race. This was the true test of literature and suddenly she wanted to be whole again so that she could experience it once more. It occurred to her then that she had not even been able to read a book since Josh's departure. Her concentration had been that fragmented, that frantic, and now this blizzard had given books back to her.

"Thank you for this," she said to the Goddess above, knowing that without this snowstorm, she would not have confronted Josh's defection, nor her own inability to let go. If she could truly let go of him and take hold of herself and her work again, then even this pain would not have been useless.

"Thank you," she said again with a nod toward that pinkly swirling sky.

The swamis and the gurus tell us that we draw to ourselves the lessons our souls require, and maybe the ending of this marriage was indeed a lesson she had drawn to herself to teach her soul to grow.

Tonight I am going to read a book, she said to herself resolutely. And she did. She reread *Dubliners*. She had come through another phase of the separation. She could read again.

Christmas arrived in due course, and Kevin announced that he wanted to spend it with her. (What had happened to the other girl friend, she did not know, nor did she inquire. Ironically enough, she and Kevin did not have the sort of intimacy which permitted her to inquire.)

The weather was cold and bitter on Christmas Eve and Kevin arrived in Westport with a large shopping bag of gifts, on a battered Conrail train where all the emerging passengers had large shopping bags of gifts.

The roads were so icy that Isadora skidded even in the Saab. Going to the station, she had just avoided plowing into a mailbox on Serpentine Hill Road. Returning to the house, she alternately slid on ice, skidded on sand—all the way home. She hated the icy roads more than anything. They made her feel so out of control and helpless about her life. She had fantasies of moving back to New York, the city of her birth—New York, where the traffic noises invaded her writing; New York, where the telephone rang nonstop; New York, where you wrote all day in a claustrophobic apartment and partied all night; New York, the city of overcommitment and creative chaos; New York, where the air was always bubbling with ideas and inventions but where you were usually too pressed to sit down at a desk and do anything about them. In New York, Isadora had never been able to hear herself *think*. But since she wasn't writing much anyway, maybe she might as well go back to New York and have fun. It would have been easier to endure this year in New York than in freezing, solitary Connecticut, in the same house she and Josh had lived in together, with the sun going down at four o'clock, and every beam, floorboard, and piece of furniture reminding her of Josh.

"How's New York?" she asked Kevin as they skidded along the roads, heading back to her house.

"Frantic," he said. "It's good to be here. You know New York on Christmas Eve—the traffic doesn't move at all. The subways are jammed. Everything has an air of menace. At least here, it's peaceful."

"I don't know whether you love me or love my house," Isadora said.

That was a risky thing to say, because she and Kevin had never yet uttered the word *love*—even in bed.

"I love you," Kevin said. "No contest."

"I love you, too," said Isadora.

They held hands and absorbed this news for a while as the car continued to skid all over the road.

"Love is skiddy," said Isadora.

Back at the house, the Christmas tree in the dining room awaited decoration and Mandy was skipping about, hugging the healed Camelia. Nurse Librium had put on a record of Christmas carols and was singing along in a demented voice. (It was the first time in Isadora's memory that Librium had taken the initiative to do anything as social as put on a record. Usually, if asked to perform such an act, she would whine, "Now, I forgot. Where's that button that you push?" Nurse Librium avoided the simplest tasks by appearing brain-damaged and idiotic—but Isadora suspected her of being crazy like a fox. She had, for example, managed to procure autographed first editions of all Isadora's books for her relatives—though, she, herself, never read a line of anything—unless it was the *National Enquirer* or the *Star*—which really couldn't be called *reading*. Isadora loved these publications, though, and stole them from Librium to read on the can. They were perfect toilet reading—absolutely guaranteed to keep your brain in beta while your anus did the thinking.)

While Kevin unpacked (to the tune of Mandy ceaselessly repeating "I hate him—he's not my daddy"), Isadora made martinis.

What a middle-aged drink, she thought while mixing them. Her parents drank martinis and gibsons; she was more inclined to vodka and fresh grapefruit juice or white wine. But still, since Kevin had reappeared in her life, she had gotten good at mixing them. She'd make a gin martini for him—straight up, heavy on the vermouth, for that was how he liked it, and a vodka martini on the rocks for herself, with almost no vermouth. She could live without vermouth. The only time she liked vermouth was in that e. e. cummings poem where he praises some girl's vermouth-colored hair. How she had puzzled over *that* one. Was it supposed to be white vermouth or red? What an intriguing hair color to have!

Let's see. Who was the girl? It was Marjorie, of course . . .

in making Marjorie god hurried
a boy's body on unsuspicious
legs of girl. his left hand quarried
the quartzlike face. his right slapped
the amusing big vital vicious
vegetable of her mouth.
Upon the whole he suddenly clapped
a tiny sunset of vermouth
-colour. Hair. he put between
her lips a moist mistake, whose fragrance hurls
me into tears, as the dusty new-
ness of her obsolete gaze begins to. lean. . . .
a little against me, when for two
dollars i fill her hips with boys and girls

"A tiny sunset of vermouth-colour. Hair." Oh, how sentimental cummings was! There is no sunset in vermouth—and the metaphor doesn't quite work, but the "moist mistake" of mouth more than makes up for it. No one, not even a cummings heroine, has vermouth-colored hair. But how delicious of him to yearn for such a girl and in his yearning to make her real.

Isadora wandered into her bathroom, where Kevin was changing into jeans. She presented him with the martini.

"Merry Christmas," she said. "Let's get looped."

He put the drink down and wrapped his arms around her. He kissed her with a very gentle, very wet, openmouthed kiss. This was no moist mistake. His kisses were lovely, but rather thin, not full-bodied, and in the background, the undertaste, the subtext as

218

it were, there was the faint taste of rot, of death beginning to take him before he had really done much of anything with his life.

What was it about Kevin? There was a sadness about him underneath all his sweetness. A sadness and a sweetness both together—like some dated perfume of the twenties. He looked young and handsome, yet somewhere inside he was *old*; he was lacking in energy, in *élan vital*. It was as if his face had stayed young but his spirit had aged—like Dorian Gray, as if (in reverse of most people) his soul had grown old while his flesh remained young.

"I love you," Kevin said, drawing back a little and holding Isadora's face between his hands.

"I love you, too," Isadora said.

But even saying this, she did not think she would wind up with him. She did not think she would "wind up" with anyone ever again.

They pretended they were a family and decorated the Christmas tree. Kevin pined for not-very-merry Andrew, who was with his mother that weekend. And Isadora secretly pined for Josh.

She and Mandy and Kevin decorated the tree together, but that did not make them a family.

"Where does the angel go?" Kevin asked, referring to a silly-looking gold-foil angel that Isadora and Josh had received one year from an artist friend of theirs in Denmark. If Kevin had really been her husband, he would have known.

"She perches on the top of the tree," Isadora said.

"And where does the New Year's baby go?" Kevin asked. He referred to a dangling porcelain baby, dressed in a diaper that said "Happy New Year."

"She goes here—Knockhead," said Amanda, seizing the baby and letting her fall to the floor before she could be snagged upon a branch. The baby shattered on the oak floorboards—just as Isadora always worried Amanda might do.

Amanda began to cry. "Are you mad, Mommy?" she asked.

"No, no," said Isadora, "not as long as you didn't do it on purpose."

"I'm sorry," Amanda said, running to her arms.

Isadora gathered her up and kissed her. What a sad Christmas this is, she thought. What a sad Christmas.

The little New Year's baby had been a gift on Amanda's very first Christmas. She had come attached to a package that bore a romper suit, long since outgrown. Sometimes Isadora saw all the clothes Mandy had outgrown stretching out behind her as if in some symbolic collage of corporeality and the metamorphoses it imposes upon us on the long voyage toward death. Mandy had been an infant, three months big, then six, then nine. Then she wore one-year sizes, then two, then three, then four, then five. At three, she wore size-five clothes. Next year, it would be six. As she outgrew all these clothes, some phantom child walked behind her picking up and wearing her worn-out garments. This phantom child was death, wearer of hand-me-downs. Clothes, flesh—it was all the same. None of them fits after a while. We finally walk clad in nothing but spirit.

Not so the Christmas tree, which is festooned with lights and ornaments for a time, then drops everything, including its needles, and succumbs to the fire. When the fire takes its carcass, does its soul return to the primal woods? Oh, what melancholy thoughts were in Isadora's head this Christmas Eve!

"Do you want the Thanksgiving turkey on the tree?" Kevin asked.

"What an alarming statement," said Isadora. Then she remembered the ornament he was referring to.

It was a very campy roast Thanksgiving turkey, made of baked play-dough, then painted in the appropriate roast-turkey colors with acrylic paints.

The Christmas Isadora was pregnant, the Christmas she and Josh got married, she had bought this ornament and a host of others made by a neighborhood woman who specialized in fake cookie-dough ornaments. She had bought dozens and dozens of them—Christmas wreaths, reindeer, Santas, angels—and the cookie-dough lady had, as a gift, made her two special ornaments depicting her two dogs—Chekarf and Virginia Woof. The miniature pets were still there in the Christmas ornament box, nesting in red tissue paper—though both of the dogs were gone. Virginia Woof had moved out with Josh, and Chekarf of course had moved out with death. The whole little family they had been then—the dogs, Mandy *in utero*—was no more. Mandy would never again be that close to her, and the dogs were either divorced or dead. Virginia Woof sometimes came over to visit with Josh, but she sniffed Isadora like an alien creature, almost as if she did not remember that Isadora had rescued her from the pound and nursed her back to health from near-extinction.

Isadora took the roast-turkey ornament from Kevin and hung it on an upper branch of the tree. Then, tenderly, she took the little effigies of Chekarf and Virginia Woof out of the box and hung them, too.

"Someday I have to tell you about my dogs," Isadora said to Kevin. "I loved those two dogs so. I feel that I'll never love any dogs that deeply again." Or any man, she wanted to add, but she didn't.

"What happened?" Kevin asked.

"It's a long story," said Isadora, though of couse, if he were really her husband, he would know.

"Woof, woof, woof, woof," said Mandy, getting down on the floor and impersonating a dog. She was bored with tree trimming, and besides, she had already massed about thirty ornaments on the few low branches she could reach. The branches were so weighted down that all the ornaments threatened to slide off and break.

"You're the sweetest dog I've ever had," Isadora said to Mandy.

"Why can't Daddy be here?" Mandy asked out of the blue. And Isadora suddenly began to cry.

"Because Mommy and Daddy don't live together anymore," said Isadora.

"Why?" asked Mandy.

"I don't really know why," said Isadora.

Kevin put his arms around Isadora to comfort her, and Isadora panicked. Every time Kevin tried to embrace her while Mandy was around, Isadora froze, imagining custody suits.

"Don't hug Mommy," Mandy said.

But Kevin ignored both Mandy's directive and Isadora's panic.

"It's okay to be affectionate," Kevin said. "I promise you."

Isadora was not convinced.

What a ragtag melancholy family they made! One heartbroken child, one panicky mommy, and one daddy who was not with the child he longed for. Isadora kept thinking back to Christmas of last year when Josh had bought her diamond earrings in an attempt to return some sparkle to their love. They were in the midst of their crisis over their supposed open marriage, his failed expectations, her successes, and all the deaths that had attended their passage through the previous year. If only—Isadora now thought —they had tried a little harder and been a little less inclined to indulge their *spilkes*. Isadora often thought that her tragic flaw in life was her Arien impatience. Perhaps all these problems with Josh could have been solved with just a little waiting. *Warten*— Kafka supposedly had hanging over his desk—*Wait*. It was profound. Many problems in writing are solved just by waiting and allowing the unconscious to do its invisible work—and many problems in life are solved that way, too.

She thought that, and then she thought—was she *crazy?* Just a few days ago, Josh had stomped out of her house in a blizzard and a blackout, leaving her to cope with baby, house, and snowstorm without even the loan of a car which he didn't need at all—but which, in spite, he had chosen to lend to one of his girl friends. How could she be so self-hating as to long for a man who treated her that way? Surely, she deserved better. But deep down inside, she did not *believe* she deserved better. Maybe she even believed she deserved worse. *There* was the crux of the problem: until she could really believe in her right to be well treated, she would never be well treated—or not for long.

Mandy went to bed after endless delaying and interrogations about Santa Claus (whose milk and cookies had been duly laid out).

When Kevin and Isadora were alone finally, they sat down to the Christmas Eve dinner Isadora had prepared—roast turkey with chestnut dressing, turnip purée, sweet potatoes, two kinds of wine, Perrier-Jouet champagne, and a chocolate fondue with fresh fruit. At dinner, by the roaring fire, to the tune of Nat "King" Cole, they discussed high school, as if to obliterate all the experiences that separated them and put them somehow on common ground.

They played Did You Know? and Do You Remember? They remembered some of the same characters from high school, but not nearly enough of them to prolong this game.

In the rosy firelight, with the snow outside and the music inside, they should have been far more entranced with the scene (and each other) than they were. Oh, they were comforted by each other, fed by each other, amused by each other. But Isadora had the sense that Kevin had somewhere been so wounded in his vitals that he could never quite give himself again, whereas she—she was in the process of giving up romance—but when she gave that up, what on earth would come to take its place?

Romance, passion, the quest for the fiery demon lover who obliterated all reason, the quest for the magic spindle—these things had marked her life. Yes, she had lived to write, had applied herself to her writing with ferocious discipline—but even more than living to write, she had lived to love. Even the books that provided her with her livelihood all chronicled females questing for love. Without her quest for love, she would also have nothing to write about; it was what linked her to other women, what stirred her vitals not only to sex but also to poetry, what made her—despite her oddness in being famous and affluent—exactly like other women, exactly like her friends, her sisters, her readers.

And now she was looking at a life without love. She was looking at Kevin, whom she *almost* loved, and thinking that a man like this spelled the end of passion. Oh, she could easily enough live with him. She could probably even write with him around—but what on earth would she have to write *about*? To settle for Kevin would be like settling for middle age. And yet she could not go on being buffeted by love as she had been for her first thirty-nine years. It was just too tough. She had loved Josh too completely, too finally —and his departure had left her too bereft.

"What are you thinking?" Kevin asked.

"Just that I've lived my life being buffeted by love," Isadora said. *"Buffeted by Love*—there's another title for my autobiography."

"Yes," said Kevin, taking her hand and looking into her eyes with his big hazel eyes. "Yes. But you'll never do that again."

Isadora shuddered with fear when he said that. Despite her fantasies of total self-reliance, of living in Connecticut alone and resetting her own furnace, she knew of no other emotional life than the ups and downs of romantic passion. What a dilemma! She might be as independent as Jane Eyre, but she was still in search of her Rochester.

"You see," Kevin said, "when we fall in love this time, at this age, we'll fall in love with real people, not fantasies. In the past, we always fell in love with fantasies."

"But *all* romantic love is fantasy," Isadora said. "Once the person is tamed and domesticated, something goes out of the love."

"Not necessarily," said Kevin, picking up another piece of sweet potato on his fork. "Couldn't life be peaceful, just like this?"

Was this a proposal? Isadora couldn't believe her ears.

"Yes," she said, "very peaceful, but I don't know if I'm ready for such peace."

"But are you ready for more pain? Of the sort you had with Josh?"

"No. But the peace seems somehow deathlike. I long for it, but —dare I say it?—it seems boring."

"That's because you haven't got your head together yet," Kevin said, patting her cheek. "There will come a time, I promise you, when it will seem attractive . . . a nice fire, a nice meal, a nice little *shtup* after dinner . . ."

Which is exactly what they had. But as they were having it, Isadora thought, There is something essentially wrong with any *shtup* that can be described as "nice" and "little."

Kevin's favorite adjectives were *nice* and *little*. His life was nice and little, his aspirations nice and little, even what he desired for Isadora was nice and little. But she, burned as she was by the attempt to live without a net, to live by her wits and by her passions, could not settle for nice and little. No, she did not want to get hurt again, but neither did she want a life without risk. Every time she had opted for what seemed like risklessness, it had proved to have its own pains. She had alternated between wildness and safety in choosing her men, and who could tell which was better, which was worse? Brian Stollermann had been a madman; Bennett Wing had been a staid doctor; Josh Ace had been a "younger man" (in the benighted days—the midseventies—when six years younger was thought to be of some consequence). Now Kevin was the safe "old school friend," the antidote to the hurt and torment of the last year. Who was next? Given her history, a demon lover was next on the agenda. And would there (after that) be an antidote to *him*, and then an antidote to the antidote, and so on until she died? No. She was about to be forty. This *couldn't* go on forever.

Would forty spell the end of love and its derangements? Would she slide peacefully into her slippers (puffing on her metaphorical pipe) and nod by the fire for the next forty years? (For she came from a very long-lived family.) Would she take to writing vague philosophical essays with no men and no women in them but only grand abstractions and long latinate words? Would she stop wearing her crazy designer clothes of lavender velvet and fuchsia silk and begin to dress out of the redoubtable catalogs of Bean and Bauer? Would she trade in her soft contact lenses and outsize sunglasses for tortoiseshell Ben Franklins or bifocals? Would she start knitting in lieu of fucking? Would she take up gentlewomanly crafts like making pictures of dried, pressed flowers or baking madeleines to sell them for outrageous tariffs at the local gourmet shop? Would forty mean the end of love—and if so, what on *earth* would she write about?

"What are you thinking?" Kevin asked when they had finished making love.

"I don't even know how to put it into words," Isadora lied. How could she tell him what she was thinking? He had comforted her, helped her, healed her; was she so ungrateful as to reject these not inconsiderable gifts?

"I feel," Isadora said, "as if I've been set adrift, as if all the givens of my life have suddenly changed, and I don't know what assumptions will come to replace them."

Well, this was true—though perhaps a little vague. As she approached forty, Isadora felt that a great shifting of gears was occurring in her life. But whether she would fly downhill after this —or laboriously climb uphill for the rest of her days, she did not know. Probably neither. Probably she would find some new way of living, halfway between self-reliance and endless love (which always, alas, ends). But was there a halfway point between those two? And what on earth would it *feel* like?

She had always adored those eighteenth-century novels in which the hero and heroine wind up, in the closing scene, cultivating their garden. That was what she craved, and yet she seemed as far from it as ever.

"What do you want most," Kevin asked, "for the next half of your life?"

"To cultivate my garden," said Isadora, "to flower again, to root myself in earth and flower again . . ."

"Then you will," said Kevin. "The ground is only temporarily frozen—so you're adrift—if I may mix a metaphor. But when the spring thaw comes, you'll root again and flower. That I promise you."

"Thank you," said Isadora, really touched. "I love you for saying that. Good-night."

And they fell asleep in the undulating waterbed with their arms around each other.

Would she and Kevin still be sleeping in each other's arms when the spring thaw came?

Best not to ask that question, but just to live this winter one day at a time, as the A.A. folk say.

11

Good Nightings for Christmas

I would like to step out of my heart
& go walking beneath the
enormous sky.
—RAINIER MARIA RILKE

ON Christmas morning, it was snowing again. Each flake struck terror into Isadora's heart, because the snow, in Rocky Ridge, meant isolation. Isadora had invited an ill-assorted group of lonely friends and acquaintances to spend Christmas with her and Kevin and Mandy, but they were not due to come until three o'clock, and by then the roads might be impassable.

It was seven when Mandy pounded on Isadora's door, waking her and Kevin and summoning them out of bed to confront the presents beneath the tree.

Kevin groaned and rolled over in the waterbed. It was not his child who summoned, after all, and Isadora thought it just as well to let him sleep while she opened Mandy's presents alone with her.

"Go back to sleep, darling," she said to Kevin. "I'll wake you at a more civilized hour."

He seemed happy enough to do this, so she put on a warm bathrobe and followed Mandy out to the tree, where a cornucopia of gifts awaited her. (Oh, how we indulge our children that first Christmas after a separation, hoping to make up with material possessions for the one gift that they desire most and that we cannot give them—two parents to open presents with.) Of the many things one takes for granted in a marriage, a partner to share the present-ritual with seems fairly trifling—until it is taken away.

Isadora and Mandy sat beneath the tree and began searching for boxes bearing Mandy's name. Mandy was happy enough to tear off the paper and embrace each new stuffed animal, each toy, each game—but Isadora was totally desolate. All she could do was remember back to Christmases past. She seemed incapable of centering herself in the present moment and enjoying what was going on. She could not stop thinking that Mandy was only three and already half fatherless. A man the little one could barely tolerate was sleeping in the waterbed, not even getting up to see her glowing face as she pillaged her presents.

Isadora put on a record of Christmas carols, as if that would infuse cheer into the cheerless scene. She put it on low so that Kevin would not be awakened. She and Mandy sang along erratically as they searched through the presents, and Isadora was charmed by Mandy's interpretations of the lyrics. "Good nightings we bring to you and your friends," she sang tunelessly, "good nightings for Christmas and a Happy New Year."

At least I have Mandy, Isadora thought—that should be a great comfort to me. And of course it was. If Mandy were to be taken from her, she would have nothing to live for. But still, something precious had been lost: the ability to share Mandy with the one person in the world whose investment in her was as great as her own. It was an immense loss and Isadora did not yet know what gains would come to replace it, if any.

The party that afternoon was a sad affair. Lola Birk Harvey turned up in her red Cherokee, with husband, Bruce, and lover Errol Dickinson, the Rhinestone Cowboy. What a curious—if unwitting—*ménage à trois* they made. Sylvia Sydenheim-Rabinowitz came escorted by son Roland. Isadora's parents also turned up, as did her sister Chloe, with kids in tow. Other than that there were a variety of lost souls: one eccentric woman writer who lived in Ridgefield with seventeen stray dogs and twelve cats (the dogs were in a kennel; the cats roamed the house); an elderly gentleman writer who did books on lexicography and was definitely a little weird; a lesbian couple in their seventies who bred borzois; the widow of a famous playwright; the widow of a famous actor; the widow of a famous producer; the widow of a famous poet. Oh, Connecticut was a great state for widows. Isadora felt a little like one herself. This odd assortment of people embraced, unwrapped presents, and got roaring drunk at once—as if to block out the possibility that they'd all be snowed in together as if in some venerable Agatha Christie melodrama. Were they due to be murdered one by one? The afternoon had that feel about it. Several of the people there had slept with other people there—though Isadora was the only one who knew it (save for Lola Harvey, who knew nearly as much as Isadora and was hugely titillated by it). Lola was glowing, animated, turned on. She loved the fact that she and Isadora shared Errol and that she was there with her husband while Isadora was there with her old school friend. But Errol, what did *Errol* think? Errol was so stoned his unmatched eyes were glazed, and Roland was equally stoned. All of these people—who were connected only by Isadora—milled around in her living room and made merry. They simulated family feeling. They did a pantomime of yuletide joy—or did Isadora only feel that way because she was so depressed? Perhaps the others were having a splendid time.

Isadora watched Bruce Harvey make small talk with Errol Dickinson. Never had two men less in common. And more! Bruce was a venture-capitalist—and Errol Dickinson was a cocksman, disc jockey, and doper. Bruce knew everything about Silicon Valley—and Errol knew everything about Bruce's wife's valley. What on earth could they be talking about?

Isadora wandered over to them.

"Hello, lovely lady," Errol said.

"Hello, gorgeous," said Bruce.

"We were just saying this is the best Christmas ever." Errol said.

Well, that just went to show how little Isadora knew about anything. Errol was thrilled to be invited to Isadora's house at normal hours (rather than sneaked in and out in the dead of night). He didn't even notice that two of her other boyfriends were present. Also, he had adored Mandy from afar and was thrilled to be able to finally meet her.

Isadora tried to perk herself up and catch some of the good mood.

"I'm glad you're having fun, Errol," she said to him.

"It's a *blast*," he said, pinwheel-eyed.

She waved to Kevin, who sat on the couch sipping a martini and staring off into space. Kevin was a party observer, a life observer. He liked to watch the passing scene. He was one of history's spectators, rather than one of its participants. He would have watched at Waterloo, at Bull Run, at the Bay of Pigs. He would have watched while Rome fell, while London was blitzed, while the Bomb was detonated at Hiroshima. Kevin was comforting to have around, like a teddy bear, yet he didn't seem entirely alive.

Mandy was the opposite—a pistol. She seemed to have been born (as Isadora's mother had also said of *her*) with an extra shot of adrenaline. She was running around like a maniac, gathering up the presents people had brought, stuffing herself on all the goodies from the buffet, grabbing at candy canes, jelly beans, and chocolates. There was a sort of frenzied quality to her running, more than just the usual three-year-old-at-Christmastime frenzy. Isadora had the feeling that her daughter spent too much time around adults, that she was too much the showpiece, the clever child, the little adult. Somehow she felt it not fair to Mandy. She had been forced to grow up too soon. Isadora herself had grown up as the second of four sisters, wedged in among siblings, always having to fight for her bit of attention, but she had never been lonely. Mandy, for all the adults paying her court, seemed lonely and Isadora didn't quite know what to do about it. Ever since she and Josh had separated, she had longed for another baby, longed for it all the more since her time to have babies was growing short. But who would be the father of her fantasy baby? Pinwheel-eyed Errol? Calm, semicatatonic Kevin? Angry, passive-aggressive Josh, who was in Vegas with Ms. Emanon? Well—why not just have a baby and the father be damned? She was likely to wind up raising it alone anyway. Maybe she *would* have another baby when things settled down a bit, when she calmed down, when she got back to work. Maybe she would even write the Papa novel and have a baby at the same time—have a little boy that she could name after her grandfather. There was a thought: write the baby and have the book at the same time.

Suddenly, there was a bloodcurdling scream from the dining room.

It was Mandy. Isadora's heart turned over. Her stomach went all gooey with terror. She ran into the dining room to see her screaming three-year-old sprawled out on the floor over a broken plate which had just a little while ago been full of ice cream. Now it was full of blood.

Mandy's face was red and contorted with pain.

"She ran into the dining room carrying the plate of ice cream and she tripped and cut her finger on the plate," said Roland.

"Let's look at it," he said.

Mandy resisted, but he and Isadora were able to look at her right hand, which spurted blood like a diminutive geyser. The little finger had been sliced open below the first joint and was gaping right down to the bone. The little white and tender place that gleamed inside the wound found a responsive gleam inside Isadora's heart.

"Oh god," Isadora said, gathering up the screaming child. "Dear, dear god."

"Can we borrow the Cherokee?" she yelled to Lola and Bruce.

"Of course," they yelled back. "What happened?" Everyone rushed over to see.

Not answering, she wrapped the screaming Mandy in a blanket, grabbed her coat, and headed out the door.

"I'll drive," Errol insisted, throwing on his cowboy hat and long silk scarf.

"You're too stoned," Isadora protested.

"I'm *fine*, lady," said Errol, bounding out through the snow and taking the wheel.

Roland followed, insisting that he, as a medical student, knew what was to be done. The stoned leading the stoned, Isadora thought. But there was not a moment to spare and Errol was already helping Isadora into the Cherokee with the screaming Mandy.

Roland had brought a clean white dish towel to wrap loosely around Mandy's finger.

"What about a tourniquet?" Isadora asked in a panic.

"A tourniquet can damage tissue," Roland said. "Just hold this towel on loosely."

"Can you drive?" Isadora demanded of Errol.

"Absolutely," he insisted. Had he risen to the occasion and overcome his dope-stupor for Mandy? He adored the little girl, and being allowed to be near her had made his Christmas. Isadora trusted to the gods that they knew what they were doing in sending her these couriers.

Her parents and Kevin had just gotten wind of the accident and came running out in the snow to see what was the matter.

"We're off to the emergency room at Norwalk Hospital," Isadora said. "Meet us there. We haven't a second to lose."

It was still snowing; large crystalline flakes were fluttering down from a pinkish sky. The driveway was thick with snow and icy underneath. Mandy was screaming in terror. Blood flowed everywhere.

Isadora sat between Errol and Roland with the shrieking child on her lap.

"Don't worry," Roland said. "They have great microsurgery techniques nowadays. If we can only get there in time, I'm sure we can save the finger."

But Isadora was not to be so easily comforted. She prayed until she thought her brains would break with the effort of concentration. She prayed for passable roads and time to get Mandy's finger back together. She could not help remembering a similar ride with Chekarf and how it had come out. She prayed. She prayed.

Errol started up the driveway, got to the icy curve, and spun his wheels uselessly in the snow. Then he backed up, started again, and spun his wheels again. Then, on the third try, he gained some momentum and roared up the driveway, skidding on the icy patches under the snow.

They reached the top of Serpentine Hill Road, made a very skiddy turn, went slowly down the hill (skidding all the way). Then they plowed through deep snow all the way to I-95.

The child was still shaking with fear and the dish towel was absolutely soaked with blood by the time they got to the highway. Isadora's pale-pink silk shirt was soaked with blood; so were her pink satin sandals. The blood was sticky between her toes, and the feel of it made her think of Jacqueline Kennedy in Dallas wearing pink and covered with her husband's blood. Except that Isadora was covered with her child's blood—which was rather like being covered with blood from her own body. Better to have severed her own finger than to see Mandy's almost severed. It was as if she herself were bleeding and screaming in that car.

Despite the deep snow, Errol ran all the tolls on I-95, hoping to pick up a police escort to get them to the hospital. Isadora remembered Josh having done the same when Mandy was about to be born, but this time, too, there was not a single policeman to be seen.

The emergency room on Christmas night was no pretty sight. There was a young black man lying on a litter moaning. He seemed to have been knifed in several places, and he was bleeding profusely. Children wandered about forlornly as if they had lost their parents. The benches were full of the bruised, the beaten, the wounded. From the look of the emergency room, you would not think that Christ's birthday was being celebrated. The Prince of Peace seemed to celebrate his coming into the mortal coil with blood, gore, and human dissension. But Isadora didn't give a damn about all these other people. She only cared about her daughter and her daughter's finger. Usually accustomed to being very laid back and leery of asking for special favors, she strode into the emergency room, announced her name to the head nurse, and asked for a plastic surgeon to see her daughter.

The child was still shaking and sobbing. She held the wounded hand under its bloody towel as if it were an alien object with which she could not identify.

"My name is Isadora Wing," Isadora said, "and this is my daughter, Mandy. She has sliced open her little finger on her right hand."

The head emergency-room nurse, a pretty, curly-haired for-

234

tyish woman, said firmly but nicely, "I know who you are. I read all your books. Have a seat and we'll send a pediatric medic."

"I think we should send for a plastic surgeon right away," Isadora said, feeling like the Jewish mother of the Western world.

"I'll see if Dr. Settecampo is in the house," the nurse said. "But please, go into that room and wait for the medic. And try not to worry so." She put her hand on Isadora's comfortingly. Then she indicated a small consulting room where Isadora could take her shaking child.

Errol was out parking the car, and Roland had taken command of the paperwork and was busily filling out forms. He came into the consulting room to get Isadora's health-insurance card. Isadora was utterly amazed to see him functioning with such alacrity under the circumstances. Either he was immune to all the dope he smoked or he had suddenly snapped into clarity because of the gravity of the circumstances.

"Can she bend her finger?" Roland asked.

"She won't let me near it." said Isadora, who couldn't bear the sight of her child's rended flesh.

"Make her try to bend it," Roland said. "They're going to ask you if she has any mobility in the joint."

"I'll try," Isadora said. "Listen, could you try to reach Josh after you make out the forms? Call his parents or his sister for it—they're in the book. I don't have a number for him."

"Right," said Roland, "though the shit doesn't deserve it." He walked out of the room.

Isadora turned to her terrified child.

"Mandy, honey," she said, taking off the blood-soaked towel, and holding back a shudder at the sight of the finger, "try to bend your finger."

"I can't! I can't," Mandy screamed. She couldn't bear to look at the finger either. She turned her face away.

"You *must*," Isadora said, "you must."

"I *can't*, Mama!"

A thousand thoughts raced through Isadora's head. Her daughter was going to lose a finger to the divorce—or even her life, as Chekarf had. Josh would have a change of heart when he realized what had happened in his absence and come back so that never again would Mandy's flesh be jeopardized. Mandy was going to refuse to cooperate with the doctors and lose not only her finger but the whole hand because of her stubbornness and lack of discipline. Isadora thought of the scene in *Sophie's Choice* where Sophie

235

sacrifices her daughter. She thought of Iphigenia sacrificed by Agamemnon for a fair wind. She thought of all the little girls, maidens, young mothers, sacrificed, raped, and maimed throughout history because of the vanity of fathers—fathers who did not bear them, did not nurse them, but who presumed to decide their fates—even *in absentia.* She thought of the long line of bleeding women, of which her daughter was merely the latest. And then she bid herself *shut up.* She willed all the gloomy, pessimistic thoughts in her head to stop, and she attended to the business of trying to get Mandy to bend her finger—and of trying to get herself to look at the process. Never had she prayed so ceaselessly in her life.

The pediatric medic arrived. He was a sweet young man named Bruce with a jet-black handlebar mustache and very gentle manners.

"What happened to you?" he asked Mandy.

"Don't touch!" she yelled.

"I'm not going to touch your hand," he said. "I just want to look at it."

"No!" screamed Mandy.

"Honey—bend your finger for me, will you?"

"No!" screamed Mandy.

He presented a tongue depressor to the screaming child and forced her fingers around it as the wound bled still more profusely.

"Now, are you going to bend that hand?"

Mandy cooperated at last. Isadora looked away, wishing she could undo this whole chain of events. If only it were not Christmas, not snowing, not the worst year of her life. *Stop it,* she said to herself. *Grow up. Think of all the worse things people have had to endure.* And then an amazing thing happened. As she took command of herself, grew if not calm, then at least calmer, her mood was communicated to her child—as if they were still connected. Mandy was allowing the medic to look at her finger. She had almost stopped crying. The little mouth still blubbered, the little eyes were still red and bleary, but Mandy, frightened as she was, was cooperating.

The whole ritual had to be repeated, of course, when the plastic surgeon arrived. And then there were tough decisions to be made.

Dr. Settecampo was the plastic surgeon she had called for. He was brusque, businesslike, but not unsympathetic. He informed Isadora that he could sew the hand right up—not knowing

236

whether the tendons and nerves had been severed—or he could perform exploratory surgery. To do that he would have to put Mandy out and take her to the O.R.

"When did she last eat?" he asked.

"All day long," Isadora said.

"Then we'll have to wait at least six hours for her digestive tract to clear—or she might throw up and aspirate the vomit."

"Is it safe?" Isadora asked.

"Anything requiring anesthesia involves risk," the doctor said.

"And if we don't do the exploratory surgery?"

"Then the finger *may* regenerate—but if the tendons are cut, she'll probably never have mobility in the joint again."

"Never? Even though she's so young?"

"Even in a very young child, tendons don't always regenerate. Look—do you want to talk to the anesthesiologist before you make a decision?"

"I guess so," Isadora said.

The anesthesiologist was brought and he duly outlined the risks of anesthesia for a young child. They would have to wait until Mandy had digested her food. They would have to hope that she wasn't allergic to anesthesia—a terrifying prospect for the mother of an only daughter, of any daughter, any child.

Isadora wished with all her heart that Josh were there. She was furious at him. She felt abandoned, adrift, betrayed—but he was, after all, Mandy's father and he should have had a part in the decision. Since she didn't know where to reach him, she bit the bullet and took the decision herself.

"We'll do the surgery," she told both doctors. "I want Mandy to have the use of her right hand."

In the back of her head were fears of all sorts—death by anesthesia, death by vomit, death by medical negligence. Isadora feared hospitals as much as the next sane person. She knew a hospital could kill you by mistake and then just say, "Sorry—we goofed." But she wasn't going to let her fears deprive Mandy of a functioning right hand. Life is risk, she thought. Motherhood is risk too. And since Mandy isn't yet old enough to take responsibility for the risk, I have to—whatever the consequences for us both.

The decision having been made, the doctors departed. Mandy was transferred to the pediatric ward and provided with a temporary bandage and an angelic white gown. (The very thought of it as angelic made Isadora shiver. *Engelhempt,* they call this sort of hospital shirt in German, and the term never fails to evoke images of death and transfiguration). The little girl was somewhat calmer now, but still basically terrified. Roland and Errol appeared with books and toys from the playroom and did their best to amuse her. Errol even offered to go back to the house and call for Mandy's own toys, but by then Isadora's parents and Kevin had arrived, bringing armloads of Mandy's familiar things, so it wasn't really necessary.

As they waited for the hours to drag by and for Mandy to digest her food, Isadora tried to explain to her daughter what was going to happen to her. She was going to be put to sleep and her finger was going to be sewn up. Did she understand?

"Will you be with me, Mama?"

This was the hardest question of all.

"No," Isadora said. "Mommies aren't allowed in the operating room."

Mandy's lip trembled. Her eyes looked fearful enough to break your heart.

"You'll be asleep, darling," Isadora said. "You won't feel a thing —and when you wake up, Mommy will be right there."

"And Daddy?" Mandy asked. "Will Daddy be there?"

"I know he'd *like* to be here and if I can reach him, he'll come right away."

"Daddy will be here?"

"I don't know, darling," Isadora said. "I can't make promises for Daddy—but I know he *wants* to be here. And I know he loves you very much."

"Oh," said Mandy, her lip trembling.

Six hours later, Isadora stood and watched as her little girl was strapped to a litter, given sedation, gowned, capped, and wheeled down the long hospital corridors, and finally taken through the double doors of the operating room.

Mandy would have to do this one alone, just as Isadora had had to make her decision without Josh. Born alone, we die alone, and whatever companionship and love we get between those two events is pure luck, but not necessarily our birthright. Aloneness is our only birthright. With any determination we can turn aloneness into independence—but nobody guaranteed us love.

As Isadora watched the tiny figure of her child wheeled into the huge, menacing operating room, she thought: Go, little girl, and Goddess bless. Motherhood is an endless process of letting go. So is life.

The operation took seemingly forever. Isadora, her mother, her

238

father, Roland, Errol, and Kevin, waited in the playroom of the pediatric ward, making strained conversation. What could Errol and Roland and Kevin talk about, after all? The only thing they had in common was Isadora's body. In the past, this would have embarrassed Isadora, but now it seemed utterly inconsequential. Sex seemed inconsequential. Everything seemed inconsequential except Mandy's hand, Mandy's destiny.

The men turned to talk of football; Isadora turned to her mother.

"Do you want to take a walk?" Isadora asked her mother.

"Yes, darling. Maybe we can get some coffee."

Well, it was something to do to pass the time. And fortunately, the cafeteria was far enough away from the pediatric ward to make the procuring of coffee a major effort. Isadora and her mother had to walk down a long corridor, take an elevator to the basement, follow red lines on the floor which threaded their way from one wing to another, from old building into new building, from new building into an annex, and so on. When they got to the cafeteria, it was closed. Good. The quest would take even longer.

They walked and walked, retracing their steps, now seeking another cafeteria, an automated one promised by an orderly (who seemed in their state of heightened awareness to be a sort of messenger of the gods). The red line on the floor seemed to be Mandy's destiny and Isadora and her mother seemed to be tracing it—almost as if they were the Fates, weaving the web of a mortal's future. Isadora's awareness was so sharp, so cosmic that she felt almost stoned.

"I remember the night you were born," Isadora's mother dreamily said, preparing to retell an oft-retold tale.

"Yes—what time was I born?" Isadora asked. (This was a sore point between them, since Isadora frequently received offers to have her astrological chart done by willing astrologers who read her books—but since her mother could not remember the hour of her birth, Isadora could never give them adequate information for a detailed horoscope).

"It was during the war," Isadora's mother said. "How should I remember the time?"

"What does the war have to do with it?"

Isadora's mother looked cross—as if Isadora ought to know that the war had *everything* to do with it. (Oh, the gap between generations! Isadora would never quite know the *feel* of the Second World War the way her mother knew it, nor had her mother ever

239

quite known the *feel* of the First World War the way *her* father, Isadora's grandfather, had known it; nor would either of them ever truly know what Mandy knew of *her* moment in history—starting with now, her lonely experience in the O.R., her first major war.)

"Well, of course the war had *everything* to do with it," Isadora's mother said. "In the first place, there were no doctors, only nurses —which was fine with me. I could have delivered you in a half-hour, I was that dilated—and you were a second child—but the nurse was afraid that I'd sue the doctor if I knew he wasn't there for the delivery, so right after the baby slid out—after *you* slid out, she slapped an ether mask over my face to try to cover up for the doctor's not being there. Well—I was livid. I was enraged! You were already born, of course, and I wanted to hold you. So I bit the nurse's hand . . . Too late. I heard her scream as I went out cold . . ."

They had found the automated cafeteria. It was brightly lit with bluish fluorescent lights which flickered as in some technicolor nightmare. Pictures of crullers, donuts, cups of coffee, chicken soup, hot cocoa with marshmallows were displayed on the vending machines as in some Pop Art fantasy. The whole place was beautiful, Isadora thought—beautiful in a grotesque sort of way.

Isadora and her mother busied themselves with making change at the change machine, with pressing buttons for extra cream, extra strong, extra sweet. Going through this mechanized feeding ritual (always with the hovering awareness that Mandy's fate hung in the balance upstairs), Isadora was reminded of some of the most visceral memories of her early childhood. They all dealt with food, of course. Patriotism, says Lin Yutang, is the memory of foods eaten in childhood. Food evokes our strongest loyalty.

Isadora remembered running through the underground arcade at Rockefeller Center when she was just a tiny child, no bigger than Mandy—tall enough to see the world as a forest of legs, a forest of kneecaps, but too short to see the faces that belonged to these legs and knees. She is holding an adult hand and running as fast as her baby legs can go. She is afraid of losing that hand and being irretrievably lost in the bowels of the earth like some baby Persephone, erring irredeemably in letting go of Demeter's hand. She is running, running, following an adult stride belonging, of course, to her mother (who would never willfully lose her—or would she?), when all at once a smell of halcyon sweetness overtakes her, overtakes her nostrils, her tonsils, even, it seems, her eyes—and then a large hand comes down from above and pops a piece of gooey chocolate fudge into her mouth: fresh-made fudge from some underground candy stand, and she receives the fudge sacramentally from her mother's (the Mother Goddess') hand.

Now it is thirty-six years later and they are exactly the same height. Goddess and disciple grown into equals. They are buying coffee together to fill the time until they hear the fate of their little offspring—the mutal sprout on the tree of both their lives—Amanda.

Isadora gulps her coffee, burns her tongue, then puts down her cup on one of the tables. She embraces her mother tightly.

"Thank you," she says, "for biting the nurse's hand. Thank you for bearing me. Thank you for everything, everything."

She has said the one thing most mothers never hear, most daughters never say—because blessings embarrass us, while curses always come readily to our lips.

Isadora's mother is touched—yet she draws away, abashed by her own surfeit of emotion—and her daughter's.

"Well—" she says huffily, "what did you *expect* me to do?"

Mission accomplished, they go back upstairs to the playroom in the pediatric ward and find the men still discussing football.

"Has the doctor come out yet?" Isadora asks.

"Not yet," says her father.

"Not yet," says Roland.

"No," says Kevin.

"Soon," says Errol.

They sit and wait.

Isadora thinks of Mandy, her little life so new, yet also so firmly rooted in her, in everyone around her. If Mandy were to be taken away, nothing would ever restore Isadora's will to live. Art would not compensate. Religion would not compensate. Good works would not compensate. It was unthinkable, yet she thought of it. Josh had given her this child—yet now he was gone, leaving the decisions, the consequences, almost entirely to her.

"Did anyone reach Josh?" she asked.

"I reached his sister," said Roland. "She promised to try to get him."

"Poor Josh," said Kevin, "he'll be sick at heart when he realizes what happened in his absence."

"Poor Josh!" said Roland. "Poor Josh? That pig! If Mandy were *my* baby, I wouldn't have left her and her mommy for the world. What a fool that man is! He deserves anything he gets."

Just then the plastic surgeon appeared at the playroom door. Isadora's heart seemed to miss two beats.

"Mrs. Ace?" he said. "Mr. Ace," he said, addressing Roland.

"No—" said Roland, "unfortunately, I'm not Mr. Ace. Mr. Ace is not here."

"Well," said Isadora, "how is she?"

"She's going to be fine," said the surgeon, "just fine. And it's a good thing we made the decision to operate because both tendons had been severed and both nerves, and even a little piece of bone had been sliced off. You made the right decision."

"When can I see her?" Isadora asked.

"She's in the recovery room now," said the surgeon, "but she won't wake up for a while. You can go up and wait there."

Isadora embraced the surgeon in a great bear hug, and her father, Roland, Errol, and Kevin broke out in a spontaneous round of applause.

Later, when Isadora waited outside the recovery room for the sleeping Amanda to awaken, she thought: Well, I got through it without Josh. This is another milestone.

But she missed him; she still missed him. And when Mandy opened her eyes, her first words were:

"Where's Daddy?"

12

Bean, Botkin, & Bum Dreams

Some for the Glories of This World;
and some Sigh for the Prophet's Paradise
to come; Ah, take the Cash,
and let the Credit go, Nor heed
the rumble of a distant Drum!
—*The Rubáiyát of Omar Khayyám*

Every man over forty is a scoundrel.
—GEORGE BERNARD SHAW
Maxims for Revolutionists

JOSH flew back immediately to see Amanda. Flying from west to east always seemed interminable (because of the time change) and especially at Christmas, flights were unbearably delayed.

By the time Josh got to Connecticut, Amanda was home, ably manipulating all her Christmas presents with one hand and seemingly not much the worse for wear.

The snow was still high and deep everywhere—though the driveway had been plowed and sanded not once but several times. Josh drove down the driveway in the Land Cruiser as before, but his demeanor when he entered the house was quite different. In tears, looking as if his legs could barely support his own weight, he threw his arms around Isadora, and wept. His body shook with great sobs.

"Is she okay?" he asked. "Is she okay?"

"I think she'll be *fine*," Isadora said, comforting him, comforting this man who had tried to kill her in her motherhood, kill her in her art, kill her in her womanhood. All right then, she *would* comfort him. He felt guilty enough. She would not twist the knife.

"We did everything we could for the finger," Isadora said. "The tendons and nerves have been repaired. I think it should heal well."

"You made the right decisions," he said. "I can't fault any of the decisions you made."

"Thanks for saying that, Josh. It means a lot. It really does."

"Were you very angry at me for not being there?" he asked. "I started back the minute I heard."

"Not really," she said. "More sad than angry. After all, the accident was no one's fault."

He began to sob and hold her again, and she had the distinct impression that he had been cruel to her not out of strength but out of weakness—and that everything she had suffered from him was the tyranny of his weakness. A stronger man would not have had to leave her. A stronger man would not have been threatened by the things that threatened him. He was a big, overgrown, bald-

ing child. His parents' killing legacy to him was utter infantiliza-
tion. *They* needed him to be a baby and he had obliged by never
growing up. That did not make him a bad person, it only made
him a weak one. And Isadora's curse was that she was strong. The
strong got to bear the greatest burdens—that was the way of nature. She did not hate Josh; she merely saw him—perhaps for the
first time. His weakness was only a criminal failing because Mandy
was involved. Had he merely sinned against Isadora, it could have
been borne.

But would she want to bear it? Would she want him back now,
if he wanted to come back? For once she couldn't really answer
that question affirmatively. She didn't know. She was beginning to
think she'd be better off alone. She had no fantasies of a different
kind of man. For the first time in her life, her fantasies did not
involve a man at all; they involved herself, merely herself. That
was a lot.

It was the dour, dull week after Christmas, when the relief of
the holiday being over almost compensates for the drabness of the
weather. Christmas has been removed from one's chest like a
hundred-pound weight in the *peine fort et dur*—that charming medieval torture imposed upon accused witches in merry olde sixteenth-century Germany. Oh, there is still the horror of New
Year's Eve to come—another medieval torture—but soon all the
dread pseudo-gaiety will be behind one, and life will begin again
in all its ordinary wonderfulness.

Isadora often thought that something in her inner core was
attuned to the solstices and equinoxes (perhaps all sensitive people
were this way—or perhaps she was really a witch) because she
grew depressed right before Christmas when the sun was farthest
from the earth, and she cheered up after Christmas when the sun
began its gradual return (or rather the earth's elliptical migration
brought it closer to its nourishing, life-giving star). The day after
Mandy's accident, Isadora's best friend, Hope, sent her a basket
of spring flowers with a card that read "Spring is ever near."
Isadora was almost beginning to believe that spring *would* come
again. Mandy's hand would get better. The snow would—eventually—melt. Isadora's driveway would be passable again and all
would be—if not right with the world—at least brighter.

She would welcome spring by getting healthy, she decided. If
she couldn't really write again yet, she would get into shape for it
the way a boxer gets into shape for a fight. For writing, she knew,

246

was physical labor. Not just the mind, but the body had to be in trim.

In celebration of Christmas being over and Mandy's hand healing, Isadora went on a fruit-and-vegetable purification regime and she resolved to join a health club and attend it regularly. *Le Chaim* —to Life! she thought. So a few days after Christmas, she accepted the offer of a friend of hers to take her to a Nautilus club in one of the nearby towns and teach her how to use the machines.

It was a spiffy Connecticut club—full of thin-lipped WASP ladies who were getting in shape for love affairs they would never have, tennis matches they would lose, Caribbean vacations that would only reveal how empty and silent their marriages were.

Isadora was wearing a black and fuchsia harlequin-style leotard and gray sweat pants with fuchsia stars printed on them. She felt good in her body the way one does on a fruit-and-veggie binge. She had her period, too, but it felt like a cleansing rather than a loss—as periods sometimes do. She had dropped seven or eight pounds since Christmas and she walked with a bounce, glad to be alive, glad Christmas was over, glad Mandy's right hand would function, glad she could get through a day without thinking of Josh. Josh was not entirely gone from her thoughts—but she no longer made all her decisions with reference to him, and she was beginning to enjoy her independence mightily. As she tried the machines in the health club, she was looking over all the attractive sweating men and thinking that she could choose this one or that, spend a weekend with whomever she pleased—or even spend a weekend alone if she chose. She was beginning to feel strong enough even for *that*. Her sap was beginning to run again; her life-force was coming back. Her bravado—so long in abeyance— was starting to return.

The friend who took her through the club was a good man, a good pal—a handsome black-bearded journalist named Steve Rinaldi whom she had met and become friends with when both he and she were married to other people. They had flirted with the idea of having an affair but never really got past preliminary fumblings. It was not meant to be, perhaps—or not yet. They had retreated gratefully into platonic friendship, having dinner together at Westport dives, sitting up all night before the fire, drinking wine and speaking of poetry. They were really fond of each other. They confided in each other about the post-divorce crazies each was going through. They talked on the phone late at night (oh, how would we get through divorces without the telephone?), but they were determined *not* to be lovers. Lovers were a dime a dozen in the days after divorce; it was friends that were rare.

Steve showed Isadora how to use all the machines. They worked up a good sweat together, then sauna-ed, hot-tubbed, and were preparing to go out to lunch—when they were stopped at the door by a very tall young man whose name Isadora didn't quite catch at first. But she did catch his blinding blue eyes which had a look that was both slightly mad and very vulnerable.

"Isadora—this is Bean," Steve said.

"Bean?"

"Berkeley Sproul the Third," said the young man. 'Bean' is what I got stuck with, a corruption of my baby name—that's the trouble with giving kids ancestral names . . . Berkeley was my mother's maiden name—like the square where the nightingale sang . . ."

A nightingale was singing to Isadora, too—a very Keatsian nightingale who was making her heart ache and a drowsy numbness pain her sense. What was this opiate she tasted? Was it LAFT? —or Lust at First Sight? Was it an earthquake or was it merely a shock? Was it the real turtle soup, or was it merely the mock? Was it Keats—or was it merely (merely!) Cole Porter?

Bean had dirty-blond hair, as tousled and flyaway as a kid's, and he had an utterly dazzling smile. Isadora looked at him and had one thought and one thought alone: how to get his phone number. Drat. She didn't even have her engraved business cards with her.

"Bean's an actor," Steve said.

"Oh—what a coincidence," said Isadora, "my sister happens to be a casting director. She's always looking for new faces."

Now, Isadora's youngest sister, Chloe, had, it is true, worked as a casting director for a few years, but she had long since gone into another line of endeavor—and was studying to be a psychotherapist—but Bean didn't have to know that.

Steve stood there amazed while Isadora and Bean fixed each other in their blinding blue gaze. Their eyes were exactly the same color—navy blue with yellow flecks. They locked eye-beams as in some metaphysical poem by John Donne. (In that scene in bodice-ripper romances where the vulnerable heroine meets the rakehell hero, this is the moment when she notices that his eyes are gray and his lower lip "curls"—meaning, one supposes, that he sneers slightly, due to years of debauchery and the lack of the love of a good woman or "one true love" to set him—and his lip—straight. But Bean's lip curled only in delight, not cynicism.)

"I didn't get your name," he said.

"Isadora W . . ." Steve started to say, but in his confusion over being in the midst of this electric embrace of auras—if not of arms —he mumbled the last name.

"What an unusual name," Bean said.

"I might say the same to you," said Isadora.

"Do you have a piece of paper?" Bean asked Steve. "I want to give this lady my phone number—for her sister, of course . . ." He looked at Isadora, beaming gleefully.

Steve-the-Cupid produced a tattered piece of paper and both Bean and Isadora scrawled numbers on it. Then Bean tore it carefully in half. He took the half with Isadora's number on it and gave her the half with his. (Isadora had given him her answering-service number, not her private line—but she seriously hesitated before making that choice. Something in her head kept saying "private line, private line, private line . . .")

And then they parted—as suddenly as they had met. Bean waved good-bye as he went to work out, and Steve and Isadora went to lunch.

"Who's that guy?" Isadora asked Steve as they were walking out to the parking lot.

"I don't know him very well," Steve said, "but I run into him a lot at the health club. He's good news. I get very good vibes from him. I'm not sure why because I really hardly know him."

"Oh—one can tell about people," Isadora said.

And it was true, too. Isadora had great instincts about people, rare intuition, but sometimes—quite often, in fact—she let her intuition be clouded by her need. Just as she was able to create people out of whole cloth—create a demonic lover because she needed one, create a steady daddy because she needed one—she was often misled in her secondary judgments of people by her neediness—or her *spilkes*.

File Berkeley Sproul under "forget," she thought walking at Steve Rinaldi's side. The last thing you need, old girl, is another lover . . . But even as she thought this, she thought of a nickname for this new friend: Bean Sprout, Bean Sprout the First.

Back at home, there was trouble—trouble right there in Rocky Ridge. There was nanny trouble to begin with—and then there was—heaven help us—tax trouble. The very last thing one needed in this period of calm after Christmas was nanny trouble, but there it was. Apparently one no sooner laid one demon to rest than another popped up. That was life in the fast lane. Or perhaps just life. Just life itself.

Isadora walked into her house at about four in the afternoon to be informed by her secretary, Renata, that they had big problems. While she was at the health club hearing nightingales sing, Alva Libbey was apparently scaring Amanda senseless with stories of hellfire and damnation.

"I couldn't help overhearing Alva saying to Mandy that she'd cut her finger as punishment for her mother's sins. 'The sins of the mother are visited on the child,' she said. I really think we ought to be looking for a new nanny. Apparently this isn't the first time she's scared Mandy with hellfire stories."

"How do you know?" Isadora asked.

"Because," said Renata in her usual understated nonalarmist manner, "Mandy has come skipping in here saying, 'Alva says I'm going to hell—what's hell?' "

"Oh god," said Isadora, "she wouldn't do that, would she?"

"She not only would—she *does*," said Renata. "Not that I think Mandy knows what hell *is*—but she's certainly scared by the *tone* of this stuff. And Alva also tells her that she dare not go out and play on her swing set or kidnappers will get her. Alva's just lazy. She doesn't want to watch Mandy outside."

Isadora trusted Renata's judgment almost completely in most matters. In the matter of children, she trusted her completely. She breathed a deep, soulful sigh. The great nanny search was on again.

Isadora couldn't fire Alva or even intimate that she was going to fire Alva until she had another nanny on the hook. So while they trod water and began the always agonizing process of going through the employment agencies, seeking the halt, the lame, the blind (why in a society that pretended to worship children did people feel that taking care of children had a status akin to being an untouchable in India?), Isadora tried to gird Mandy's loins by telling her 1) that there was no hell, 2) even if there was one, she wouldn't be going there, and 3) Alva's warnings about kidnappers were groundless.

Mandy said: "The people who steal children go to hell, right, Mommy?" Well—what could Isadora say to that?

"Wrong. There is no hell, Mandy. And no people around here are stealing children, either."

"Oh," said Mandy vaguely, as if she didn't know what to believe. "Can I watch the Muppets?"

It was a wonder Mandy was asking this since Alva let her watch television all day and all night apparently. Alva believed in the video-wallpaper method of baby-sitting. Why Isadora had kept Nurse Librium this long was an astonishment anyway, but maybe the answer was to be found in the preceding cavalcade of nannies. Isadora had come to believe that any elderly stable person *had* to be better than a young English chick with jangling ovaries, but in truth Alva Libbey was probably the least stable nanny of all. A virulent Catholic who read the *National Enquirer* for its prose, Alva Libbey was at once obsequious to Isadora's face and horribly judgmental behind her back.

"I don't care what you think of me and my life," Isadora said to Librium, "it is not your job to give my child instruction in *your* religious theories."

"Oh—I would never do that, Miz Izzydorry," said Librium. "I would never in a million *years* do that."

"Well—see that you don't," Isadora said menacingly.

And she went upstairs to Renata's office to begin—again—the long search for the perfect nanny. Or at least for a relatively imperfect one who would stay.

Between phone calls to employment agencies, friends who had Swedish *au pairs* (who had other friends in Sweden), friends who had Danish *au pairs* (who had other friends in Denmark), and friends who had Finnish *au pairs* (who had other friends in Finland), Renata buzzed Isadora with some news that might make the whole question of nannies academic forever.

"Call Mel Botkin," Renata said. "It's important. Something about a tax audit . . ."

Is there a phrase in the English language more fraught with menace than *a tax audit?* If there is, it is probably, *Is it in?* or *malignant neoplasm.* In fact, there are few phrases as ominous as *tax audit*—unless they are the sort you see on medical charts at Memorial Hospital.

"God," said Isadora, "Mel Botkin. What on earth would lead Mel Botkin to intimate the existence of a problem on the phone?"

"A big problem," Renata said, "shall I get him for you?"

"Mm-hm," said Isadora, imagining an eighteenth-century debtors prison (a Newgate straight out of *The Beggar's Opera*) where she and Mandy and Dogstoyevsky would live out their productive years cadging food and favors from the avaricious turnkey, who only granted them same because he lusted for the now nubile Amanda and her aging—but still peppy—Mom.

Mel Botkin was Isadora's business manager. A bouncy rotund Jewish CPA whose ancestors came from that town in the Ukraine where a whole generation of Jewish grandmothers must have been raped by Tartars, he had slitty Asiatic eyes, high cheekbones (like an obese Pan), a huge Afro of curly black hair (which he called an "Isro"), a wife in Long Island, a mistress in Soho, and dozens of show-business clients who depended on him as slavishly as they depended on their analysts.

Isadora had come to Mel at a time in her life when her affairs were in a total mess. To her astonishment, she had just begun earning large sums of money and she hadn't the faintest idea what to do with it. She had no receipts for anything, no canceled checks, could not read a ledger, and certainly was not equipped to deal with those densely printed little pamphlets the IRS seems to issue every other day. It is a paradox that in the country of self-reliance, *Poor Richard's Almanack*, not to mention the puritan forefathers (and foremothers), our government has managed to reduce all but her totally destitute citizens to utter dependence on their CPAs. And we call that democracy!

Mel Botkin was Super-CPA. His clients were a Who's Who of neurotic Jewish show-business types (with a few neurotic WASPs thrown in for good measure). Ham Garland was perhaps his biggest client, his ur-client. Ham Garland, né Herman Grabowsky, was a little, skinny, redheaded nightclub comedian turned moviemaker. By dint of sheer wit and force of personality, he had managed to parlay his pasty-faced, freckled geekiness into sex appeal (in a country where fame translates into sex appeal for even the ugliest man—though it does not necessarily do the same for the ugliest woman). Ham Garland was in some ways pure genius and in other ways pure asshole. It was he who had managed to make a silent movie one of the biggest box-office hits of the seventies. It was he who managed to get great reviews in *The New Yorker* and also keep the *National Enquirer* guessing about which Swedish sex symbol was currently living in his "gracious" West Village townhouse. It was he who had perfected to a high art the trick of spurning Hollywood while taking its money.

But Ham Garland was the perfect client for Mel Botkin. Ham Garland didn't want to know from money and Mel Botkin was great at the "don't-worry-your-pretty-little-head-about-it" (or, in

Ham's case, "your-balding-little-head-about-it") school of money management. Ham Garland was renowned for never carrying even a dime to make a phone call. His chauffeur (who trailed him down the streets of New York in a black Jensen-Healey with plates that said—God help us—AUTEUR), carried dimes the way Queen Elizabeth's ladies-in-waiting carry *her* shillings and pence. Isadora was often in Mel's office when Ham's secretary called from various points abroad to ask that money be transferred to Venice or Paris or Rome. Sometimes she sneaked a peek at Ham's ledger and was amazed to see that in one year he had earned fourteen million dollars. Now—*there* were tax problems compared to which Isadora's were small potatoes.

Mel—in his kindly, avuncular way—never really demanded that his clients become simpering infants in his care, but his practice was structured in such a way that it was hard not to. Mel had teams and teams of little gremlinlike sub-CPAs, and hand-holding secretaries whose main function was to make you leave it all to them and feel good about it. Did you have a deadline on a book, a film to edit, a play in rehearsal? They would pay your bills, file your taxes, invest your money, argue with your landlord, buy you that car you needed (get the vanity plates for it, have it insured, even have it custom-striped at a special place Mel alone knew about). Were you moving to the Coast for six months? They'd find you the house, sublet your apartment, make all the travel arrangements, and even get your dog crated and shipped without letting the airlines kill her in the process. There was no way that busy, neurotic, absorbed, obsessed, creative types wouldn't have been seduced by the range of services Mel offered. He was nothing less than Sugar Daddy or God. After a while you got so used to saying to your spouse, or secretary, or lover, "Send the bill to Mel" that you began to think Mel was *making* the money for you and kindly permitting you to live high off his hog.

Not that Mel ever did anything to dispel this illusion. On the contrary, he promoted it. Charming, chatty, with a wonderful bedside (audit-side?) manner, he always had time for his clients—time to come to Connecticut and spend the whole day talking about whether or not you should put in a hot tub, time to go house hunting on West Tenth Street if you decided you *had* to have an historic brownstone, time to plan your vacation in Venice with you, time to help you shop for a Rolls or a Jensen-Healey—or even a Ferrari.

It was years before Isadora understood the psychology of Mel's practice, and by then it was too late. Creative people—to use that terribly belabored phrase—cannot really see what they produce in relation to money (let alone in relation to densely printed IRS pamphlets) because they do not produce it *for* money. It comes to them as pure gift and they give it out as a tree gives leaves. They cannot, in truth, hold it back—whether there is money for it or not. Just as Shaker artists used to call themselves "instruments," anyone who has ever had the experience of a poem or a song or a play coming through her fingers knows that the gift is not really hers to sell. It is passed along, given out, given back to the stream of creation from which it comes. Of course, one has to eat and pay the rent, landlords notoriously refusing to take poems and songs instead of checks, but the artist's relation to money is always queer because the production of art is not *for* money; one would do it even if one got paid nothing at all. (Isadora, for example, wrote poems and novels long before she had any expectation of selling them to publishers and she still values most the work she does without pay, without contract, without advance: her poems in particular). Because of this paradox of art as gift in a money society, it is not surprising that many artists feel the need of an intermediary to deal with the world of money for which they feel so ill equipped. And in Isadora's case that intermediary was Mel. He was like the *Shabbes goy* who lights the fires for the religious Jew on the day of prayer. He dirtied his hands with money so that she did not have to. His fingers alone touched the till. His fingers alone were *in* the till.

Well, what did you expect? Did you expect to get a Jewish *Shabbes goy* for nothing? Just as you wrote the books because you had to (and never expected to make a nickel off them), you were like a child when the money began pouring in—and what *else* would you do but find a daddy to give it all to?

Besides, Mel was wonderful about money—as free and open-handed with money as poets are with words. It was *he* who really taught Isadora how to enjoy money, how to *live*. "Why fly tourist" he'd say, "when Uncle Sam picks up half when you fly first class?" "Why *not* buy that designer dress for two thousand dollars—your image on TV demands it." "Sixty bucks for a haircut—why not? After all you're a 'personality.' " All the things Isadora felt guilty about spending money on—namely her own *pleasure*—Mel absolved her of guilt for, saying it was important to her work, her image, her peace of mind. He was instant cure for the Protestant ethic. He was Mr. Generosity—with her money. Whenever Isadora called him up in a panic asking, can I afford this or that, Mel would say, "We can afford it." Isadora figured that as long as Mel said "we," everything was okay. When he started saying "you"—as in "*you* can't afford it," she'd know she was in big trouble.

Did she never have misgivings about Mel? Of course she had misgivings. She would have had misgivings over *anyone* having power of attorney over her money. (Mel took care of everything except the trust for Mandy, which was in Lowell Strathmore's care.) But she felt sort of helpless about it. First of all, she didn't understand those IRS pamphlets. Secondly, she was always so busy writing, was always so obsessed with the next book or the next—that the IRS pamphlets seemed like flies buzzing at her ears —and Mel became her flyswatter. She was always trying to get to page 200 by Christmas, or to page 400 by July fourth. Or else she was pregnant and racing the book against the baby, trying to see if she could get at least a draft of *Tintoretto's Daughter* done before she went into labor (she couldn't). Nor did she have a husband to take over these tasks. If anything Josh was even *less* business-oriented than she, and more than happy to leave it to Mel! *Leave it to Mel* became the theme of their lives. *Leave it to Mel* also became a way of their never having to deal directly with the fact that she was supporting their ménage. Mel paid the light bill, the gas bill, the mortgage, the school bill—not she. Mel's existence was a salve to Josh's delicate, threatened ego. If Isadora had had to sit down and write the actual checks, Josh would have floated away even sooner than he eventually did.

From time to time she had a fantasy about Mel absconding to a country from which there was no extradition. Mel was a great sailor who kept an oceangoing sloop—and Isadora often thought that one day she would arrive at his ratty little office on West Forty-fourth Street—in the kind of old theatrical office building where the doors are glass and have names lettered on them—and find that Mel Botkin had boarded up the door, left a crudely lettered sign that said, GONE FISHIN', and departed for Venezuela. As Isadora stood there pounding on the door, suddenly all Mel's other clients would appear—Matthew Myers, the gorgeous, green-eyed, lantern-jawed talk-show host (who also did commercials for Atari); black-haired, be-knickered Lola Thornton, that refugee of the sixties (with her rainbow of little kids and her various twenty-year-old lovers—most of whom had been drummers with her band); Hassell Frumkin, the chubby comedian who toured colleges doing imitations of Ronald Reagan and Richard

Nixon; Jennifer Hines and Stedman Stillman—the grand old couple of the American theater; Hilly Workman, the dwarflike screenwriter; and of course Ham Garland (who had never actually come to the office before—Mel came to *him*—but was making an exception in this case). As they all assembled there, the horrible truth would dawn: *Mel Botkin had sailed away with their money!* Then and there they would organize an expedition—"organdize an expotition" as Pooh Bear says—to Venezuela to snag the fraudulent Mel and return him to justice (possibly with the help of Superman?) on America's shores. It would all be done as a sort of Jean-Paul Belmondo caper movie. All these various *fartootst* intellectuals and theatrical types would suddenly turn into slick French adventurers (dangling Gauloises from their mouths) or Caribbean pirates with sabers between their teeth. Off they would go on the Great Venezuelan Caper, becoming persons of action for once instead of *luftmenshen!* Great battles and great danger would intervene. Mel would be brought to justice; contrite, he would kneel before them and promise never, *never* to take their money again. Then they would sail triumphantly back through the Bermuda Triangle (having made their money *un*disappear), return to New York, and everything would be copacetic as before, a chastened Mel now doing their business honestly. Hah!

So much for fantasy—reality is always a little more unbelievable.

"Hi, Mel," said Isadora, "what's up?"

"Nothing much," Mel said avuncularly, "but I think we should have a little talk."

"Why? What's the matter?"

"Well, I think we should talk about it face-to-face. Shall I come up to Connecticut or are you planning a day in New York anytime soon?"

He said this most casually, but Isadora could hear the panic underneath—but was the panic hers or Mel's?

"How soon do we have to have this little talk?" Isadora asked.

"Oh—any time would be okay," Mel said, as casually as possible —"but the sooner the better. Are you coming to New York tomorrow?"

"I will," Isadora said, "it it's that important." (She was secretly relieved that Mel had not insisted on coming to her; if he had, it would probably have meant the problem was even worse.)

Great. She had to go to New York the next day—go to New York and leave the child with a woman who was telling her hellfire stories. Isadora thought about it for a while and then decided that it was impossible to keep Alva Libbey one more day. The damage had already been done to Amanda's psyche, perhaps, but keeping her another day with full knowledge of the hellfire tales was something her motherhood could not countenance. If need be, she would quit work cold and take care of Mandy herself till she found a decent replacement. In the meantime, she would make do with temporary part-time sitters—of whom there were a few in the neighborhood.

Alva was astounded to be fired—"I dint do nothin' wrong, Miz Izzydorry," she said. Isadora contemplated bringing up the hellfire question once again and then decided it would do no good. She packed Alva off as soon as possible—to the tune of Mandy screaming, "I don't *want* a new nanny! . . . I don't want a new nanny!" (had the kid been brainwashed?)—and got in feckless, redheaded Danae as the temporary sitter so she could go off to New York and see Mel.

Danae was the sort of character you only find hanging around towns like Malibu or Venice, California, Woodstock, New York, or Rocky Ridge, Connecticut. She was a beautiful, slightly loony Englishwoman (from the North—Lancashire, to be exact) who waited tables in various health-food joints, catered dinner parties, baby-sat, did gorgeous needlepoint, taught yoga, and passed bad checks. She was only thirty-five, but had four grown kids from various unions (the kids were as lovely as the unions apparently hadn't been), and she seemed to float from one odd job to another, from one man to another, from one house-sitting stint to another. She had no visible means of support and yet she seemed, somehow, to keep afloat. Kids adored her—she was, after all, Lady Madonna—and Amanda was no exception. She had been a part-time baby-sitter for Amanda since her infancy. So Isadora left Mandy in Danae's somewhat chaotic (but basically sound) care and drove off to New York to see Mel.

Mel's office had always reassured Isadora that he must be, at bottom, honest. If he were a crook, would he have had such a modest office? Here was no Hollywood money manager with chrome strips on the art deco walls and chairs that cost $7,000 in the D and D Building (or at the West Coast Design Center). Here was no fantasy out of *Architectural Digest*. Comfortingly enough, Mel had no sauna, no device for hanging upside down, no brown suede couches, no cactus garden under spotlights, no "collectibles" (like antique quilts) staring at you in the waiting room. No—his office smelled of old cigar smoke and looked like a set for *The Producers*. (And, of course, you remember that the last scene in that movie takes place in *jail?*)

The one couch Mel had was an old, saggy brown leather affair with springs that had come untied many tax seasons ago; the chairs were 1930 vintage walnut office chairs that squeaked when you tried to lean back in them; and the filing cabinets were army khaki. Old copies of *Variety* and *The Hollywood Reporter* were strewn around (with a few *Wall Street Journal*s thrown in). The receptionist chewed gum and had a green stripe in her hair. Since so little was done for show at the offices of Botkin and Son (oh yes, Mel Botkin had a son he treated like a lackey and never allowed to have any contact with the clients) you had to assume that basically sound and sensible things were being done with your money.

Isadora was ushered into Mel's inner sanctum. As usual, he seemed to have all the time in the world for her and absolutely nothing of a business nature to discuss.

"So how's the gay divorcée?" he asked, getting up to give her a great bear hug. Bear hugs were Mel's specialty. He had a big belly that got in the way, but that only made him more of a Poppa bear.

"So-so," said Isadora, "slowly getting my sealegs back."

"It's a tough transition," Mel said, never having made it himself —since he had a wife of thirty years and a mistress of ten. But he was all empathy and warmth, and truly Isadora felt warmed and happy to be here, sitting in his office. He had called her in, supposedly, to talk about a tax audit, but all he seemed to want to do was chew the fat about other, more pleasant matters. Since Isadora had a reputation for having written books that were said to be racy, Mel always wanted to poll her about phenomena like sex clubs, massage parlors, soft-core cable TV, the latest racy books. Today he wanted to report a visit to New York's most famous sex club—Eros Anonymous—which he had apparently made with his mistress. (Mel never alluded to his mistress directly, but there was a special phone under his desk that he answered in a tone reserved for someone who elicited all his erotic yearnings. Isadora thought of this as the "mistress phone." And she knew from Mel's various winks and leers when he answered it, that there must be a secret companion he took to all the places that Florence Botkin of Cedarhurst, L.I., wouldn't be caught dead in.) Actually, *Isadora* wouldn't be caught dead in a mattress club either. She had gone once (out of a sense of duty as a cultural reporter)—when Eros

258

Anonymous had just opened—and her distinct impression was that religious orders ought to send monks there in order to help enforce their vows of chastity. The place, in short, had made her want to give up sex. She and Josh quickly found that they couldn't even make it with each *other*—whereupon they fled into the night. But Mel adored Eros A. He had taken some Japanese business-men there with girls from an escort service, and they had all had, apparently, a jolly old time.

"Did the businessmen bring their cameras?" Isadora wanted to know. (She could just imagine two diminutive Japanese in three-piece suits, clicking away, while two naked mile-high chorus girls loitered on their arms.)

"No," said Mel, laughing merrily. "I don't think they allow pic-tures."

"When I was there," Isadora said, "I kept thinking I'd catch athlete's foot. Athlete's foot *all over* my body."

"And to think that you invented it—" Mel said.

"Invented athlete's foot?"

"No—I mean sex," said Mel.

"Invented sex? God—you flatter me."

"No—I mean, weren't you the one who first coined the term *the unzippered fuck?*"

"Zipless," said Isadora. "And lived to regret it. On my tomb-stone it will probably say: 'Here lies one who first said Zipless Fuck' —and all the poems and novels will be so many stones thrown into the water."

"I doubt it," said Mel.

"Guess I'm just still depressed," Isadora said. "Okay, Mel— what's this tax-audit thing?"

"Well," said Mel, "it's nothing *very* bad . . . or nothing that can't be fixed, most likely . . . Remember that investment called Lotus Limited?"

"No," said Isadora, "sounds like a Chinese restaurant."

"Well, I'm sure I told you about the investment. It was basically a straddle."

"What's a straddle?"

"It's basically a sort of hedge," said Mel.

"What's a hedge?"

"Well, you take a position on both sides of a transaction, go long and short at the same time . . . It's rather complicated—but if you want, I'll give you all the prospectuses to read. They're immensely long and totally baffling, but . . ."

Here Mel produced several heavy xeroxed tomes that had what seemed to be hundreds of pages bound in clear plastic covers.

"So—what happened?"

"Well, you had quite a lot of money invested in Lotus Limited . . . and you see, most of the money . . . well, due to poor management, the shelter . . ."

"This was a tax shelter?"

"Yes . . . Well, due to things in the management which we couldn't control, most of the original investment has been . . . well . . . dissipated."

"You mean I lost a lot of money. How much?"

"Well, you can't really look at it as a loss, because you got a huge tax write-off . . ."

Isadora's head was swimming. Here was Daddy, Poppa Bear, who was supposed to protect her, announcing to her that he had lost all her money.

"How much, Mel?"

"Well—the original investment was only two hundred thousand dollars, but if the investment is disallowed, you could owe as much as a million in back taxes . . ."

"I could owe—*what?*"

This was a nightmare out of Kafka. She could wind up owing more than she'd ever known she had.

"Do I have the money to pay the back taxes?"

"Well, I don't think the case will be decided for years and years and years, and by then, you'll be paying out inflated dollars which are worth less than today's dollars and meanwhile you've had the use of the money, which otherwise would have gone to the IRS."

"I don't understand."

"Well, you see, you have the *use* of the money now . . ."

"But what's the good of that if the investment has been dissipated?"

"You see, you don't pay back the taxes until the case is settled and by then you're paying back in dollars that are worth much, much less . . . Do you understand?"

"No . . ." Isadora said. All she understood was that she was in big trouble. The eighteenth-century debtors prison loomed closer.

"Probably," Mel said, furiously backpedaling, "none of this will ever come to pass. If the government disallows the tax shelter, we'll fight it, and if the time ever comes that you need to pay back the money, it will seem like very little . . ."

Isadora was thunderstruck. The only occasions when she felt

she had money were those when she went out and bought a designer dress or a new car. Her concept of money was not much different from a ghetto black's. If she couldn't *wear* it or *drive* it, she didn't believe she *had* it. All the rest was a matter of inscrutable ledgers and even more inscrutable tax regulations. That was why she had turned it over to Mel—and now she discovered that Mel had seriously fucked up. Perhaps Mel had even liquidated Mandy's trust. He had the power to—on paper. And she had been too busy with the upheavals in her life to ask.

Of course, she never thought to ask Mel the pivotal questions either: Had Mel or his company received a fee for promoting Lotus Ltd.? What *was* Lotus Ltd. anyway, and who ran it? But Isadora was so overwhelmed by a sense of panic, of being alone and exposed in the world, that she was nearly speechless. Oh, she knew full well that there were no guarantees of daddies to protect one. Josh had promised to help her raise Amanda—and he had fled. Mel had promised financial sensibility (if not total security) and now it seemed he had gone and put her money into something that sounded like a fortune-cookie factory.

That's the way the cookie crumbles . . . she thought—but her very next thought was: What on earth to do? Problems have to have solutions—and this was a problem to be attacked.

"Well—what do we do next?" Isadora asked Mel.

"Nothing for now," Mel said. "I just wanted you to know the parameters of the problem."

"Is there anything more you're not telling me?" Isadora asked.

"Just that I couldn't be more sorry this happened," Mel said— and he got up and gave her a big bear hug.

Isadora wandered out onto the street like a deranged waif. She had QUIM parked in a garage on Forty-sixth Street, but she wasn't even walking toward it. Instead, she walked toward Broadway, observing the bars, the bums, the cacophony of life in this sleaziest section of the city. This might as well be eighteenth-century London, and Mel a highwayman who had robbed her and left her freezing in the road, for that was how exposed she felt. She had no husband, no one to share in the support of her child, and the one thing she knew how to make money at—writing—she had not been able to do for the past year because she had been so depressed. She had felt her strength slowly returning, but now it was as if someone had rabbit-punched her in the stomach all over again. Losses, losses, losses. First Papa, then Chekarf, then Josh, then her nest egg—what would be next? Of course, she could get

261

a job teaching again and slowly pay off her debts. She'd be five hundred and six before she paid off *this* debt on a professor's salary, but still maybe she could move to some pretty little Vermont town like Middlebury, teach poetry, live in a white farmhouse, send Mandy to public school, and eventually marry an absentminded professor who would cherish her for herself alone and not her fleeting fame or fortune. It was a pleasant fantasy. She loved teaching and truly she'd be happy to have a good man who loved her regardless of her assets and her glitter. Or maybe, she thought—wildly switching gears—she could snag a rich husband *before* the government took back everything—much as that went against the grain. Okay, old girl, she thought, why not *try* to be attracted to men in suits, men with gold watch chains, men whose angle of erection is inversely proportionate to their bank balances? Hopeless. Isadora *never* had been able to peddle her ass for security. She was too straight—in her kinky way. She cared too much about sex to pervert it into some kind of commodity exchange. Oh, she knew that she could snare a rich husband if she wanted one—but the trouble was: she'd have to love him. She was incapable of marrying *just* for money.

This was a great district of the city to be walking through while having such gloomy thoughts. The bums were out in force. Isadora felt about bums the way she felt about dead animals in the Connecticut roads: heartsick. She saw the chilblains on their fingers and she wept. She wished the bums of New York had gotten that $200,000 and spent it on sweaters and hats—instead of Mel Botkin spending it on Lotus Ltd. If she'd ever known how much money she'd had in one place (before the crash of Lotus Ltd.), she'd have distributed it freely among the bums. The truth was— she identified with them. Homeless, seeking shelter in doorways, sticking out their reddened hands for the quarter that might or might not come along, they were as dependent on the vagaries of the Great Goddess as any artist.

The book would come—or not—in its own sweet time. The public would buy—or not—depending on the fickleness of public taste, the vagaries of reviewers, the happenstance of newspaper strikes. You could write your heart out and have the ill luck to publish during a strike, a flood, a fire, a plague. Isadora might as well be a bum, she thought, as be an artist. And then she thought of her grandfather, her grandfather who had lured the bums off the streets and taken them home to his studio to paint them. They had eaten her grandmother's chicken soup, warmed their toes on her Oriental rugs, stank up her velvet upholstery, and Papa had painted them, caught their pathos for all time—or at least for a little while, until the canvas rotted or was lost.

Isadora stopped in a doorway and stared at a sleeping vagabond who reminded her of one of her grandfather's paintings. His nose was red and covered with exploded capillaries. He wore a tattered green ski cap and he rested on a pallet of old newspapers, snoring loudly. What did he dream of in his addled bum-brain? Bum dreams? Dreams of foods eaten in childhood, of hellfire tales told by an old nanny (was he a formerly *rich* vagabond?), of loves lost and fortunes slipped through his fingers? The bum stirred, heaved, muttered something unintelligible like a sleeping child. Isadora wrapped her coat tightly around herself and ran all the way back to the garage where QUIM was parked.

While she was driving home, it began to snow again and the road grew slippery. There was a huge wreck on I-95 and she sat in traffic for nearly an hour while the police cleared away the wreckage of two jackknifed trailer trucks and three smashed cars. When she finally got back to Serpentine Hill Road, she was exhausted and it was nearly suppertime. Mandy was happily watching "Sesame Street" in Danae's care (oblivious of the fact that she and her mother might soon be broke) and Renata had gone home, leaving two pages of phone messages. Mel Botkin's office had called three times since she'd left; her agent had called; there were various calls from various boyfriends; a call from Kevin; two dozen nuisance calls concerning celebrity auctions (Isadora always thought they meant to auction *her,* but they only wanted her old clothes or manuscripts) and the sort of free speeches she was always asked to give at fund-raisers; there were also three phone calls from Bean Sproul (aka Bean Sprout).

The first thing she did was call Mel's office. No answer. Then she called Renata at home.

"Isadora . . ." Renata said gravely, "Mel died of a massive coronary this afternoon—not less than two hours after you met with him. He was at the office of another client on Fifth Avenue. That's really all I know about it."

"You're kidding—" Isadora said, sitting down and pulling off her boots.

"Would that I *were,*" said Renata. "You can call his secretary at home if you want more information about it."

"Should I really call *now?*" Isadora said.

"She said to. I think she'd like to talk to you. Let me know what happens. The number is on your desk with the messages I left."

Isadora called Gladyce, Mel's secretary, a chubby lady in her fifties who was as motherly as Mel had been fatherly. Isadora's psyche was a mass of conflicting emotions. Here she had always been expecting Mel to sail away to Venezuela—and instead he had sailed away to Hades—leaving her affairs in utter turmoil! Isadora was too shocked to register grief or loss. The whole sequence of events had such an air of unreality about it that it *had* to be true.

"Gladyce," she said, getting Mel's secretary on the phone, "I just heard the news. What exactly happened?"

"He went over to Ham Garland's office to go through some computer reports on the new movie and he apparently had a heart attack. I came right over and arrived just about when the medics did. But he was already gone. He passed on about four in the afternoon."

"It's unbelievable," Isadora said. She noted the delicacy of the euphemism *passed on.*

"It certainly is," said Gladyce. "He was such a wonderful man. No one will ever take his place."

"We all loved him," said Isadora. And it was true, too. She *had* loved him. What a cheat to discover at the last moment that he was not all he appeared to be. She felt a little the way a loyal wife must feel when she goes through her husband's effects and finds that he has left his whole fortune to some doxy. (Speaking of which—Mel's wife would now be in for quite a little surprise, too.)

"When's the funeral?" Isadora asked Gladyce.

"Well—the family hasn't made arrangements yet. In the next few days I should think."

"Let me know," Isadora said.

"Of course, dear," said Gladyce in a voice that implied that everything would still be taken care of as usual. Mel might be in heaven—or hell—but you could still send the bill to Mel and Mel would still pay. He was only promoting tax shelters in heaven—in between strums upon his harp. Had God made too much money this fiscal year? Was He in hock to the IRS? Mel would take care of it. *Leave it to Mel.* Of course, the Almighty might wind up owing back taxes *somewhere* along the line—but the main thing was: He had the use of His money. Or should we say: His Money?

The absurdity of Mel's dying at a time like this suddenly

changed Isadora's mood from gloom to mad abandon. It was so insane—first to be told your affairs were in a total mess and then to have the perpetrator of that mess die and leave you high and dry. Isadora would have to sort it all out somehow without his paternalistic guidance. What a lesson in impermanence and letting go! What a lesson in the unreality of worldly things!

The phone rang again just as Isadora was sitting near it. Though it was the answering-service line and not the private line, she picked up at once. What *more* could have happened? Were Ham Garland *et al.* organizing an expedition to heaven to get Mel to return their money? It would be something like the Warren Beatty version of *Heaven Can Wait*—sets full of fleecy clouds and she and Ham skipping arm in arm through heaven singing like Judy Garland and Ray Bolger. No, wait—that was *Wizard of Oz*. What matter? Mel Botkin had proven to have his share of humbug, too. They had followed their own yellow brick road straight to disillusionment.

"Hello, Isadora?" came the voice on the other end of the phone. "This is Berkeley Sproul—you know, Bean . . ."

"Oh, hi," said Isadora.

"I just happen to be in your neighborhood and I'd love to come by for a glass of wine. Would you invite me?"

Well, he certainly was direct about it. Normally, Isadora would have said no. She had an ample stable of young men to choose from and she wasn't planning to add Berkeley Sproul III to it. He was too beautiful, too appealing, too much potential trouble. Unemployed young actors spelled trouble. So did employed *old* actors. So did everyone, in truth—after a while. Young men were trouble. Old men were trouble. Life was trouble. So was death. But Isadora felt so giddy with abandon following Mel's sudden death and the sudden disappearance of her assets, that she heard herself saying to Bean:

"Sure, come over. Maybe I'll even give you dinner."

"Great," said Bean. "I can't wait."

"Me, too," said Isadora.

She put down the phone and gazed out the window. It was snowing even harder now and her icy driveway—which had melted during the day and refrozen at sundown—was covered with fresh powder, making it still more treacherous than usual. Was she *crazy*—to invite a total stranger? She was drained from the day's exertions—drained and disillusioned. Her period was at its heaviest; great quantities of blood had been pouring out of her all day—growing more copious with each new stress she faced. She had no nanny—only the irrepressible Danae, who hadn't been planning to stay the night, but now, seeing the snow coming down, decided to.

What the hell, Isadora thought. If I'm about to be broke, might as well have fun. So she put her kid to bed with stories and kisses, lent Danae a nightgown and gave her fresh sheets for the nanny room opposite Amanda's nursery, reapplied her makeup, changed her Tampax, doused herself in Opium, turned on the hot tub optimistically, put a dreamy George Shearing record on the turntable, opened a bottle of wine, and waited for her gentleman caller.

13

On a Skid

the boys i mean are not refined
they go with girls who buck and bite
they do not give a fuck for luck
they hump them thirteen times a night

one hangs a hat upon her tit
one carves a cross in her behind
they do not give a shit for wit
the boys I mean are not refined

they come with girls who bite and buck
who cannot read and cannot write
who laugh like they would fall apart
and masturbate with dynamite

the boys I mean are not refined
they cannot chat of that and this
they do not give a fart for art
they kill like you would take a piss

they speak whatever's on their mind
they do whatever's in their pants
the boys i mean are not refined
they shake the mountains when they dance
—E. E. CUMMINGS

The Road of excess leads
to the Palace of Wisdom.
—WILLIAM BLAKE

HE came into her life on a skid, she always said after that night, and it was true. If Mel hadn't invested her money in Lotus Ltd. and then dropped dead, if Alva Libbey hadn't gone the way of all nannies, if it hadn't snowed *again,* if she hadn't been exhausted, drained, bleeding, and yet also oddly exhilarated at the prospect of starting life afresh totally broke—would she have ever let as disruptive a force as Berkeley Sproul into her life? Probably not.

He arrived in a motley van, painted, like his own temperament, in red, purple, yellow, and day-glo orange—one fender of each color and a mélange of spray painting on the side panels, like a bad LSD trip. He had, anyway, the air of a merry prankster, or a court jester—twinkling blue eyes, dirty-blond hair that flew in every direction, a smile to make you melt. His socks were two different colors—one red, one gray. His clothes were disheveled and smelled slightly of mothballs. He wore a big white fisherman's sweater that was unraveling under the armpits (from all the life-force bursting out?), a long woolen scarf (red), and no overcoat, so much the air of a vagabond did he have. And he carried a white orchid in a silver bud vase, which he presented to Isadora.

"Orchids—at this time of the year. Where do you get them?" she asked.

"My mother grows them in her greenhouse in Darien," he said, "Da-rien: *yes* in Russian and *nothing* in French. *Yes, nothing!* That about describes the place. It's the land of the wasted WASP, home of the sore winner."

Isadora laughed. She had the sense that she had written him in a book and then witnessed an astounding metamorphosis as he came to life. He might have been Marietta Robusti's suitor, not hers. No—not even Marietta Robusti's, but a character out of an even earlier age—the age of Arthurian legend, perhaps, the mists of prehistory. Sir Lancelot—or Gawain.

"What were you doing in the neighborhood?" Isadora asked.

Bean looked at her blankly.

"I *wasn't* in the neighborhood," he said. "I was at my parents' in Darien. I just thought I'd never see you again if I didn't act fast. First of all, when you gave me that piece of paper with your name on it, I *freaked out*. Here I merely thought you were an outrageously beautiful woman, and you turn out to be my favorite author, too."

"Flattery will get you everywhere."

"I mean it. Your pictures don't do you justice. I never would have guessed you were *that* Isadora."

"Are there very many *other* Isadoras?"

"There's Isadora Donkey . . . as the joke goes . . ."

"Oh god—possessed by the bad-joke demon . . . You're the man of my dreams. One bad pun and I'm yours forever . . . Would you like a drink?"

"And dinner," said Bean, "if you're still offering . . . What you don't know is that I have called your secretary about a dozen times in the past twenty-four hours—and she keeps telling me you're out or you're in the shower, or in the sauna. Either you're the cleanest woman in Connecticut or you give out your phone number and then change your mind a lot. I didn't leave *too* many messages because I didn't want to seem pushy, but I *had* to see you again." He smiled that dazzling smile.

"Let me get you a drink," Isadora said, and she bounced off into the kitchen to get the wineglasses and the chilled wine. She was exhausted; she had cramps—but she was also exhilarated.

"Would you like to make a fire in the living-room fireplace?" she called to Bean.

"Sure," he called back. "I'm an old Connecticut boy. Grew up here and in New York," he said. "That was before the crash."

"What crash?" she called out.

"Well—I'll tell you if you promise to come back."

"I'm coming!" Isadora called from the kitchen.

"I should hope so," called Bean.

She came back into the living room with wine and cheese to find him on his knees expertly laying the fire.

"That's a well-laid fire," she said.

"I won't even dignify that with a response," he countered.

"You make me merry," she said, "and I've had one hell of a day. Anyway—tell me about the crash."

"Well—there were two," he said. "The crash where my family lost most of their money to the IRS . . ."

"What an astounding coincidence . . ." said Isadora.

"And then the car crash . . . Which would you like to hear about first?"

"I don't really know," Isadora said. "Have some wine. It's a lovely Trefethen chardonnay which I may not be able to afford for long . . ." She handed him wine in a crystal goblet, and then, as an afterthought, she asked:

"How old are you, Bean?"

"Twenty-five," he said. "Does that disqualify me?"

"For what?" Isadora asked.

"To be your friend," he said gravely. Suddenly, she looked in his eyes and she knew he meant it. His eyes could be merry, but they also had a very vulnerable look. Was he possibly scared under all his banter?

"I want to be your friend," he said. "I feel, from reading your books, that I already am . . . Do people say that to you a lot?"

"Not the way you said it," she said. "What they *usually* say is that I've been their sexual fantasy for seven years—and then we get into bed—and *pffff* . . ." She made a gesture with her right index finger which indicated a penis going into profoundest detumescence.

Bean laughed. "Actually, I thought your supposedly scandalous first novel not nearly so good as your second or third, or *Tintoretto's Daugher* . . . There was so much self-hatred in that first book. Don't you ever stop beating up on yourself? You *should*. You've got more balls than most of the men around. You're a real hero— in the classical sense."

" 'What is a hero?' " Isadora quoted. " 'Primarily one who has conquered his fears.' "

"That's it," said Bean.

"That's Henry Miller's definition, not mine," said Isadora, "and by that definition I'm *not* a hero because I feel fear all the time."

"Ah—you may *feel* it—don't let the fear control you," said Bean. "I'll bet Odysseus felt fear, too. In fact we *know* he did. It isn't the presence or absence of fear that makes a hero—it's the action completed in *spite* of the fear. And you never stop the action. You go on right into the teeth of the storm. That's why you're my hero."

"Thanks," said Isadora. "It's nice to hear in the midst of the worst year of my life. I nearly died this year. I never thought I was suicidal, but after my husband walked out, I was ready to throw myself in front of a car. In fact I did. I threw myself in front of *his* car."

Bean looked at her intently, as if he knew exactly what she was saying.

"I'm an accident looking for a place to happen," he said. "I have more scars up and down the length of my body than anyone you'll ever meet."

"I'll match you scar for scar," she said.

"Done," said Bean. "Let's get naked."

"Have I been your sexual fantasy for seven years?" Isadora joked.

"No. Only for the last seven minutes."

"You're looking at a wreck of a woman," Isadora said. "I've almost given up my profession—and not by choice either. I, who have never been blocked in my life, find myself suddenly unable to write at all."

"You're merely shifting gears," Bean said, "or lying fallow for some great, new flowering. I don't for a minute believe that you're really blocked. Art is not mechanical—it's organic. You can't produce it the way a factory produces nuts and bolts."

"Thank you for reminding me of that," Isadora said. "I've never felt so used up, so finished."

"You must be doing something right," said Bean, "to be so alive and so beautiful."

She looked at him with gratitude, if not with total trust, and said:

"So tell me about the two crashes."

"I will," said Bean, "if you give me dinner."

"Spoken like a true vagabond," said Isadora. "Next you'll want a bed for the night."

"The floor will do," said Bean, and laughed.

At dinner (which Danae had made and which was consequently delicious), Bean spilled out the story of his family *mishegoss*. Oh boy—Jews love to delude themselves that they have cornered the market on *mishegoss*, but they don't hold a candle to the WASPs in the realm of the *meshugge*. Bean's family history was rife with shootings (accidental and purposeful), squandered inheritances, family manses and antiques fought over (as in some Cheever story), alcoholism, incest, greed, embezzlement, lawsuits, prison terms, heroics, and mock-heroics. His ancestors had fought in the Revolutionary War, the War of 1812, the Civil War. His immediate family's fortunes had fallen from five houses (New York, Paris, Palm Beach, Martha's Vineyard, Darien) to one—a crumbling manse in Connecticut crammed with crumbling furniture and crumbling collections of books and paintings that were all, anyway, in immediate danger of seizure by the IRS for back taxes. As far as Bean's own hope of personal booty, he had long since quashed it by his insistence on pursuing a career as an actor.

"There are no actors in the Social Register, my mother is fond of saying," he said.

"Not true—there must be *one*. How about Dina Merrill?"

"Well, I guess," said Bean. "One ac*tress*. It's anyway the profession of whores and vagabonds. I've never known a woman who could tolerate an actor's life. Not even actresses can stand it. We work all night, sleep all day, cavort with beautiful young women who are usually half naked, have no fixed addresses, don't wear suits, seldom shave, have ambiguous sexual habits—or voracious ones—and usually have no money at all—but love to spend other people's. Also, we eat like slobs."

He dangled a chicken leg from his teeth for emphasis while making a mustache out of a lemon rind (it was Danae's fabulous lemon chicken with sesame seeds).

Isadora laughed.

"So tell me about the crashes," she said.

"Well, the first is the conventional tale of the fall of the family fortunes, told by the would-be seducer to the astonished young maid."

"Young? I'm more like an old maid—"

"Not after three marriages, you're not."

"How do you know?"

"I? I only know what the world knows. Your life is an open book."

"Do you have any idea how old I am?"

"I figure you've got to be older than me or you wouldn't have written all those books—but I can't imagine how you did it without it aging you."

"Hah," said Isadora. "More flattery. I reached puberty the year you were born."

"Yes—and now I'm going to make it all worth your while."

"You're really potential trouble," Isadora said, laughing. "Tell me about the second crash."

"Oh yes—*that*. Well, quickly passing over the tale of fortunes lost and great houses fallen in ruins—"

"The one you tell the potential seducee."

Bean nodded and continued. "—I go on to the tale of my at-

273

tempted self-slaughter, as they said in Elizabethan times . . . You see, I've been trying unofficially to kill myself ever since *I* reached puberty. Maybe it's because I have too much energy—and no place to put it—or maybe it's because I realized then that my father had been trying to off *me* since I was born and I had somehow—according to my shrink—internalized his wish to do it. But anyhow, I seem to have these very nearly fatal accidents all the time. The last one was two years ago when my head flew through the windshield of my car, my chest flew into the steering wheel, my spleen flew all over the inside of my body, and I hovered between life and death for two weeks, having out-of-body experiences, while my parents went bananas, and one young nurse tried to suck my cock while I was conversing with God and the angels . . ."

"And what did you learn while you were conversing with God and the angels?"

Here Bean became very serious, almost solemn.

"That God and the angels do not care who sucks your cock— but that a life without love is not worth living—even if you have fame, fortune, and lemon chicken to eat. So when I saw you at that health club and you looked so beautiful, so succulent, but something in your eyes looked destroyed, betrayed, haunted—I knew I *had* to see you again . . ."

"Sir Galahad to the rescue. Are you one of those men who only falls in love with damsels in distress?"

"No," said Bean. "I usually do not fall in love with anyone. I usually fuck my brains out and go home emptyhearted—but with you, I have a feeling that even if I never get to fuck you, you will fill my heart each time I see you."

This brought tears to Isadora's eyes. She blinked them back. She was not sure whether she was hearing honesty or blarney. It was her curse to be moved by a man who could turn a phrase, however flowery, and it was either curse or blessing (she was never sure which) that she was so vulnerable. She girded her loins. She would *not* sleep with Bean, she decided—however he might appeal—or however appealing he might be. His openness, his emotional vulnerability was either very close to her own—or else he was *really* a good actor, and a bit of a con man (as all performing artists must be—and perhaps even writers?).

"Lately, I have also been doing a lot of fucking my brains out and going home emptyhearted," Isadora said. "It gets boring really fast. I never did *enough* of it before to know that—whatever my reputation. But I've decided to give up promiscuity."

Bean snapped his fingers. "Damn—just my luck to meet you *now*, on the round heels, as it were, of that decision."

Isadora laughed again. She was trying to figure out how much sincerity was here, and how much humbug. Without a doubt, Bean was one of the most charming people she had ever met. He could charm birds out of trees, candy from babes, money from misers. But she was determined not to let him charm his way into her bed.

They had left the fire to smolder in the living-room fireplace, and were now putting one log after another on the blazing fire in the dining room. Outside, it kept snowing lightly and the sky had that wonderful pink-as-a-baby's-bottom look it gets during a snow-fall. Usually, snow in Connecticut panicked Isadora, but this snow-fall was warm and friendly because Bean was here. Perched in the big wooden house on the cliff, at the end of the treacherous, snaky driveway, at the end of Serpentine Hill Road, Bean and Isadora talked on.

"Why do you think you're so self-destructive?" Isadora asked. "I mean, *really*? Is it only your relationship with your father? Don't get me wrong—I *believe* in that sort of thing. I think that a man who never slays his father, never grows up—as witness my last ex-husband, Josh—but why are you slaying *yourself* . . .?"

"Because I want to kill *him*, so I turn the aggression inward?"

"Too glib," said Isadora. "Listen, I spent the first twenty-five years of my life accumulating scars, too. Scars, broken bones, broken marriages. I nearly crippled myself being thrown from a too-spirited horse in Texas. I broke my tibia in twelve places following my inscrutable Oriental second husband down an icy slope in the Austrian Alps—which I *knew* I shouldn't be caught dead on. But I think I was always punishing myself because I felt so guilty, guilty for being more talented than my sisters, guilty for using my talent the way my mother didn't use hers, guilty for being so blessed."

"So you admit it—you *are* blessed."

"I guess."

"Like being born with a little extra spin on the ball—as the WASPs say." (Here Bean imitated a tight-lipped WASP accent— the sort of accent Isadora thought of as "Locust Valley Lockjaw.") It was so uncharacteristic of him, it made her laugh.

"Or an extra shot of adrenaline—as my mother said of me when I was a child," Isadora said.

"Precisely," said Bean, still mimicking a real WASP. "Hey—you like that? You like when I don't open my mouth to talk?"

"I love it," said Isadora. "It's so unlike you. You're the most openmouthed man I've ever met. But still, you're going to have to go home."

Bean looked utterly crestfallen. His shaggy eyebrows drooped. His blue eyes suddenly lost their sparkle. Even his perfectly pointed WASP nose (the sort that Romance novelists call *retroussé*) seemed to retreat toward his upper lip as if in pursuit of sudden Semitism.

"But there's so much more to *say*," he said. "We have to discuss Nietzsche, Schopenhauer, and sex."

"We've *already* discussed sex. Nietzsche and Schopenhauer will have to wait."

"But don't you *need* sex to power your creativity?" Bean asked.

"Not tonight," said Isadora. "My business manager just dropped dead, leaving me with horrendous tax problems. I have my period and I'm utterly exhausted. I'm going to stand up now—if I still can after all this wine—and ask you to go home."

"What can I do to dissuade you?"

"Nothing," she said, standing up and reeling slightly from the wine. "I swear it. Nothing."

Bean looked suddenly like a very tall Holden Caulfield. He seemed fifteen, not twenty-five. His upper lip trembled as if he were about to cry. His enormous blue eyes grew watery. Suddenly, Isadora *could* imagine him killing himself. He had already told her that he owned a revolver and knew how to use it. He had also told her that he used cars as lethal weapons—and the roads were certainly treacherous. Ought she ask him to sleep in the guest room?

No. Impossible. Impossible to have so sexual a presence in the house and not fuck him. Well—if he was so self-destructive—it was his problem, she thought. She was tired of taking care of the whole world. She was tired of taking care of young men. Josh, Roland, Bean—they would all have to fend for themselves. But were old men much better? Apparently she had taken better care of Mel Botkin than he had taken of her.

"I think you should go home," Isadora said. She held onto her chairback for support. She could feel the cramps in her belly dragging her downward and she was wondering whether the last Tampax was beginning to seep. In about a minute, trickles of menstrual blood would begin inching down her thighs.

"I loved tonight," Isadora said, "but I really think you should go home."

Why she was so determined not to sleep with him she didn't really know. After all, she had slept with plenty of men she liked less. Maybe she sensed the hold he might come to have over her; maybe she really *knew* what a formidable presence he might become in her life. When a woman is powerfully attracted to a new man, sometimes that is just the moment she chooses to flee. But when a man is just so much chopped liver—she can bed him and go her way unhooked.

"Let me at least give you some autographed books," Isadora said to the misty-eyed Bean. It was the old ploy: books not bed. Or books as a prelude to bed—she wasn't sure which. At fifteen, she had written poems to men instead of bedding them. At twenty-five, she had done the same. At twenty-eight, she had written a whole novel just because of a man she could not have (for he was impotent with her out of spite)—and when, in her thirty-first year, the novel was published, the world became hers for the asking, but still not that man. At thirty-nine, she had substituted bed for books, and always come home dry-eyed and emptyhearted. What was the final solution to the book-bed dilemma? *Was* there one? Did she only love the unattainable man, the man under the bed, the impossible object—finally Daddy?

"Come upstairs," she said, leading Bean to her tree-house study. She walked carefully, rubbing her thighs together in her jeans, to keep the blood at bay.

They mounted the spiral staircase that led to her studio. Up there, in her gray-carpeted sanctuary, lined with her books, she could see his astonishment at the quantity of volumes she had produced. He saw her as a woman, not a book machine—but clearly she was also a book machine. She had laid waste forests on sundry continents to proliferate her words in a multitude of languages.

"French, Spanish, German, Italian, and what else?" he asked, amazed.

"Japanese, Hebrew, Dutch, Danish, Swedish, Finnish, Norwegian—and even Serbo-Croat and Macedonian—but not Swahili," she said drunkenly. Why was she so proud of her foreign editions? She had no way of knowing if their texts even remotely resembled anything she had written. Well, in the French and Italian and

277

German, she had *some* way of knowing, but the other languages were all Greek to her. And yet, there was such a gap between intention and effect anyway, that her books were never quite what she intended, even in her own native tongue. It was as if she meant to draw a unicorn, but produced somehow a goat with a pasted-on horn. The result was always so far from what she intended that she could derive little pleasure from it. The best part was the writing itself—the flow of words on the page, the joy she found in covering her yellow legal pads with multicolored inks. Let other authors stare at video screens. She needed the visceral feel of paper and ink; she needed the sheer physicality of writing.

But the end product? That was not for her to enjoy or even to judge. It was artifact to her: the process was all. Surely all authors must feel this way; surely they must feel the painful gap between intention and effect, and even when the readers raved, one wanted to say: No, no—life is much more interesting, complex, and rich than prose can ever be.

"Here," she said, grabbing a hard-cover copy of *Tintoretto's Daughter.* She began to inscribe it for Bean.

"To Berkeley Sproul III. May you live to see the IVth and Vth and (even) VIth. And may you fall in love in Venice someday—as Marietta Robusti did—but not have to die for it. With much affection, Isadora Wing."

She handed him the book. He read the inscription, and looked even more misty-eyed. Then he grabbed her suddenly and hugged her very tight. She could feel his hard-on under his jeans, and she could feel his very large, very gentle hands cupping her ass and then moving up along her back, fondling her as if he wanted to press her body into his. But it was the way he touched the back of her neck and her hair that astounded her. His fingers found the very place on her neck that always caused her the most pain when she had her terrible tension headaches and they began to massage it with infinite tenderness. How did his fingers know just where to go? It was uncanny. One hand remained on her neck, and the other moved up to her head and rubbed it with such gentleness and love that she might have been a child again, having her head rubbed by her grandfather as she fell asleep.

Now she was really panic-stricken. No man (except her grandfather) had ever found those parts of her body before; no man had ever known to rub her neck and head that way. If he knew that—what other, more volatile knowledge of her body might he have? She was afraid to find out.

"You have to go home," she said to Bean, breaking away. "You really do."

He nodded sadly. She took his hand and led him down the spiral stairs, wondering, Was she *mad* to let him go, or was she sane? No more love, she had promised herself, no more beguiling young men whose hearts are "wax to receive and marble to retain" (as Byron says).

"That's right—throw me back in the gutter, where vagabonds belong," Bean said histrionically.

Downstairs in the foyer Isadora handed him his long red scarf and his fisherman's sweater. She even found an old ski cap of Josh's to offer him, but he refused.

"No thanks," he said, "I'd rather freeze to death if I can't have you. I'd rather die in the gutter."

" 'We are *all* in the gutter,' " Isadora said, " 'But some of us are looking at the stars.' " She opened the heavy front door and snow swirled in.

"That's from *Lady Windermere's Fan*," said Bean. "Now let me quote you something even more relevant from *The Importance of Being Earnest*." He walked out onto the snowy flagstone path, flung the red scarf dramatically around his neck and declaimed: " 'I *hope* you have not been leading a double life, pretending to be wicked and really being good all the time. That would be hypocrisy.' "

"*Touché*," said Isadora. "Now go!"

Though she was wearing only a sweater over her jeans, she walked out to the van with him, reveling in the pinky, snowy night, which was really not very cold after all.

"Careful," he said, "don't slip." He held her arm with great tenderness.

When they reached his flamboyant van (which was lightly dusted with snow), he opened the door and looked at her again sadly.

"Go home," she said, hugging him briefly. He leaned down, took her in his arms again, and kissed her on the mouth with a tongue that knew the inside of her soul. He might have been kissing her cunt not her mouth for the excitement that it generated in her. His tongue knew everything about her mouth, as his fingers had found the sensitive place on her neck. She felt she could come just kissing him.

"Go home," she said again, breaking away. She was wondering why she was so determined to get rid of him. What we all want most is to be *known*, and Bean certainly knew her. Was that why

279

he had to go? She stood on tiptoes and playfully stuck her tongue in his ear. "Go home," she reiterated.

Without a word, he got into the van, revved the motor, and began to back up. She waved, and walked back to the house, feeling that she had just narrowly escaped with her life, her freedom, her soul.

Thank Goddess, she said to herself, deeply relieved to hear his engine roaring up the driveway.

Inside, she stripped off her clothes, changed her Tampax (just in time to avert a bloody disaster), and put on an old flannel granny gown. She lathered up her face with black soap, enriching the estate of Dr. Lazlo—wherever he might be—in heaven, perhaps, doing deals with Mel Botkin?

Bean's arrival in her life had cheered her immeasurably. What the hell if I'm broke, she thought. I'll make it again as I made it the first time. She felt reckless, enterprising, fearless, exuberant. She felt that her life was beginning again—all the more so perhaps because she had to start from scratch. She would declare bankruptcy, sell her possessions, simplify her life. The classic car would go—maybe *both* cars would go—and so would the diamond earrings Josh had bought her. She would be perfectly happy with a smaller house and smaller car—even no house or car at all. Writing was what mattered, not money, not fame—writing and Amanda. And what about love? No. It wasn't time for love yet. Good thing she had sent Bean home. He was a real threat to her resolve to stay free, a real threat.

Isadora finished her Lazlo regime, turned on the light in the bedroom, and prepared to curl up in bed with a book—preferably a classic rather than the masses of importunate galleys that crowded her bedstand, seeking blurbs. "Read not the times, read the eternities," Thoreau says, and on the eve of bankruptcy, one needed the classics more than ever. Well then, she would read Thoreau. She would reread *Walden,* as a prelude to selling the house and cars and moving even deeper into the wilderness. She could certainly face life without black soap!

American literature was upstairs in the attic, the room where she had written *Tintoretto's Daughter,* now Mandy's playroom. The adult books had not yet been moved out. Isadora put on her funny old red Eddie Bauer goosedown slippers (the ones that made her look like she had clown feet) and she padded to the main stairs and thence to the attic in search of Thoreau. Just as she passed the front door, she heard a most persistent knock.

"Isadora!" came Bean's voice. "Isadora!"

"Shit," she muttered to herself. "I must look like holy hell."

She threw open the front door.

Bean stood outside, teeth chattering. His hair was covered with large snowflakes. His nose dripped slightly and was very red.

"What happened?" Isadora asked.

"I slipped off the driveway and the van got stuck in a snow-bank," Bean explained. "I can't push the damned thing back onto the road."

"A likely story," she said.

"It's *true*," said Bean. "I drove off the road and just missed plowing into a tree."

Isadora looked at him cynically. "You drove off the road on *purpose*," she said, immensely relieved that he was not dead, and that he had come back.

"I swear it—I did not," Bean said. "I skidded backwards off the icy curve."

"Sure," said Isadora laughing. "Anyone who wants to get laid that badly must be absolutely incredible in bed."

And she took him by the hand and led him into her bedroom.

They threw off their clothes—sweater, scarf, granny gown, goosedown slippers, jeans—and fell into each other's arms as if their whole lives had been a preparation for this moment.

Talk about the Zipless Fuck! Talk about the impossible fantasy come true! Bean took to bed as a duck to water, a polar bear to snow, a starving man to a hunk of mutton. You'd have thought—from the way he went at Isadora's body—that he'd been starved for female bodies his whole life, though clearly that was not the case. He was so hungry, so horny (yet so oddly pure in his hunger and horniness that she wanted to say, "There, there—nobody's going to take it away from you," but she refrained, out of fear of being flippant about his prodigious sexuality). Nor did he have any kind of hang-ups about taste or smell. It was clear that he relished smells, juices, sweat, blood. He dove into her muff with great exuberance, parted it, found the white string that dangled chastely there and pulled her Tampax triumphantly out with his teeth.

"Aha! A string!" he said between clenched teeth. He chewed on the Tampax lightly, savoring its taste, then tossed it to the floor and dove in again, tongue-first. He played lusty tunes on her clitoris, plunged a practiced finger into her snatch, and reached all the way in until he found, on the anterior wall, the sweetest spot. By rubbing her expertly there, while his tongue trilled on her clit and the other hand pressed down on her belly, he brought her swiftly to the most palpitating climax she'd ever known.

She tried to close her legs to rest a while, but he forced them apart (ignoring her protestations) and rammed his cock inside her. He rocked her from side to side, touching parts of her insides she could have sworn were untouched before; then he pulled back suddenly, and rammed it in again. Now he began to pound her mercilessly. Raising himself on his arms, he went at her cunt with his ferociously hard cock as if he meant to annihilate all trace of any previous lovers. "For Josh," he said, ramming it in, "for Bennett, for Brian, for all of them." He pounded her so hard that she was about to come again, but just at that moment, he pulled back saying, "Not yet, baby, not yet," forcibly turned her over, smacked her hard on her bottom, and plunged into her from behind. He drew her up on her knees, and fucked the daylights out of her while his fingers found her clit and she came and came and came, screaming and covering his cock, the sheets, the quilt, the pillows, with blackly red menstrual blood.

He was triumphant. The sheets were mad with blood. His face, his cock, his belly ringed with it. He wore a mustache of blood, a beard of blood, war stripes of blood on his cheekbones; and she wore blood all over her belly.

She tried to eat him, to lick off her own blood, but he pushed her back, threw both her legs over one of his shoulders, and began to fuck her again with outrageous determination and spirit. She had never known anyone—except herself, perhaps—to give himself so wholly. Usually in sex, there is a part of the other that tries to hold back, seeking detachment, cynicism, judgment—anything rather than a complete fusion with the lover. But Bean had no such need of detachment; he was wholly unafraid of sex, wholly confident of his own manhood in a way that Isadora supposed must have vanished with the Vikings. His face bore the most intent expression: he would have killed himself by skidding into a tree if he couldn't fuck her, and now he fucked her as if fucking her were a matter of life and death.

Holding her legs aloft, pinning her ankles behind his ear, he fucked her wildly. She could not choose the position, nor control it. She could not lead with this dancing partner—but curiously enough this excited her more than ever and she came repeatedly in positions which she had previously thought were not propitious for her.

282

He chortled and laughed whenever she came. He could feel her orgasm squeezing his cock—so perfect was their fit.

"You're my fit, my mate," he said, eyes wild with delight. "Have another one on me."

He kneeled above her, brandishing his cock like a lethal weapon. It was very red, covered with her blood, and it had a tantalizing curve to it, almost a bend at midpoint.

"I want to fuck the daylights out of you," Bean said, plunging in again. "I want to obliterate all the other lovers, all the other husbands," he said, "I want to be your *man*," he said on the next plunge, "your *man*, your *man*, your *man*."

Isadora gasped as he plunged into her. She gasped with pleasure and astonishment. Bean's eyes were wild.

"You madman," she said. "You maniac."

"I haven't even *begun* to fuck you," he said, pulling out, rolling her over, and starting to smack her bottom again.

"What a beautiful ass you have—but not red enough. I'm going to make it red."

He smacked her until the whole room resounded with smacks, until her buttocks smarted and tingled and the fiery feeling seemed to pass to her cunt. Then he rolled her over again and whipped her pussy with his hard cock. Again he thrust his cock into her and then pulled it out. Again he whipped her clit. He kept this up until she was begging for him to plunge in again.

"Not yet, baby, not yet," he said.

He lowered himself between her legs and started to eat her again, revolving his tongue on her clit, filling both cunt and ass with fingers.

"I'm going to stick one finger deep inside until I can feel all the dark of you," he said; then he went back to eating her.

She was wild with desire, fatigue, desire. She wanted to fight it, not to favor him with another orgasm. She had lost count of how many she'd had—but she was somehow sure that it was the next one which would bond her to him forever, which would finish her, finish her freedom. She was determined to hold back. She tried to think of Josh, of Kevin; she even tried to conjure up a headache —but it was in vain. She felt herself going over the shuddering edge into another orgasm, an orgasm which seemed to raise the *kundalini*, and which made her legs go into convulsions and her hands grip the back of his neck until he cried out in pain.

Then he mounted her again and fucked her with an intensity even greater than before. He turned his head to one side and his face became contorted as if in pain. He raised himself on his arms again and slid, glided, flew in and out of her body as if he were blasting off into space.

"Fly, darling, fly!" she said.

"Baby, baby, baby, baby," he screamed, as he thrust into her, coming like mad, his pelvis and thighs convulsing as he came and one artery pulsed hotly in his thigh. He collapsed on top of her.

"My darling," he said, rubbing her head and neck again. "My darling, darling, darling, darling, darling."

They lay for a while in each other's arms, astounded by the intensity of their own coupling, astounded by the third creature they had made with their two bodies.

"I knew you were trouble," Isadora said, "but I didn't know you were so *much* trouble." She felt like Venus with Adonis in her arms, like Ishtar with her young consort, like Cleopatra with Mark Antony. This was the primal erotic experience, she knew—a woman in all her ripeness, and a young man who had not yet begun to lose the juice of life. Men forfeited so much for their worldly power that their life-force, sex-force, began to leave them sooner than it left women. Women were powered by their years, by their babies, by their passage on the planet; men grew oddly depleted. So a woman of thirty-nine and a man of twenty-five met at an equal point sexually. This was the great truth the French novelists knew—but we Americans resisted. Colette had known this when she bedded Maurice, who was thirty-five to her fifty-one. She had known it when she married him at sixty-one, calling him her best friend. It was the secret of wise women that they knew they held the life-fuse longer than men.

Just as Isadora was having these thoughts, the telephone rang.

"It's my business manager—in heaven," she quipped, giggling. "Hello?"

It was Kevin.

"Oh hi," she said, feeling embarrassed, as if he could see her with the dried blood all over her belly, "how *are* you?"

Bean giggled.

"Shhhh," she cautioned, putting her hand over the phone.

Bean picked up the discarded bloody Tampax from the floor and began to suck on it again.

"Mmmmmm," he said.

"Shhh," Isadora went again, hand cupped over the phone.

"Listen, Kevin?" she said. "I was just drifting off to sleep—can I call you in the morning? Okay?"

284

"Is something the matter?" Kevin was asking. "Are you *sure* you're all right?"

"Perfectly fine," Isadora said.

"You sound very weak, very faint," said Kevin.

"Just falling asleep, that's all . . ." She feigned a sleepy, rather than fucked-out, voice.

"Sure you're all right?"

"Absolutely," she purred, looking at Bean, who was still cutting up with the Tampax. Was he mad—or only merry? It was a definite possibility that he was crazy. Who but a crazy man could abandon himself so totally to the dark gods? But then, that made her crazy, too. Kevin, on the other hand, was *not* crazy: Kevin— the master of nice, little after-dinner *shtups*. Kevin would never take away her soul, but neither would he bring out the bacchante in her, the madness in her, the sheer animal insanity.

"Call you in the morning," she said to Kevin, looking at Bean. "Hugs and kisses." She hung up.

"Who was that?" Bean asked.

"My main man," said Isadora.

"Your *what?*"

"My main man. Want to make something of it?"

"I wish *I* were your main man," Bean said.

"You're too young for me," said Isadora, knowing in her soul it was not true.

"I have a feeling you'll age me fast," said Bean. "Which reminds me—I have something for you."

He was hard again and raring to go.

"Here," he said, taking her by the hand and helping her out of the waterbed, "lean over the bed."

He heaped the pillows in front of her for her to lean on, and cupping her breasts, he took her from behind, ramming her harder than before. Her cunt throbbed, ached, tingled. She screamed for him to ram her even harder, to smack her, to pound her. When Bean entered her, it was as if she were possessed by a dybbuk. When he rammed her, she found herself urging him on in a voice that didn't even seem to belong to her—as if she had truly become a bacchante, as if the boundaries between pain and pleasure had totally dissolved and he were her master, her priapic god, pounding her soul as well as her body.

Ah—she claimed to worship the Great Mother, but she was in thrall to the penis, cock-bound, cock-mastered, cock-unsure. Always she had known that men had this potential power over her, but never had she so surely met her sexual mate—a man who never tired of fucking, who liked to fuck until the point of soreness and exhaustion, a man who had as few hang-ups about sweat and smell and blood as she had, an earthy man, who knew that only through earth can we become divine.

"I want to be your *man*," he growled, fucking her wildly from behind, filling her ass with his middle finger, her cunt with his hard, hooked cock, her soul with his passionate need, his intensity, his certainty, his desire.

She had never come before in this position—but when she did, it was as if thirty-nine years of comes were released and she howled and growled like an animal—whereupon he was aroused beyond containment and he began to come with a pelvis and cock gone wild, pounding her fiercely, filling her with come, until they both collapsed over the bed, panting with exhaustion.

"Come, let me hold you," he said, climbing up on the bed and leading her to do the same. He put his arm around her and she nestled in the hollow of his body while he rubbed her head. Even lying together, they had the perfect fit. Though she was five foot three to his six foot two they lay in each other's arms as if they both belonged, had always belonged there. It was amazing how rarely that happened in life—a good fit between bodies. The only positive thing to be said for promiscuity was that it taught you that —with a vengeance.

"You're my fit, my mate," he said. "Now that I've found you, I'm never going to let you go."

"My darling," Isadora said, fighting back the feeling that there might be any truth whatever in his words.

After tonight, I'm never going to see him again, she thought. He's a mirage, a dream, a demon out of an I. B. Singer story, the devil himself impersonating an angel. Passion like this cannot be clung to, cannot last, cannot keep. A man as charming as this could romance his way right into your heart, then leave you flat. She was not ready for that after the recent heartbreak with Josh. She might never be ready for it again.

"What are you thinking?" he asked. "What?"

"Nothing," she said.

"You're a woman who's never thought nothing in her whole, entire life," Bean said. "Of *that* I am certain."

"I'm only thinking that you're trouble," she said, "big trouble."

"Just a very wild young man," he said. "Your standard, garden-variety rake."

286

"The garden of earthly delights," she said. "Besides—a re-formed rake makes the best husband—or so they used to believe in the eighteenth century *vide* Tom Jones."

"Gadzooks, wench, are you proposing?"

"Hardly likely," she said. "I've been married more than enough already."

"I'd marry you in a minute," he said, "and I don't even *believe* in marriage." He stroked her head with a very gentle hand. He was as tender with her now as he had been rough before. Which was real—the tenderness or the roughness? Or were they *both* real? Unstoppered sex brings out all the extremes within us—angel and animal, angel and ape. She felt that unmistakable sign of a cosmic connection, a diminutive sun glowing inside her pelvis, a radiant spot of warmth two inches below her navel, at precisely that point upon which Zen masters meditate, the Chakra between navel and pubis.

"What am I going to do with you, Bean?" Isadora asked. "Am I going to have to adopt you?"

"Shhh—darling," he said, "let's drift . . ." and they fell asleep sweetly in each other's arms, sleeping entwined without the slight-est strain, wrapped in each other's sweat and come and blood, utterly blissed, utterly peaceful.

Isadora slept as she had not since Josh's departure. She slept without Valium, without booze, without dope. She dreamt herself back in the old West Side apartment where she grew up, climbing the stairs to Papa's studio, looking over the balcony into the dou-ble-height living room, trying to balance there (although the rail-ing was mysteriously missing), and not to fall into the abyss where her parents were entertaining their friends. They were toasting with French champagne in trumpet-shaped, hollow-stemmed glasses. The bubbles rose in the stems to the strains of tinkling cocktail-piano music. They were merry and gay and tittering about things kids could not understand. But now, out of the blue, they were talking about her, not knowing she was there. "She will have to learn it the hard way," they were saying, "the hard way."

Suddenly, those vague parental words struck terror into her heart. She wanted to say, "I'm here, I'm listening," but she was eavesdropping and it was long past her bedtime, so she couldn't disclose her presence. She lost her toehold on the balcony and began to fall. She floated through the air, borne on air currents, like a winged seed pod, lazily circling down. She knew that even-tually she would crash into the floor of that parental living room

—and her terrible secret, her terrible guilt, would be exposed. Just before she hit bottom, she woke up with a start.

She awakened in a panic to feel the blood gushing between her legs and a strange face on the pillow beside her. The beginnings of a ruddy sunrise gleamed at the edges of the roman blinds which shrouded her bedroom windows. The digital clock said 5:59. Her daughter sometimes rose at six.

She bounded out of the waterbed and into the bathroom, where (like Lowell Strathmore impersonating a Keystone Kop before running home to his wife), she began to wash up. She found a Tampax, inserted it, washed her legs and belly with a cloth, splashed cold water on her face, sprayed Opium all over her, brushed her hair, dabbed on some makeup, and ran back to the waterbed to shake the sleeping stranger who had somehow landed there.

"Darling," he muttered, "darling."

"You have to *go*," she said. "My kid may wake up at any minute." She was in a sweat, a panic—whether from the dream or from the bacchic exertions of the night before, she did not know. All she knew was that she had to get rid of him—and fast, fast.

"Please, Bean, please," she said, shaking him.

He opened his eyes sleepily and reached for her to kiss.

"Excuse my dragon breath," he said.

"No problem," she said, kissing him tenderly. Then she broke away, saying: "You really must go." She went and got his clothes for him. Lazily, lazily, like a man underwater, he put them on.

"Is this the bum's rush," he asked, half hurt and half amused.

"My kid's going to wake up any minute," she blurted out. "I had a *great* time last night—you're wonderful—but what am I going to do when Amanda toddles in here?"

She held open the door to the dog run, where little Bichon-Frisé turds lay twinkling under the new-fallen snow.

"Oh, god—the van," she said.

"I'll push it," he said. "I'm good at manual labor—don't worry. Lady—I *adore* you. Will you please remember that?"

He bounded into the dog run, flinging the red scarf around him.

"Out amongst the turds where I belong!" he said merrily, skipping over the frozen dogshit.

She watched as he sprinted up the driveway, found his van (which was gleaming kaleidoscopically in a snowbank), and began to push it back onto the road. It looked like an impossible task—

but either his strength was so great or the power of the Goddess who had first stuck him, then unstuck him, was so strong, that in a minute or two he was able to push the van a few feet closer to the road.

He trudged over to Isadora's sand barrel, picked up the banjo shovel which was poised priapically there, and began to spread sand and salt under the wheels of the van. Then he got into the outrageously painted vehicle, revved the motor, and began rocking back and forth, trying to get a hold on the road. Even the way he drove was sexual! Goddamn, Isadora thought, this man is going to be a distraction. She couldn't *wait* for the sand to take hold and for his wheels to skid him out of her life forever.

When that happened, she almost burst into a solitary round of applause. Out, out, out, out of my life forever, she thought—like the mirage, the demon, the dybbuk you are! But even as she saw his van take off up the road, she was singing. She was singing love songs to herself as she stepped into the shower. "I've ne-ver been in love before . . ." she sang, and then she laughed at herself, lathering blood and come out of her pubic hair, and watching it turn the shower water rusty as it whirled, whirled, whirled down the drain.

14

In Vagabondage

A novel about love
cannot be written while
making love.
—Colette

O thou blyssed Lady,
Hyde hem that flen
unto the for helpe
& that be vagabonde
dyscoure hem nat.
—John Lydgate
Déguileville's *Pilgrimage
of the Life of Man*

As luck would have it, neither Mandy nor Danae awakened until eight o'clock. Isadora, although exhausted, was humming happily as she made oatmeal in the kitchen, stoked up the fire in the dining room, and generally awaited the new disasters the day might bring.

What next? No nanny, no money, no Botkin, and no Bean. He had vanished from her life as precipitously as he had come, leaving skid marks in her icy driveway, blood all over her sheets (she'd already bundled them into the washer), and indelible marks on her heart. (Well—she *thought* it was her heart—though, admittedly, our heroine had a bit of a problem distinguishing between her heart and her cunt.) Her midnight and morning visitor had taken off, leaving her unsure that he even existed—so much an apparition did he seem. Nor could she really make sense of his character. On one level, he seemed a rake, a bounder, a madman; on another a sweet knight from a vanished age of chivalry, valiant in bed and in battle, ready to bleed for lady fair (as she for him). All she knew was that he had left her singing—a sure sign of *some*thing, possibly love—whatever *that* was.

"Good morning, Danae!" Isadora said as a disheveled Danae came skipping down the stairs, with a brushed and washed Amanda behind her.

"Well, aren't *we* cheery this morning, luv," Danae said. Had she been eavesdropping all night—or had she seen the vagabond depart at dawn?

Isadora kept mum, sang dumb. The nanny and baby rooms were far from her bedroom and a floor above. There was no reason to assume they could have heard the wild blood-fucking transpiring in her bedroom.

"Mommy, Mommy, Mommy!" sang Amanda.

Isadora was never more relieved that Bean was gone.

She fed Danae and Amanda their breakfasts, wondering whether Bean had made it home alive, whether he actually existed or whether he was really a character she had invented, a projection of her own need for an ecstatic release from the troubles besetting her—Botkin's death, the tax troubles, the nanny troubles.

Whenever she was left alone in her isolated snowbound house without a nanny for Amanda, she felt a sense of primal abandonment and panic—as if someone had socked her in the gut. It was hard enough to mother a baby *with* a father around, but without one, and without another mother helping to mother *you*, it was well-nigh impossible. True, one did not need a man to raise a child, but one did very much need a network of *women*—mothers to mother the mothers who mothered the babes, mothers to refill you as you emptied, mothers to stroke you as you stroked the fevered head of your child.

Isadora could well imagine an ancient matriarchal age. She could well imagine networks of mothers and grandmothers and aunts mothering each other. But we were as far from this in our isolated single-parent households as we were from the moon. Isadora's mother was in New York; her sisters were scattered around the globe. Her friends with children were mostly married—or else their children were much older, for they had begun bearing sooner—so their problems were hardly the same as hers. Few of her friends wrote novels; fewer still wrote novels and bore babies at the same time—and fewer still were breadwinners. This might be the common lot of women today, but her friends seemed to have avoided it. Also, when she had moved to Connecticut seven years ago it was with a man she was madly in love with; they had bought their house specifically *for* its isolation from the outside world. Poised on a cliff above a river valley, down the steepest of driveways, it was the sort of house two lovers bought when they were (or *thought* they were) self-sufficient in their *folie à deux*. It was also a hell of a house for kids—steps and balconies everywhere, decks poised above a steep ravine. At that point in her life, Isadora had needed such a house in which to research, then write *Tintoretto's Daughter*. She had needed to close off the outside world and live within her own dreams and fantasies of sixteenth-century Venice. Poring over her maps of canals, her floor plans of *palazzi*, she had been able to re-create Venice in her head—in part because of the isolation of her Connecticut house. When she needed more stimulation, she flew off to the real Venice, or drove up to Yale to molder amid rare books in the Beinecke Library. She wanted none of the world which, to her kind, New York represented. She wanted no part of the media gossip, the fund-raisers, the benefits, the posh parties, the screenings, the gallery openings, the opening nights. She had had her fill of these dubious pleasures after her first novel was published. She had had her fill of being cultivated by people who had previously scorned her, of having to explain herself to people who never had to explain themselves, of having to be witty in the face of dullness, thick-skinned in the face of gratuitous cruelty. For Isadora had been through the whole celebrity cycle—adulation followed by attack, wholesale demolition followed by cautious reconstruction—and it wearied her. She was too sensitive a plant not to run from it. And she had run to Connecticut—that nourishing "nutmeg" state—that state of colonial charm with eighties kink underneath, that state of winter emergency (power, snow, flood), that verdant summer Eden, that blessed retreat from Gotham's grinding cares.

But alone with a three-year-old child in winter, that same house which had previously been such a refuge became a trap. One was dependent on one's household help to a degree that made them arrogant. One's boilerman and snowplow driver held the keys to one's kingdom—with a vengeance. And snow tires, four-wheel drive, and wood stoves became more important than bread, wine, and love.

What problem should she tackle first this morning? The nanny-replacement marathon or the search for a new business manager (and a lawyer, perhaps to file a lawsuit against Botkin's estate)? Or should she simply sit down and write as if none of this were going on—since it was her writing, after all, that always rescued her? But life, alas (or perhaps, amen), always comes before art. And life was staring her in the face in the person of Amanda.

"I don't want a new nanny," Amanda said. "I want Danae!"

Danae smiled blissfully with her sexy gap-toothed smile. She shook her auburn hair. Amanda had loved her since infancy, and Amanda was absolutely clear on the fact that there were two women to love in life—a mommy and a mommy-substitute, chief baby-maker and comforter and assistant baby-tender.

"I want Danae to be my nanny," Amanda said. "Danae-nanny, Danae-nanny, Danae-nanny!"

"Well," said Isadora to the smiling redheaded North-of-England lass (who always came down like a shower of golden rain in nanny emergencies), "would you like to stay for a week or two while I attend to some urgent business in New York?"

"Sure, luv," said Danae. "Just let me take off and get my things."

Isadora took charge of Amanda while Danae borrowed the Saab

and sallied forth into the world in search of her suitcases, her children, her various and sundry lovers.

Of course, Isadora knew that having Danae move in—if only temporarily—would mean great cuisine and great disorder both. Sometimes Danae would take care of Amanda; sometimes her sons would; sometimes her lovers. The house would be bustling with activity, the food exotic, the music loud. Danae would either take Amanda along as she made her rounds (fulfilling her various other part-time jobs) or she would leave her boys to baby-sit Amanda. But there would be no hellfire stories—that was for sure. And Amanda would thrive under Danae's benignly neglectful care.

Isadora was exhausted by the night's exertions and her mind boggled at the day's duties. Where to *begin* to solve the mess Mel Botkin had left her heir to?

In the meantime, she would put *Sesame Disco* on the turntable, have a little morning dance with Amanda, take her to nursery school in QUIM (if the driveway got resanded in time), and then think about it all. "I'll think about it tomorrow," Scarlett had said, but here it already *was* tomorrow!

"Want to dance, Amanda?" Isadora asked.

What a question! The kid was born to dance!

"Me lost me cookie at the disco," Cookie Monster sang as Isadora and Amanda stomped and whirled and shook their hands in time to the music—after which they flipped past "The Happiest Street in the World" (which they both thought was nerdy) and a few other undistinguished numbers to that old favorite, "Doin' the Trash," starring Oscar the Grouch.

Amanda danced like her mother—with natural rhythm— though she was just past toddlerhood and not awfully well coordinated. She danced—like Isadora—with the total abandon of childhood. Blue eyes flashing, pink palms slapping the air, sneakers pounding the ground, she danced like a kid who was bound to follow in her mother's footsteps—heaven help her! Taking in her daughter's unmistakable sexuality, her life-force, Isadora was thinking that she, too, would have to learn for herself all the lessons Isadora was just now *beginning* to learn. How to make demonic passion jibe with domestic responsibilities, artistic responsibilities, financial responsibilities. What a hell of a job *she* had done! What kind of model was she for her child? A model of perplexity, a model of chaos, a model of confusion! She had tried to live her life with openness to all aspects of being a woman, of being a *mensh,* and where had it led her? Here—to this perplexed passage! Three months before her fortieth birthday, she knew less than ever about where the serpentine road was leading her. She had danced the night away with a vagabond and now she danced away the morning with her daughter!

Renata arrived to find mother and daughter madly disco-ing in the foyer.

"Good morning, ladies," she sang. Well—wasn't everyone cheery and manic this morning? Is that what death did—at least the death of a business manager? Actually, Isadora knew other people who reacted to death this way—even the deaths of loved ones. Far from making you mope, it made you manic and merry —at least for a little while—before the finality of it sank in.

The snowplow and sander followed close upon Renata's arrival, so Isadora decided to take Amanda to nursery school after all, even though it was late.

As they drove slowly along the icy roads, Amanda chattered happily of one thing and another. Nurse Librium's departure seemed not to make much difference to her—unlike, say, the departure of Cicely aka The Naked Nanny. In general, it was the young nannies, the ones who related to Amanda as older sisters rather than grannies, who made the biggest impression. They fought with her like siblings at times; they made arbitrary rules— but they bonded to her most ferociously—and their departure left her bereft.

Isadora so wished she could make life perfect and stable for her daughter. She had some foolish fantasy of the perfect bourgeois life—the life she had so assiduously *avoided* for herself—a rose-covered cottage, Amanda playing on a swingset, and Mommy and Daddy within, being domestic. All the ideals she had pursued in her life as a writer—to live like a picaresque heroine—ran counter to the stability she wished for her daughter. She was tempted to say to her daughter what her mother had, in fact, said to her: "Do as I say, not as I do." *Be stable, though all I have taught you is instability. Be calm, though all I have taught you is frenzy.* Her mother had been similarly contradictory with her. *Go out and conquer the world of men,* she had said, *though I have not done so myself. Do as I say, not as I do.* Isadora's mother had once even gone so far as to say: If you become a famous writer, all else will follow—money, beautiful clothes, and the love of beautiful men. Well, Mother knew best, after all, didn't she? But like the Chinese curse "May you live in interesting times"—fame, money, designer clothes and the love of

beautiful men all had their own built-in problems and disappoint-
ments. Beautiful men, in particular, though they left you humming—at both ends.

Isadora's rump and cunt felt sore from last night's madness. But
it was a sweet soreness, an eighteenth-century rake's soreness—
without, however, the incipient fear of clap which so plagued
those boozy buggers. Gadzooks! *Ought* she to worry about clap?
Bean was certainly a rake, in the fine old John Cleland–Henry
Fielding tradition. Or was it herpes you were supposed to worry
about these days? Things had changed so drastically since her
adolescence that she hardly knew *what* to worry about! In *her* adolescence in the fifties, pregnancy was the big worry, the big P. It
was hard to lose yourself in sex when you were thinking that you
might die on some abortionist's kitchen table in Jersey City (why
were they always in *Jersey?*) just for enduring the fumbles and
pokes of some pimply adolescent from Horace Mann (or Trinity
or Collegiate). Then, in her twenties, the pill became the big P, so
you didn't have to worry about the *other* big P anymore—until
(just a scant two years later) it was proved that you better *start*
worrying again, but this time about blood clots and embolisms.
Pretty soon, society suffered a collective expulsion from Pill Paradise, and diaphragms and condoms returned—but by then venereal disease had become epidemic—and resistant to antibiotics.
Just as everybody was absorbing the news of *that*—herpes hit the
press, then AIDS—what would it be next?

Isadora and Amanda had reached the Blue Tree School, but
the session was well in progress, so no children were to be seen
(bundled like little Michelin men) outside. Isadora parked QUIM
adjacent to a snowbank and trundled her daughter into school,
walking down a corridor which celebrated Christmas in all Third
World nations: Iranian New Year, Madagascan Twelfth Night,
Chinese Candlemass, Maori Halloween, and the like. The Blue
Tree School would celebrate *anything* as long as it wasn't Judeo-
Christian!

Coming upon the three-year-old's room—called (without political connotation) "The Pink Room"—Isadora paused a moment to
put her daughter's parka in a cubby (decorated with Amanda's
adorable photographic visage, as well as with pictures of Mom and
Dad). Amanda allowed her red rubber boots to be pulled off, and
then she ran forward to greet her peers.

There they were—the knapsack children, the children of the
two households, the children of the divorce Olympics.

298

Jeremy, Lauren, Moses, Elihu, Jennifer, Jennifer, Allison, Alison, Alyson, Noah, Simon, Caleb, and Kimberley—they were called—and eight out of the fourteen (Amanda made fourteen) were from fractured families. (Isadora hated the term *broken homes* because actually the homes *increased* rather than diminished with divorce.)

Like true children of the late seventies, they were named after biblical patriarchs, paper products, Chaucerian heroines (the Wife of Bath, after all, yclept "Alisoun"), and English gentry (Jennifer and Amanda). Someday, Isadora thought, I will do a phenomenological essay on kids' names and how they betray the pretensions of their parent's generation. In Nazi Germany, for example, everyone called their kids old Teutonic names like Holgar, Heike, and Gudrun. The guilty post-Nazi generation named their kiddies Old Testament names like Rebecca and Rachel, Abraham and Isaac. Easy to account for *those* trends—but what of post-Vietnam America and its generation of little Noahs? Were we expecting a flood momentarily? And what of names like Kimberley and Stacy and Tracy? Nobody, thank heavens, ever named their kid Isadora —even when *Candida Confesses* rode the best-seller lists—though Candida did have a brief flurry of popularity in the midseventies.

Isadora waved good-bye to her knapsack child (who was already cuddling a rabbit named Peter—animal names had become oddly conservative in the seventies and eighties)—waved hello and good-bye to her teacher, Simba, aka Arnold Greenspan, and her other teacher, Karma, aka Diane Grossman. (Simba had shoulder-length hair and wore one emerald earring; and Karma lusted for him in vain. Well, it certainly was an adequate preparation for life in the postnuclear age that the kids were getting right here in Westport.) Then she found QUIM again (what about *car* names in the seventies and eighties?) and headed back home to Serpentine Hill Road (and street names?).

At home, the phone had already been ringing off the hook.

Bean had called a couple of times; Kevin, who was worried about last night, had also called. Mel Botkin's office had called; and Hope (who, in her usual psychic way, knew something was up) had also called. Renata was womanning the phones while Danae was moving in with bag and baggage, tape decks, gourmet cookware, and rubber checkbooks. She was singing as she moved her stuff (oh, why couldn't *Isadora* be as blithe a spirit as Danae?). Why? Because she was Jewish—that's why—and worrying ran in her blood. Danae was broke and happy. Danae wrote bad checks and cared not. If Danae were in hock to the IRS, she wouldn't lose a moment's sleep over it. The only time Isadora felt as carefree as Danae was when she was fucking—which maybe was why fucking was so important to her. It was her Valium, her dope, her addiction. It was her muscle relaxant, anxiety quasher, her poison and her antidote both.

"Who shall I get for you first?" Renata asked. "Hope? Bean? Mel's office? Kevin?"

"Get me Hope," said Isadora. When in doubt, she called her mentor, her fairy godmother. Theirs was a friendship like no other—a friendship of souls, a friendship of the heart. The fact that Hope was twenty years older eliminated all stress and competition, and made their karmic connection absolutely pure. That they had been together for many lifetimes was clear every time they talked.

"So," said Hope, "what's up? I've been thinking about you all night—couldn't sleep a wink."

"I was up all night, too," said Isadora, "but not sleeping."

"So—who is he? Someone new or someone old?"

"This young actor who skidded off my icy driveway."

Hope laughed her rich throaty laugh. "Well—that's *one* way to meet men—just build a steep driveway and wait for them to skid in."

"I have to tell you all about it," Isadora said. "It was absolutely incredible."

"So tell me—when can I see your beautiful face?"

"I don't know," said Isadora. "Yesterday all hell broke loose in my life. I had to fire Nurse Librium for telling Mandy hellfire stories. Then Mel Botkin announced to me I was in terrible tax trouble and a few hours later he dropped dead. After that this young actor skidded off my road."

"Have you checked your horoscope for *today?*"

"I don't even want to. Frankly, Hope, I don't know where to *begin.*"

"Take a deep breath, and then gather information. Do nothing *yet.*"

The oracle had spoken. Hope *was* Isadora's deep breath. She knew her friend's tendency to act, act, act rather than meditate. She knew that these problems needed a different approach and that the answer to them might not be immediately apparent.

"If I were you, I would start seeking counsel—see other business managers, talk to lawyers, but don't do anything drastic yet."

Isadora knew that was good advice.

"Okay," she said. "If I wind up in your neighborhood, I'll drop in—okay?"

"I'd love to see your beautiful face." They hung up with many kisses.

While Renata and Isadora were setting up appointments with various counselors and advisers (including Lowell Strathmore) for the next couple of weeks, the private line rang again.

Isadora picked it up—out of force of habit.

It was Bean.

"Hello," came his beautiful, resonant voice.

"How'd you get *this* number?"

"Off the telephone. I figured if your 'main man' called on it, it must be *the* number."

"You tricky bastard."

"Not one of my more complex tricks."

"Certainly not—I saw a few of those last night."

"You ain't seen nothin' yet, lady. I *have* to see you again. How about tonight?"

Isadora's heart began to pound at the very thought—she, who was determined not to see him again.

"I can't. I have to go to New York and see millions of boring financial advisers. I have no idea when I'll be free."

"Then call me when you are. I'll hang out in New York and wait for you."

"I'm not sure I'll be free at all."

"Then I'll come to Connecticut."

"When?"

"Tonight, tomorrow night, the night after, the night after that. Just say the word. Lady—I *adore* you. I have to see you."

Isadora's resolve weakened. She would have gladly canceled the day's activities and spent it with Bean—but simply *because* of that, she resisted.

"How about Friday night, in Connecticut?"

"That's three days off—an eternity!" Bean protested.

Isadora felt the same, but these uncontrollable feelings *had* to be controlled somehow.

"Look—" said Isadora, vainly trying to assert *some* control, "if I get free before that, I'll call you."

"Promise?"

"I promise."

And she took off for New York to start to gather information.

Driving down the highway, watching her windshield splatter over with slush, with snow, with muck from the roads, Isadora wondered what on earth a normal person (which she admittedly *wasn't*—but then, who was?) ought to be thinking at a time like this. Was she blessed or was she cursed? Where was *The Divorced Woman's Book of Etiquette* now that she needed it most? What ought a woman to do when, faced with overwhelming financial problems, she meets an astounding young man and wants nothing more than to fuck.the days away with him?

Was this an etiquette problem for her imaginary book of etiquette, or did it fall, rather, into the province of one of her imaginary game shows? Isadora was forever making up the names of books she would never write, TV shows she would never produce. In moments of extreme crisis, a book title or television series title would come to her, as if that were the answer to her problems—and perhaps it *was*.

Not long ago, while goofing around with a friend who was a TV talk-show host, she had come up with two crazy ideas for game shows. "Shiksamania" was the first. It was a highly competitive game show in which Jewish guys had to vie with each other in singing the praises of their resident *shiksas*. The show would have a split screen and on each side would sit *shiksa* and Jewish consort, the Jewish consorts both competing in describing their ladyloves' excellent *shiksa*-like qualities—ski-jump Draw-Me-girl noses, perfectly conical breasts, small waists, high, firm asses. The mirror image of this show would be called "Shaygets-o-Rama," in which two Jewish girls would appear with their *shkotzim*. (Isadora, of course, would now be ready to open the season with Bean!)

The other fantasied show—which Isadora found strangely comforting while driving down the highway deeper and deeper into financial ruin—was called "People Are Desperate," also a game show but one in which miserable people competed with each other for the dubious honor of being the most truly wretched. While they told their sad stories—of AIDS, of financial distress, of romantic losses—to the weeping studio audience, their misery would be measured on a huge Angstometer built into the set. The needle would have several settings: Miffed, Miserable, Wretched, Agonized, Grief-stricken—and only the most miserable of all the contestants would win.

Just thinking of the Angstometer, Isadora began to giggle. Where did she fit on the scale of misery? Did tax trouble qualify you for Grief-stricken? Not bloody likely. She had her health; her kid was alive and well; she had met a man who made her hum. So what if her next three unwritten books already belonged to Uncle Sam? Books were only lent, not *given*—like life. They came through you, not of you—like children. They were for the world, not their authors to enjoy and to profit by. What the fuck, Isadora thought, feeling undeniably cheerful. She had never felt *more* cheerful, in fact. Every time she thought of Bean, she wanted to sing.

So she did. She put a Manhattan Transfer tape on the tape deck and sang along with "A Nightingale Sang in Berkeley Square." Oh, she could chart the passage of her post-separation crisis through the music she selected. At the worst point in pain over Josh, she listened obsessively to Billie Holiday's bluesy maunderings over mean men. That was her "Ain't Nobody's Business If I Do" period. Then, as things got a little cheerier, she moved into the bittersweet Berkeley-Woodstock world of Michael Franks— "Popsicle Toes" for good days and "Burchfield Nines" for melancholy ones. She knew she was really on the comeback trail when the music on the tape deck switched to the Manhattan Transfer. "Twilight Zone," "Spies in the Night," and "A Nightingale Sang" represented considerable emotional progress over Billie Holiday and her songs of female masochism. "I swear I won't call no copper if I'm beat up by my poppa" was some fine lyric for an avowed feminist to be listening to (and with such an approving heart!). And yet that was the essential female paradox, wasn't it? It was precisely the most passionately *independent* woman who longed most to be mastered by men. Aphra Behn, Mary Wollstonecraft, Colette—they'd all had more than their share of beastly male chauvinists for whom they'd lusted and suffered. Intelligence in a woman did not necessarily translate to her emotional life. In fact, it so often seemed to work the other way around: the more intelligent the woman, the more of a dummy she was in her dealings with men. Yeats had got it exactly right in "A Prayer for My Daughter":

> It's certain that fine women eat
> A crazy salad with their meat
> Whereby the Horn of Plenty is undone.

Amen.

Once in New York, Isadora parked in a garage on Fifty-seventh Street and began making her appointed rounds.

First, she saw a bald, chubby business manager named Hillel Marantz, who wasn't much interested in what Mel Botkin had done or not done, but promised, if she made him her trusted adviser, to do "everything but marry her."

"And maybe that, too," he said with a wink. He'd invest her money (what might be left of it), deal with audits, mortgages, insurance, reinsurance, bills, and bank balances.

"I can promise you everything but stud service," he said with another wink—this one even more loathsome than the first. Isadora thanked him and went on.

Next she saw a tall, skinny Dickensian lawyer-CPA named Marcus Marcus, who was as bellicose and litigious as they come and who said:

"Sock the widow with a lawsuit—and do it now before the corpse is cold or you'll never get a penny—mark my words."

"I mark them, Marcus Marcus," Isadora wanted to say, but she thought better of it and went on to:

Lionel Lowry—a very distinguished, silver-haired business manager with very plushy offices on a very high floor of 30 Rockefeller Plaza—offices festooned with glossies of rock stars. He implied (politely, but clearly) that Isadora (and indeed anyone with an income of less than a million a year) was too small a fish for him to fry, so Isadora thanked him sweetly and went on to:

Oliver Glascock, Jr., a WASP CPA—whom she mistrusted for that very reason: What sort of peculiar WASP mother encourages her son to become a *CPA?*

Her final consultation was with Seymour Wolitsky, of Wolitsky, Werfel, and Ruben. Seymour was a bearded fellow with an ample belly, who unhelpfully implied that if only she'd come to him years ago, she'd be rich and secure today.

By five o'clock, her head was swimming. She'd have to give these decisions a little time, and see other advisers in the coming weeks, but meanwhile, should she call Bean for solace, or should she call Hope? Bean first, she decided (he would not be in); then Hope. With a pounding heart, she tried Bean's number, hoping indeed that he wouldn't be home. The phone rang and rang. Just as she was happily about to give up, he picked up the phone.

"Lady," he said. "I thought you'd *never* call. I've been sitting here debating whether or not to jerk off—or whether to save it all for you."

"Will you buy me a drink?"

"Of *course*—why don't you come and meet me at my humble dump—or, as I'd rather call it, my dumble hump."

"Gadzooks, sir—come to a man's apartment? Surely, you would not wish my vartue to be compromised thus?"

"My lady, you do me a great disservice to assume that I would even *try* the vartue of one so pure as you. Or is't 'thee'?"

"Then meet me at a Publick House, sirrah, and not your scurvy batchelor quarters."

"Milady—I swear, upon my Honour. . ."

"What Honour?"

"The Honour I shall acquire for thee, if thou wilt but inspire it. Come but briefly here. We'll out anon."

"A likely story."

She was finally persuaded, but swore in her heart not to let him take her to bed. Women—surely some sage has remarked—have this curious magical belief that if they let a man take them to bed once but not twice, twice but not thrice, thrice but not four times, it will prevent their becoming enthralled. Three, after all, is a charm, and Isadora had often felt that if she succumbed only once or twice to a beguiling man, then she would be safe from his emotional clutches. Three or more times meant danger. Three or more and you were deeper in than you wished to be.

Bean's fifth-floor walk-up in the East Twenties was a revelation of his character, like his van. It was also a revelation of his status —not quite single; a woman's shoes and makeup, mail and photographs were everywhere. (Isadora was actually glad of this—she would rather be the mysterious mistress than the live-in lady.)

He greeted her passionately at the door to his digs. Clothes were flung on every available surface. A double bed with leopard-printed sheets lay unmade. The kitchen was in the center of the living room and greasy pots were ubiquitous. It was the apartment of a college kid, a prep-school boy. Barbells and jock straps supplied the decor. Improving literature and trashy tabloids; roaches; the smell of old grease and new sinsemilla; a few pieces of old family furniture festooned with dirty clothes.

Taking it all in (while Bean was embracing her), Isadora thought: How nice, how nice, how nice. I keep starting life again and yet again. One of the great pleasures of having new lovers, young lovers, was that she kept getting the chance to start over— over and over again. For the first time since the separation, she saw the upheavals in her life as positive rather than negative. She was almost jubilant. It was as if she kept going back to her twenties and beginning again. Would she possibly get it right this time?

She and Bean kissed and kissed. His kisses made her stomach turn to mush and her cunt drip. Before she could protest, before she could rationalize or even speak, he tore off her clothes and fucked her madly on the unmade bed. She had wanted to believe that their perfect fit last night was only a mirage, a delusion, a passing fancy—but that was not the case. Their fit was astounding, incredible, whether they merely lay in each other's arms or fucked like animals gone wild.

Nor did their sex ever seem to have a beginning, a middle, an end. They helped each other to deep-purple portions of sex, portions that seemed to begin anywhere and end nowhere. After they finished, they would begin again. There was never a moment when it was over and ecstasy succumbed to interrogation ("Was it good for you, too?"). They never had to ask. It was clear that their link was cosmic, enormous, deep as the reaches of space. They seemed to give off blue light as they fucked, the blue light Wilhelm Reich claimed he could see around copulating couples. If there was such a thing as orgone energy, *kundalini* energy, they had discovered it. All the cares of the world were as nothing as compared to this force, this fire they made with their bodies. It was unstoppable, irresistible, the pulse of the cosmos. Lost as she was in this tornado that had overtaken her life, Isadora didn't care about tax troubles, money troubles, Josh troubles. All troubles were suspended as she lay in Bean's arms. Dimly, a disembodied voice (her own?) came to her as she floated out of her body. *It will be all right,* the voice kept saying. *It will be all right.*

She and Bean had dinner afterward at a Japanese restaurant in Murray Hill. They sat together on the floor of a small private room with paper walls and couldn't keep their hands off each other, or their eyes off each other.

"I adore you. I adore you. I adore you," he kept saying between bites of sushi.

Some demon seized hold of her sanity and she was led to do mad things like putting sushi in her cunt, and making him retrieve it before the demure kimonoed waitress reappeared. They laughed so loudly that even the party of Japanese businessmen in the adjacent paper room tried to peek in when the waitress slid their paper door ajar. Gold teeth aglint, cameras dangling from their necks, they tittered before the paper door slid shut again.

Bean and Isadora drank sake and stared into each other's eyes

—which were, astoundingly, the same color: cornflower blue with yellow flecks.

"Bean—you are the sweetest man I've ever known," Isadora said.

"Impossible," he said. "I'm just a *man*. Maybe you've just never had one before. I hardly deserve you. If there weren't so many wimps and nerds in the world, I wouldn't have even had a crack at you."

"A what?"

"A crack," he said reaching his hand under her skirt and finding the object in question.

"A crack, a quim, a quente, a bottomless pit, a honeypot, a slit, a gash, a gravy giver, a boy in a boat . . ."

"How do you know those terms?"

"I love sexual slang—especially the sexual slang of Shakespeare's day. I studied it in grad school."

"How astounding—so did I. I nearly did my master's thesis on Shakespeare's sexual slang, but then I switched to eighteenth-century lit."

"Extraordinary," said Bean. "Listen, lady, we are linked in more ways than you dream—even though I am a guiltless WASP and you a guilty Jew."

"Not guilty at all with you."

"That's why you need me. I'll teach you guiltlessness—if you'll teach me guilt. Is it a deal?"

"Why should anyone *want* guilt—the curse of the Jews?"

"Because all artists need a healthy dose of it to give a finer point to their suffering and their art. My race of guiltless WASPs is dying out. We have nothing else to tell the world—or nothing that they want to hear."

"And what do the Jews have to tell the world? Guilt?"

"The world has never needed guilt more. Or conscience, as I'd rather call it. And Jews—in case you haven't noticed—are the conscience of the world. That's why they're so hated. Since we met, I've longed to be one. Listen, lady, if they were lining up the Jews to march them into the ovens again, I'd sooner go with you than walk this world without you by my side. I love you, lady. I've decided I can't live without you."

Isadora looked at him quizzically. "It's awfully soon to fall in love," she said.

"Not soon enough," said Bean, holding a forgotten piece of sushi aloft in his right hand. "I fell in love the moment I saw you in the health club. Last night only awakened my lust and told me what I never knew before—that lust and love can sleep in the same bed."

"I think I love you, too," Isadora heard herself saying in a voice that seemed not to be her own. "It's either love or vagabondage—but one way or the other, there's no turning back now—damn it . . ."

"Why '*damn it*'?"

"Because falling in love is the first step toward heartbreak."

"I swear I'll never break your heart," he said. "I'm here to heal it."

"So they all say—at first."

"Oh, you are cynical, aren't you? What makes you so cynical anyway?"

"Living on planet earth. Three marriages. Four decades."

"And you believe that cynicism is truer than hope, do you?"

"That observation would seem to be borne out by experience."

"Only if you write the end of every story and then live your own creation to the bitter end."

"Slick. Very slick. I wish I could triumph over cynicism—but I would not want to be a fool again."

"And when were you a fool before?"

"With Josh. Because I loved him so totally."

"And is that bad?"

"Not bad, but pretty excruciating when it ends."

"And so you'll never begin, and that way never have to end. What a solution for a hero! What a solution for the most courageous woman of your generation!"

"Don't goad me—especially not with flattery."

Bean looked genuinely penitent. "I'm sorry," he said. "I know it's hard to trust again when you've been badly hurt. But promise me one thing—it's all I ask . . ."

"What?"

"You'll give me time. I'll prove to you how much I love you—no matter how long it takes. I only want the time. Is it a deal?"

"I have to think about it," said Isadora.

"Okay—think," he said and kissed her until the paper door slid open and then slid closed at once as the waitress realized her intrusion and went away in a rustle of silk and straw.

15

More Vagabondage & a Lagniappe

Oh, what a dear ravishing thing
is the beginning of an amour.
—APHRA BEHN

From outrage (matrimony) to
outrage (adultery) there arose nought
but outrage (copulation) yet the
matrimonial violator of the
matrimonially violated had not been outraged
by the adulterous violator
of the adulterously violated.
—JAMES JOYCE
Ulysses

ISADORA was indeed in vagabondage—in bondage to a vagabond, that is. The OED may define *vagabondage* as "the state, condition or character of being a vagabond," but Isadora preferred her definition, with its vaguely sadomasochistic implications. Vagabondage is bliss, she thought, and I am a vagabondager—or is it vagabondagess? She would swear to stay away from Bean, not to call him, not to take his calls—but then he would phone, or appear out of the blue in his skiddy van—and all would be lost. Just when she was most convinced she had invented him, he would turn up in her driveway either in the van or in an old red MG that had no backward gears, and she would drop whatever she was doing just to be with him.

She tried to restrict him to Tuesday and Friday nights (Kevin still had weekends and various other "eligible" swains commandeered various other nights of the week), but little by little he began to encroach on her life, always calling at the last minute, appearing or disappearing with the unpredictability of a true vagabond.

One night he appeared at the house just as Kevin was about to arrive at the train station and she had to send him away though it broke her heart to do so. (That night she went to bed with Kevin dreaming of Bean.) In fact, her nights were full of Bean dreams, and days full of Bean fantasies. She had all the unmistakable signs of infatuation: singing in the streets, skipping everywhere, unaccountable cheer in the face of financial ruin.

When the phone rang, adrenaline flew into her veins. When he wasn't at the other end of it, her mood plummeted. When he called, she was frantic, counting the hours till they might meet. When he did not call, she was frantic, lest he never call again.

She read horoscopes—his first, then hers. (Then, belatedly, Amanda's.) She was sure her stars were about to herald a sudden turn for the better.

Aries: March 21—April 20

This year the Sun enters your birth sign on March 20th and puts the influence of Mars, your ruler, to flight. All questions pale beside this one: Can you finally come to terms with the fact that a relationship still fraught with difficulties and conflict must end? After all, it seems you have had less choice in the matter than you would have wished; others have been attempting to cut loose. March and April will be decisive months. Now all the rest is sweetness and light. Beautiful planetary influences relate to finances and long-term business interests, but more important still, the New Moon on March 25th is certain to herald a truly remarkable phase for travel and connections with people far, far away. Wholly unexpected events will restore your optimism and give you the courage to start life afresh.

Beautiful planetary influences relate to *finances,* Isadora thought. Finances! Surely this must be wrong. And yet she was absolutely certain—in that blithe way that fools and children have —that everything was about to improve.

She had not been idle. She was busy scaring up as much work as she could handle: magazine pieces, book proposals, lectures, treatments for movies. This is what her grandfather would have done in a similar situation—paint his heart out—and she had been well trained by her family. They were not only artists, but artisans. They did not wait for luck, they made it with their two hands.

Though all she could think of was Bean, Bean's eyes, Bean's cock, Bean's voice, she knew she had to work. She was simultaneously trying to untangle the tangled business affairs Mel had left and trying to drum up work. *Arbeit macht frei,* she thought. It was what the diabolically ironical Nazis had put over their particular gates of hell—Auschwitz. It might not be as poetical as what Dante put over his—*Lasciate ogni speranza voi ch'entrate*—but it had a certain ring to it, didn't it?

Work would save her; work would redeem her; it always had in the past.

But it was not easy to work when you were always throbbing at the heart, the cunt, and the telephone (surely in the twentieth century, the telephone had become an organ of the body—and an erogenous one at that!). While Danae continued in residence as temporary-permanent nanny; while Danae's sons and lovers supplied Mandy's surrogate family, Bean and Isadora were forever sneaking off to lose hours, afternoons, whole days and nights in

ecstatic embraces. Isadora had a host of houses to choose from—
both in Connecticut and in New York. Since her separation from
Josh, she had collected proffered keys to second homes from a
variety of friends and relations (whose pipes she monitored
against frost and whose mail she collected—in exchange for perfect playgrounds for illicit sex).

What can be sweeter than an empty house on the Sound on a
gray and blustery February day when no sailboats dot the horizon
and no kites wing across the sky? The two illicit lovers tiptoe in
(though no one at all is there to hear their footsteps—no one but
the skeletons in the family closet).

"Hello? Hello?" she calls.

"Nobody here but us sex maniacs!" he growls.

And often before the door is properly shut or before the ther-
mostat has been turned up to seventy, they have fallen to the deep
shag carpeting in the living room (with its view of the blustery
Sound and dipping seagulls), and are hungrily eating each other
as if they had been starved for years—though it's only been two
days. In between bouts of passion, they refuel on the picnic they've
brought: icy white wine, lobster salad, crabmeat stuffed back in its
shells. They pass the wine from mouth to mouth, the joint from
mouth to mouth.

"This time I'm going to give you a pearl necklace," he says,
jerking off slowly, and slowly spraying her with his pearly come.

"This time you'll have to crack your own crab," she says, spreading wide to let him stuff her with crabmeat, then lick it out.

Everything is salty, tangy, sweet, and sour—like the Sound itself
at low tide. They are the flotsam and jetsam of the beach, coming
together to make music with their bodies, to make blue light, white
foam, sweet and sour hope. The ordinary organs which join them
—join them at one pulsing point on both their bodies—are mere
appendages of flesh, shared by apes (if not angels). And yet these
foolish, vulnerable appendages can carry them into the cosmos.

Astounded by their love, by its mere physicality (which seems so
spiritual), its spirituality (which seems so physical), they are suddenly alive to all the world as well. The Sound delights them with
its blues and grays; the taste of crab seems newly minted for their
tongues; the wine from Napa Valley seems grown especially for
them from bursting grapes.

They notice everything as if with Edenic newness. Alive only to
each other and their own stoned senses, somehow they still see the
family pictures in the hallway (and laugh over them), the leftover

313

Valium in the bathroom, the little bottles of nail polish left on the bedside table—for they fuck from room to room—and their poetic names: Etoile, Misty Lilac, Pennies-in-a-Stream, Disco Platinum, Fire and Ice, Mocha Polka, Cocoaberry, Mochaberry, Kumquat Peach, and Mango Pink.

"Clitoris Pink," she says.

"Foreskin Fuchsia," he counters.

They have become silly in their love, silly in that intimate way lovers have that means as much to them as sex.

Starved for such intimacy for so long, Isadora thrives as much on the private jokes and hijinks as on the fucking. Random sex, lottery sex, does not supply what an *amour* supplies—the jokes, the looks, the tender teasing. How to sustain life without it? Well, she has done it, but *how*, she does not really know. Life without intimacy is a desert which stretches out to the last syllable of recorded time. To have been so intimate with Josh—and then to have that intimacy cut off—has left her with a bleeding stump. Bean's love has begun to cauterize that stump. Lust itself can cauterize an amputated limb—and yet and yet, the hunger for the intimacy with Josh has not really left her.

But her love affair with Bean has something strange about it—death clings to their violent coupling. She is always somehow sure that he will die before they meet again; he will swerve off the road for good, skid on the ice as he did that time he nearly died, smoke one joint too many, pop one pill too many, fry his senses until they betray him utterly.

For they are both sensation seekers, unstoppered in their lust. Neither holds the other back. Their lust is like flowing wine unconstrained by any cup; their coupling threatens to invade their lives until all there is in life is coupling—coupling and death. And is there more to life than that, anyway? Isadora has her doubts.

They fall upon each other hungrily—as if this were the last fuck on earth. Isadora pierces his back with her nails; he falls sobbing into her arms after his orgasm. His thighs shudder and pulse. She weeps when he enters her, weeps when he fucks her, weeps when he stops. They meet in abandoned houses in part because their sex is so loud and so uncontrollable. The growl that rises from the throat extends the orgasm, makes it more powerful. The scream redoubles the come. Lovers like this cannot live in condominiums—newly built with ticky-tacky walls. They must have solid plaster houses by the Sound to contain their screams and cries.

And yet, and yet—he will be dead before his thirtieth birthday.

314

She knows this almost as if it were a proven fact. And so she clutches him all the tighter, knowing that they are doomed to drift apart; history separates them. The history of death.

Waiting for him, she sometimes shakes with fear—fear of his never coming back, or fear of his death? Ah, what's the difference, really? If she and Josh could be so close and then could part—then parting is death and death is parting and she has already died many times—and then come back to life.

Although the love affair with Bean seemed to be absorbing most of her life, she also had other tasks to perform, and she did not shirk them. The meeting with Lowell Strathmore, in particular, had been on the books for some time, but, oddly, he kept postponing it. Originally, they were to meet in New York at his office, but he put it off again and again—until one day he called, asking—could he come to her house in Rocky Ridge, for dinner? This was indeed a peculiar request for a man who was so powerfully afraid of his wife.

"Leona must be out of town," Isadora said to him on the phone.

"How did you guess?" Lowell asked.

"There's no other way you'd even *consider* coming for dinner."

"She's with her sister in Southampton." he said. "Her mother died and they're clawing each other to death over the family jewels."

"Are you sure she's not driving home unexpectedly?"

"Not a chance. She has to stay there and keep watch over those canary diamonds."

"Then come to dinner," Isadora said. Danae would provide.

Danae came up with a fabulous meal—roast quail with wild rice; mango mousse; cappuccino. She threw the meal together cheerily enough, while Isadora got Amanda ready for bed, then Danae took off for the movies with her twenty-two-year-old struggling-rock-singer lover. Her kids were scattered around town, peddling dope, doing their homework, getting laid.

Isadora read Amanda not one, but three bedtime stories. *Big Bird Gets Lost* (an epic of scratch and sniff—ah, someday she herself would write an *adult* scratch and sniff book to end all scratch and sniff books!), *Let's Eat* (a very simple, beautifully illustrated book in which Amanda could participate by picking out all her favorite foods), and Bemelmans' *Madeline and the Bad Hat* (one of Isadora's favorites—and Amanda's). Then she went through Amanda's bedtime ritual with her—certain lights had to be left on, others left off; certain doors had to be left open, others left

315

closed; Camelia had to be safe in her arms—and went downstairs to get herself tarted up for Lowell.

Remembering that he loved Opium, she doused herself in it—powder, body cream, perfume. She wore a pink suede shirt, the color of white baby's skin; brown suede jeans, the color of black baby's skin; and crushed suede boots with fur tops, the color of chicano baby's skin. She brushed her mane of blond hair, did her makeup slowly and elaborately, put on a Fats Waller tape on the machine, and danced out into the foyer, singing along with "Your Feets Too Big."

Pretty soon the doorbell rang and the Big Foot in question arrived.

Now, Isadora had not seen Lowell since the advent of Bean—but she dimly remembered Lowell's particular brand of WASP lust and she remembered it with fondness. He was a masculine man—in the manner of Bean—a passionate man, a priapic maniac underneath his reserve. Supposedly he was coming over to advise Isadora about her future course of action in the wake of Mel Botkin's mess—but Isadora had the feeling that Lowell had other fish to fry as well.

She opens the front door. Dogstoyevsky growls lethally. (Since the separation, Dogstoyevsky has become even more antimale than usual—attempting to defend Isadora from her hosts of motley suitors.)

He looks just as she remembered him: that stooping tallness, red hair parted amidships, Ben Franklin glasses, a crisp new shirt (which *must* be from Turnbull and Asser) with the addition of a jaunty silk paisley bow tie, tied to perfection.

"I always admire men who can tie bow ties," Isadora says.

"And I admire women who can untie them," says Lowell, scooping her into his arms. He picks her up as if she were nothing more than a paper doll and presses her to his huge torso. He is such a *big* man; his bigness alone is exciting.

"Don't . . ." says Isadora.

"Why?" says Lowell. "No one who smells the way you do really means *don't!*"

"My kid's upstairs," says Isadora.

"Is she asleep?"

"Presumably," says Isadora.

"Good," says Lowell. "I had such a hard-on driving over here from Southport that I thought I'd have to stop and jerk off or I'd drive off the road."

"I seem to inspire that in men," says Isadora.

"I'll bet you do."

He slings her over his shoulder and carries her into the bedroom, where he drops her on the waterbed and begins peeling off all her clothes.

"Suede, suede, suede," he says. "I thought you were a Friend of Animals."

"Only animals like you," says Isadora, undaunted by his attempt to make her feel as guilty as he probably does. She feels no guilt toward Bean or Kevin (both of whom are probably with their other girl friends tonight—although she does feel useless guilt toward the animals who gave their lives for her ensemble).

Toward Lowell she feels mostly curiosity. Will she still lust for him passionately now that Josh is no longer on the scene? Or will he seem superfluous to her? The adulterous antidote you choose in the midst of a poisoned marriage does not usually work very well once that poison is out of your system and the marriage is over. People who marry adulterous lovers are fools, Isadora thinks; they're just reacting against the marriage they're in, not truly choosing afresh. And then she remembers that she herself did that with Josh!

Lowell has got off all the skin-colored suede and is down to Isadora's own skin—which is lacily covered with beige bikini pants and a beige lace camisole.

"I had forgotten your fabulous nipples," says Lowell, pushing up the camisole, "the pinkest nipples between here and München." Lowell is recalling their first tryst—though Isadora's memory has dimmed. "Do you know I dream about your nipples?" he says, sucking on the left and then the right. "Do you dream about my big cock?" he asks, kicking off his tasseled loafers and then adroitly pulling off his trousers and boxer shorts with one hand, and exposing the glorious pink object in question.

Isadora eyes it curiously. Is it bigger than Bean's? Who cares? Can it make the same magic? Well—this should be an interesting experiment.

Lowell is growling with passion, mad with his wife's fortuitous absence. He grabs her by the hair, by the shoulders, by the flesh on her buttocks. He tears off her bikini pants and spreads her legs as if he were attempting rape.

"I've missed you," he says plunging in.

"And so have I missed you," she moans, curiously detached as he is fucking her.

The cock goes in; the cock goes out. Oh, Bean, she thinks, I love you. How I love you.

Lowell thrusts and thrusts like a madman, getting her somewhat excited at the last—just before he comes.

Winded, spent, he falls upon her. Absurdly enough, he is still wearing the bow tie and shirt.

"I guess I've forgotten how to make you come," he says. "Sorry."

"Oh darling—it's okay," says Isadora. "I'm distracted tonight, not really all there. It has nothing to do with you."

The act of sex with Lowell is so inconsequential tonight that it may as well never have happened.

"I'm so sorry about your not coming," says Lowell, scooting down between her legs to eat her dutifully—as Leona has probably trained him to do.

The practiced tongue flicks at her clitoris; the fingers explore the purple cave within; another hand wanders up to flick a nipple. This is textbook sex, Southport sex, Wall Street's version of *The Joy of Sex,* Isadora thinks. And yet she is determined to have an orgasm just for *auld lang syne.* But somehow she can't get into it. All the buttons are being pushed, but something is wrong. What can it be? She used to find Lowell Strathmore so sexy—in his ur-WASPy way.

Aha—the ur-WASP, she thinks and in her mind's eye sees Bean as Lowell lies between her legs. Gone is the middle-parted hair, gone the bow tie, gone the watery blue eyes usually protected from the world by Ben Franklin glasses. Instead, it is Bean lying between her legs, Bean flicking her, Bean licking her, Bean fingering her nipples. Having got the fantasy right at last, she comes tumultuously, screaming, "Bean!"

"What?" says Lowell, getting up and picking a pubic hair from between two front teeth.

"Oh darling—it's just a private joke," she says. "Josh used to say that sex was better than bean sprouts—remember how he was a vegetarian? So sometimes, to twit him, I used to make vegetable references when we made love. 'Bean' came to stand for the greatest orgasm of all—the ten on a scale of one to ten.
And, boy, was *that* it!"

Lowell looks moderately convinced by this specious explanation

—which is, after all, absurd enough to possibly be true. He cradles Isadora in his arms.

"I had forgotten what a piece of ass you are," he says. "God damn it. This will have to hold me for a year."

"Till some other relative of Leona's dies in Southampton?"

"She died in New York," Lowell says, humorlessly. "They're just dividing up the booty at the Southampton house."

"What a lagniappe for you," says Isadora.

"A what?"

"A lagniappe—something unexpected, an extra treat, a little gift," says Isadora. "It's a Creole word meaning an unexpected gift."

"A piece of ass with a fantastic vocabulary." says Lowell. (His vulgarity in bed is, after all, part of his charm.)

"So I'm told," says Isadora. "That and a token will get me on the subway."

"You're a fabulous woman," Lowell says. "I'd marry you in a minute if . . ."

"If I weren't quite *so* fabulous?" Isadora asks. "After all, you told me in Germany—and also once in Fort Lee, that all my accomplishments intimidated you—you who remain Leona's grumbling slave."

"Well, wasn't *I* the fool?" Lowell says, not so rhetorically.

"You'll never be able to leave her now," says Isadora. "She's probably *so* rich now that her ma has died, that being married to her is like being married to Fort Knox."

"In more ways than one," Lowell says.

"And I'm broke," says Isadora.

"Well—not really," says Lowell, sitting up in the waterbed, reaching for his glasses, and adjusting his shirt and bow tie (which absurdly enough is still tied—though askew).

"Remember the Mandy Trust?" he asks.

"Damn straight I do."

"Well, the Mandy Trust, if I may say so—immodest though it seems—has been invested by a very talented investment adviser."

"And a very talented lover, too," says Isadora, flattering him as a matter of course, "albeit an infrequent one."

Lowell smiles. "Better have me as an investment adviser than a lover," he says. "As an investment adviser, you get my services daily. And it just so happens that your inattentiveness to your own business affairs gave me the freedom I needed to play my hunches. Other clients call me up and bug me all the time—and it throws me off. I'm trying too hard to please and second-guess. But with you—you fabulous piece of ass—I just fantasize about you and pick any stocks I please. And it turns out to be a fabulous system."

"What's the Mandy Trust worth?" Isadora asks.

"I can't give you an exact figure till I get into the office tomorrow morning—but it's got to be several times what you put into it. I'll call you tomorrow morning with the figures."

And with that, he gets up off the bed, strips off his bow tie and shirt, and heads for the shower.

"Why are you showering," she asks, "if Leona's away?"

"Don't want to get Opium on the sheets. She uses Arpège," Lowell yells from the shower.

"I would have thought so," Isadora mutters, wandering into the bathroom. "Leona's the type to use Arpège."

"What did you say?" Lowell asks.

"I said: She's the type to use Arpège."

"What type is that?"

"Dippy," says Isadora.

"Can't hear you with the water running," yells Lowell.

"Good," says Isadora.

She is admiring his huge pink body lathering in speeded-up motion behind the steamy glass door of the shower stall.

"You're a gorgeous man," she says, meaning it truly—but thinking how little he stirs her now. She readies a big bath sheet for him and wraps him in it as he emerges from the shower.

"Sir, your towel," she says, serving him like a geisha, just because it pleases her to do so.

"I've got to get home," Lowell says, with his old fear of Discovery.

"For heaven's sake—why?" she asks. "I thought Leona was in Southampton."

"She's going to call at ten-thirty. If I'm not there, she'll suspect something."

"For heaven's sake, Lowell," says Isadora, "you astound me."

"I often astound myself," he says throwing on his clothes—boxer shorts, shirt, trousers, bow tie, glasses, silk socks, tasseled shoes. She, in turn, puts on a caftan to walk him to the door.

"You're not as broke as you think," says Lowell, combing his hair.

"Are you suggesting I rob my daughter's trust?" Isadora says.

"You wouldn't be the first mother in history to do it—would you? Anything that floats the sinking ship has got to be considered."

"Is it legal?" Isadora asks.

"I don't know how the trust is written," Lowell says, putting on his outer clothes now and opening the door, "but there's no trust under the blue skies of Connecticut that can't be broken."

"What blue skies?" Isadora asks.

Dogstoyevsky has come out from under the living room couch and is barking ferociously.

"You know—we've forgotten all about dinner," Isadora says. "Won't you stay and dine with me? I've got quail and wild rice, and a fabulous dessert."

"I can't," Lowell says. "What if she calls and I'm not there?"

"It's only nine-thirty," Isadora says.

"What if she calls *early*?"

"True, true," says Isadora, wondering whether she can snag someone else for dinner at this hour. Otherwise what a waste of Danae's feast!

Lowell runs out the door.

"Your daughter's well fixed—though you may be broke," he says. "God—you turn me on. I could start all over now."

"So could I," says Isadora, watching him fold his long body—like a collapsible umbrella—into his little black Porsche.

" 'Bye!" he shouts, revving the motor.

" 'Bye!" she shouts, waving.

He roars up the driveway to his phone call, while she goes in to nibble at the quail alone and think and think and *think* about her life and its absurdities.

16

Take Him

Take him, I won't put a price on him.
Take him, he's yours.
Take him, pajamas look nice on him.
But how he snores!
—LORENZ HART
"Take Him"
Pal Joey

For this relief, much thanks.
—SHAKESPEARE
Hamlet

As promised, Lowell called the next morning to tell Isadora that if he continued to invest it luckily, Mandy's trust might eventually cover a portion of the back taxes. How large a portion depended upon when Uncle Sam called in his markers and the vagaries of the stock market. So if Isadora's ledger was not exactly back to zero again, she was not as much in the red as she feared (unless of course Mel Botkin had left other little surprises, which was not unlikely). But somehow Isadora cared far less about all this than she had before. Debtors prison no longer loomed. Broke or not, in the red or not, she was working, and work always made her optimistic. Anything could happen. Hits, flops, fortunes gained, fortunes lost—the only thing to fear was stasis. She was well and truly out of her depression.

She would start again, working her ass off—once again saved by her daughter and her random lusts. Lowell might not be a dependable lover, but he was a dependable friend and adviser. The main thing was that she had been unblocked by her financial emergency. She was writing love poems to Bean at the rate of two and three a day (though love poems certainly would never pay the tax man); the Papa novel had come unstuck and was moving again; and she was writing the treatment for an original screenplay called *The Vagabond and the Movie Star*—about a well-known thirty-nine-year-old actress who takes up with a twenty-five-year-old actor.

Isadora loved being flush with words again. She still had no proper nanny for Amanda; Bean still invaded her life and her peace of mind on a completely unpredictable schedule. But at least she was writing again, so she felt moderately sane—as sane as she ever did anyway. The daily bloodletting of words on the page kept her from going bonkers.

Of course, it was not easy to balance this with domestic duties, trips to New York, erotic trysts, and the like—and Isadora always felt as though she lived in the midst of a travelling circus. There never seemed to be enough time for anything. She felt like one of the Keystone Kops—now writing for three hours, now playing with Amanda, now shopping for Amanda's clothes, now feeding the dog, now taking Amanda to the pediatrician or the dog to the vet, now driving to New York to consult with more lawyers and business managers, now arguing with Josh over the divorce, now meeting Kevin, now meeting Bean.

She had figured out a way to be faithful to Bean without ever really *saying* she was going to be faithful. Whenever Kevin came up for the night (or they met in New York), they would have dinner, get into bed, and she would promptly fall fast asleep. She would sleep in Kevin's arms, dreaming of Bean. In the morning she would always think of an appointment she had to run off to. How ironic, she thought, to find fidelity vaguely forbidden and exotic after all that promiscuity and to have to find excuses (even with *herself*) to be faithful.

The fact was: she didn't *want* to be promiscuous anymore. What was the point? She was a loyal person, and she had found her sexual mate. She did not want to be in bed with Lowell screaming "Bean!" or in bed with Kevin, dreaming of Bean, or in bed with Roland or Errol making up excuses that sounded like recipes out of a wok cookery book. Enough was enough.

But Bean made her crazy. He appeared and disappeared with utmost unpredictability. He lived with another woman to whom his weekends were promised (though at times this, too, seemed unpredictable). He was often unreachable by telephone because he pulled his phone out of the wall and left it that way for hours and hours. Sometimes it seemed they met by sheerest accident. She would have a meeting in New York, and the meeting would get canceled—and then, by happenstance, she'd run into him on the street, whereupon they'd sneak off to his lair to lose hours in bed.

They both began canceling everything for each other—meetings, auditions, work commitments of every description. When they were together, they never wanted to part. When they parted, they feared they'd never see each other again.

Isadora kept up the semblance of her old life—Kevin, Roland, Errol—because she still felt that Bean was an invention of her imagination, not a real person. The way he abruptly arrived and vanished and her difficulty in reaching him gave him the air of a dybbuk or a faerie person (in the lovely old-fashioned sense of the term). When he disappeared, where did he go? Into an earthen hollow? Did he slip behind the hedgerows? Between the rain-drops? Did he fall into a purple shadow between snowbanks?

But whatever was happening to him (and whether or not she had invented him), he was gradually giving her back her will to live and her belief that she could love again. After Josh left, she had all but stopped writing. The first night she met Bean, she told him that she expected never to write again and she meant it. He took her hand, squeezed it, and said, "Of course you'll write again." But she was still convinced that she was finished. Why write, she thought, if writing only loses you the one you love? For Isadora no longer believed that art was more important than life. She did not believe that artists who made their families miserable were justified if their books were great enough. She felt that it was incumbent upon one to be a good human being first, an artist second. She had not felt that way in her twenties; perhaps she had not felt that way before having a child humanized her; but she certainly felt that way now. The demands of life are nearly always antithetical to the demands of art. The crying baby does not ex-actly enhance the daydreaming state needed for writing poems. The trip to the vet or the pediatrician does not exactly prepare one for writing a chapter describing *palazzi* in sixteenth-century Venice. Or *does* it? They had cats and dogs and babies in those sixteenth-century *palazzi*. And doubtless they felt about them the way we feel about our cats and dogs and babies. Even the most unexpected occurrence at the pediatrician's or the vet's turns out to fuel the book one is writing. The look of an animal in pain. The *feel* of a wet baby. How can any artist believe that by excluding the clutter and commotion of life he is somehow enhancing his art? Women artists don't believe it. They know that the crying baby somehow has to be accommodated with the manuscript that cries out not to be left. For whatever one loses of concentration, one gains immeasurably in the richness of observation. The force of life is with one—the everyday, the ordinary miraculousness of life.

Isadora had truly believed she would never write again, but Bean became her Muse. She had also believed she could never love again after Josh, but slowly she was starting to see that loving was a capacity, not necessarily an exclusive club. As she tentatively came to love Bean, always denouncing herself for loving him, doubting herself, doubting her sincerity, his sincerity, the pain over Josh began to lessen and fade. Perhaps she and Josh were not as fated as she had thought. Or perhaps they had been fated for a time. Perhaps, in lives that compressed many lifetimes into one, it was necessary to have many mates. Oh, what a blasphemous thought! And yet maybe it was true.

Bean came like a breath of fresh air to a shut-in, like Mr. Browning to Miss Barrett, like a cataract operation to an old woman getting blinder and blinder every year. The fuse of life is passed along through human flesh. We are plugged into the world of spirit through our decaying, dying flesh. Sex is the motor. Skin makes the electrical connection. Those who scoff at sex, who laugh at flesh (perhaps because it is not permanent?), do not know that it is not permanence that determines whether something is real or unreal. Molecules change patterns, rearrange themselves—but still the dance of life goes on. Through our skins, we become messengers to each others' molecules. As long as those molecules move, we are alive.

One night, lying in Bean's arms, she had a dream which marked how far she had come. The dream was elaborate: in color, with music. The stage was set for a musical of the thirties or forties. A brass band on stage was tuning up. Isadora was pulling on her costume and tap shoes.

Suddenly she mounted a Plexiglas staircase festooned with red neon lights. She wore a white top hat and carried a Plexiglas cane. Her white tailcoat flapped in the breeze and her little white satin boxer shorts gleamed. Her tap shoes were red patent leather. As she broke into her song and dance, the band played with her.

> "Take him, I won't put a price on him.
> Take him, he's yours . . ."

She sang Vera's mock-plaintive lines from *Pal Joey*.

> "Take him, pajamas look nice on him.
> But how he snores! . . ."

Bean, Josh, and Josh's no longer nameless lady, Wendy, were in the audience. Bean applauded wildly. Josh looked stunned and tentative (as he often did in life). And Ms. Emanon rushed up to the stage like a rabid dog and bit Isadora on the wrist.

Isadora laughed as Ms. Emanon's big buck teeth sank into her wrist.

"If they asked me, I could write a book . . ." she sang. And then the dream faded.

328

She woke up in Bean's arms with the most wonderful sense of relief. She was actually laughing.

"Darling—what is it?" he asked, stroking her hair.

"I'm almost free of him," she said, "almost. And what a blessed relief it is." She was euphoric. Bean held her very close and she smelled his delicious smell. She loved the smell of his sweat, the taste of his semen, the taste of his tears.

"I love you," she said. "After that dream, I can love you even better."

So what, if it lasts or does not last? she thought. This is what we have now. Life is only now—not then, not when. We delude ourselves in thinking that past and future really exist.

"What dream?" Bean asked.

So she told him. And the amazing thing was that he understood.

"Your life is just beginning, not ending," he said. "At forty, you'll shift gears and be launched into a whole new phase of your life."

"How can you know that?"

"I can't. It's just that I *do* know it because we're linked. I can't tell you how."

And indeed, as February wore icily on, there were murmurs of spring in the air. Isadora found a new business manager and lawyer to deal with the IRS mess and slowly they began to unravel Mel Botkin's tangled skeins. The law is sometimes just, but never swift. Meanwhile, invitations arrived. Invitations to speak in San Francisco, and other points west; invitations to travel to Russia that summer to partake of "cultural exchange"—whatever *that* was. Struggling as she was with the Papa novel, there was no question that she would go to Russia. (The invitation even coincided with the very month Mandy was going to stay with Josh—so surely she was meant to go.) She had been interviewing relatives about their memories of Papa, memories of Russia; she had been trying to track down that great lost painting presumed to be in that mysterious Midwestern warehouse. But the invitation to go to Russia was just too fortuitous; of course she would go. She would travel to Odessa and try to find her grandfather there.

Meanwhile spring *was* ever near. February in Connecticut was as treacherous and icy as ever, but on odd days, another wind blew from the Sound: a warmer wind, a wind that promised the blessed seasonal return of mud and all things that squirm under it. Roots, worms, tubers, and runners would aerate the mud of Connecticut. Connecticut itself would heave out from under its shroud of ice and once again Persephone would return from the underworld and her rejoicing mother would make things grow again.

In truth, there is no place in the world where spring does not come again. Even Malibu (where Isadora lived for one fateful year) has seasons—though at first they are not visible to the easterner. But the tides on the Pacific shift; whales migrate; phosphorescent organisms tint the water neon blue and pelicans dip and dive-bomb into these shining waves. When that happens even the gray and beaten-down screenwriters who earn millions a year (but dream of novels they will never write), and the stoned and sun-streaked surfer boys and girls look up and acknowledge the birth of a new season.

Spring comes to the desert with a rush of mustard flowers on the dusty slopes of the arroyos. Spring comes to the ocean with a change in waterlife and a change in the air. Spring comes to frozen Connecticut even in February, when the ice looms more menacing than ever. By March, when the winds blow and the rains begin to soften the winter mantle of prehistoric ice, even the thickest snowstorm cannot deny the crocuses pushing up below.

Papa had survived almost two winters underground; it was time to write his story and get on with it. She and Josh were through as lovers (would they someday become friends?—oh, it was too soon to tell), and she and Bean were just beginning. Isadora had somehow to find the courage to follow all these paths to the places where they led. So she cut her losses. She stopped arguing with Josh over whether or not he would support Mandy. She decided she would support Mandy—and be grateful she was working again. That was the example she would set for her daughter. Josh's childishness was Ms. Emanon's problem now, not hers. And good riddance.

From time to time she had an absolutely clear vision of him as her enemy, and that was helpful to her. He had undercut the two things dearest to her in life: her child and her writing. Not that she still did not *wish* to be friends with the father of her child (that dream never dies), but she did not expect it. She expected nothing from him but trouble. Already that was a help.

Once she ceased expecting, she ceased being angry—for anger is really disappointed hope. She hoped for nothing from him but a little civility. And even if that did not come, she would not be surprised.

She and Josh had long phone conversations about Mandy, but they tended to avoid each other in the flesh. Still, one day in

March, as her fortieth birthday was approaching and she was trying to come to terms with the news that her life was half over, they happened to confront each other in Westport.

The stuffing fell out of the hole in her heart. She went weak in the knees. He had a laundry bag slung over his shoulder and was on his way to the laundromat. She was carrying an antique lamp she wanted to have rewired.

The lady with the lamp met the man with the bag.

"Want to have a cup of coffee?" she asked.

(Mandy was at the Blue Tree School till two that day and it was only noon.)

"Sure," he said.

They went into a Westport dive that they had often frequented when they were together. It was called Gone Fishin' and it was a seafood place decorated in a tacky nautical motif—fisherman's nets, blown-glass balls—that kind of cutesy stuff.

The lady with the lamp put down her lamp. The man with the bag put down his bag. A helpful hatcheck person checked these unwieldy items. The man and the lady thanked her rather too kindly. (They were nervous in each other's presence.)

"So?" he said.

"How about lunch?" she said, aware that people were looking at them, recognizing them, wondering if this was the great reconciliation scene she (and they?) had dreamed about so many times.

Josh looked very bald to her after Bean, very bald and somewhat silly. He was not comfortable in his skin—that much she knew. And she also knew that she was beginning to be comfortable in hers. Not in the old way—because she had a man tucked away somewhere—but in a new way, a radical way—at least for her. She was comfortable just because she was who she was and centered in her soul. She had gone to hell (like Persephone) and come back up into the light of day. She was ready to flower again just as Bean had predicted.

They made small talk.

Josh loved gadgets and talked about the new decoder dish he had bought to intercept cable TV programs, the new telescope he had, the new word processor.

She realized that he was as thrilled about these things as a boy of ten would be thrilled. He wasn't even in adolescence; he was in latency! The idea of helping to support Mandy was not only alien to him—it scarcely even struck him as his responsibility. He was like a bonsai tree his parents had carefully cultivated and grown.

They needed to remain the parents so they stunted him accordingly—for their benefit, not his. And he had obligingly remained a little boy. Still, there was always some woman ready and waiting to take care of the most infantile boy-man.

But here was the amazing thing: he did not protest. He only protested Isadora's attempts to free him from his little root-bound pot, not his parents' attempts to keep him there. It was amazing; he would go on tinkering with his gadgets forever, but she would get on with her life.

"So? How are things?" she asked.

"Better," he said. "I'm going to a yoga workshop next month in Colorado, and then next summer—after Mandy comes to stay with me, I'm going off to a Zen retreat in the Caribbean with Wendy."

Isadora saw red. The blood heated up behind her eyeballs and her heart began to pound. Here was a man who turned his back on almost every opportunity to take care of his kid financially, who pleaded poverty at every opportunity, yet who seemed to be spending his life at a series of retreats—in every sense of the word.

"I thought you were totally broke," Isadora said, as calmly as she could. (She remembered that he hated this. One of the things he always assailed her with when they lived as man and wife was her ability to keep her voice low and soft even when she was agitated and angry. He always wanted to goad her to throw teacups and fling food, as if such violence were the proof of involvement.

"Well—I'm just about scraping by with help from my parents and Wendy, but . . ."

"But you always seem to have money to indulge yourself," she snapped.

Oh, why had she said this? She had promised herself to *drop* the issue, to let him be a wimp if he wished to be, to let him grow up or not grow up in relation to Mandy—not to assume the maternal role with him, not to fall into the trap of saying judgmental things.

"There you go again—hocking me," he said, getting up to leave.

They hadn't even ordered yet (all that stood on the table was ice water) and here he was: leaving. She felt cheated by his refusal to confront her on it. She would have liked to have it out once and for all. The discharge of feeling would at least be salutary for both of them, but he wouldn't deal with it.

"I'd better be going." he said.

She panicked. Just a moment ago, he had been sitting down with her, about to break bread, and here he was already getting up to leave. The repetition of the leaving yet again was so unbearable that she did what she had never done before in her entire life: she picked up her glass of ice water and flung the contents in his face.

He looked shocked, then contemptful, then mocking. Their neighbors sat there all around them gawking at them. A few drops of ice water hung from Josh's beard, a drop of water from the tip of his nose.

"Good-bye, Isadora," he said, and walked out—clearly the victor in this round. *She* was the one who had lost her dignity. *She* was the one who looked like an idiot. *She* was the one who had vowed not to be angry, not to assail him, not to make demands on him—and she had failed.

As he put on his ski parka and walked out, she buried her head in her hands on the table and openly wept, not really giving a damn who saw or heard.

Then she got up and ran out of the restaurant.

She found QUIM and began to drive like a maniac, the tears blinding her, the unexpressed longings (to hold him, to love him, to protect him, to win him back, to maim him, to kill him, to drive a stake through his heart and bury him) rising up in her chest like an indigestible meal. She was still in a welter of confused and conflicted emotions. Eight months was not long enough to make the psychological separation from someone you had loved that deeply, shared pregnancy with, animals with, births and deaths of every sort.

Isadora blamed herself for still being on a roller coaster of emotions, yet she also knew that she should be good to herself, give herself more time. She *wanted* the mourning time to be over, but it just wasn't yet. She wanted to be completely forgiving and understanding and then to get on with her life, but she was still furious with Josh for having left her and left Amanda. When he moved out she had thought he would shape up and come to appreciate her the more; all he had done was slide deeper and deeper into self-indulgence. She could not believe that she was no longer her husband's keeper. She was the keeper of her own soul now.

As she drove, she suddenly remembered something she hadn't thought of for the longest time—Mandy's siege of terror during the spring before she and Josh split. It was as if the child (and the animals) acknowledged something she and Josh could not yet acknowledge: that their whole world was falling apart.

It was just after Josh had returned from that Zen monastery in Kyoto and just before Cicely-the-Naked-Nanny ran over Chekarf. Mandy was two and a half. With no apparent warning she began to be terrified of bugs—invisible bugs, bugs that weren't there, bugs that seemed to be projections of her parents' impending split.

At that point the baby—they still called her "the baby"—slept in a bright red youthbed with removable sides. She would wake up in the middle of the night in a panic, screaming, "Bugs! Bugs!"

Terrified, Josh and Isadora would run upstairs to her room. They would find her face contorted in fear, her mouth open like a black tunnel in an Edvard Munch painting of a screaming child. Her body shook as if she were going into a seizure. Her face was white with fear.

"Bugs!" she would scream. "Bugs!"

"Where? Where?" Daddy asked.

"There aren't any bugs," Mommy affirmed.

"Bugs!" the child would scream.

At first they denied that the bugs were there. That did no good. The child still screamed their existence to the very rafters. She still shook and trembled.

Then they thought up a new stratagem: participate in the child's fantasy.

"I'm going to get a broom and kill all the bugs," Mommy said.

"Yes, yes!" said Daddy.

Mommy ran downstairs to get a battered straw broom. Like a deranged old witch, she flung it about the room.

"Bugs!" she screamed, whacking the corners of the nursery. "I'm killing the bugs. Oh—there goes another one . . ."

Whack!

"I got him!"

Whack!

"There goes the last of them."

Whack!

The child would usually be convinced for about a minute and then she would begin to scream again in terror.

"There, Mandy, *you* kill the bugs," Mommy said, taking the toddler out of her bed and giving her the broom.

Mandy seized it and began to go after the bugs herself, whacking them, screaming at them, chasing them. The two parents urged her on with apparent enthusiasm, as if they were fans at a baseball game and their little offspring had just hit repeated home runs. But in their hearts they were deeply troubled—as only parents can be troubled when they think they have done irreparable harm to their little one and they do not know how on earth to remedy it. Finally, the child would collapse with exhaustion.

"All the bugs are gone now," Mommy said, picking Mandy up and putting her into bed.

"Bugs," the child would mutter sleepily, dropping off. "Bugs," she would mutter, conking out.

The two parents, co-conspirators in making both the child and her problems, joined hands and tiptoed down the stairs. They each prayed silently for the extermination of the "bugs"—whatever they were. They each yearned for a house free of bugs. They each hoped that their child would sleep through the night and wake up in a world without bugs.

Remembering this siege, Isadora was comforted that she and Josh had not stayed together. Mandy was better off now—for all her problems in dealing with Daddy's absence. She was self-confident, spunky, free of imaginary insects. She cried for her daddy, missed her daddy—but her feelings and her fears were appropriate. She was sad when Daddy left, happy when he arrived. Though she felt torn between Mommy's house and Daddy's house, she did not see bugs where none existed. That in itself was a blessing.

And what of the infestation of imaginary insects? It had gone the way of their marriage. Oh, Isadora still loved Josh, still wanted to see him grow and change and come back to her a better man, a stronger man, but in some sense she had given up on him. She and Mandy had to get on with it. Better to be broken and stronger at the mended places than to live one's entire life in an impending fracture.

Stop crying, she said to herself finally. This is all for the best.

She glanced at her watch. It was almost time to get Mandy at the Blue Tree School.

Drat, she said to herself. I forgot the lamp at the restaurant.

She would go back and redeem it later, she thought. The lady with the lamp would have light again.

"Let there be light," she said, driving to get her daughter.

17

Witches & Goddess Worshipers or May You Never Lack for Magick

Considering that, all hatred driven hence
The soul recovers radical innocence
And learns at last that it is self-delighting,
Self-appeasing, self-affrighting,
And that its own sweet will is Heaven's will;
She can, though every face should scowl
And every windy quarter howl
Or every bellows burst, be happy still.
—W. B. YEATS
"A Prayer for My Daughter"

Whirl is king.
—ARISTOPHANES

SHE had been invited to California to speak at a convention of contemporary witches and goddess worshipers. They had gotten wind of her interest in the Mother Goddess and wanted her to address them—in lieu of the Goddess herself. If they couldn't have Ishtar in person (or Isis, or Persephone, or Demeter), they would take Isadora. Some bargain. The conference—called "Isis Emergent"—was to be held late in March, right after Isadora's fortieth birthday. It would take place outside San Francisco in the funky county of Marin (where Isis would surely emerge—were she *intent* on emerging in the U.S. in the early 1980s).

Isadora could hardly face such a junket alone. The Goddess herself only knew what nuts would accost her there. She had long ago vowed not to make these trips without a kindred spirit in tow. One was entirely too vulnerable otherwise—or at least she was. Alone in a strange hotel room, prey to the intrusions of whomever happened to knock and seek admittance, Isadora found conferences full of strangers a trial. She was not good at the unbridled rudeness or chilly hauteur required to keep lunatics at bay; she was too friendly, too accessible. So she tended to get swamped by ill-wishers. Her celebrity skills were lacking. After all these years she still tended to assume that most people were decent and well meaning—in spite of a host of experiences to the contrary. So she invited Hope to come along, but Hope was busy. Then she invited Kevin, but Kevin was to be with his kid that weekend. Finally, on a lark, she invited Bean; Bean delightedly accepted.

Up until the last minute, she wasn't even sure he would turn up at the airport—that was how unpredictable he always was about schedules.

But there he was, flashing his blue eyes at her from under the brim of the most boyish gray flannel cap. He looked like a kid, and here she was two days past her fortieth birthday. In truth, she had never felt younger. Her birthday had been a festival of spring. Baskets of flowers arrived from far-flung friends to adorn her house. Dozens of roses, balloon bouquets, cases of champagne all heralded her passage into her fifth decade. Once the day itself was in progress, forty seemed the best age in the world to be. It was only the day *before* forty that was bad. Once forty was actually there, it proved to be delicious. One could counter every trepidation, quiet every qualm with the knowledge that one's life might be half over. Better go for it, grab it, seize the day, savor the sweetness—who knew what decrepitude tomorrow might bring?

Isadora had given up on finding the perfect nanny and had invited Danae and family to live with her and Amanda. She had decided that her quest for Mary Poppins was an anachronism— some aberration picked up from reading too many old novels. There *were* no nannys in America in the eighties; there were only "arrangements." Communal living was the answer. If you had a big house in an isolated spot, better to share it with people who could help you dig out in case of blizzards than to go on vainly pursuing the dream of perfect "help." Nobody wanted to *be* help in America in the eighties—at least not for hire. With Danae in residence, Isadora could take off and do a lecture in California knowing that Mandy would be well (if erratically) looked after. It was much better than having Nurse Librium, zonked in front of the TV, or Cicely-the-Naked-Nanny in the hot tub with her boyfriend, or Olive-the-Scientologist forever on the phone, or Bertha-Belle busy padding the butcher's bill and talking to God— hallelujah.

When Isadora met Bean at the airport, she was blithe in the knowledge that Danae was with Amanda, that the house was full of kids coming and going, and that for all the chaos, there was camaraderie and laughter.

She and Bean astounded each other by traveling together as if they had always traveled together. They both kept expecting to wake up and find that the other one was a colossal pain in the ass, but it never happened. From the moment they embraced at the airport and boarded the plane, they were happy in each other's company—happy, easy, and unruffled. As for Isadora's terror of flying, it had long since turned to elation. She sometimes felt she was happier in the air than on the ground.

In California, the weather was glorious. Blue skies in Marin, the green hills humping off to nowhere, even the usually misty Golden Gate Bridge gleaming like a fairy-tale span leading to the pot of gold at the end of the rainbow.

She and Bean checked in at the Stanford-Court, where she had often stayed with Josh and even more often stayed alone. Everything seemed like an extension of her birthday. There was champagne waiting in their room, bags of sinsemilla sent by the organizers of the conference, another basket of flowers sent by a friend in California.

"To us," Isadora said, toasting Bean in champagne.

"To us," he said.

Oh, she didn't really believe any of this was permanent. Happiness is fleeting, pain unforgettable. But life was not permanent either. Better to live in the present than to fret about the future or rehearse the past.

There are times in life when the curse seems lifted, when existence seems as pure and uncomplicated as a drop of spring water dangling at the end of a crystal mixing rod, when great suffering has suddenly fled, leaving in its wake only great joy: this was one of these times.

"My mothball fleet," Isadora said, embracing Bean.

"My baby, my bounce, my darling," he said, hugging her.

She called him her "mothball fleet' because his clothes always smelled vaguely of camphor—in true old-WASP family fashion. He called her "bounce" because of her bouncy, loping walk. "Loping de Vega" he also called her, after the most prolific (and happiest?) writer in human history. Oh, they were mad for each other, mad for San Francisco, mad for the hills, the Bay, the dope, the champagne, the food, and each other's bodies. They devoured each other in bed, gazed into each other's eyes until it seemed they would drown in their mutual blues, ate and drank and smoked together until all of life seemed suffused with sweet sensation.

Isadora, who had felt so much pain for so long, who had lived the last eight months with an aching hole in her heart, was strangely filled by *this* love, *this* sensation. It was not just sex (as if such sex can ever be "just")—it was also protection, caring, concern. Bean had a sweetness she had never known in any man, a tenderness (for all his passionate roughness in bed). He wanted to protect her. She felt his protectiveness as a force around her body. She felt the force of his manhood, the tang of his sex. He was the first man she had ever met who did not confuse sweetness with being a wimp. He was tender, but there was no question he was a man.

The conference itself was a gas. Run by a large mustachioed brunette (with enormous pendulous tits) who called herself Lisa Goddess-Priestess (or Lisa G-P for short), the conference was full

341

of feminist witches, hippie-agriculturists (who were growing sinsemilla in the hills of Humboldt County), hippie-animal husbanders (who were raising unicorns that looked suspiciously like one-horned goats), hippie children costumed for Arcady—or a northern California production of *A Midsummer Night's Dream*. Isadora was hugely amused by it all (and also very glad she'd brought Bean). Nuts abounded at the conference and each and every one had a bone to pick with Isadora. One stopped her to declare that *Tintoretto's Daughter* was a sexist book. "Why didn't you call it *Marietta's Father?*" a very bellicose Goddess-person demanded.

"Because no one would have kn   n which Marietta I meant."

"But naming it after Tintoretto panders to the very patriarchy you are criticizing."

"Not really. Anyone who *reads* the book *knows* I'm not on the side of patriarchy."

"Well—I would have called it *Marietta's Father*," the Goddess-person said.

"Then," said Isadora (more kindly than she felt), "maybe you should write your *own* book and call it that."

Bean was furious at the wholesale hostility that greeted Isadora from some of the very people who'd invited her.

"Why'd they ask you here if all they wanted was to assault you?"

"Oh, darling," said Isadora, "that's my *function* as a writer—to be a lightning rod for people's fantasies, their fears, their feuds with the world. I'm used to it."

"I'm not," said Bean. "You need protection. Someday, you're going to walk outside your door and find that the same thing happens to you as happened to John Lennon. But not while I'm around. I'd lay down my life for you."

Isadora could see he really meant it.

Bean was still young and innocent enough to believe that fame meant honor rather than a complex combination of attention and attack. Isadora privately congratulated herself on having brought along her own ally so that she could enjoy the trip.

As they explored the exposition site—set up as a medieval fair on the green hills of Marin (not far from Mt. Tam)—it occurred to Isadora that ten years ago she'd been at a convention of Freudian shrinks in Vienna, and now she'd "progressed" to a convention of feminist witches and Goddess worshipers in Marin. Then, she'd been with a man eight years older; now she was with a man fourteen years younger (a man who'd been in prep school when she was gallivanting around Europe with Adrian Goodlove), a man who'd learned about lovemaking in part from reading her books! It all seemed so unreal. Her very life seemed unreal. She had created books out of her own substance and out of those books had come the outer trappings of her life—houses, cars, the means to support the child she bore—not to mention crooked business managers, crazy nannies, complex tax troubles—the lot! It was as if she'd dreamed the world and then seen it come to life. But was it a nightmare, or was it a euphoric dream? Could she choose, or was the choice thrust upon her? And was the stock market, the world of mergers and acquisitions, or the world of academe any less of a dream?

Today, it all seemed like a comic dream—a comic dream out of the mists of pre-Arthurian legend. Who were these costumed figures wandering across the greensward? Had she invented them, too, and invented the companion with whom she viewed them? They were a ragtag group—part Monty Python, part sword-and-dragon epic, with special effects. The Goddess worshipers wore filthy *shmattes* that grazed the ground; from underneath peeked orthopedic sandals. The feminist witches sported the double-bladed ax from Crete—the labyris—which they hung as amulets around their necks. And little children frolicked amongst unicorns (why spoil the Magick and call them one-horned goats?).

The conference was as tacky as it was cosmic. Vendors were busy selling everything from astrological charts to perineal prints (yes—it was indeed claimed that if you sat bare-assed upon an ink pad and then upon a sheet of rice paper, your perineum would give a print predicting your future far better than any mere palm-print!). Other medieval-looking mountebanks sold "pyradomes" —little wire pyramids to wear on the head—"to concentrate the cosmic rays and increase both inspiration and intelligence." It didn't *seem* to have worked for the dudes who were selling them (who merely looked like your average northern California stoners). Herbal remedies were for sale at other booths, as well as magic potions, herbs to be used in doing incantations and spells, carob-covered cookies in the shapes of zodiacal signs, and even "solar-powered" vibrators (for the ecologically minded masturbator!). Good new neopaganism didn't seem to have resisted commerciality any more successfully than bad old Judeo-Christianity. Apparently, whether God was male or female, the pursuit of lucre was equally sacred to Him/Her. Not to mention the pursuit of sinsemilla. The sweet smell of sinsemilla was everywhere. Isadora hardly knew how much of what she was seeing was contact high and how much was "real"—whatever "real" might be.

She gave her speech on the female aspect of the deity—and it was warmly received. Like many people, Isadora tended always to concentrate on the few people who hated her rather than on the many who loved and admired her. In truth, most of the audience was delighted to hear her—delighted and appreciative. A great rush of applause followed her speech—but even without it, she would have felt the pleasure of the listeners.

"Why am I so negativistic?" Isadora wondered aloud to Bean when her gig was over. "I always seem to anticipate criticism and to focus on that rather than on all the affirmation I receive."

"There's probably no artist on earth who doesn't," Bean said. "Except for the real fools and four-flushers. They're *never* self-critical."

Bean came as balm to Isadora's soul. He was so supportive, so accepting. He had the wonderful optimism of youth, the optimism and innocence that betrayals and divorces and IRS audits manage to wear away in time. At forty, the true lover of humankind must be a cynic: so many hopes have been dashed. But at twenty-six, the optimism is fresh. Bean was an innocent, for all his sexual bravado. His heart—the organ that mattered most—was pure. That was why Isadora loved him so: he restored her faith in innocence, her faith that the poet's vision (not the taxman's) was the true one.

Once her gig was done, they fled the conference and headed for Muir Woods. Drunk with their new love, intoxicated with San Francisco, with weed and wine, they drove to the Muir Woods and reveled in its green.

A light rain misted their faces as they walked the pathways between the ancient redwoods. Rejoicing in the green, imbibing the green, absorbing the green through their pores, they both felt reborn, renewed, reconnected to life. Love is green (as Shakespeare knew). The lovers' sleeves are green (as the Elizabethans sang).

From time to time the rain would grow heavy and they would run for cover under the towering trees. The tree trunks were kissed with moss; the rocks were as wet and slippery as lovers' thighs; the sky was obscured by the monumental trees.

The rain had driven away the other tourists, so it was as if they were walking in an enchanted forest, sprung up exclusively for

344

them, more state of mind than material reality, more Brigadoon than California. They saw fantastic animal heads in the mossy fallen tree trunks and rotting roots: basilisks, griffins, green unicorns. These seemed to be the true imaginary animals, and those at the conference merely the bogus. The vegetable world here seemed in the process of metamorphosis into the animal, the mineral world in the process of metamorphosis into the vegetable.

"It's an enchanted forest, out of time," said Bean; "it will vanish when we do."

And so it seemed—though they both knew full well that *they* would vanish and the forest would remain. They walked on a little ledge of time above the abyss of eternity. But in their budding new love, they felt secure and strong—as if they could hold the demons at bay for a time.

" 'On the world island we are all castaways,' " Bean said.

"That's beautiful," said Isadora.

"I know—it's Loren Eisley, not me, unfortunately. But with you, for the first time in my life, I *don't* feel like a castaway. I feel I *belong* . . ."

"Belong where?" asked Isadora.

"Belong in your arms," said Bean, taking her and kissing her as the rain drenched them.

Their tongues intertwined and they were lost in the wet sweetness within (and the wet sweetness without). Their kiss was like a bolt of lightning in a torrential rain—fire conveyed through water. Often, when they kissed, the intensity of connection was so great that they both experienced vertigo.

"I never feel lonely with you," said Bean when they stopped kissing. "I keep *expecting* to feel lonely or shut out or irritated, but the more we are together, the more *right* it feels, the more we seem to belong together."

Isadora felt the same, but she feared admitting it. She feared the commitment it implied, she feared the heartbreak, the entanglement that leads to bitter loss. Bean waited for her to pledge herself to him in turn, but she remained silent through fear and the recentness of her heartbreak.

She looked up at him.

"You're beautiful," she said.

He shook his head. "I'm just a man who loves you," he said. "But I love you completely. You'll see. Just give me time."

They clasped hands and walked on in the rain not caring at all that they were both drenched, that they had ruined their shoes, and that they had begun something they could not easily repudiate.

Isadora had had doubts about her relationship with Bean from the very beginning. Born in demonic passion, it seemed doomed to end as it began: suddenly. So many of their nights were booze-soaked, weed-hallucinated, that it seemed she would awaken one morning and find that it had all been a dream—as in the ending of the corniest "Twilight Zone" tale. "Was it all a dream?" the protagonist wonders—but then she finds some material remnant of the dream zone which she has somehow carried back intact. It is the oldest of literary devices: the twelve dancing princesses find their shoe leather worn out; Mary Poppins's wards, the Banks children, emerge from the world of the Royal Doulton plate on the mantel, but discover they have dropped a woolen scarf which now remains in the world of the plate, trapped forever under its glaze. An old literary trick but one which never fails to haunt. What would Isadora bring back from her sojourn in the world of fantasy with Bean? Clap? Herpes? Or a heart that healed and was somehow whole again?

Right now she didn't care. The present was so beautiful that it obliterated all fretfulness. Always accustomed to agonizing over the future and regretting the past, she released herself to be entirely in the present. She gave herself permission to enjoy San Francisco, her companion, her life.

They rode the cable cars and walked the waterfront. They slogged uphill and down; they bought silly trinkets in Chinatown boutiques; they sat at the Top of the Mark and watched the lights of the city, the boats on the Bay, the bridges, the procession of cars that seemed from this distance like tiny illuminated insects crossing a bridge of grass. They explored Marin by car, driving up the winding ways of Tiburon and Sausalito, the serpentine roads of Mill Valley. On a road somewhere they stopped and found a roadside marker that read: Isadora's Way.

"I wonder if it was named after Isadora Duncan?" asked Isadora.

"After *you*," said Bean.

"I doubt it," Isadora countered, never believing in her own power.

"Then it's magic," said Bean. "That sign's been waiting for you for years." Somehow the discovery of her name on a signpost seemed a good omen, but then everything seemed a good omen during those days in San Francisco. Bean and Isadora never stumbled over each other in their hotel room, never got in each other's hair in restaurants, in bars, in cars. He never complained if they took a wrong turn, nor razzed her if she stopped to pee too often. He was nothing at all like the other men she'd known: not peevish, not controlling, not fretful.

"What's wrong with us?" Isadora wondered aloud. "We get along so well."

"You'll see," said Bean. "You'll see. There's nothing at all wrong with us. And sometimes perfection is harder to take than imperfection, and love is harder to take than heartbreak."

And yet there was also chaos and anarchy in Isadora's idyll with Bean—a sense that Pan the prankster was ever near and that Whirl was king.

On a cablecar in San Francisco, Isadora had her wallet picked— three hundred dollars in cash, credit cards, driver's license, everything. The wallet vanished in part because she and Bean were kissing and not paying attention to the world around them. She had to call home and have Renata cancel all the cards and wire money to the hotel—and the incident gave Isadora a pang of doubt about this wildly world-obliterating love and where it might be leading her.

Later that night, when they were madly fucking in their hotel room, Bean nibbled off one of Isadora's earrings—diamond studs her mother had bought her for her fortieth birthday. Either he swallowed the stud, or it fell into a crevice of the bed and they could never find it, though they searched all over for it. Again she felt a pang of demon doubt. Not that she cared a hoot for cash, or credit cards, or diamonds, compared to Bean—but from time to time the bourgeois demon of her childhood would come to haunt her, perching on her shoulder and calling her a bad girl, a bad mother, an irresponsible hedonist, a wild woman, a tramp, a trollop, a tart—predicting financial ruin, venereal disease—all the things that happen to bad girls who seduce and support younger men.

She'd feel a stab of longing for Amanda then (Amanda who she knew was perfectly well looked after for these three days she was away), but in her childhood world, mothers did not go away even for three days (though *her* mother surely had) and they certainly did not go away with men who were fourteen years younger.

Sometimes, when she and Bean were making love, Isadora

347

would think gloomily that their idyll was doomed: she would be fifty when he was thirty-six; her allure would be fading; he would be in his prime. They were passing each other on the escalators of their ages—she going down toward menopause, he climbing to the prime of manhood. The explosiveness of their lovemaking had something frightening about it—frightening and evanescent. Part witchery, part fantasy, it seemed to belong to that class of things which must perforce vanish—like the Banks children's idyll in the Royal Doulton plate or the twelve dancing princesses' wild nights in faeryland.

Their lovemaking surely had something of the realm of faery about it, but also it was the product of the immense changes in the world of sex that had occurred in the fourteen years that separated them. In fourteen years, the mores had changed just enough so that a man of Bean's generation had perhaps never had a woman as accepting, as open to his loving as Isadora. He was of that generation—raised to manhood on *her* books—that expected women to throw fits (and their partners out of bed) if they didn't have three orgasms in rapid fire before the man even began to think of his own pleasure. And she—despite her public reputation (or perhaps *because* of it)—was just enough a child of the fifties to think that cosseting a man, pleasing a man, nurturing a man was more important than her own immediate pleasure. Consequently, she must have struck him as the most obliging woman he had ever known in bed, and he certainly struck her as the most obliging man. As she had discovered with Roland, men born in the fifties were so used to young women who seemed like traffic cops in bed that a woman in her thirties or forties seemed like a revelation in old-fashioned femininity.

None of which prevented Isadora from sometimes feeling like an old bawd, the Wife of Bath, or a dirty old woman. Certainly she was not that estimable but somewhat intimidating creature "a good woman."

Not long ago she overheard—from a friend of a friend of a friend—her ex-mother-in-law's judgment of Josh's new lady friend, Ms. Emanon.

"She's not beautiful, god knows," Josh's mother had said, "but at least she's a good woman."

What a withering judgment—annihilating *two* daughters-in-law with one economical blow! Implying, of course, that Isadora had *not* been a good woman, that she had been too career-obsessed, too passionate about writing to be anything *resembling* a good

348

woman. A good woman was one who squelched her own career in favor of her husband's (even if she was the breadwinner—well then, she worked in *secret* so as not to make him feel bad about it). A good woman was one who killed her own creativity rather than ever threaten her man (even if she was the more talented of the two). A good woman was one who set her daughter the example that women always curb and prune their talents, make themselves into half-living bonsai trees—for the love of a man.

Of course this was what Josh's mother had done, what nearly all gifted women of her generation had done—no matter how large their talents. A splendid pianist, who'd studied with the most legendary teachers and had a great concert career predicted for her, she'd shucked it to coddle Josh's father, nurse him through his plays and screenplays, even become his collaborator at the typewriter, sneaking to that other keyboard only when he wasn't around (which was almost never, writers being a notoriously homebound lot), for he would invariably develop a blinding headache whenever she played. And she had accepted this as her fate—to indulge and pamper an artist less gifted than herself only because *he* had the prick. Eventually, she'd become his writing partner, rather than practice an art that took her from him. Naturally she disapproved of Isadora for not being able to do the same—for not being, in short, "a good woman."

Oh, many was the time that Isadora had longed to be a good woman, to be still married to a doctor (as all good girls from Central Park West are bound), to have a life in which brilliant studs did not get nibbled off by brilliant studs—but the demon of her destiny had forced her to follow a different path: the bad girl's path, the serpentine path of the artist. Good women died—in childbirth (like Marietta Robusti), of suicide (like Virginia Woolf), or else they died into marriage (like Josh's mother)—but bad girls lived entirely too long, some of them outliving even their looks, their health, their fortunes, their husbands, their lovers. Colette was a bad girl; most survivors were. Only the good girls died young. For women, the artist's calling had the highest stakes: life or death. One stunted one's gift at peril of one's very life, but even if one followed the serpentine path, one's childhood and its bourgeois teachings haunted one forever. Always, there was the nagging sense of being a freak, a trollop, a tramp—and all the mothers-in-law of the world conspired to confirm one's worst fears.

The fact that Isadora was to be paid for this gig, that she sorely needed the money, that she was committed to supporting a child and a ménage, in no way lessened her guilt. When she went away from her child to work, she always felt remiss; when she took care of her child exclusively, she knew she was neglecting her work, her professional and financial responsibilities. There seemed no way out of this dilemma, and Josh and his family lost no opportunity in making it even more painful for her. Sometimes she thought that Josh's main impetus to leaving her was somehow to sabotage her work just when it was going well. She had had too much—her books and her baby—and he, seething with jealousy because his books remained obscure, wanted to place as many obstacles in her path as possible.

So he had, and, predictably enough, she had stopped working when the demands of her life and Amanda's were simply too great. Now she was getting back the lust to work, and what was she doing? Sabotaging *herself* with the good girl/bad girl dilemma!

"The hell with being a good girl!" she suddenly said to Bean, as they still crawled around on the floor, looking for the lost diamond stud.

"What the hell are you talking about?" he asked.

"All my life I've suffered about not being a good girl—regretted my marriages, my travels, even my books—because they don't conform to some silly middle-class Jewish childhood notion of what a good woman ought to do!"

"You're the best woman in the world," Bean said, "don't you know it? You're even the best mother, setting your daughter the best possible example. What should you have done? Stayed with a man who never would have been satisfied unless you stopped writing? That would have been some hell of an example to set your daughter!"

"You're right!" Isadora said with great bravado, but in her heart, she still nourished the little worm of doubt that perhaps the naysayers were right, and that perhaps even Bean would someday betray her. Her prayer for her daughter was that Mandy would grow up without this conflict, that she would never have to choose between a man she loved and work she loved, that she would never have to stunt herself, battle with herself, waste hours in dialogue of self and soul.

She would know her gifts and seize the fruits of them. She would be beautiful, kind, burning with talent, and full of the courage required to follow the talent to the dark place where it always leads.

350

Going home, Bean and Isadora nosed around the airport shop, which was amply supplied with copies of *Tintoretto's Daughter* and even Isadora's first novel, *Candida Confesses*, about which she felt properly ambivalent (as she supposed all authors *should* feel toward their maiden efforts). She had the odd experience of watching a plump elderly lady with silvery half-moon glasses and hair of a distinctly bluish hue, open *Candida*, glance desultorily at the first few pages, and put the book back, picking up in its stead a copy of *Love's Raging Tempests* by Melissa Mallow and *Scullery Days* by Rhonda O'Toole (a modern retelling of the Cinderella tale with explicit S-M scenes between the stepsisters and Cinderella). Isadora, who supposed herself indifferent to the fate of her old book, felt a stab of rejection when the utterly unknown woman put it down, like a girl who is not asked to dance at her first college mixer. She wanted to walk over, shake the woman by the shoulders, press her own book upon her, and say, *"Here*—read *this,"* but she could also laugh at herself for feeling this way.

Since she'd become a published author, all the joy of browsing in bookstores was lost to her. Either she was pissed because her books were not in evidence, or if they were, she became absorbed in the drama of whether or not anybody wanted them. Oh, she longed for those innocent days of her adolescence when the lofty *dream* of being an author far exceeded the grubby reality!

Going through the barrier, with its metal-detector and X-ray machine, Bean was stopped. Bells went off and various attendants gathered to inspect him. Bean waved to Isadora to go on ahead, not to wait for him, but she stood riveted to the spot, suddenly terrified of losing him.

From a little distance, she saw him being frisked, saw the troubled expression on his face, and then saw him extract a large knife from his pants pocket and surrender it. All the attendants examined the knife. Then they called over a man in uniform who did the same. Isadora could see Bean's lips moving (but she could not hear what he was saying) as he explained his way out of this predicament. Her heart was banging in her chest, her mouth was dry, she was actually praying.

After what seemed like an interminable delay, they let him go (keeping, however, his knife).

Looking distinctly upset, Bean strode over to her.

"Why didn't you take off?" he demanded. "If I get in trouble, I want you to pretend not to know me. The *last* thing I want is to get you in trouble."

Isadora looked up at him, her eyes filled with tears.

"Then why'd you bring the knife?" she asked, thinking of the lost wallet, the lost earring, and now his narrow escape from being thought a hijacker. Incipient lawlessness lurked behind Bean's sweetness. He was the sort of man who'd carry dope across the borders of barbaric countries and wind up rotting for years behind the bars of a Saudi or Turkish prison—or in a frozen Soviet stalag. But did she want to be there, sharing his fate when that happened? Not bloody likely. Then why was she with him? Why was she risking her neck? For a sexual obsession?

"Why'd you bring the knife?" she asked a second time.

"To protect you from all your admirers," he said. "I can't let you go out into the world unarmed. You think you can write incendiary books and then walk this jungle we call the world without a bodyguard. My love,—you're a sitting duck. But *I'm* not. I have no intention of letting you (or your little girl) be destroyed."

"I don't need you to carry knives for me," Isadora said.

"Like hell you don't," said Bean, looking at her with those very blue, very tender eyes. "You think that because you're sweet, the whole world is. I may be young—but I know far more than you do about the world. You need somebody to take care of you and I don't know why there aren't more applicants for the job."

He put his arm around her and they walked briskly to the waiting plane.

Taking off from San Francisco, watching the peninsula and the Bay recede beneath them, Isadora knew that something had shifted irrevocably in her life as a result of this trip, taken almost by accident. It was as if cylinders in a combination lock had accidentally fallen into alignment and she was open to Bean in a way she never would have been had they stayed home in Connecticut or had she chanced to go with Kevin or Hope. It was more than a sexual obsession, she knew—far more than that.

Bean was revealed to her in San Francisco, and what was revealed—despite all her misgivings, all the scar tissue that covered her heart—was somebody who really loved her and would fiercely protect her no matter how quixotically. He wanted to be her Lancelot and he adamantly refused to take no for an answer. He understood that underneath her peculiar notoriety (which Josh had finally found so intimidating) there was only a woman who

352

wanted and needed loyalty and love. He was not put off by her fame, did not see her as either a forbidding fortress or a potential acquisition. He saw her only as a person, strong, yet vulnerable.

"If they are really together," Bean said, "really partners, a man and a woman make the most invincible force in the universe."

"Do you really think so?" asked Isadora, still burned enough by Josh to think the notion of a man and a woman as partners was a pleasant fiction, which could last three years motivated by passion alone, seven years motivated by passion and sadomasochism.

"I really think so," said Bean, "but I don't expect you to. Not yet. But I'm damned persistent. Just give me the requisite seven years. You'll see."

18

The Russia
of the Heart or
The Pink Notebook

Make no mistake. Everything in
the mind is in rat's country. It
doesn't die. They are merely
carried, these disparate memories,
back and forth in the desert of a
billion neurons, set down, picked
up, and dropped again by mental
pack rats. Nothing perishes, it is
merely lost till a surgeon's
electrode starts the music of an old
player piano whose scrolls are dust.
Or you yourself do it, tossing in
the restless nights, or even in the
day on a strange street when a
hurdy-gurdy plays. Nothing is lost,
but it can never be again as it was.
You will only find the bits and
cry out because they were yourself.
—LOREN EISLEY

No one but a fool trips
on what's behind him.
—YIDDISH PROVERB

So he said—yet when they got home and resumed their anarchic affair, it was more maddening than ever. He had somehow become indispensable to her and the days without him dragged by interminably. She only managed to get through them by writing poems to him and she sat waiting for the phone to ring like an adolescent having her first fierce attack of puppy love. The fact that Connecticut had exploded in a riot of spring hardly made things any better. The very breeze was sexual—flowers bursting out all over the place: crocuses triumphing over snow, daffodils and jonquils trumpeting over the muddy fields, followed by the fluttery pink blossoms on the weeping cherries, and the white confetti of the apple blossoms.

Three robin's eggs appeared in a nest cradled in the crotch of the weeping cherry outside the rectangular stairwell window of the house on Serpentine Hill Road. While the tree bloomed, dropped blossoms, came alive with livid green leaves, the mother bird busily prepared for her babies' arrival. Whenever Isadora opened her front door, the mother flew from the nest and perched on her door lintel; a moment after the door shut, she flapped back to the nest and settled upon her triumvirate of bluish eggs.

When at last the babies poked out—all starving beaks and pulsating red throats, Isadora took it as another omen that all three hatched and all three survived. From their staircase, she and Mandy had a perfect view of the feeding frenzies of the young and the dutifulness of the mother. Hand in hand they stood and watched while mama-bird poked fat worms down the babies' desperate red gullets.

"Look, Mama," Mandy would say, "she's feeding the babies."
Yes, thought Isadora, so she is, and so am I, so am I.

Nor was this the only omen of hope. Two of the little fruit trees (which Isadora had given up for dead during the long winter) actually bloomed. And a diseased oak-maple (which Isadora's tree man had given up for dead last fall but allowed the grace of one more spring) suddenly began to burst forth with new branches and masses of new leaves. Isadora felt that she also had allowed *herself* the grace of one more spring. Nearly dead last fall—here she was improbably blooming at forty. Even the branches of the ficus in the living room seemed to leap up and almost scrape the double-height ceiling. And Dogstoyevsky (that waggish fellow) knocked up a neighbor's dog. Spring was certainly bustin' out all over.

Bean and Isadora met in New York to amble through Central Park amid blossoms, or else they drove around Connecticut in her vintage Mercedes with the top down. By the Sound, they got stoned and ate cracked crab and drank white wine. They lolled in her hot tub late at night or danced until the wee hours in tacky Post Road discos where even Bean seemed too old for the rest of the crowd.

"Let's get physical—physical . . ." went the inane lyrics, but they needed no urging. They fucked the nights away as if fucking had just been invented and might soon be taken away as quickly as it was given.

She felt that he had given her back her life—and yet her life seemed just beginning. She was like a child in her fretting over this love, a child who knows that if Mommy and Daddy go away, all is lost. She had no doubt that loving and being loved were the most important things on earth—far more important than the vanities of art.

Sometimes it struck her as ironic that after having fought so hard for feminism, she had come to this—the humbling acceptance of love as the only life-giver. Not that she expected it to last. She expected her child and her work to last and this love to go the way of all loves. And yet she knew that without this renewal nothing was worthwhile. Let cynics doubt it. Let the antisex league denounce it, this linkage of lovers alone defeated hopelessness, defeated death, defeated defeatism.

Spring whirled on in a rush of blossoms and wild fucks. Isadora was still researching the Papa novel, dealing with the tax and legal mess, trying to position herself to absorb the blow of her indebtedness to Uncle Sam whenever it came. But she was not hysterical anymore—merely determined. This was a challenge, a problem to be solved; in some strange way, having come so close to utter breakdown and disaster, she was able to put something as trivial as money problems in proper perspective.

Roland and Errol were pretty much out of her life by now;

Kevin was there but more and more as a friend. She and Josh were behaving in a relatively civilized manner for Mandy's sake, and Bean was as unpredictable as ever. It was not even a year since her breakup with Josh, and from time to time she still wondered whether they mightn't wind up together. But less and less. His bitter resentment of her seemed now a fact of life and her escape from it seemed providential—a reprieve. The dream of reunion was not wholly gone, but Isadora had come to accept it as just that —a dream. She thought it would be good when a full year had passed, as if the turning of a year would mean she was that much closer to healing.

By the time that fateful anniversary arrived, she was in Russia, home of her ancestors.

Everyone had warned her against going off to Russia in search of her ancestors.

"Papa is not to be found there," her French publisher—a very wise and beautiful lady with a long red braid down her back and a tendency to chain-smoke—had said. "You are writing about the Russia of the heart, not the beastly Russia of the *aparatchiks*." But Isadora did not want to hear this. She *had* to go to Russia if only to discover that the Russia of her grandfather no longer existed.

Mandy was with her daddy for the requisite month the separation papers required. Bean was house-sitting for her in Connecticut and it was he who drove her to the airport in QUIM. The night before, he had presented her with a notebook for her to record all her impressions of the trip. "The Pink Notebook," he had waggishly written in the front flap. It was in homage to Doris Lessing, whose *Golden Notebook* he knew she loved above all contemporary novels about women. She loved it because it had the anarchy and chaos of life itself. She loved it because it took a heroine of "middle years" and approached her as a real person (though everyone *knew* that women of "middle years" were over the hill, finished, not worth writing about). She loved it because it was crammed-to-bursting with the contrariness of experience—which no mere book can ever really reduce to "order."

She was traveling to Russia with a delegation of American writers, who had been invited by their Soviet counterparts to a conference in Kiev. The American delegation included a three-hundred-pound lady poet who wrote anemic haiku, a fiercely intellectual woman essayist who wrote for *Commentary* (and who cultivated a disdainful attitude toward absolutely everything—as

359

if disdain must, of necessity, be more true than praise), a courtly silver-haired historian of the Second World War, a popular historical novelist whose books were translated into all the Soviet languages, a waggish novelist of manners (whose books were not), an amiable critic of contemporary mores who also played the balalaika. Typically enough, all the women were traveling alone; the men were married and accompanied by useful, note-taking, camera-toting wives. The delegates had been told that they could not bring companions who were not legal spouses—Russia being a notoriously puritanical country—so Isadora was traveling solo as were the other women. (Ah, why were the women writers all spouseless and the men amply spoused? Was writing an unforgivable "sin" punished with loneliness only in women?)

She missed Bean sorely. In the last few weeks, he had all but moved in with her and she had come to love the comfort and pleasure of going to sleep with a man and waking up with him, of living with a lover again despite all her previous protestations that she would never, never succumb to domesticity. Bean had slipped into her life, without ever really announcing that he was moving in. Suddenly one day she realized that his wet jock straps ornamented her bathroom and his barbells her bedroom floor. And she was actually glad. She was glad even to see the cap he habitually left off the toothpaste tube, because this reminded her that he was there and was coming back. She had heard her divorced women friends complain of the irritations of a resident male once they had truly become used to living alone again, but (to her amazement) she found nothing whatsoever irritating about the jock straps and barbells and toothpaste caps. On the contrary, they comforted her—as did his shaving creams and lotions, his dirty underwear, his jeans and sweatshirts. She was happy to have the chaos and disorder of Bean's presence in the house. *Life* was chaos and disorder. One found order only in the grave. Like having a child, having a man meant a certain amount of dirty laundry and disorder. She would find that final order soon enough, she figured. Meanwhile, she was still in the midst of life.

Parting from Bean at the airport was particularly hard—as parting from Amanda had been the previous day. Much as Isadora wished she were one of those asexual nuns who lived for literature alone, she had to admit that men and maternity still stirred her very vitals. What to do? Leaving Bean was like an amputation. She still felt the phantom limb. The first stage of the journey to Russia took them from New York to Copenhagen, and even that flight had a surreal feeling about it. At one point she woke up from a deep sleep and found an unknown man with his face next to hers. Thinking it Bean, she said, "I love you" and kissed him several times, then she fell back to sleep. When she woke up in the morning, she realized what she had done and was horribly embarrassed, rigid with fright. The man had one of those skull-like, Scandinavian faces—a death's-head with skin stretched over it. Isadora couldn't speak to him. She was mortified, silent. He shook her brusquely to awaken her when the stewardess came with orange juice—as if the somnambulistic sexual encounter gave him rights over her which turned immediately to violence. She had become so accustomed to having Bean there that she thought it *was* Bean. The confusion frightened her. Had she kissed death at some point during the night? This surreal encounter seemed to prepare her for the dreamlike quality of Russia itself. It also made her think of that crazy flight to Stockholm last September when she had necked madly with a total stranger. How the year had come full circle! But she was not quite as desperate as last September. The hideous pain of parting from Josh was gone. The constant ache in the pit of the stomach had become only an intermittent hollowness.

When the delegation arrived in Moscow, Isadora had the strange sense of being at home, yet also in the most alien place in the world. All the American writers were relieved of their passports and presented instead with wilted roses and little packets of worn-out rubles.

Not wanting to part with her passport, she complained to the head of the delegation that she felt identityless.

"Darling," he said, (he was the silver-haired historian and his name was Charles Cochran), "we have *all* given up our passports —the Writer's Union will take care of us."

This didn't seem very convincing to Isadora, but what could she do? She relinquished her passport to a smiling functionary with gold teeth, never expecting to get it back or to leave Russia alive.

From that moment on, she was annexed to the group, dependent on the group and also dependent on the various guides the Russians provided. The American writers traveled through the country as if into the inner world of a dream. There was something courtly and nineteenth-century about Russia—like entering a time machine rather than a nation. Everywhere one heard the gorgeous, liquid sound of Russian (which Isadora did not understand, but which somehow sounded so familiar—like the illegible language of books read in dreams). There were the red skies, the overarching train stations at dusk like the insides of whales, the women in babushkas, everything at once familiar and strange, like a homecoming, but also like a final departure.

The first hotel they were taken to was reminiscent of *Anna Karenina:* a huge nineteenth-century pile with long windows, old, high-ceilinged rooms, large wooden armoires, and creaky beds. It seemed she had been there before in another life.

They were given an afternoon to rest and change clothes, and when Isadora found herself alone in her cavernous room, she looked around in wonderment at the brocaded walls and dark wooden furniture, expecting to see "bugs" and other evidence of KGB activity. They were nowhere to be found. Ah, she had been in the USSR too short a time to understand the precise nature of the spying that goes on there. (Later she came to understand that all of Russia was a sort of army base where everybody worked for the same employer. In that context, the word *spy* took on a new meaning, a different one than it might have in the West).

In Moscow, they were given their first celebratory meal—divine greasy grayish caviar served in little butter blossoms, icy vodka served cold and neat to ease the pain of passportlessness, cabbage soup, blini, stewed beef and rice with endless glasses of Georgian wine served throughout. At the postprandial toast, (with Georgian champagne) several of them were called upon by Cochran, their delegation leader, to assay a politically correct greeting.

The waggish novelist of manners (whose name was Quentin Lawrence) safely toasted the Moscow sunset. Isadora herself carefully lifted a glass to Pushkin, and the *Commentary* intellectual (whose name was Clarissa Cornfeld and who sported those clunky negative-heel shoes so beloved by traveling American hippies) topped them all in the leftier-than-thou department by proposing a toast to the kitchen staff that prepared the meal. Isadora could already see that delegations were a tricky business. It was not only your opposite numbers among the Reds who were shifty—but your own compatriots, who were scoring points for future literary football matches.

After dinner, they were shepherded to the railroad station where the overnight train to Kiev awaited.

A midnight departure, a rocking compartment with sliding glass doors. Red plush, antimacassars, feather pillows, *chai* (tea) in glasses, and everywhere the faces of *her* people: high cheekbones, curly hair, liquid tongues that spoke the language of her dreams.

Crammed into a sleeping compartment with the immense lady poet (who was named Rya Dubinsky and who mercifully—and doubtless inevitably—took the lower berth), she drank vodka from a gift bottle to get to sleep and listened to the mournful balalaika music from the next compartment (where the critic of contemporary mores was wooing Clarissa Cornfeld to let down her primly pinned-up hair, remove her wire-rimmed glasses, and perhaps sweeten the Russian night for him—but whether he succeeded or not Isadora never found out, for the train—and the vodka—put her to sleep long before that).

They were awakened brusquely at six with a sharp rap on the door of their compartment, which then flew open to reveal a white-sleeved arm and at the end of it a glass of tea. Another glass followed; then two boiled eggs; then hunks of bread and cheese all served contrapuntally to the clacking of the train against the track.

"My goodness," said Rya, seizing the first glass of tea. "A feast."

More Writers' Union dignitaries with wilted roses and faded rubles greeted them at the Kiev train station. They were transferred *en masse* to another rambling hotel (this one sleazy and modern as a West German airport hostelry), where hydrant-shaped women in white coats guarded each floor, officially dispatching elevators and garnering clanking bouquets of keys.

Isadora remarked to herself how impossible it was to get in or out of one's room without witnesses in the form of these matrons of key and elevator. Another dimension of the notorious Russian spy system was revealed to her. It seemed that all the citizens of this country had been reduced to the status of elementary-school classroom monitors, as she had known them in her youth. They were spies in the sense that all ten-year-olds are spies. What secrets of hers could they hope to gather? Her life was an open book. (Although, like Nabokov, she sometimes thought she had lived her whole life in the margins of a volume she had never been able to read.)

Kiev proved to be beautiful—the wide gray-green Dnieper bisecting a gracious tree-lined city where golden domes glistened above pastel-candy churches. The conference was held in the powder-blue palace of an eighteenth-century prince, which was now claimed by the Soviet state. The dark-suited delegates assembled on the candy parapets of a pale-blue wedding cake with white icing. All the Soviet delegates were male; most were over sixty. Little women in colored dresses—translators, editors, journalists —fluttered around them, attending to their needs. In the USSR, as in the USA, women were prized for utility and decorativeness, not so much (apparently) for the practice of literature. There were three women writers on the American side, none on the Soviet.

A U-shaped conference table, a glass translator's booth, high blue candy walls, white candy swags and gold rosettes. Isadora was painfully aware of the time lag in translation. A wall of frozen faces greeted her across the U-shaped table. And then the faces unfroze and the poets' features succumbed to the spring thaw of language.

The conference began with dozens of long, boring speeches on the part of the Soviet delegates. They spoke (from prepared texts) about "The Great Patriotic War," "The War Against Fascism," "The Growing Nuclear Threat." They spoke as if they expected every word to be monitored by the Party, as if no impromptu remarks could be risked, as if every word were a potential coffin nail. But at night, walking along the banks of the Dnieper, under the influence of Georgian champagne, the poets boozily recited their verses (and Pushkin's), the novelists confessed their frustrations, and all the round and *zaftig* translator ladies (many of whom were divorced) unburdened themselves to Isadora about the dire difficulties of being a woman in Russia. Of course they all had children (usually *one* cosseted child) that they had to raise alone, and they dreamed of a world in which women could stay home with their babies and be taken care of by men. The irony of it! The revolution had come full circle. These women lusted for the dependency that Isadora's baby-boom generation had been struggling *against* for twenty years! And Isadora herself empathized with them. Raising a child and making a livng were no easy feats. One always felt divided. One always felt that one's vital organs were being torn apart.

"We have been liberated to work twenty-four hours a day," one Russian woman said.

"We, too, have been liberated to be eternally exhausted," Isadora agreed.

The American men and the Russian men had politics to argue about. The American women and the Russian women were wholly united in their common concern about raising children while also managing to earn their bread. There were no political disputes

364

between the women—just a mutual recognition of mutual problems. Meanwhile, the world of men spun pointlessly onward, building bombs and arguing abstractions. They argued the insane logic of competing death machines and seemed wholly oblivious of the problems the women confronted. They saw the women sentimentally, as monuments to abstractions called "Womanhood," "Motherhood," and "Love."

There was one poet in particular—a chap called Anatoly Klimov who had flat Tartar features, eyes so slitty they almost disappeared into his cheeks, and grimacing gold teeth—who kept grabbing Isadora at official receptions, gazing into her eyes, and reciting acres of poetry, poods of poetry, steppes of poetry in Ukrainian and Russian. His breath was as powerful as Soviet missiles, and his English so limited that he and Isadora could only converse by means of sporadic "thank yous" and "you're welcomes," but he seemed to have this burning need to grab her and recite poetry to her whenever he passed her. As she heard the rhythmical but unintelligible words tumble out, as she saw the yearning look in his slitty Asiatic eyes, she felt she was receiving a message from her grandfather, but what message she did not know.

Prompted by the rigid formality of the Russian delegation, Isadora became gayer and gayer, freer and freer in her speech. She wanted to smash this blasted bureaucracy, shake up these official stone faces, to make the conference somehow human, a real exchange of loves and fears. She began to realize that she was seen as a faintly fabulous figure at the conference—even though her time to speak had not yet arrived. (Nor was it hard for a stylish Western woman to seem fabulous in Russia, where everything was so drab.) The Russian ladies marveled at her designer clothes, her shoes, her perfumes. The poets kept courting her with unintelligible verses. Since her works were prohibited in Russia, but word of their supposed scandalousness had traveled, she was viewed as a colorful presence—the youngest member of her delegation and the most enigmatic. The elderly Soviet poets did not know whether to court her as a sort of demimondaine or treat her as a figure of literary eminence. How could she be "literary" when she smelled of French perfume, had blond ringlets, and wore brightly colored dresses? Wasn't literature a dusty thing whose true practice was revealed by the drabness of one's dress?

"My dzear lady," they would say, wagging an admonitory finger, "my dzear lady, you must read us your poems."

And so she did. After making her own formal speech on the status of women in the USA (which all translator ladies cheered but the men received with stony or flirtatious faces), she read to the Soviet delegation the very same poem about her grandfather that she had read at Papa's funeral all those many months ago. She had even titled it: "The Horse From Hell," it was now called, and she spoke informally about her grandfather and his life before she propelled it—on the winds of her breath—into the heart of her audience. She felt that by speaking about her grandfather here, in the country of his birth, she was bringing his spirit home to rest in the land of his ancestors.

The Horse From Hell

A dream of fantastic horses
galloping out of the sea,
the sea itself a dream,
a dream of green on green,
an age of indolence
where one-celled animals
blossom, once more, into limbs,
brains, pounding hooves,
out of the terrible innocence
of the waves.

Venice on the crest
of hell's typhoon,
sunami of my dreams
when, all at once,
I wake at three A.M.
in a tidal wave of love & sleeplessness,
anxiety & dread . . .

Up from the dream,
up on the shining white
ledge of dread—
I dredge the deep
for proof that we do not die,
for proof that love
is a sea-wall against despair,
& find only
the one-celled dreams
dividing & dividing
as in the primal light.

O my grandfather,
you who painted the sea
so obsessively,
you who painted horses

galloping, galloping
out of the sea—
go now,
ride on the bare back
of the unsaddled horse
who will take you
straight to hell.

Gallop on the back
of all my nightmares;
dance in the foam
in a riot of hooves
& let the devil take you
with his sea-green brush;
let him paint you
into the waves at last,
until you fall,
chiming forever,
through the seaweed bells,
lost like the horses of San Marco,
but not for good.

Down through the bells
of gelatinous fish,
down through the foamless foam
which coats your bones,
down through the undersea green
which changes your flesh
into pure pigment
grinding your eyes down
to the essential cobalt blue

Let the bones of my poems
support what is left of you—
ashes & nightmares,
canvases half-finished & fading worksheets.

O my grandfather,
as you die,
a poems forms on my lips,
as foam forms
on the ocean's morning mouth,
& I sing in honor of the sea & you—

the sea who defies all paintings
& all poems
& you
who defy
the sea.

Here no rabbi sucked in his breath, but clearly the audience was
moved. They were with her. Even the translators in the glass

booth were charmed. Feeling her audience's intensity, warmth, even love, Isadora went on, drawing them in, drawing them toward her. Suddenly she remembered, in its entirety, the very first poem for her grandfather she had written, as a freshman at Barnard. She recited it to her Russian colleagues with all the passion she could summon.

The Artist as an Old Man

If once you ask him, he will talk for hours:
How at fourteen he hammered signs, fingers
Raw with cold, and later painted bowers
In ladies' boudoirs; how he played checkers
For two weeks in jail and lived on dark bread;
How he fled the border to a country
Which disappeared, wars ago, unfriended
Crossed a continent while this century
Began. He seldom speaks of painting now.
Young men have time and theories; old men work.
He has painted countless portraits, sallow
Nameless faces, made glistening in oil, smirk
Above anonymous mantelpieces.
The turpentine has a familiar smell
But his hand trembles with odd, new palsies.
Perched on the maulstick, it nears the easel.

He has come to like his resignation.
In his sketchbooks, ink-dark cossacks hear
The snorts of horses in the crunch of snow.
His pen alone recalls that years ago
In dreams he met a laughing charioteer,
Who promised him a ride around the sun.

When she finished, the dour, dark-suited Russian writers burst into applause. Poetry had taken them from generalization about "Soviet Man" and "The Nuclear Threat" to the singular life of one singular artist. This was something they could understand.

From then on the conference became a torrent of poetry readings. Not an hour passed when someone did not stand up at that U-shaped table and declaim reams of poetry (while the simultaneous translators in the glass booth scrambled madly to translate all the similes, all the metaphors, just as fast as they could be uttered).

The whole character of the meetings changed. In the halls, on the stairs, on the balconies of that candy palace, poets were now collaring each other and babbling verses. Even the novelists began reciting poetry (since most novelists have written poetry at some time or other), and the journalists and translators began reciting other people's poetry just to join in the fun. The blue wedding-cake room became a great marriage of literary styles and languages. Poetry had aerated the conference. The pale-blue palace had become a Tower of Babel.

In mid-July, Kiev is hot and dusty; the spreading chestnut trees are in dark-green leaf and the city is reminiscent of Paris. Down these chestnut-lined boulevards their bus took them—to Babi Yar. On the first anniversary of her split from Josh, Isadora found herself walking gingerly over the bones of the dead at Babi Yar as if she were walking on those same bluish eggs she had seen hatch in Connecticut last spring. Circling slowly with the members of her delegation, she looped around the ravine where so many had been buried—dead or alive. Anyplace where so many souls have given up the ghost is a holy place, and Isadora felt the strong desire to kiss the earth at Babi Yar, but self-consciousness restrained her.

A little child toddled over the green grass—greener than all the other grass of the Ukraine because of the many deaths that fertilized those blades. High above the living child (who walked in the headlong, drunken manner of all toddlers) there loomed another child—a huge bronze baby, taking leave of a huge bronze mother whose monumental hands were tied behind her back. The bronze baby was frozen forever in an attitude of leave-taking; the living baby was running toward its mother's arms. Isadora thought of Voznesensky's line: "Children are the periscopes of the dead." She thought of Lisa Erdman in *The White Hotel*, who had dreamed this scene, then lived to see it come to life, come to death, come to transfiguration. She thought of the unimaginable slaughter (which had occurred in part because the victims had found it so unimaginable).

"What a splendid monument," Isadora said to Anatoly Klimov.

"Thank you," he replied, he always replied.

If Papa had lived here, Isadora thought, looking up at that monumental mother and babe who soar over the bones of the victims of Babi Yar, he would have been the most celebrated of artists, since representational art is still all the rage in Russia. But then she realized that if Papa had lived here he would probably not have survived the Revolution at all. (Most of her known relatives had perished of starvation.) Or even if he *had* survived the

369

Revolution, he would surely never have survived Babi Yar. His paintings, then, would have been quite as lost as they were now. Paper, canvas, flesh, she thought—none of it stays. We are not immortal, nor are our creations. Is that why the human race is having a collective temper tantrum and threatening to blast all life off the face of the earth? Because they have never come to terms with their own deaths? Surely that was the case with the patriarchal elders who serviced the war machine. If *they* couldn't live forever, then nobody else could either. And yet, their representatives could weep for her grandfather poems.

At Babi Yar the air was very pure and the grass the most livid green she had ever seen. So much death makes for the best gardens, the sweetest air. You can't grow roses without shit, the French proverb goes. Omar Khayyám, her grandfather's favorite poet, had said much the same thing:

> I sometimes think that never blows so red
> The Rose as where some buried Caesar bled;
> That every Hyacinth the Garden wears
> Dropt in her Lap from some once lovely Head.

But not after nuclear war—no, not then. At Babi Yar, where so many had died so unspeakably, the air was the clearest and most aromatic in all Kiev. She thought of her own Amanda running across the greensward, her red-gold hair a banner behind her, triumphing over all these corpses. And then, with a pang of longing, she thought of Bean and imagined fucking like mad on the grassy lip of the ravine where so many nameless corpses lay. Tears squeezed from the corners of her eyes; her cunt moistened. She wanted to throw herself on the ground, to smother it with kisses, to inundate it with tears, to cover it with poems.

Instead, she knelt down and chastely gave the ground one dry kiss.

"It won't help now," said Clarissa Cornfeld, the unofficial Cassandra of their delegation.

That night she called Bean in the States. It was early morning in Connecticut and his voice sounded foggy and sleepy.

"I adore you, lady," he said. And then, unbidden, he added: "I'm true to you because I want to be. There are no random ladies in the hot tub."

This was more than she expected of him—though she was true to him, too, and true out of desire, not guilt. There were no random gents in her narrow bed in Kiev (though one of the Russians—a tall slender bearded chap with merely *one* gold tooth— had clearly been assigned to seduce her).

"I'm true to you, too," she said, thinking how silly this old-fashioned romantic talk sounded, yet how deeply felt it was. "I'll call you from Odessa."

Calling from Odessa proved to be easier said than done, for Kiev and Moscow had phone communications unheard of in the rest of the country. Nor did Isadora realize during the first few halcyon days of the conference that in Kiev they had been accorded a "Golden Spoon treatment" unknown in the rest of the USSR.

The Soviet government had kindly provided each American writer with a translator-guide and tickets to any Russian cities they wished to see, but once they got away from the conference and began traveling the way the Russians themselves traveled, the jollity and courtliness of the wedding-cake conference evaporated and there were only queues, late (or nonexistent) flights, no phone or cable connections, and the usual chaos that marks travel in the Soviet Union when it is merely Soviet citizens who are doing the traveling.

To take her to Odessa, the Writer's Union had assigned a fellow named Vladimir Glotarchuk—a Soviet Mr. Gradgrind whose answer to every question was: "We must ask proper authorities."

When Isadora was introduced to him in Kiev and realized that she would be marooned with him for god knew how many days, she was desolate.

Glotarchuk was an American Studies expert who had never been to America, and declared that he never wanted to go because he had read everything about the United States and already knew it "by heart." He thumped his chest as he said this.

"But aren't you even curious to visit?" Isadora asked.

"I have been to Poland and Cuba," said Glotarchuk, "and I have read all books and newspapers on USA."

Glotarchuk had a body shaped like a fireplug and curly ash-blond hair that made damp ringlets on his forehead. His eyes were a drab Soviet blue. His little gold-rimmed glasses glittered in a sinister fashion.

"I am guide," he said, "interpreter, professor, passport into the interior."

"How'd you draw me?" Isadora said, "By lottery?" But Glotar-

chuk had no funny bone whatsoever: the Soviet state had amputated it. Or bred a whole race without them.

"Draw you?" he asked. "Draw you? On the contrary, I wish to
write you. I wish to show that your *Candida Confesses* is a bourgeois
decadent novel and a danger to the good socialist woman."

Aha, thought Isadora—so it is the same here as there: the good
woman—whether of the socialist or capitalist variety—is equally
endangered by my books.

"So you are traveling with me to write a hatchet piece?" she
asked.

"A what?" asked Glotarchuk.

"Hatchet—one of those things you chop down trees with. If I
were you I wouldn't show my hand so early. Even Sally Quinn
romances one a bit before she strikes."

"Sally who?"

"I guess the *Washington Post* is prohibited here."

"Not at tall, at tall," said Glotarchuk. "We may read *everything*
what we wish. I know all things about United States. I read *New
York Times*. I read also *Wall Street Journal*. And, of course, *Post*."

"Of course you do," Isadora said mischievously. "But did you
know that there are some people in my country who question
whether reading the organs of the capitalist establishment necessarily gives one a perfect picture of life in the United States?"

Glotarchuk looked mystified.

"Then what should a scholar read if not *New York Times* and
Wall Street Journal?" He looked like a little boy who has just been
told there is no Santa Claus.

"Oh, you *should* read those papers, but you should read everything else, too, and you should certainly visit the U.S. You should
also read the *National Review*, say, and *Mother Jones. The Nation,
Commentary, The New Republic, Rolling Stone, Playboy, Penthouse,
Harper's, Atlantic, The New Yorker*—and of course the more bourgeois decadent novels the merrier—since only novels really give
you life in all its perplexity." (Isadora saw Glotarchuk's eyes light
up when she mentioned *Playboy*. Glotarchuk would have *killed* for
a copy of *Playboy*—harder to get in Russia than a First Folio of
Shakespeare. Only in the U.S.—and possibly Scandinavia—was
sex ubiquitous enough for people to grow bored with it. Only in
the U.S. had we *enough* promiscuity to realize that promiscuity is
no panacea. The Russians still titillated their people with puritan-
ism—the great titillator.)

"But which is One True View of the USA?" asked an astounded and salivating Glotarchuk.

"There are some who say there *is* no one true view of the USA. In my country"—wasn't it *amazing* how in the Soviet Union one found oneself saying things like "in my country"?—"we don't *believe* there is only one true view. In fact, we strenuously believe in *many* true views. That's why our country sometimes seems so chaotic and violent to outsiders. In our chaos is our strength."

Holy cow—Isadora sure was becoming fueled with patriotic fervor. The more she talked with Glotarchuk, the more she stayed in the USSR, the more wildly patriotic she became. She had never loved America as ardently. Today she even loved the IRS: what a small price to pay for being an American, she thought, her brain softening and her vestigial patriotism rising to the surface.

Her passport and tickets home were still with the Writers' Union officials in Moscow and a rigid "cultural programme" for her trip to Odessa had been planned. Now that she knew what motivated her guide, she wanted to cancel the junket, but, it could not be done. Without consulting her, the Writer's Union had scheduled her for two weeks in Odessa with Glotarchuk, and after that, a whole rambling odyssey through Russia with him as her guide. The timing was impossible. She was planning to meet Bean in Italy on the first of August and her child was coming home on August fifteenth. Though she had cabled these schedules to the Soviets *months* before her departure for Moscow, they had blithely disregarded them and made their own plans for her. They wanted to keep her in the Soviet Union for the whole month of August, and they saw no reason why they had to consult *her* about it or take either her kid or her travel plans into account.

Elaborate negotiations with officials at the conference (who had to negotiate with other officials in Moscow) ensued. Finally a compromise was reached. She agreed to spend a week in Odessa with Glotarchuk, then return with him to Leningrad to meet her delegation. After that, back to Moscow, then (if she was lucky), Milan.

When she and Glotarchuk left Kiev for Odessa, she still did not have any assurances that she could leave the country on August first.

"When will the tickets be approved?" she asked Glotarchuk.

"When proper authorities deem it advisable," said Glotarchuk, smiling spitefully.

373

"Why can't we get an answer about it now?"

"How womanlike and hysterical you are," replied Glotarchuk. "The Soviet Union is a rational country. It does not recognize female hysteria. When proper authorities are consulted, we shall get tickets. If proper authorities do not agree, we shall not get tickets."

Instead of throttling him, Isadora took a swig of Kiev pepper vodka (a gift from another boozy, love-struck poet). She was beginning to understand the dimensions of the famed Soviet drinking problem. After a week with Glotarchuk, her liver might never be the same. Not to mention her brain.

The departure for Odessa was about as cheery as deportations described in books about the Second World War. Without the drivers and guides the conference had provided, the airport at Kiev was revealed in all its horror. Squalling children, pasteboard suitcases falling open to reveal somebody's entire life crammed into a box, queues that inched along with no apparent destination, people who shoved and pushed each other as if in line for a reprieve from some sort of Kafkaesque doom. ("There is hope, but not for us," said Kafka. Never had Isadora really understood that line until she flew Aeroflot.)

Three hours after the announced departure time, they took off over the golden wheatfields of the Ukraine bound for Odessa, home of her ancestors. Although the passengers were deliberately starved, the crew was to be watered and fed. (In a stunning reversal of American airline practices, Aeroflot serves no drinks to the passengers, but only to the crew!) Suddenly there was a hopeful commotion of stewardesses in the back of the plane, which seemed to portend lunch.

"Are we going to get lunch?" Isadora asked hopefully.

"No—that is for the crew," Glotarchuk said.

Minutes passed. The plane completed its ascent. Little by little a funny smell reached Isadora's nostrils. She turned around to see great clouds of black smoke issuing from the galley. The stewardesses had set fire to lunch!

"They've set the plane on fire!" Isadora said to Glotarchuk.

"I am sure proper authorities will remedy situation," said he, turning paler than usual.

A co-pilot burst out of the cockpit, ran to the back, tore a fire extinguisher from the wall. He was followed by another co-pilot. Isadora turned around to look. The galley was full of people all struggling in the smoke to get a fire extinguisher to work. Al-

374

though the plane was now filling with clouds of black smoke, not a word of explanation was offered to the passengers.

Isadora gazed into the depths of the vodka bottle where the genie of calmness resided. At that moment of absurdity beyond despair, when the whole inside of the plane reeked of burnt blini, burnt upholstery, soggy carpets, these lines came to her:

> The Genie in the vodka bottle
> has twinkling eyes and a soul of pure
>   pepper.
> He burns the tongue.
> His eyes glow
> like blazing coals.
> He says:
> I bring forgetfulness
> with no headache.

Was she becoming Russian? She felt powerless to do anything but stare into her vodka bottle!

Glotarchuk looked disdainfully at Isadora for having taken refuge in the vodka.

"Would you like some?" she asked.

"Wodka is no answer," said Glotarchuk like some beastly Soviet social worker.

"Are you crazy? It keeps the plane aloft! In the USA, no one would fly without alcohol."

Her guide gave her one of those "aha—I knew it!" looks that always signaled his views of American culture. Terrified as he was, he was congratulating himself on the superiority of the Soviet system because the Soviets did not serve alcohol on their airplanes —except of course to the crew. "Air travel in the U.S. is *wonderful*," Isadora said. (*What* had she *said*? Was she *mad*?) She was suddenly lost in a reverie about American airline travel and its peculiar joys. How cunning were those little trays of reconstituted food! How munificent were the beauteous stewardesses who dispensed the flowing liquor! How stalwart the captains with their manly Marlboro-man accents, their broad shoulders reminiscent of American football victories, their turned-up WASP noses, their long, virile strides, their wonderful hats filled with golden spaghetti . . . Russia was really driving her bonkers if she was nostalgic for American airline travel, airline *food*, and even the IRS! There was no telling *what* she would miss next. Would she start missing Conrail and Amtrack? Would she grow nostalgic for the Long Island Expressway at five P.M. on a Friday night? The subway at rush hour? The lower reaches of Forty-second Street where the vomit and jerk-off houses are? Yes, yes, a thousand times yes! She missed them like crazy. She yearned for the blessed silver birds of Pan Am, the gorgeous blue-tailed jets of Eastern, the regal wide-bodies of TWA with their crimson markings. She, who had so often cursed American planes, who booked all her trips around DC-10s (and sometimes got stuck with them anyway), was now madly in love with *all* the airlines of her native land. Let them fly DC-10s! Let them fly *anything* at all! Their food was manna, their service bliss, their politeness legendary. If one trip on Aeroflot could do *this* to her, imagine the state she'd be in by the time she left this godforsaken country—*if* that time ever arrived. Every American leftist should be forced to fly Aeroflot, Isadora concluded—or try to get served tea in the snack bar of a Russian airport. Russian snack bars made even Chock Full o' Nuts seem like havens of racial amity and humanity—not to mention McDonald's and Burger King, which now appeared more gracious than the old Pavillon in its heyday. One week in Russia and her politics were slightly to the right of William F. Buckley!

The commotion in the aisles of the plane had become a parade by now and the black smoke was still belching forth.

"Why don't they announce what the problem is?" Isadora asked her guide.

"It would only make things worse," said Glotarchuk stolidly. "People would be nervous."

"And they're not nervous now?" Isadora said. "Are you kidding?"

"It is Russian proverb: 'If they're beating you by hand, be glad they're not beating you by stick.' "

"Jesus H. Christ," said Isadora, "now I know where my grandfather's whole philosophy of life came from—submission, submission, submission—that's all you ever talk about . . ."

"What do you mean *submission*," asked Glotarchuk, "and who is Jesus H. Christ?"

"Don't you people believe in *optimism*? Don't you believe in *action*?"

Glotarchuk looked at her, uncomprehending.

"Here—hold this," said Isadora, handing him her vodka bottle (in which one lone red pepper bobbed).

She flew out of her seat and ran to the back of the plane, where no fewer than five coughing people were trying to get a fire extin-

376

guisher to work. One of the co-pilots had apparently cut his arm on a metal band that had once held the extinguisher to the wall, and two clumsy stewardesses were trying to bandage him. The black smoke was still billowing out.

"Can I help?" Isadora asked.

Baffled looks—since none of them spoke a word of English.

Isadora seized the fire extinguisher out of one of the stewardess' arms, pulled the pin, squeezed the handle, and began spraying foam in the direction of the stove.

"Open the door of the stove," she shouted—but nobody knew what she meant.

The stewardess wrestled the fire extinguisher back and began uselessly spraying foam on the *outside* of the closed stove, as the steward before had done. Meanwhile, one burly steward and someone who looked like a co-pilot grabbed Isadora by the arm-pits and dragged her bodily back to her seat. Did this mean she would be arrested on arrival in Odessa and interned in the USSR forever? What matter—since the plane would probably blow up long before they arrived anywhere *near* the Black Sea!

"What have you been doing?" a very panicky Glotarchuk asked. He was responsible for her and her behavior in his country, so he was understandably concerned. So what! They would probably die together anyway, this curious duo, this oddest of odd couples, this inverted reprise of *Ninotchka*.

"I tried to show them how to get the goddamned fire extin-guisher unstuck—then they wouldn't even let me point it at the base of the flames. It won't do any *good* if they just keep spraying it randomly around the galley. They have to *open* the stove and spray the foam at the *base* of the flames. Trust me—I'm not terri-bly technologically-minded, but I *do* know how to operate a fire extinguisher. Living alone in the country with a little kid teaches you a *few* things! Please, Vladimir, *please* go back there and tell them that they have to open the stove and foam the inside. And please tell them to point it *under* the flames—would you?"

"It would be arrogant of me to presume to tell captain what he will do."

"It would be stupid of you to sit here and let the plane blow up just because you're afraid of what they'll think of you. I'd do it myself, but I can't speak Russian."

Reluctantly, timidly, like a schoolboy who is afraid of being struck, Glotarchuk got up and shuffled to the back of the plane. Isadora took his aisle seat and craned her neck to watch. She saw

Glotarchuk tap the captain on the shoulder and begin talking to him rather diffidently. She saw the captain listening. She saw them open the stove—whereupon the smoke became denser. But that was all Isadora could see.

By now all the passengers were sputtering and coughing. Some were praying. Others were sitting quietly, gripping their armrests with white knuckles. There was no doubt they were done for. But what did Isadora feel at that moment?—she who had so often imagined death in flight? She knew that if she died on an Aeroflot flight, her death might not even be reported to her next of kin. And yet, all she felt was a terrific sense of lightness, of transparency. All anxiety was gone, somehow, as she prayed to the Goddess to take care of Amanda, take care of Bean, take care of her parents and sisters. So this was her personal Babi Yar! So be it. To go home to Mother Russia to die. What a strange karma. To die at forty, having produced one masterpiece—Amanda. (Oh, she would also stand behind *Tintoretto's Daughter*. That book, she thought, would last, as would some of her poems—though who ever knew for sure about one's own work?)

Glotarchuk returned. "They have put out flames," he said, "now it is only smoke without fire, contrary to Russian proverb."

"Are you sure?" asked Isadora.

"Absolutely," said Glotarchuk, "I showed them how." He said this smugly, taking Isadora's seat near the window and refastening his belt.

"Oh did you?" asked Isadora. "Are you about to become a Hero of Socialist Labor?"

"I think they are grateful," he said. And sure enough the two co-pilots and four stewardesses were proceeding down the aisle to congratulate him. They slapped Glotarchuk on the back heartily, babbling congratulatory greetings.

"I am satisfied," Glotarchuk said when they had gone. "I have —how do you say?—saved the day!"

Isadora smiled hatefully at her guide. She would almost rather they had crashed.

At the Odessa airport, Isadora and Glotarchuk were met by a contingent of Odessa Writers' Union dignitaries, headed by Mikhail Berezny, a bluff, white-haired, pink-cheeked fellow with blazing blue eyes, who looked amazingly like some of Isadora's own Russian-Jewish relatives (particularly those she had met on childhood sojourns in the environs of Golders' Green).

"Madame Poet," said Mikhail, presenting Isadora with the requisite wilted roses and the damp packet of rubles (expense money courtesy of the Soviet state), "your fame has preceded you. We have been reading and reading your *great* poems to your grandfather, which were sent to us by our colleagues in Kiev."

(How ironic it was that here in Russia, where her books were prohibited, her few lines of hastily translated poetry were almost more valued than in her native country, where volumes and volumes were freely available. In Russia everyone craved books, and no one could get them. In America, the best books piled up on the remainder tables while the populace played Pac-Man.)

"Thank you," said Isadora, "thank you." She accepted the roses and rubles and was ushered into a waiting car—courtesy of the Writers' Union—for transportation to the Black Sea Hotel. Checking to see if her luggage was with her, Isadora noticed that it had been tagged "Addis Ababa" rather than "Odessa"—and yet somehow it had *arrived!* Ah, the Goddess has plans for us (and our luggage) that she does not divulge. Our fates are in her (baggage-handling) hands!

First impressions of Odessa: the whole city smelled of sea and mildew. Its atmosphere was boisterous, Jewish, Breughelesque. Even Kiev seemed goyish and reserved by comparison, and Moscow icy and arctic.

Mikhail Berezny was Jewish. He was the first Russian she had met who peppered his speech with Yiddishisms. (Oh there had been one official KGB Jew at the conference in Kiev—the one who had been assigned to seduce her and had failed—but he was more Russian than the goyim and never would have risked the colorful abyss of Yiddish. His job description was Official State Jew, and he went around the conference swearing that the Russians were *not* antisemitic—just anti-Zionist—and praising the PLO). Here, on the contrary, Mikhail was proud of his Jewishness; he might even have admitted to Zionism, if pushed. Isadora was not about to push him, though.

"Welcome to the most Jewish city in Russia," he said, ushering Isadora out of the car at the Black Sea Hotel, "our beloved Odessa. We welcome you home as if you were a daughter of our city."

The hotel lobby was swarming with East German tourists, and even some American Jewish tour groups in search of roots. Isadora and Glotarchuk discovered that their rooms would not be available for them until much later. In view of that fact, Mikhail suggested that they check their luggage at the desk and make an excursion to the Black Sea itself, since this was presumably why people came to Odessa. Isadora and her guide hastily removed bathing suits from their Addis Ababa–tagged luggage and followed Mikhail back into the waiting car. (The other members of the welcoming committee dispersed, pleading other engagements; they would all regroup later at the opera.)

The ride to the Black Sea was breakneck and torturous. Mikhail talked on and on about the sunny southernness of Odessa—the Naples of Russia. And indeed, Isadora could detect something of the boisterousness of southern Italy, the mildewed sea smell of old resorts along the Amalfi coast, the openness and rowdiness of people who were determined, with the desperation of New Year's Eve revelers, to have a good time.

When they came to the seashore, they parked at the top of a steep dune and half-slid, half-walked down to the beach. There, beyond a wall of porcine, virtually naked people, Isadora could see that brackish blue-green apparition itself, the Black Sea. It was the sea where Jason sailed to seek the Golden Fleece, where *The Potemkin* had sailed into history, where her grandfather had first sniffed liberty and found it sweet.

Several huge women, with mountainous bellies and triple rolls of fat at their sides, stood planted in the sand conversing. One of them, monumental legs spread wide and rooted in the sand, methodically chewed little nuts and spat them out at syncopated intervals. Isadora hadn't seen so many huge women since her days in Germany. It was as if the Black Sea were bounded by a wall of women who guarded it against entrance like gorgons.

Mikhail and Glotarchuk ducked into a cabana to change into suits, indicating where Isadora might do the same.

Soon they all reemerged, Glotarchuk looking pasty, pale, and vulnerable without his clothes, like the proverbial creature who has crawled out from under a rock. Isadora had brought her Nikon and was madly snapping pictures—as if photographs could ever really capture the essence of a place.

Noticing her touristic avidity, her fashionable American bathing suit, a huge dark-haired man with a long nose, a black beard, and an immense hairy belly toddled up and cordially demanded:

"*Americanski?*"

"*Da,*" said Isadora.

"Relatives in Brookleen," said the man cordially. "*Mishpocheh.*"

"Me too," said Isadora, marveling at this open confession of Jewishness and the ubiquity of "relatives in Brookleen."

"Brother-in-law drive taxi," said the man, but after that, English failed him. How did he know she was Jewish and why had he approached her? Was this another message from Papa?

Glotarchuk jogged to the water, beckoning Isadora and Mikhail to follow. They ran past the walls of half-naked women and threaded their way to the very edge of the sea.

With Chaplinesque pantomimes of invigoration and seaside delight, Glotarchuk stooped to the water and began rubbing his pallid, hairless body with seawater.

"Brrr," he said theatrically. Then he pranced into the waves.

Isadora and Mikhail followed, and for a little while this curious trio bobbed together in the Black Sea like matzoh balls in soup. The water was very salty, very buoyant. Isadora let her mind wander to the battleship *Potemkin,* to her grandfather's samovar stories, to her grandmother's cooking. Why had she come all this way and what was she really looking for? She had—somewhere in her luggage—a little notebook with the names of possible Odessa relatives, the names of streets where Papa may have lived—all as yet unverified. But she knew she was not really looking for relatives or streets. She was looking for the spirit of the place, the *Geist,* the breath of Black Sea air which her grandfather had breathed into her own lungs.

Back at the hotel, they were finally given quarters. Isadora drew a damp and mildewed suite, with huge armoires and overstuffed furniture much too big for the rooms. The water in the tub was brackish; none of the drains worked (so both sink and tub water leaked depressingly on the floor). The toilet also leaked when it was flushed and there was no toilet paper whatsoever. Ah, Eastern Europe—where a plumber could be king!

When Isadora came to unpack her luggage, she had the definite impression that both her large folding dress bag and her book bag (which had contained all the notes for *Dreamwork,* poetry worksheets, yellow pads, "The Pink Notebook," and another small notebook containing Odessa names and addresses) had been rifled. She went through both bags in a hurry. Neither "The Pink Notebook" nor the little address book was anywhere to be found. Her elegy to her grandfather had also been stolen, and indeed so had the whole Grandfather memoir she had read at the funeral. Yet she was *sure* she had packed all those things in Kiev.

"The Pink Notebook" contained her jottings on the conference (she could live without those—the memories were so vivid—and at home she had other copies of the Papa memoir and the elegy), but without the book of names and street addresses, her trip to Odessa was virtually useless as research. Why would anyone have taken these things? Why, indeed. Isadora knew that a police state does not have to conform to reason in the confiscation of written materials. A police state confiscates writings just because they carry the word (and the word represents power). Whether it has any *immediate* utility is not the issue. Seize first and question later is the rule.

Panic claimed Isadora. First the fire on the plane, then this. Were they planning to confiscate *her* next? She hastily redid her makeup, changed clothes (damp, creased, and smoky as all her garments were), and went down to the bar to meet Mikhail and Glotarchuk. What should she say? Anything? Was she possibly *imagining* the loss of her notebooks and writings? Could she have left them in Kiev by mistake? Not a chance. She would have sooner left her clothes and cosmetics, her cameras and jewelry. Her book bag was always the first thing she checked on departure, the first thing she reclaimed on arrival.

Glotarchuk and Mikhail were waiting at little tables in the lounge to welcome her with warm, sweet, Georgian champagne (which tasted, for all their raving about its quality like poor German *sekt*). They were exhilarated by their swim, by the prospect of dinner, and by the anticipation of seeing Rimski-Korsakov's *The Czar's Bride* at the opera that night. Isadora couldn't have cared less. She was obsessed with finding a way to call the States, especially to get in touch with her cousin, Abigail (who had given her some of the names and addresses in the lost notebook), and also to warn Bean that she might be in danger. His family knew State Department types who could possibly bail her out, but perhaps even more than that—she just wanted to talk to him to prove to herself that America still existed.

"Do you think I can call the States?" Isadora asked Mikhail.

"We shall inquire," he said cordially. "Sit down, my dear, sit down."

So, despite the fact that she was trembling with an incipient anxiety attack, Isadora sat down and quelled her anxiety in Georgian champagne, followed by a mediocre dinner served as slowly as possible by a waitress who seemed to be walking underwater. ("Typical inefficient female behavior," said the charming Glotarchuk—but Isadora no longer even rose to his bait; she had other worries now.)

On the way out of the hotel, they enquired at the desk when

382

they could call the States. After considerable cumbersome translations and further enquiries by telephone to invisible "proper authorities," it was concluded that there *were* no international connections out of Odessa except one day a week and even that appeared doubtful.

"You see," said the cordial Mikhail, "the phone is on—how do you say?—relays. No direct lines."

"Oh," said Isadora, doubting him, doubting everything.

"But we can send a cable tomorrow morning if you please. Now —to the opera."

It was hardly likely she could say what she wanted to say by cable (which Mikhail would have to translate and god knows who else would have to approve), so Isadora merely shook her head and they left for the opera to see *The Czar's Bride*.

At the beautiful, columned opera house, with its rotund façade, its rampant rooftop statuary, Isadora's anxiety attack reached major proportions. Her heart began pounding as if it would fly out of her chest. Her mouth went dry, her hands cold as the grave.

They had been given a red plush box where other Odessa Writers' Union dignitaries were already ensconced; down below, the opera had already commenced. A very threatening-looking Ivan the Terrible was about to ax his umpteenth mistress so he could take the umpteenth plus one.

"The heroine is a pure Russian type," Glotarchuk whispered to Isadora, pointing to the bejeweled, beauteous soprano who played the new mistress (in actuality, number seven), "obedient and passionate." He looked at Isadora with a mixture of hostility and lust. Isadora knew full well from talking to the Russian women at the conference that this was pure Russian rubbish—Russian women were no more obedient than American ones—but she was too far gone with anxiety to argue the point. She felt that *she* was Ivan the Terrible's sixth mistress and was about to get the ax. She remembered one of her grandfather's favorite lines: "In Russia they used to have Ivan the Terrible and in Russia they *still* have Ivan the Terrible." How would she ever sit through this opera, she wondered, feeling the way she did? She reached into her bag, hoping against hope to find the little bottle of five-milligram Valiums she usually carried in anticipation of hotel-room insomnia. There was one left. (She had only brought a dozen.) She popped it in her mouth and swallowed. It stuck.

As Ivan the Terrible thundered on, as the mistresses trilled and chorused, the Valium slowly made its way down her dry gullet. It

383

seemed, in her present state of panic, big enough to choke her. But maybe that was the lump in her throat.

The opera was interminable—and dreadful. Despite the fame of the Odessa State Academic Theater of Opera and Ballet, the production was ghastly: stagy, stilted, old-fashioned, and not even very well sung.

Isadora felt she *had* to escape. Sitting still was impossible for her. So, she escaped to the ladies' room. Then she paced the marble rotunda, found a water fountain to take care of the lingering effects of the stuck Valium, and finally trudged up and down the broad marble stairs in her spike-heeled shoes, hoping against hope that all of Russia would prove to be "only a dream" and she would fall asleep and wake up home in her cozy waterbed in Connecticut (wake up to find herself merely facing an IRS audit rather than Ivan the Terrible!).

It was not to be. Soon Glotarchuk and Mikhail came looking for her. She had been away too long—and they were assigned to monitor her.

"What is trouble?" asked Mikhail. "You have some *tsuris?*" Did she have *tsuris! Tsuris* was her middle name!

"Only a terrible headache and a disc in my spine that makes it hard for me to sit."

They both clicked their tongues sympathetically. Oh, the universality of the "bad back" as an excuse to get out of everything from bad operas to bad sex!

"Then let us go at once without further ponderment," said Glotarchuk.

"No—I couldn't ruin your good time," Isadora said. "Not to mention the other writers'."

"Nonsense," said Mikhail. "We come to entertain you. They may stay. If you are not entertained, then we are not either. Let us go then. More champagne! That is answer!"

The three of them strolled out of the opera house (admiring its noble architecture), then they returned to the hotel, where they put away two bottles of Georgian champagne and listened to a group called The Sevastopol Four play twenty-five-year-old American rock music in a style that could only be described as Eastern European.

"Nice music," Isadora said.

"Bourgeois decadent American music," Glotarchuk riposted, eyeglasses twinkling. He was apparently still hoping either to rile her or to arouse her (perhaps he was one of those men who think

384

both are the same?) but Isadora no longer cared. She was merely hoping now to become so blotto that she could get to sleep. She did not relish the thought of tossing and turning all night while she speculated about why her notebooks had been taken and what that might portend. Finally, when she thought she was somnolent enough, she excused herself. Both men insisted on accompanying her to her room, as if to tuck her in.

"Good night and thank you," she said as they redeemed her key from the matron of keys.

"Good night," Mikhail cheerily sang as he walked her down the hall.

"Good night, sweet princess," Glotarchuk said, helping to open her door. "It is from *Hamlet* by your William Shakespeare," he added.

"He's yours as much as mine," said Isadora. "Let's just say— ours."

The two Russians waved good-bye cheerfully and went down-stairs to resume drinking.

She staggered into her room (half expecting to see jackbooted secret policemen out of some Hollywood movie) and closed the door. Quickly she stripped, put on a blue and white yukata she always used while traveling, removed her eye makeup, washed in the dingy water with her black soap (how silly the conspicuous consumption of Lazlo products seemed here in Russia—sillier even than in the U.S., if such were possible), and crashed on the lumpy mattress. A momentary fear of not sleeping seized her, but she was drunk enough and she drifted off almost immediately.

In her dream, Papa and Mama were not dead, and when they turned up and realized she had sold their apartment on West Seventy-seventh Street, they were dismayed. Their furniture was all gone, dispersed among relatives, sold at auction, stolen by Isa-dora's ex-husbands, but their mail had been piling up for years (as if everyone but she knew they were not really dead). They wan-dered aimlessly around the old apartment, waiting for Isadora to ransom their home. For her part, she was vaguely guilty; she should have known they were not really dead. Everyone else seemed to.

She woke up with a start. Though the metal shutters were closed, an eerie blue light was filtering into the room. The room was unnaturally cold—like a cold spot in the sea. Papa, she was sure, was there. Somnambulistically, she got up, opened the shut-ters, and walked out on her balcony. Her bedroom window faced a church with two silver domes, flanking one larger rusted iron dome that resembled a rotting red onion whose outer peel is half decomposed. Onions had figured in her early poems. They were metaphors of the self, with its endless introspection, its pursuit of the pungent green heart (which also peels away in layers leaving nothing but scent and spirit).

"Papa," she said. "Papa."

She looked up at the domes, down at the street. Then she put on low-heeled shoes, a sweater, and slacks, and she quickly left the hotel.

The blue dawn was coming up and she walked briskly through the unknown streets (with their illegible street signs), led by she knew not what force. She walked over bluish cobblestones, over gleaming trolley tracks, past shadowy marketplaces where the first few produce trucks were arriving from the country and huge bluish women in babushkas were carrying buckets of bluish cherries, buckets of bluish apricots. She walked past public buildings, past rows of apartment flats, always smelling the sea, always feeling Papa around her like a prickle in the scalp, like a cold chill at her shoulders.

Alley cats crossed her path, and scrawny dogs followed her for a while, seeking scraps. She had none to give them. Her trek continued as the sky grew lighter and lighter blue. Finally, she was led, as if by an invisible string, to a battered four-story house on a narrow street (where vegetable refuse and animal offal lined the gutters and two mongrels fought over a bone in the street).

She looked up. On the fourth floor, one lone blue window had a flickering bluish light. A young man with bushy black hair, a bulbous nose, and a droopy mustache came to the window. Did she only imagine it or was he carrying an oblong wooden palette in one hand and a bouquet of brushes in the other? But he had to be at least twenty-five and Papa had left Russia eleven years before that birthday. As she watched, the youthful figure in the window turned into a fretful, stolid householder of forty, a pink-cheeked man of seventy, and finally a bent, pale wraith of ninety-seven with an open fly and his underwear showing under his jacket.

A baby cried mournfully in the night. Dogs growled. A man and woman shouted, somewhere, then began to make noisy love. She realized she was almost ninety-nine years too late for *everything;* he had already been born, grown up, grown old, died. (But that was only assuming time existed.)

"Papa?" she called to the fading figure in the window, who now vanished, taking with him the house, the street, the baby, the lovers, the dogs, the refuse, the offal, and also the chill. Bluish streets beckoned her back past a market already bustling with life. Under the onion domes, she undressed and went back to bed. She slept the sleep of the dead, dreamless and deep.

In the morning, she and Glotarchuk had sweet rolls and *chai*.

"Well—shall we search for your grandfather today?" he asked, as if he did not know her notebooks were gone, as if he were innocent of everything.

"I think I may have already found him," Isadora said.

She, Glotarchuk, and Mikhail Berezny returned to the Odessa market, where, under metal canopies, huge peasant women in babushkas were weighing out buckets of sour cherries, sweet apricots, tomatoes, carrots, cucumbers, peppers. The women had faces as wrinkled as maps of the moon: with their hard and glittering eyes, they seemed almost sibylline as they weighed the shining fruit, and their dangling old-fashioned earrings bobbed and danced from their long earlobes. There would be another week in Odessa, another week in Leningrad and Moscow, art treasures to see, Pushkin's house, Tolstoy's house—but Isadora already knew what she needed to know. She understood that she was not Russian, but American, and that she was rooted not in Odessa, but in her own soul. She knew that lost notebooks didn't really matter, nor lost paintings nor lost manuscripts; that we pass the torch along through human flesh; through our lusts, our loves, the poetry of our daily existence. How vain we are to think anything else is more than a dream! Even our ancestors are dreams, created to explain us to our own selves. She knew she was not her grandfather's shadow, but herself: the creation and the creator both, the poem and the poet, the written and the spoken voice—both in one body that was destined to die.

19

A Venetian Ending or The Greenest Island

Can one then have the heart,
the impudence to visit Venice? Is
that the reason Proust would
never go? For against this, if it
might be too hot by day or the
stench then too great, by contrast
it would seem only too easy to set
out by moonlight so that no
couple, if given the miraculous
chance, could fail, intent on their
two selves, to sink Venice, as can
be done tomorrow by the Gondola
covering a moonlight lane of sea.
Yet to leave her thus is but
to come back to bed in Venice.
—HENRY GREEN

It is my intention to remain at Venice
over the Winter, probably as it has
always been (next to the East)
the greenest island of my imagination.
It has not disappointed me. . . .
I have been familiar with ruins too long
to dislike desolation.
—BYRON

SOMEHOW, she got out of Russia. Somehow she got through the endless days with Glotarchuk, the endless days without Amanda and Bean, the travesty of having to share the white nights of Leningrad with the dread Glotarchuk, the absurdity of sharing Pushkin's house and dueling site with this ghastly Soviet Gradgrind.

She remembers walking along the luminous Neva embankment with him at midnight, wishing for Bean, thinking of Bean, feeling Bean in her fingers and toes, her cunt and her womb.

Leningrad was the most beautiful city she had ever seen. The Neva outshone the Dnieper, the silver Seine, the glorious Thames, the glittering Arno, the dappled Danube, the fabled Neckar of Heidelberg, and the majestic Hudson (on whose shores she was born). From river to palaces, from palaces to parks, nothing about Leningrad was overrated—not the White Nights, nor the Golden Treasury of the Hermitage, not Pushkin's dueling site, nor the Haymarket, where *Crime and Punishment* is set, not the Neva Embankment itself, with its pale pewter paving stones, its low golden palaces, its luminescent light (combining the best of Paris light, Copenhagen light, Amsterdam light in one northern sky), its glorious Winter Palace, lying low, green, and columnar beneath astounding river clouds, not its art treasures, nor its kvass trucks (around which people group, boisterously drinking), nor its leafy verdant parks where statues stand.

Yet all of Leningrad was somewhat spoiled for her by the anxiety about tickets home, by the constant companionship of stolid, stolidest, stolidisimma Glotarchuk, and by her creeping sense (which grew with every day in the USSR) that here was a society as sinister, as subtly devastating to the soul, as anything Kafka had created.

She never knew whether her notebooks had been stolen or, if so, by whom. She imagined that someone in the Soviet state did not want her to meet her Russian relatives (if they were alive) or discover they were dead (if they were dead). What these putative relatives could have told her, she did not know—nor, probably, did the Russians. They withheld the information, most likely, by pure reflex. All information is, by definition, to be withheld—for information is a means to freedom. "Liberty," said Camus, "is the right not to lie." He also might have said: "Liberty is the right to information, to notebooks, to addresses." *Droit de cahiers,* one might call it, as strong as *droit moral.*

True, her government had shredded documents, had perpetrated Watergate, had killed Vietnamese, had interned Japanese-Americans, had supported hideous bloodthirsty regimes in Salvador, and points south, but even these atrocities were balanced by a degree of domestic freedom unknown in the whole rest of the world. If Papa could have seen Soviet Russia, he would have given up even the last, lingering vestiges of his Marxism—as indeed most *Soviet* Russians had. But he left the country before the twentieth century even dawned, and all he knew of communism was from books. As he painted in Paris, in Edinburgh, in London, in New York, he dreamed of a Marxism which never came to pass—except in theory—and the proof of whose pudding he'd never tasted.

The Writers' Union had not wanted to let her out of Russia. She waited day after day at the old, regal Sovietskaya Hotel in Moscow while various officials debated her fate. Finally she broke down and wept to one of the round motherly ladies of the Writers' Union (which seemed to specialize in round, motherly ladies)—a red-ringleted translator of English and American poetry (with several wens on her face and large buck teeth).

"I am in love," Isadora said, weeping, "and I must meet my lover in Venice; then I must meet my daughter at home. Please see what you can do about the tickets."

In Russia, love and children are still sacred abstractions and tears are potent as vodka. The translator lady, Larissa Yahupova, began to weep herself.

"I have read your grandfather poems," she said, "And I know you have great heart." Those same poems were still her passports home—as they had been her passports here!

Miraculously, the tickets arrived. Miraculously, Larissa Yahupova brought her to the airport. Miraculously, the Aeroflot flight from Moscow to Milan awaited. Miraculously, she was allowed to board the plane (though not without the usual confusion and delay).

All she could think of was the fictional Henry Bech, alter ego of Updike in his nostalgic, literary yearning for *yiddishkeit,* as she tried to think of what to do with all the rubles she had collected from Writers' Union welcoming committees in four cities, but had never had any place to spend. The *beriozkas* (gift shops) were always closed, it seemed, when she had a moment to frequent them. All her expenses were paid in each city. And leaving Moscow she was held up for $312 (in American money only, please), supposedly for overweight luggage. Her luggage was underweight, she wanted to protest—(her notebooks had been stolen)—but of course she did no such thing. In every city she visited, she had been heaped with heavy gift books, art books, autographed poetry books, so perhaps her luggage *was* overweight. All that Russian poetry weighed a ton. Ah—when she got home, she was going to start studying Russian at once.

What to do with the rubles? She had consolidated them all into one envelope and they made a damp, thick packet. She wanted to toss it in the garbage, but she was afraid somebody would see and think it her comment on the Soviet state. She held the wad of rubles in her pocket, terrified of the consequences of throwing it away, and of the consequences of carrying it out of the country. She was paralyzed.

Two weeks in Russia had reduced her to a quivering mass of anxieties about the most simple, ordinary tasks. The fantasy of being under constant surveillance was perhaps a more potent force for control than the *reality* of being under surveillance. It was illegal to carry Soviet money out of the country (Larissa had warned her before hurrying to her mysterious duties at the Writers' Union, leaving Isadora to wait for the plane alone), even though the currency was nonconvertible—and it was probably some kind of crime against the state to throw it in the garbage.

She paced about the airport, waiting for the flight to Milan to be called, the wet wad of rubles seeming to show through her pocket as through a fluoroscope screen. She considered going up and giving it to a policeman—but then she thought that maybe she could be arrested for that, as if it might be misconstrued as bribery. (But bribery for what? Her mind was not functioning rationally; her paranoia was rampant.) Suddenly her flight was called. She went to the designated gate, marked with the correct number of the flight to Milan, and for some time she waited in a long line. But after waiting there for quite a while, she chanced to ask the only English-speaking person on line and she realized that the flight she was waiting for was bound for Odessa! (Did they now want her back in Odessa? And if so, why?)

She ran around wildly, shlepping her heavy book bag until she saw, waiting at another, unmarked gate, a tour group of elderly Italians (she could tell by their beautiful shoes, their brown-tinted glasses, their friendly, extroverted ways that they were Italians (even before she got close enough to hear *la bella lingua*). She asked one of *them* where they were headed.

"Milano," came the reply from a sweet gray-haired lady who, it turned out, was as eager to leave Russia as she.

"Quel buona fortuna!" said Isadora. And then, in the pure bliss of being immersed in a sea of Italian, she began to quote—out of the mists of her freshman year at Barnard, the first canto of *La Divina Commedia:*

> *"Nel mezzo del cammin di nostra vita*
> *Mi ritrovai per una selva oscura,*
> *Che la diritta via era smarrita.*
>
> *Ahi quanto a dir qual era e cosa dura*
> *Esta selva selvaggia e aspra e forte*
> *Che nel pensier rinova la paura!"*

"Lei parla Italiana!" the lady exclaimed with that true joy which is one of the great delights of studying Italian (the inverse of the humiliation of learning French—for in France speaking French badly is as big a sin as speaking Italian badly is a virtue in Italy).

"Non parlo exactamente—ma posso recitare la poesia!"

"Ah, signorina," said the lady, taking Isadora back, back, back to her student days in Italy (where she looked so young she was always *signorina,* never *signora*) . . . *"Ah, signorina—la Russia a me non piace. Andiamo insieme all Italia!"*

Isadora couldn't have agreed more. They waited on line for the plane—the right line—chatting happily in Italian of the joy of leaving Russia. But even as they spoke, Isadora wondered whether they mightn't be overheard and arrested. And she still fingered the damp rubles, wondering what to do.

Why had Larissa Yahupova scurried back to the Writer's Union and left her in this predicament? If she were Henry Bech—or any male author, real or fictitious—she would have had a whole *committee* bidding her farewell, as she had had a committee welcoming

394

her, when she traveled with the delegation. But no, she had been left to fend for herself. Suddenly the gate opened up and the flight to Milan was boarding.

What to do with the rubles? Bech had tossed them insouciantly onto the runway in a crumpled ball. What a free spirit! Clearly he had not been as terrified in Russia as Isadora. His terror lurked elsewhere—in the Deep South perhaps, or Israel.

On boarding, Isadora summoned up the courage to offer the rubles to a stewardess. The stewardess declined. (Would she also call the police and have Isadora dragged from the plane like a disorderly drunk and locked in a Russian dungeon forever?) Isadora briskly walked to the back of the aircraft where the lavatory was and carefully closed the door. After looking around for hidden cameras, she stuffed all the rubles in the garbage can, and covered them with brownish paper towels. Still, she was fearful of arrest—but what else could she do? It was already time to fasten seatbelts. She went to her seat and sat down.

As the plane ascended over Moscow, all the Italians (and Isadora) let out a burst of applause. Her heart became lighter with every minute that carried her away from the baleful influence of Russia.

What *was* it about that country? It was as if an invisible gas invaded your bones, making you paranoid, suspicious, wary of any false step. You didn't feel it at first, but little by little it crept up on you; little by little it took over; little by little it invaded your consciousness. After two weeks in Russia, Isadora understood Kafka's *The Castle* and Nabokov's *Bend Sinister*. She understood Orwell's *1984*. She could *feel* the principle of the police state in her fingers and toes, in her gut and lungs.

As the plane moved on its way out of Soviet air space, Isadora began to grow less paranoid, more rational again. Was it *possible* that she had given up her Papa novel just because the notebooks were stolen? That was absurd! She was a diligent researcher. One false lead had never stopped her in the past. The first trip to Russia was clearly only a beginning. She would go home, learn Russian, get the names and addresses again, and return as soon as she could. She would really prepare herself this time—prepare herself properly (she'd even *memorize* the names and addresses as Nadezhda Mandelstam memorized Osip's poems)—and then she'd be back. She swore it. Now at least she knew where Papa's fearful consciousness had come from; she knew that Eastern Europe was heavy with death, chockablock with corpses in a way the

American soil wasn't—not yet—and that these layers of death, histories of death, had affected Papa's consciousness, made him negative where she was positive, made him mournful where she was cheery, made him defeatist where she was intent on victory.

But would she really go back? For all its sublime natural beauty, Russia was the most unpleasant country she had ever visited—unpleasant in a way you couldn't even put your finger on. It was unpleasant in a way she would probably scarcely even be able to *remember* once she left there. The invisible gas would fade and only the beautiful sights would remain.

Not quite. The fearful consciousness would remain with her forever. Papa's fearfulness. His terror of risk-taking—and yet his great gamble in walking across Europe at fourteen. Without that gamble, she would not exist, nor Amanda. She owed her life to his paradoxical fear, his paradoxical courage. She *would* write his story after all.

The plane rose higher. They were over Romania, then Austria, then blessed, beautiful Italy. As the Adriatic coast appeared, the Italians cheered. And so did Isadora. Never was she so glad to be revisiting her spiritual home—*Italia.*

Would Bean be in Milan? Centuries ago, they had made these plans, centuries ago in Kiev, she had called him to tell him to hang in, to wait, to trust that the Russians would let her out. Nothing seemed certain. She might even be arrested for throwing away rubles. As the time of descent approached, she was less and less sure he'd be there.

The airport in Milan was a mess—as Italian airports tend to be during prime vacation time in August. Mobs of Italians flowed out over the barriers, pushing, shouting, shoving. The nice thing was: Bean was taller than everyone. Isadora looked longingly for his tousled mop of dirty-blond hair, his blazing blue eyes, his incandescent smile. Nowhere to be found.

She had her heavy book bag *and* her large suitcase (which had come off the plane in record time—the first instance of Aeroflot efficiency she had seen to date), so she was greatly encumbered. She pushed through the barricade, dragging both suitcases, looking for Bean. No Bean in sight. And here she'd been so sure he'd be waiting for her, waving madly on her arrival.

She checked out the arrivals-and-departures board. His Alitalia flight from New York had long since come in. (Her flight number, however, was nowhere posted—par for the course). Well, maybe he had never *taken* the plane from New York. Maybe something had come up. He'd met some girl, gotten stoned, taken off to fuck away three days and nights—as in the early days with her. He was just as rotten and unreliable as she'd always feared—another Adrian Goodlove (pure cad masked by a winning smile); or else he was another Brian Stollerman (a madman who could make *any*thing sound convincing, even phony commitment); or else he was another Josh Ace (sweet-seeming younger man with the soul of a user). She'd been had again. He'd probably even cashed in the plane ticket and used the money on some tootsie—or, more likely, on cocaine or sinsemilla (probably both). She was a pure idiot where men were concerned. Oh *why* couldn't she learn to like the eligibles—the men in their fifties who bought you life insurance; the men in their forties who paid *your* bills instead of you paying *theirs;* the men in their sixties with mansions in Palm Springs and money (not to mention liver spots) to burn! "I'd rather be an old man's darling than a young man's slave," her mother used to quote to her when she was little. (It sure hadn't worked, had it?) All her life, she'd done the opposite of what her mother said. "Don't wear your heart on your sleeve," her mother had always said—and she knew nothing else but bleeding heart on dripping sleeve (not to mention dripping cunt, and bleeding pocketbook—for her men, in addition to everything else, always left her poorer than before—and usually cleaned out most of the furniture, video and sound equipment into the bargain).

So, she'd done it again—found another heartless bastard to justify her incurable masochism. Forty more years of analysis! She'd go to the *grave* still in analysis! "Next time I'll try Lourdes," says Woody Allen in *Annie Hall.* Maybe *she* ought to try Lourdes, too. She'd tried everything else—including Woody Allen's analyst. Maybe she could convert to Catholicism like Graham Greene. Ah —*there* was something she hadn't tried.

Suddenly, she spotted Bean.

He was waving madly and flashing those blue eyes like beacons. He struggled through a crowd of Italians and clasped her in his arms.

"Darling, darling, darling," he said, weeping. "I never thought I'd see you again."

She was crying, too—overcome with the relief of being out of Russia, still alive, back in what she now knew really *was* the free world. Or at least, the freer.

"I never thought I'd see *you* again either," she said.

They wept and hugged, hugged and wept. Since they had three hours to wait before their flight to Venice, they decided to go at once to the airport hotel.

In their room—a boxy modern one like a futuristic cell or a pullman compartment on a spaceship—they stripped naked and showered madly. Isadora didn't know what she wanted more—a Western-style shower that worked, or Bean's arms (and legs) around her.

Both, she guessed.

Clean and still somewhat wet, they fell onto the bed. He held her face between his two palms.

"I had such a sense I'd never see you again," he said. "I was half mad without you. I wrote you reams of letters which I couldn't send—you never would have gotten them."

"Where *are* they?" Isadora asked, always one for preserving the word, the word, lest the flesh should flee—or fail.

"I'll give them to you later," said Bean.

"Oh god—I'm glad to see you," Isadora said, the tiredness and despair and fear melting away, the paranoia of Russia dissolving with the touch of his body.

"I love you with all my heart," she said. "I never want us to be parted again." (What had she said? What had she promised—she who had sworn off promises?)

"I know now that I can't get along without you," he said, weeping.

"Oh—I have so much to tell you," she said. "So much, so much . . . I don't know where to begin."

"Did you find your grandfather?" he asked.

"Well, yes and no," she said. "But yes, yes I did!"

They made love in that careful way lovers do after a long separation, relearning each other's bodies, relearning love itself, retracing their steps along each other's skins.

It is death that propels us to these dangerous promises, these dangerous commitments, Isadora thought, as they were making love. If we thought, like adolescents, that we'd never die, then we could go on from lover to lover never confessing ourselves wholly for love, never committing to love, never pledging ourselves. But death's proximity gives love its value. Life is too short to spend it in shallowness, in avoidances, in fear of flying, falling, catching fire. Isadora had felt the full history of death in Russia; in Odessa, by the Black Sea, in Kiev, by that sea of spirits which is the sealed-up gulch called Babi Yar. And she knew that what Auden had written (in a poem she loved in college long ago) was true: "We must love one another or die." (Though, of course, we love one another *and* die anyway. But do we die in spirit, too? No. Not if we love. That is what Papa's Russian ghost had taught her.) When the deathmakers and deathmongers had had their way with the planet; when they had annihilated every living thing—even grasses and insects—would the poems of our extinguished species still orbit around the globe in the irradiated ethers? Isadora liked to think so.

The two hours in the hotel flew by. Washed and dressed in clean clothes, they took off for Venice.

"You're not going to believe Venice," Isadora said.

"If you can exist, then so can Venice," said Bean, hugging her.

They arrived at Marco Polo Airport as the sun was slanting across the lagoon in its final daily descent.

The sense of freedom and fantasy, the sheer euphoria of being in Italy alive and reunited with Bean was so great that Isadora wondered at the last minute whether Venice would be a disappointment. She had been to Venice many, many times—the first time at nineteen (when she had come alone from Florence and stayed in the student hostel on the Isola del Giudecca for two dollars a night). On that occasion, she had wandered through the city with a copy of *Childe Harold* in her hand and she had sat in the Piazzetta reading and dreaming of a Byronic lover to come and take her—if not away (for what was Venice if not the very essence of "away"?), then at least to *take* her.

" 'I stood in Venice on the Bridge of Sighs,' " she read. " 'A palace and a prison on each hand.' "

Sitting in the Piazzetta, nubile and nineteen, hunched over her cappuccino and its sweetened foam, she muttered those lines from Canto the Fourth aloud (for Byron cries out to be read aloud—the essence and the test of poetry):

"I stood in Venice on the Bridge of Sighs,
A palace and a prison on each hand:
I saw from out the wave her structures rise
As from the stroke of the enchanter's wand:
A thousand years their cloudy wings expand
Around me, and a dying Glory smiles
O'er the far times, when many a subject land
Look'd to the winged Lion's marble piles.
Where Venice sate in state, throned on her hundred isles!"

399

And a Byronic lover, as if bidden by the poetry itself (and the Muse contained within it), arrived.

He was a young, slender Chinese doctor from Australia, tall, handsome, the harbinger of the slender Chinese-American doctor she would someday meet and marry. (Was it really true, or did Isadora only imagine it, that every one of the major men in her life had had an antecedent, a harbinger, a forerunner? First one met the forerunner, or one wrote him into a book, then one met the real man—as if there were indeed *two* of every man, the real man and the man of dreams. These phrases *real man* and *man of dreams* were not so idle after all, then, were they? Women still wrote home: "I've met a real man" or "I've met the man of my dreams." Unfortunately, Isadora tended to invent the characters the epic of her life demanded—and then to be disappointed when the character she imagined and the person she had met did not coincide. All writers did this: it was partly why their marital histories were so entertaining and expensive—entertaining, that is, if you didn't have to live through them. Writers fell in love with characters and characters do not necessarily make good mates.)

The Chinese doctor she had met at nineteen had walked with her through the Doge's palace, had bought her violets on the Piazzetta, had recited poetry to her over spumanti at Florian's. She had not slept with him. It was 1961 and in 1961 you did not sleep with everyone (besides, she was staying in a hostel), but the encounter was all the more romantic for that. Innocent kisses were exchanged, and addresses, too (though, in fact, they never wrote). I wonder where he is now, Isadora idly thought, as the DC-9 carrying her and Bean began its descent into Venice. (She flew DC-9s but not DC-10s—though after Aeroflot, she figured she'd fly *anything* at all and be grateful.)

The next trip to Venice had been with Pia—her old school friend—and they had stayed in a fleabag near San Marco and fought like blood sisters. The next time, she went once to Venice with Bennett Wing (during their Heidelberg years) and Bennett, of course, had sulked the whole time, reading and rereading *Death in Venice* and making grim and depressing psychoanalytic interpretations. The following trip was with Josh on the crest of *Candida Confesses;* they'd had a suite at the Gritti and *papparazzi* in hot pursuit. (This time *Josh* had sulked because the *papparazzi* were not in hot pursuit of *him.*) After that whenever she returned to Venice, she'd been alone, a researcher on the trail of Marietta Robusti and her famous father. Oh, Venice was full of memories for Isadora—her own memories and her characters' memories. Her own memories and her alter ego's—for, of course, Marietta was as much an alter ego as Candida (though the world naturally did not see it, being easily fooled by surfaces, by petticoats and panniers, bodices and ruffs, wigs and masks). A novelist's memories are perhaps more layered than other people's. There are her own memories and then the memories of her character (which sometimes coincide with hers but sometimes not—or sometimes are like her own memories but with strange refractions, like the *palazzi* mirrored in the Grand Canal).

What would Venice be like this time? To go back to Venice, that unearthly paradise, with a demon lover and find—what? Ah, that was the nature of Venice, as changeable as the I Ching and just as much the mirror of one's moods. One never knew with Venice— that shimmering chimera on the lagoon of memory.

Isadora turned and looked into Bean's eyes as the plane was whizzing up the landing strip. The skin around his eyes crinkled at the corners and his irises were very liquid, very azure in this light; his pupils were large and dark enough to drown in. It had taken Bean to teach Isadora about eyes and how to read them. Bean had often told her that in his years of whoring around he finally came to know which women were dangerous and hurtful through looking closely at their eyes. "You can always tell a *snake*," Bean said. "Her eyes are cold and there is a kind of blankness or impassivity about them. I see the same thing in your photographs of Josh. His eyes look dead."

Isadora had been slow to recognize that—seven years slow, in fact—but when she did, she knew Bean was right. Josh *did* seem to have dead eyes. It wasn't that his eyes were calculating, it was just that some flicker of feeling had been turned off; the ray of life had been intercepted. There were so many things Josh did not want to look at—perhaps that was why. He did not want to look at his relationship with his father, his relationship with Isadora, his relationship with himself. And so he had shut himself off, shut off some vital receptors in his brain, which showed in his eyes.

Isadora knew his eyes had not always been dead. When she and he had first met, when he was hopeful about his life and their love, his eyes had had a sweetness about them, a willingness to see. Then he began to seal himself off; he grew blind and cold. She was sure this change had occurred—but *why* it had occurred, she did not know. Life ought to open people, not close them, make them less frightened and more accessible, make them more loving. Sometimes it does the reverse. You cannot really predict who will improve with age and who will deteriorate, though often failure and disappointment in oneself make for a tightening of the heart that never loosens.

And so they had the impudence to visit Venice. At sunset, weary from their travels, weary from their mad longing for each other, weary from their insane six-month courtship severed by Russia, united by Russia, they saw Venice together as if for the first time.

Their luggage was heaped into a *motoscafo*, the boatman took the helm, and with their arms around each other, they puttered into that watery apparition which is the lagoon of Venice at sunset. They rode and rode under a wide gray sky, seagulls weaving and dipping to greet them. They passed the buoys, the markers, the causeways. Suddenly, they entered the glittering dark snake of the Grand Canal.

The palaces wobbled downward into their greeny reflected images; the sun was caught in the waters and drowned. Isadora looked at the seawall of crumbling *palazzi* and rejoiced. Venice was still here. The waters might be rising (rather than the city sinking —as some maintained), but Venice was still here: they had not struck the set.

Bean was seeing it all for the first time. And she was seeing it *as if* for the first time because of him. This was a magic but a melancholy place, a place of cats as much as a place of people; a city where all the spirits of the past now inhabited the bodies of animals and darted through the alleyways in pursuit of other metamorphosed spirits. Bean, who was a cat person, instinctively understood this about Venice. Isadora had never quite understood before—before coming here with him—that Venice's long history of empire and long decline of revelry had left her walls alive with ghosts in a way other cities were not. "You cannot draw blood biting a ghost," goes an old Taoist saying—yet in Venice you could. The ghosts of Venice were bloody. The ghosts of Venice wanted no less than sex and death.

And Bean and Isadora gave it to them. Ensconced in a mirrored suite at the Cipriani, they astounded themselves by fucking so madly and so often that they were too sore to sightsee. Once, twice, three times, four, five, and six times a day was not enough. They'd fuck away the mornings, feast on croissants and omelettes in their garden, swim a little, and go back to bed. Their desire seemed

402

boundless, insatiable—as if all the revelry of Venice's carnivals and masquerades, all the sexual madness of Casanova's Venice, Byron's Venice, went into their passionate lovemaking. A sexual odor rose from the canals and rotting palaces and came to claim them in their huge bed at the Cipriani. In this city where revelry and vice were once *de rigueur*, where a woman married at sixteen and by seventeen took a lover, a *cicisbeo*, a *cavalier servente;* in this city where gondolas plied the dark canals and love was made under the gondola's black hood on the water, or in little hideaways on canals not even other Venetians knew about; in this city where the lovely lapping of the brackish waters suggests sex even to the celibate, suggests death even to the young and healthy, they made love with all the stored energy of centuries of lust, centuries of thwarted love.

They made the love that Ruskin and his Effie could not make, the love that Byron and his Marianna Segati only dreamed about, that Byron and La Guiccioli began to make, but shied away from out of fear that the conflagration would consume them.

"How do you spend the evenings?" Byron had asked his friend, Tom Moore, when he was growing rather bored with La Guiccioli. What a dismal (and revealing) sentiment for a lover! Bean and Isadora spent their evenings exploring the dark byways of Venice.

A city of sex, a city of death; "a fairy city of the heart," Byron had called it. Ah—it was the city where he had written that all-betraying line: "The sword outwears its sheath," to be followed immediately by another all-betraying line: "and the soul outwears the breast."

What were *they* wearing out—Bean and Isadora—in their passionate lovemaking? Were they creating a foundation for a life to come, or merely burning up the passion they'd begun one snowy night in frozen Connecticut?

Isadora didn't know. She no longer believed the *amor vincit omnias* of her youth. And yet she did not believe in cynicism either. It was true that the plots of all lives—and all novels—had somehow been invalidated by the imminent nuclear threat, but still Clarissa Cornfeld's cynicism had nothing to teach her. Constant naysaying was not the answer. One must look, but one must also leap. One *must* go a-roving late into the night.

Bean and Isadora were sensation-seekers; they would feast on life to bursting, and when death came, well then, they'd feast on death. But neither one would die of unlived life.

All day they loved and fucked, talked, read poetry, exchanged love letters from Russia, swam, ate wonderful meals in bed, drank wine, and held each other. When twilight came, they ventured out into the city like nocturnal creatures, like the very cats of Venice, like the revelers of the eighteenth century in their astonishing golden masks.

Venice, for them, became a city of shadows, a city of dark alleyways, of silent gondola rides, midnight wanderings, of rovings in the night. The dowager duchesses lounged by the pool at the Cipriani as always; the elegant homosexual poets and novelists, designers and painters, met at their *conversazioni* in *palazzi* as always during the summer season—but Bean and Isadora were deaf to *conversazioni*, oblivious of dowager duchesses and the whole madcap social whirl of Venice. They lived inside each other's eyes and hearts and bodies. They feasted on each other; they partook of those sacraments of sex that may be the beginnings of a greater life together or maybe only ends in themselves.

She understood now, in Venice, that city of dreams, that the world *was* a dream, and that the personality of the dreamer in part created it. Papa had dreamed one world, painted, peopled it and lived it. But she was able to dream another. Always in the past, she had lived in fear of the future, had lived with the legacy of Papa's fearfulness, his mournful Russian-Jewish pessimism, his melancholia. But she refused to live that way anymore. She refused to live in fear of tax audits, failures of love, failures of life-force.

She would give herself permission to love Bean for as long as it lasted. She would give love itself permission to last. If she wanted it badly enough and Bean wanted it badly enough, it *would* last. If not, not. This much was within their power.

Venice itself was an example of something human that had lived on long after its announced demise. Isadora and Bean could rebuild their lives upon this dark lagoon of death; they could shore up the crumbling palaces; they could be together if their imaginations permitted them to be together. It was a question of courage; it was a question of living like heroes. Other dreamers were conspiring to turn the world into so much irradiated rubble, but at least they could burn up flesh as long as they still had flesh to burn.

"We have only a short amount of time to inhabit these bodies," Bean said. "And then who knows? Why not inhabit them fully?"

"Because 'the sword wears out the sheath . . .' " said Isadora, quoting her favorite muse.

"Well, then, let it wear out," said Bean, taking her in his arms

404

and beginning to make love to her again. "Let's wear it out with a vengeance!" he said.

So they went back to bed in Venice, by the sibilant waters, under the luminescent sky that only Turner knew how to paint, in the city of sex and death, of cats and lovers, of dowager duchesses and dark alleyways, of gondolas and greed, of pickpockets and poetry. They went back to bed in Venice on the brink of a day that held everything in store for them—if only their imaginations could conceive it, if only their conviction could make it stick, if only their courage could make it stay.

Falling asleep, Isadora promised herself that she would start writing the book about Papa as soon as she got home. But she really did not need to find that lost painting, if it had ever existed. *She* was that lost painting, she thought. She was the periscope of his death. And she was still alive.

ABOUT THE AUTHOR

Erica Jong has attained rare distinction as both
novelist and poet. Her first novel, *Fear of Flying,*
was hailed as a breakthrough by Henry Miller
and John Updike and became one of the top ten
bestsellers of the Seventies. *How to Save Your Own Life*
was chosen by Anthony Burgess as "one of
the 99 best novels since 1939," and *Fanny* was
acclaimed by *The New York Times Book Review* as
"a quantum leap, a literary prodigy." She has also
published five award-winning volumes of poetry,
a nonfiction book, *Witches,* and *Megan's Book of
Divorce: A Kid's Book for Adults.*